A TIME LIKE NO OTHER

Audrey Howard

WINDSOR
PARAGON

First published 2007
by
Hodder & Stoughton
This Large Print edition published 2007
by
BBC Audiobooks Ltd by arrangement with
Hodder & Stoughton

Hardcover ISBN: 978 1 405 61864 9
Softcover   ISBN: 978 1 405 61865 6

British Library Cataloguing in Publication Data available

Printed and bound in Great Britain by
Antony Rowe Ltd., Chippenham, Wiltshire

CHAPTER ONE

Amalia Fraser felt herself sway slightly as they lowered the coffin that contained her husband's body into the ground but the touch of Biddy's hand on her arm steadied her.

'Bear up, my lass,' Biddy whispered, the words heard by no one but Amalia and she bore up as Biddy knew she would. Biddy was her rock, her anchor, her life-raft in this nightmare and she clung to her, for there was no one else. Biddy had been with her for as long as she could remember, giving her strength, giving stability in her unstable world, always there, comforting and yet standing no nonsense in her care, for she was a plain-spoken, level-headed Yorkshire woman with what was known as a heart of gold that she did her best to keep well hidden except to the girl beside her.

The weather was raw. It was November, which was usually dismal in the dales and on the moorlands of the Pennines. Though not exactly raining, the damp clung to the mourners like cobwebs so that they felt the need, as if they were real, to brush them away from their faces. They stood, heads bowed, hands clasped respectfully, the gentlemen in their black top hats and gloves, the ladies in black crepe and mourning veils, so many of them that the church would not hold them all and some were forced to wait outside until the service was over. After all, the eldest male Fraser had for generations been the closest thing to a squire the small town of Moorend and its surrounding parish had ever known.

1

'I am the Resurrection and the Life, saith the Lord . . .' the parson intoned, and from several ladies sniffles could be heard and black-edged handkerchiefs were lifted to tearful eyes. From beneath her own veil, from her own tearless eyes, Amalia looked about her. She, like the others, was in deepest black as she had been since they brought him back to her on a gate from Higgins's Farm. He had been at the front of the field as he always was, on his coal-black gelding and everyone behind him had seen him come off at the ditch surrounding Higgins's mangold field. Jack Hodges even claimed to have heard his neck snap, though he had the good sense not to repeat it in the company of the widow. The dead man was twenty-three years old, Amalia was twenty and had just risen from childbed after the birth of their second son, otherwise she would have been racing just as madly beside him in the hunting field. She could feel their sympathy, all those who, three years ago when she and Chris had fallen wildly in love and against all opposition had married in this very church, had shaken their heads at the folly of youth. At seventeen she was of marriageable age but he, at twenty, was far too young. A gentleman was supposed to sow his wild oats before he settled down, make his way in the world and then, when he was perhaps in his thirties, marry some slip of a thing who would bring him a good dowry and a brood of sons to inherit.

'It's over, lass.' She came from her detachment to feel Biddy's hand drawing her away from the grave, guiding her round the freshly dug soil and on to the grass verge beside the path. The path was lined with faces bearing every expression from sadness, sympathy, curiosity, to the downright avid.

Harry Sinclair was there to assist her into her carriage, his face stern on this sad occasion but his deep brown eyes were soft with sympathy and from behind her veil she managed a small smile for his benefit. He did not return it. Biddy climbed in beside her, knowing that half the men among the mourners would have offered their arm, their strength, their manly support for the fragile little widow if only their wives had not been present. Harry Sinclair was a bachelor, twenty-seven years old, his own master in his flourishing mills since the death of his father and could do as he pleased, which he always did but he was also a careful gentleman who had no desire to change his unmarried status. His brother had been a close friend of the man they had just laid to rest and, at a time like this, with Roly Sinclair abroad on business, selling Sinclair cloth, it would not be out of place to give assistance to the widow of his brother's friend.

The carriage headed off in the direction of The Priory, the Fraser family home, moving along the curving, narrow road which led to a wide stretch of gorse moor, the other carriages following on, for there were to be refreshments for those who had come from some distance. Biddy hoped Jenny and her sister, Clara, had carried out her instructions in laying the table with the custard tarts, ham sandwiches and pickles she herself had prepared before getting the lass into the carriage. She was still not right, her lass. She had suffered a grievous shock. Especially so soon after giving birth to Master Alec, three weeks old and at this very moment shouting for the nipple, no doubt, and

3

Master Jamie getting in the way of poor Jenny and Clara who would be all at sixes and sevens without her to bully them. What was to become of them all? she had time to wonder as she watched Mr Sinclair swing into the saddle of his bay and tack on to the end of the cavalcade of carriages.

Harry had decided to ride over from Mill House on his bay. Though it would have been more appropriate in the circumstances to use the gig it would have meant keeping to the roads between his home and the church where poor Chris was being laid to rest. Mounted, he could gallop across the fields and the bit of moorland which would save him time. He would, naturally, be expected to return to the Priory for the formalities that followed an interment, but he had a piece of cloth ready to come off one of his new looms which demanded his attention and though Mather was a splendid overseer he wanted to see it himself. It was well known by his shrewd, hardworking competitors in the woollen industry that you only had to let your eyes wander for a fraction of a second for the business to grind to a halt. Take Chris Fraser's father as an example, and Chris Fraser himself who had both been concerned with pleasure rather than the business of running an estate and had spent the family's wealth in the space of two generations, the wealth built up by the first Fraser, also called Christopher, 200 years ago. The sooner Harry was back at his weaving and spinning mill at High Clough the better. A glass of decent wine, if such a thing was to be had at The Priory, and he'd make his excuse to leave. No more than an hour. He begrudged the time but it was his duty to attend the funeral of the lad who had been

4

a frequent visitor at Mill House, sometimes bringing his pretty second cousin, Amalia, with him. The boys had attended Moorend Grammar School together, played together, fought together, been wild together as young men are and when Chris had announced his intention to marry Amalia Atkins he remembered how thunderstruck Roly had been. Mind you, they had both been a little in love with Amalia or Lally as they had called her, for she was extraordinarily lovely. It was hard to describe her in the usual way as her looks were exceptional. Dark, glossy hair cut in a tumble of short curls about her head, because even then she had defied the conventions of her class. Her face was like that of a kitten, with a pointed chin the colour of ivory and she had startling translucent green-blue eyes which changed colour with her mood and the weather. They were surrounded by long, thick lashes which meshed together when she laughed which was often, for she was a madcap who revelled in all the mischievous things Chris and Roly got up to. She had fought with them, laughed with them, ridden her small pony in a mad explosion of movement in an attempt to keep up with them. She had climbed trees, splashed in the busy waters of the moorland streams with them, chased Max and Dandy, the two Mill House Labradors, with them, and when they went to school waited for them to come home to join in whatever scheme they had thought up.

They had noticed at the same time, with the suddenness of boys almost grown into young men, that she was not, in fact, one of them at all, but an exceptionally lovely young woman with whom they had, as they did everything together, fallen in love.

5

It was Chris Fraser who captured her wayward heart.

She was mercurial, sunny-natured, wayward and wilful, fun-loving and wildly reckless even after her marriage, which everyone thought would surely calm her down, particularly with two babies in rapid succession. It had not, even the birth of her two sons failing to keep her occupied by the things that young married women were expected to be busy with and why it was so sad to see her as she had been drooping at her husband's grave today. Harry had stood on the other side of the gaping hole, ready to leap across it if necessary to give her his arm to cling to, wondering why he should think thus. He supposed it was because she had no one but a servant, the woman who had come with her when she married Chris. There were many there who would have been more than willing to do the same if there had been money in it, sons of the millocracy and even the lesser gentry who had known young Chris Fraser as a good sort. But there was nothing left of what had once been a fine estate, for Chris had been feckless and reckless as his father had been before him. Joe Fraser could have lived comfortably on the rents of his farms had he taken more interest in them and the farmers who rented them but Joseph had attempted to live grandly and had kept a mistress in Halifax. He had spent his time with her and at the gaming tables when he should have been overseeing the running of his estate. He ran up huge debts at his tailors—his fancy waistcoats were the talk of Moorend—and at his wine merchants and it was said that the scandal of it killed his poor wife. He followed soon after, leaving little for his only son, his only child, Christopher. And now would you look at the result! A dead landowner, a young, impoverished widow and two babies.

Harry handed the reins of his bay to a lad at the front entrance of the house, wending his way through the tangle of open carriages, gigs and broughams that were standing on the gravel drive. Coachmen muttered oaths, flustered by the confusion, for there seemed to be no one in charge of ordering their places on the drive. There were a couple of equally flustered servants, a groom or perhaps a gardener doing their best to make some sort of order out of the press but then that was typical of the Frasers, their servants as hapless as they themselves had been. It was said that until Lally married Chris and took the woman whose arm she clung to at the interment to her new home there had been nothing but chaos in the Fraser house. Servants, most of them unpaid, lolling about the place, pots unwashed, beds unmade, gardens untended, the dairy smelling of sour milk, but all as happy as the lark, comfortable and time-wasting. That is until this woman who now stood at the entrance to the house had taken control and brought order where there had been confusion. Since she had returned from the church she had tied a pristine white apron over her black dress and on her head where there had been a deep-brimmed black bonnet was now a fluted white cap. She was greeting the mourners and directing them to the drawing room. She was tall, stately, immensely dignified, her face quite expressionless. As she indicated the way he was struck by her proud, easy carriage, her clear skin and excellent teeth, and wondered where she had come from.

7

Servant to Lally Fraser's own mother until the day she died, he had heard, and the one who had brought her up as if the girl were her own. Lally's mother had been known as a somewhat odd woman who had mixed with a literary crowd, artists and writers and admirers of Goethe, Schiller, Herder and such, which was not to the taste of the plain-spoken, strait-laced manufacturing folk of the district. They supposed that was from where she got her daughter's fancy name.

Lally was seated on a sofa by the enormous fireplace in which a fragrant applewood fire blazed and beside her a thin thread of a woman nodded and murmured at the ladies and gentlemen who approached Lally with their condolences. This was the aunt, or rather a distant cousin, who had, on the death of Lally's mother, taken her to live in a modest villa in Skircoat on the southern perimeter of Halifax. The woman to whom Lally had clung had gone with her. A maiden lady, was the cousin, Harry had heard, who had had no control whatsoever over her unconventional young relative.

Two young maidservants were moving about the room offering sherry—no decent wine then—and on a table were the refreshments. Lally toyed with a glass of sherry, smiling vaguely as each of the mourners came to pay their respects. Sympathy oozing, ladies held her hand for a moment and gentlemen bowed over it, wondering, Harry was certain, what to say to a widow so young and helpless. It was not to be borne, they whispered among themselves, thinking no doubt of the man just buried in the ground and his two baby sons who were upstairs. In whose care? they wondered,

8

for it was well known that the Frasers had been unable to pay the wages of even the most inexperienced nursery maid. The house was probably mortgaged to the hilt and there would be debts, gambling debts run up by Chris who, at twenty-three, had believed he had all the time in the world to pay them off.

The house had indeed once been a priory, an Augustine priory, parts of it dating back to the thirteenth century and added on to it was an eighteenth-century mansion. It was extremely beautiful, built from the honey-coloured sandstone quarried in Yorkshire and dissected by tall flat windows across its front. A cluster of trees stood before it, old oak trees which looked as though they had been planted when the monks glided about the now derelict cloisters, the stables part of the main building with an arch that led through to the stable yard. There was a small, overgrown formal garden enclosed by ragged box hedges and to the side of that a paddock in which several animals grazed, among them the black gelding that had flung Chris to his death. An ancient donkey, a small pony and a lovely chestnut mare, probably the animal Lally rode, lifted their heads to stare at the visitors at the front of the house. A small lake lay directly in front of the old house on which ducks paddled, darting in and out of the weeds that surrounded it. The grass, a vast stretch of parkland as far as the eye could see, was uncut but an air of peace and serenity prevailed, in marked contrast to the character of its owner who had been buried this day. The front door was massive with worn stone steps leading up to it and across the façade of the old house a mantle of creeper ran wild like

9

everything else on this dilapidated estate.

*   *   *

She would remember that day for the rest of her life, the day they had brought Master Chris home and Miss Lally had sat down in the rocking-chair in her kitchen, remaining there like a broken doll until she herself had taken charge.

'Get up, Miss Lally.'

'I don't think I can, Biddy.'

'You must, lass, for your children need you. Come on, my lass, you can't sit there for ever. They've taken . . . Master Chris upstairs and there's things to be done.'

'What things, Biddy?'

'Miss Lally, get up and do as you're told . . .' and she had done as she was told, for her lass, though so delicate-looking, was made of strong stuff and here she was after putting her husband in the ground getting ready to greet those who had come to pay their respects.

*   *   *

Lally Fraser shook hand after hand, whose she didn't really know, since they all looked the same except some were gentlemen and some were ladies, friends of Chris's family, she supposed. The first hand that made any impression on her was slender, brown, strong-looking as though it were not unaccustomed to manual work, but the nails were clean and well manicured. The hand extended from immaculate white cuffs which protruded from the sleeve of a black jacket. It

10

grasped hers firmly with none of the tentativeness of others and when she looked up she found herself gazing into the eyes of a man she recognised.

'Mr Sinclair?' she murmured, allowing her hand to remain in his, aware that beside her Aunt Jane was looking on with disapproval, for after all there were many Moorend folk waiting to offer their condolences, standing behind the tall man who was holding Amalia's hand for longer than was proper.

'The same, Lally. Roly is abroad and so I came in his place. Would you care to come and sit in the conservatory with me for a moment or two?' He smiled round at the company, none of whom, even if the occasion allowed it, dared argue with Harry Sinclair, one of the wealthiest, most influential men in the district. His grandfather had built the house in which Harry still lived. His grandfather had been a merchant in his younger days, travelling to Lincolnshire with a string of packhorses for the sheep shearing, choosing his wool then bringing it back to the Pennines to distribute to the workers, combers, spinners and weavers in their cottages. Later, being an astute man of business, it struck him that it would be more profitable to keep the wool for himself, guiding it through all its processes and employ the cottagers to weave it for wages. The hills around Moorend, bare, brown uplands, had a plentiful supply of swift-flowing moorland streams which were needed to drive the waterwheels and his first mill was built and the men and women who had once woven their 'piece' and weekly taken it to the Piece Hall in Halifax, with no wool at their disposal were forced to work for Martin Sinclair or starve.

Harry and Roly, his grandsons, had three mills now, High Clough, West Heath and South Royd. Their looms no longer depended on water for their running power. Power-loom weaving of woollen cloth and the combing of worsted by machinery had presented technical difficulties but these were quickly overcome and when Harry's father died the woollen trade, which was now concentrated in the West Riding of Yorkshire, grew and prospered. Old towns like Halifax and Leeds were vastly expanded while new towns like Huddersfield were created out of mere hamlets. Robert Sinclair, old Martin's son, had built the magnificent High Clough Mill which had good lighting, warmth and ventilation and was the biggest in the area. Robert and then Harry Sinclair built West Heath and South Royd in the same manner and during the four years since 1850 the wool textile trade experienced its most rapid expansion.

Though Lally and Chris Fraser had been as light-hearted as children during the three years of their marriage, laughing their way through the days, romping their way through the nights in the depths of their big bed with no thought for their future or that of any children they might have, since they were barely out of childhood themselves, certain parts of the old house had been fairly well kept. The conservatory was one. Constructed in the early part of the century by Chris's grandmother who had been a lover of plants, it was, like the rest of the house, somewhat neglected but still had white cane chairs, a fretwork glass ceiling, dozens of plants, a glowing terracotta tiled floor strewn with children's toys for it was a favourite place at all times of the year. The

12

colour in it, the plants seeming to bloom with scarcely any help, provided a lovely setting and it was here that Biddy often sat with eighteen-month-old Jamie.

Harry guided Lally to a seat, as she still seemed in a state of shocked confusion. The mourners, left in the drawing room, exchanged glances, wondering whether it was time to take their leave but neither Harry nor Lally seemed to notice them.

'What will you do now, Lally?' Harry asked casually, bemused by her fragile beauty which was enhanced by the stark black of her gown. The background of lush foliage, a hibiscus, he thought, though he was no gardener, its frilly-petalled crimson flowers hanging down like Japanese lanterns, gave out a subtle fragrance, while to her side was a jasmine plant, beautifully perfumed. At the entrance to the conservatory he could see the housekeeper hovering, keeping a watchful eye on her mistress, and though he was tempted to lean forward and take the hand of the young widow he refrained.

'Do?' she asked hesitantly.

He knew she was still unable to think properly, and who could blame her, and he was filled with a sudden urge to protect her. An urge he had never felt before. There were no women in his life, no sisters, no mother and the only females he had anything to do with from time to time were the ones who sold their favours to any man with the money to purchase them. There was one such living in Halifax, a pretty little thing who asked nothing of him but the guineas he gave her, the relationship anything but romantic. But this one was different. He had known her for years, watched her grow up with Roly and Chris but something strange was working in him, something new and he was not sure he liked it.

'Will you stay on here or go back to your . . . er . . . relative in Skircoat? The one who sat beside you on the sofa. I believe you lived with her before you married Chris.'

She looked bewildered but something was coming alive in her eyes and she was frowning as though she were not sure to what he was referring.

'I'm not certain of your meaning, Mr Sinclair.'

He smiled. He supposed he must seem quite elderly to someone of her age though there were only seven years between them. Which was why she called him Mr Sinclair.

'This estate needs a firm hand, I would say. The farms on it—how many, and how many acres are involved?'

'I'm not sure. Chris . . . Chris and I never talked about it.'

No, I bet you didn't. A couple of youngsters playing at being grown up with no thought in your heads as to where the next penny was to come from. He knew exactly how many acres there were and how many farms and even their names, for he was a man who took an interest in what went on around him: 1,300 acres, a Yorkshire manor house, a Home Farm and five tenant farms each of between 200 and 400 acres, together with areas of surrounding woodland and common. Excellent farming, because the estate lay in a sheltered valley where the soil was in good heart. It only needed a sound agent and some money to turn it into the most productive and profitable estate in this part of Yorkshire.

'Perhaps I can help you, Lally.' He leaned forward and this time took her small hand in his. As he did so his heart seemed to flip over, for it was so delicate, so fine, the nails oval and polished and perfect. The wedding ring she wore seemed too heavy for it and he wondered for a startling moment what it would look like with a dainty band of gold and an expensive diamond and pearl ring on it.

'I'm not sure how you could help me, Mr Sinclair.' She gently withdrew her hand and seemed ready to stand up.

He was at once ashamed of himself, for the poor child was recently widowed and was still floundering in her new state. He must not take advantage of her weakened condition.

But he could not help saying, 'Harry, please. Call me Harry. Chris always did.'

'Mr Sinclair, I . . .'

At that moment the housekeeper entered the conservatory, moving in a stately glide to stand beside Lally. She took her hand and drew her to her feet, her expression one of suspicion and concern for her young mistress.

'Excuse me, sir, but people are beginning to leave and Mrs Fraser should be there to bid them farewell.' Her eyes told Harry Sinclair that she'd have no breath of scandal touch Amalia Fraser, especially on this day when they had just buried the master of this house.

'Of course, forgive me.' Harry rose and nodded courteously. 'I just wanted to let Mrs Fraser know that if ever she needs help or advice—business matters and such—she has only to call on me. She will need a decent solicitor and I can recommend

15

one.'

'That's very kind of you, sir, and if the occasion should arise we will certainly take up your offer. Won't we, my lamb?'

'We will, Biddy, and thank you, Mr Sinclair.'

She was led, as though she were a child about to move into a world of grown-ups, into the drawing room, shaking hands and murmuring and, at last, the others having departed, Harry Sinclair bowed over her hand, ran down the steps and leaped on to Piper's back, galloping off down the long gravelled drive to the gate cut into the park wall. He knew it would not be long before he was back despite what he had seen in the eyes of the housekeeper!

CHAPTER TWO

Lally left the house through the kitchen when she was sure that Biddy would be elsewhere, since she knew she would be questioned on where she thought she was off to!

It was a week since the funeral and the world still felt unreal. She had sat in the bedroom that she and Chris had shared, curled up in the rocking-chair, her feet tucked under the skirt of the black gown Biddy insisted on putting her in each morning, the two dogs, Chris's dogs, Fred and Ally, beside her. The two bewildered animals huddled against her wherever she went, for she was the nearest they could get to their missing master and she was glad of their warmth and devotion. She stared with unfocused eyes into the applewood fire—there was no coal and they had no money to

16

buy any until the rents came in—and her wandering mind wondered what she was to do with the rest of her life without Chris. She actually didn't even knowingly do that, for her mind seemed to be drowning under roaring sea waves that threatened to swamp her and she felt herself to be doomed to spend the rest of her life curled up in her chair with the feel of Chris's thick blond hair soft under her fingers as he lay motionless on the gate on which they had carried him into the great hallway of The Priory. It was a nightmare picture of the future without him and as she slipped down the back stairs she had known that if she didn't get away from the house even for a little while she would go out of her mind.

She was wearing her midnight-blue riding habit, the one Chris had liked so much. It had the usual full skirt with a train that could be hooked up at the side but underneath she wore a pair of skin-tight dove-grey kid trousers so that if she felt like it she could ride astride, which she had usually done when out with Chris. Her tall top hat with the dashing bright scarlet ribbon tied round it was left on her bed. Her hair was short, curls cropped close to her skull, and beneath it her pale face was elfin and her brilliant eyes, which Chris had likened to turquoise, were dulled with painful grief. The dogs were at her heels.

The maids, Jenny and Clara, left on their own, were busy following Biddy's directions to chop vegetables—of which there were plenty growing in the garden—ready to be made into a hearty soup for their evening meal. Biddy had gone upstairs to oversee the feeding and dressing of the babies who were in the care of Dora, Jenny and Clara's

17

fourteen-year-old sibling—of whom there were plenty in their large family—employed only yesterday. Their mam was glad of the work and the girl was experienced in the care of infants, for their labourer's cottage overflowed with them since Ned Akroyd was a lusty man. Mrs Stevens, as they called her, would not be down for a while but there was to be no lolling about, she had told them and the two sisters knew she meant it. Their young mistress's milk had dried up on the day they brought their master home and Mrs Stevens and their Dora were having the devil's own job to get Master Alec on to the cow's milk he lustily refused to drink.

The two maids looked up as their young mistress entered the kitchen, their eyes wide, their faces filled with sympathy, for it must be awful to be a widow at the age of twenty. Their busy hands stilled and Jenny, who had been with the Frasers the longest, ventured a word.

'Tha' off, Miss Lally?' They all called her Miss Lally and had always done so, for she had never looked more than fourteen even on her wedding day.

'Yes.'

' 'Appen Carly'll go wi' thi'.'

'I won't bother him, Jenny,' she answered, continuing through the enormous kitchen to the back door.

Jenny looked suitably disapproving. 'Nay, tha'll never go alone. Not . . .' She had been about to say 'not at a time like this' but Miss Lally's expressionless face stopped her and she wished desperately that Mrs Stevens would come downstairs, for she was the only one who seemed

18

able to manage poor Miss Lally.

'I won't be long, Jenny,' Lally said tonelessly, opening the back door and slipping through with Fred and Ally close to her skirt. For a moment she remembered the day Chris had brought the two setter pups home just after they were married, laughing at her delight as he tipped them into her lap. She and Chris were always laughing.

'What are you going to call them?' she had asked.

'Fred and Ally,' he had told her solemnly.

'Fred and Ally!' She had inspected them. 'But they're both bitches.'

'I know. Roly and I had a German teacher called Frederick and a French teacher called Alphonse and these two reminded me of them, don't ask me why. We were rather fond of Frederick and Alphonse, Roly and I. They were so easily diverted from the lesson and one day we saw them out together strolling across the top of Skircoat Moor thinking themselves unobserved. They were holding hands!'

'Two men?'

'Yes, there are such . . . such things, my darling. Love is not always restricted to that between males and females . . .' and he had proceeded to tell her of this condition. Chris had educated her on many subjects! Chris . . . oh Chris . . . what am I to do without you?

Carly was as startled as the maidservants. He had been tenderly grooming Master Chris's gelding, Ebony, who was restless under his hand because he had had no proper exercise since his master's death.

'Nay, Miss Lally wheer's tha' off to?' His

weather-beaten face looked as disapproving as the maids' as he did his best to hold in the beautiful animal.

'I'm . . . not sure, Carly, but if you would saddle Merry for me I'd be obliged. I might . . .'

'Wha'?' Carly asked suspiciously, for he knew Mrs Stevens would box his ears if he allowed Miss Lally to go off on her own.

'Just a ride, Carly. To get out of the house. Perhaps to the edge of Moor Wood.'

Moor Wood. That wasn't far. In fact if he stood by the paddock gate he could keep her in sight. For a moment he hesitated; after all the poor little woman had just suffered the worst thing that could happen to a woman and at the young age of twenty, so could you blame her for feeling as she did? She'd been stuck in that bloody big house all this time with all them women and if she felt the need to have a bit of a gallop across the park who was he to stop her? She had them dogs with her, big dogs, gentle, affectionate and kind, but let anyone make a move they didn't like against their master, and now their mistress—as he supposed they belonged to her now—they could be fierce as tigers.

He saddled the chestnut mare who greeted Lally with joy, whinnying a welcome, and when he opened the paddock gate Miss Lally had her out in the park and across the rough grass like a bullet out of a gun, the dogs a streak of black and white behind her. But she did not head for the trees as she had promised but raced across the parkland, leaping a dry-stone wall and vanishing from his sight. She was making for the moorland beyond Appleton Farm, the moorland that rose in a

20

shrouded mist at the back of The Priory. He groaned, for Mrs Stevens would have his hide when she discovered that the young mistress had persuaded him to saddle her mare and not only that but to open the paddock gate and usher her through. Shaking his head, he returned to the fretful gelding who tried to bite him.

'Bugger!' he swore.

*   *   *

She was sitting on an old gate when he saw her, the mare tethered beside her, the dogs lying with their noses on their paws. It was mid-afternoon but already drawing towards twilight. She was gazing out across the winter moorland, over which lay a filmy veil of soft, dull mist, but it did not quite hide the panoramic view, for the sun was not yet fully set. There was a lilac hue about the tops and a robin was singing without a care in the world, the sound mixed with the plaintive bleating of sheep on the lower folds of the hills. Her eyes were shadowed and she did not seem to hear his approach until the dogs sprang to their feet and bristled, their paws splayed, their muzzles lifted, for he had Max and Dandy with him. Piper whickered a welcome to her mare and Lally turned indifferently, giving him the attention she might have bestowed on a sheep that had wandered up from the lower slopes. For all she cared it could have been tinkers, gypsies or vagabonds, the travellers who roamed the country looking for work and who would do her serious harm for the farthing in her pocket.

It was a Sunday and he had called at the Priory

to pay his respects, or so he told himself, to the widow, only to find it in turmoil with the woman, Mrs Stevens, raging at the stable lad who stood sullenly at the back door, his attitude saying that whatever she berated him for was not his fault. He ran to take Harry's horse in great relief, touching his forelock, glad to be away from the woman's icy anger.

'Mrs Stevens, is something wrong?' Harry asked her as he dismounted.

'Indeed there is, Mr Sinclair. Lally . . . Mrs Fraser has gone off on her mare and this . . . this fool allowed it. God only knows . . .'

'Mrs Stevens, you can hardly blame the groom, for Mrs Fraser is a grown woman and mistress of this house. It is not up to him—'

'Thank you, Mr Sinclair, but Mrs Fraser, as you must understand, is not herself.'

'Of course, I apologise.'

The housekeeper was beside herself and her grey eyes flashed at him in annoyance, for who was he to interfere. At once he beckoned to the groom to fetch back his animal and the man did so gratefully, scurrying away into the enormous stable.

'I'll find her, Mrs Stevens, and bring her back safely if the groom will tell me in which direction she went.'

With the information he needed he had galloped off where the stable lad had indicated.

'Lally.' He spoke now to her unheeding back, his voice gentle, for this woman was grieving badly. 'Your Mrs Stevens is in a fearful state, giving what for to your stable lad for saddling your horse and allowing you out of the yard.'

22

'Is she? Well, I'm sorry about that but I knew if I told her where I was going she would have stopped me. You see I had to get away, Mr Sinclair. The place is empty without . . .' Her voice trailed off and there was silence as though she had forgotten what it was she was talking about.

Harry tied up his own animal and very carefully climbed up on the old gate and sat beside her. The four dogs settled uneasily on the tufted grass. There were some cows in a field further down the slope who stared at the two humans, watching them with a keen interest until one of the dogs stood up, slipped under the gate and advanced in their direction and the cows retreated.

'I hoped for a cup of tea,' Harry said casually.

'What?' She turned to look at him as though he had spoken in Swahili.

'I called at the Priory for afternoon tea. Is that not the custom? Fifteen minutes and no more and on no account leave your hat or stick in the hall. My mother was, apparently, a stickler for the conventions.' He grinned endearingly and her mouth twitched at his attempt at humour.

'My mother was just the opposite. We never knew who would call or when. That's why I'm as I am.'

'And how is that?'

She shrugged. 'I don't give a damn for the rules of society and neither did . . . did Chris. That's why we . . .'

'Roly's the same,' he said quickly.

She did smile this time as the memories of Roly, Chris and herself washed over her for an enchanted moment, then the smile slipped away and with a polite nod in his direction she climbed

23

down from the gate. At once he was beside her, reaching for the reins of her animal, handing them to her, ready to continue his gentle approach but suddenly he knew that would not do. She must be made, even this early in her widowhood, to set her feet on the path towards the future for herself and her children.

'I thought I might also help you with the farms. You have no agent, I believe, and there must be . . . be many things that need attending to.'

She turned to stare in astonishment. 'Things, what things?'

'Perhaps I could ride with you to call at each farm and see what needs doing. I admit I know nothing of farming but the tenants should know there is still someone in authority keeping an eye on things.' Though God knows, he wanted to add, Chris Fraser was the most lackadaisical landlord in the county and the tenants had probably paid not a farthing in rent for months, or even years. The old man, Chris's father, had been the same and if the tenants were not supervised as he supervised his own labourers, they would drift along, week after week, with no planting done, beasts left to themselves except for their most basic needs, and if Chris Fraser had paid no heed to the state of the farm buildings they would probably be falling down around their ears.

She looked confused and yet, as on the day of the funeral when he spoke to her in the conservatory, a small gleam shone in her eyes. It was like a tiny light that lifted the darkness, not enough to illuminate a tunnel but which nevertheless showed perhaps a way to go on.

'Your boys must have something to inherit,

24

Lally. I know they are young yet, babies really, but someone has to look after their inheritance until they are able to do so themselves and there is no one but you.'

She winced and he knew he had been brutal but with that woman at the Priory so protective of her and all the servants treading softly about her in order not to upset the new widow someone must drag her away from her sorrow, fresh as it was, and set her on a road that would not only give her a purpose in life but be of value to her children and to her.

'Mr Sinclair, you seem to forget I have just lost . . . lost the only man I have ever loved . . .'

His own heart flinched then and he turned away from her so that she would not see the expression on his face. What the devil was the matter with him? Why should he feel the gnawing in his chest which her words had caused him, for this woman, whom he had hardly seen since her marriage to Chris Fraser, was nothing to him. And why was he offering to help her run her farms, he who knew nothing of farming and, besides, had his own three mills to run? He must be off his head. What was he doing here skulking about on the moor when he had work he could be doing at High Clough where several new power looms had just been installed and a carding engine, the largest machine in the industry, was giving his overseer some problems. Taking afternoon tea! Bloody hell, if his competitors in the industry could see him now they would think he had lost his mind. But something about this girl, this woman, drew him to her, to her sadness, which he wanted to alleviate, but she had just lost, as she said so forlornly, the only man she had ever loved and how could he expect her to snap out of it in a matter of days. No more than a fortnight, less, since wild Chris Fraser had broken his foolish neck and his young widow could not be expected to . . . to . . . what . . . ? He didn't know.

'I am well aware of what you have lost, Lally, and it must seem heartless to speak of such a thing so soon after . . . after your . . . your bereavement but will it not give you an . . . a motivation, something to occupy yourself with until it becomes easier? Who knows, you may find you have a flair for it. And the tenants, who, I was told, were all present on the day of the funeral, will surely be pleased to have someone take an interest in their problems, should they have any.'

'How can I help with farming problems, Mr Sinclair? I do not come from farming stock.'

'I realise that but . . . well, it was just a suggestion. But I meant what I said. I will gladly accompany you on a round of calls. Now then, Lally, let me help you mount and I'll take you home.' He linked his hands for her to step into.

'There is no need, Mr Sinclair. I know my way.'

'I'm aware of that, Lally, but that woman of yours will wring my neck if I don't see you safely to your back door where, no doubt, she is waiting and giving your poor stable lad the rounds of the kitchen.'

'Mr Sinclair . . .'

'Harry, for God's sake. You make me feel like some old fellow who knew your grandfather.'

She smiled then, a lovely smile which smote him to his heart and Harry Sinclair, as he helped her up into the saddle, knew that at the age of twenty-seven he had at last fallen in love!

26

* * *

It was almost dark when she entered the kitchen, the paleness of her face flushed slightly at the cheeks for, with Harry, as he insisted she call him, at her heels, she had ridden hell for leather back across the moor and along the rutted lane that led to the gates of the Priory.

'You can leave me here, Mr . . . er, Harry. I shall—'

'Nonsense. I shall drop you in your stable yard,' and she had no choice but to ride on and into the stable yard where Carly was waiting to take Merry. She had no idea how enchanted Harry was that she had condescended to call him by his Christian name!

'And where the dickens have you been, lady?' Biddy greeted her, from the huge kitchen table where her efforts with the ingredients for the soup took up no more than a fraction of the surface. As Clara had remarked to Jenny when she first came to work at the Priory, you could have held a dance on its top!

'Biddy, for God's sake, let me be. Mr Sinclair found me and brought me back. Isn't that enough?' Lally sat down at the kitchen table and lifted her foot for one of the maids to pull off the boot.

'Well, have a cup of tea then. There's one in the pot. See, Clara, pull off Miss Lally's boots and then pour her a cup of tea.'

'I don't want a cup of—'

'Get it down you. You look fair crammocky and then get upstairs and see the children. Master

27

Jamie's been playing poor Dora up and that babe'll starve if we don't get something inside him. He doesn't like that baby milk the doctor recommended.'

'Biddy . . . BIDDY, don't . . . don't. I can't stand it. I just can't stand it without him. How can I manage on my own?'

Clara began to cry, her sympathy overwhelming her, for the poor little missis was so upset. She knelt at her feet doing her best to pull off the riding boot but Biddy sprang to attention, her demeanour telling them she was having none of that. She was the only one who could keep this household together, as they were all inclined to cry at the slightest thing, even the little lad who helped Barty in the garden and who was called, strangely, Froglet.

'Now then, my girl,' meaning Clara, 'don't you start. Let us try and get some order in this house and the first thing is to get these children settled. If Master Alec doesn't take to that milk we'll have us another . . .' She had been about to say 'another death on our hands', not meaning it, of course, for the infant would take the milk when he was hungry enough. He had the stubborn determination of his mother, and his father, she supposed, though she knew Miss Lally better, and once he had shown his vast disapproval of the teat and the strange milk instead of the friendly nipple he had got used to in the three weeks since he had been born, he would soon get it down him. Already, after a petulant whinge or two, he was beginning to show an interest in it.

'Now drink your tea and then get up to the nursery,' which Lally did and when she entered the

28

warm and cheerful room that she and Chris had made for this first child, their firstborn, a mischievous imp they had named James, Jamie for short, she was met at the door by a tottering, handsome boy who flung himself round her knees. Dora sat by the fire, relaxed for the first time with the baby in her arms, ready to doze off as the child sucked sullenly on the teat.

'Mama . . . Mama . . . Mama,' the boy shouted, making the baby jump. It was the only word he could say that was understandable and when she swept him up in her arms he shouted again, this time with laughter. He had his father's cheerful temperament and his joy at seeing his mother, who played with him and sang to him and nursed his drowsy body before the nursery fire, made Lally laugh too, for he and Alec were all she had of Chris. Mr Sinclair, or Harry, as he had ordered her to call him, was right. She had nothing but these two, nothing except them and the estate that was their birthright. She and Chris had taken no heed of the farms—how many were there?—nor of whether the rents had been paid or where their next penny was to come from, but somehow she must make some sort of living, for these boys were her responsibility. Hers to feed and clothe and see that they had a roof over their heads. That they were warm in the winter when the blizzards swept down from Siberia, that their summers were filled with sunshine and play, that they were brought up as Frasers, gentlemen of the county and, though her heart broke for the loss of Chris who had given her three glorious years of love and laughter, she must get on with it. Biddy would help her. Before the menace of winter on the bleak Pennines really set in she must make the rounds of the farms—Carly would know their names and where they were situated—to let them all see that though Chris had gone it was all to be supervised as was right. It did not occur to her that not once in the three years of their marriage had she ever known Chris to call on his tenants!

Tomorrow she would send word to Mr Sinclair—Harry—that she wished him to call on her and discuss the affairs of the estate and when she had the names she would ride round and if it had not been paid, collect the rent and see . . . well . . . what needed seeing to. She had no idea what she meant by that but somehow as she sat on the floor with her son in her lap, studying a book about the beasts of the jungle, listening to his incomprehensible chatter, she felt an almost imperceptible lift to her spirits. It had been the awful sensation of not only losing Chris but of not knowing what she was to do tomorrow, the next day, next week that had borne her down. Now she had something to occupy herself. A task to fill her days and at the same time perhaps keep the estate in heart for the day when Jamie and Alec could do it for themselves. In her blindness she had no conception of what that meant.

The baby slept in Dora's arms, replete at last and when Dora lifted him expertly, for she was the sister to many young children, and put him in his crib he did not stir. She looked at her young mistress who held the little demon, as Dora called him, her young heart filled with sadness for her plight. She and her two sisters, Jenny and Clara, were lucky to be employed in this big house, for there was no employment for women except in the mills and her mam had kept her at home rather than let her go into one of those. Now she was, at the age of fourteen, in complete charge—apart from Mrs Stevens—of the nursery. She'd soon have the little demon tamed because she was well used to youngsters who tried it on.

Dora sighed contentedly and began to tidy what was her domain.

CHAPTER THREE

To say that the Weaver family at Foxwell Farm were surprised to see the widow of their late landlord ride into the yard of their derelict farm with a perfect stranger was an understatement of gigantic proportions! Usually the Weavers knew what was happening within a five-mile radius of their ruinous cob farmhouse but somehow, with the landlord dead only a few weeks, they had relaxed their vigil and the whole tribe of them were ensconced in the farm kitchen, waiting for the rabbit stew which the eldest boy had poached off the 'squire's' land to be ready for eating. The Weavers lived off the land, not their own it might be said, the sons Jed and Ham selling the firewood that came from the squire's woodland, poaching his deer, rabbits, grouse, partridge and selling what they caught and did not eat themselves to the local butcher in Moorend at a profit advantageous to all. They had ninety acres of mostly scrubland which should have been under the plough and the old man, as they called Arty Weaver, spent most of his time contentedly drawing on his pipe in a patch of sunshine to the side of the farmhouse, or by the fire in the filthy kitchen. They had pigs, and chickens which rooted and strutted about the yard and as the two riders entered the chickens scattered beneath the hooves of the horses. His two eldest girls, twins about sixteen or seventeen years of age, none of them was sure, for the Weavers were not ones for recording events, worked as part-time servants or on their backs in the occasional sale of their admittedly handsome bodies. The two youngest were still babies under the age of five but already one of the twins had given birth to a child which crawled about the floor in happy unconcern.

It was the first time Lally had laughed outright, for the consternation of the family was the funniest thing she had seen for weeks. It was as though a squad of policemen had come upon them with the intention of searching for illicit goods and the panic showed itself in a wild scurrying, for while they were aware of the identity of the lovely lady on her fine mare, since they had caught sight of her with the squire, they had no idea who the man was. He carried a bulging saddlebag.

'Mrs Fraser,' Arty babbled. 'Us weren't expectin' visitors, was we, Mother,' addressing his slatternly wife, Evie, almost as if, had they known she was coming, they would have arranged refreshments.

'No, Arty, we wasn't fer we was still sad-like over't death o' poor squire. We never thought as yer'd . . .'

'I'm sure,' Harry said curtly, swinging down from his saddle, turning to give a hand to Lally.

Harry Sinclair, on receiving Lally's message that

she would be grateful if he could call on her with a view to accompanying her on a round of the farms on the estate, could scarcely restrain himself from ordering Piper out and galloping over Skircoat Moor, through Moorend and on to the Priory at once. He was actually in the carding room discussing with his overseer the revolving cylinder which teased out the blended wool into a fine web of intermingled fibres. The machine was new and as yet the mill-hand who was working it was having a problem or two which he and the engineer were doing their best to put right. The man, or 'hand', as he was called in the trade, was accustomed to working thc wool in the old way between two hand-held boards set with wires and Harry, who was prepared to, and often did, take off his fine jacket and do the bloody job himself, was doing just that in an effort to get the man to tackle the new method of carding.

'Jack, just watch me and do exactly the same, for God's sake. It's easy, man, and will save time and money and probably earn you an extra bob or two a week.'

'But, maister, tha's used ter't bloody thing an' . . .'

'Well, you'll just have to get used to it if you want to keep your damn job,' Harry was telling him when a little lad slipped up to him, pulled nervously at his shirt sleeve and told him he was wanted in the office.

'What the hell for?' Harry thundered, turning on the boy who cowered back.

'Ah don't know, maister,' the lad quavered, so Harry, muttering about time-wasting, strode across the yard to his office to find Lally's note waiting for

33

him.

Now he glared round the clearing in which Foxwell Farm was set. 'Mr Weaver, is it?' Harry asked, hefting the leather bag and fastening his gaze on the startled farmer.

'Aye, that's me bu' . . . ?'

'Is there somewhere we might discuss this farm and the rent owing on it?' though by the look of the yard the interior of the farmhouse would be just as unsavoury a place to sit down and talk about what had to be done. Lally hung back and Harry was sorry to have to put her through this but she must learn one way or the other that she was to be the new landlord and that as such she must deal with shifty-eyed men like this. That she must oversee the farms, see to repairs that might need to be done, collect rents and make sure that her sons' inheritance was being cared for.

There was a great deal of shouting, denials, false whimpering on Arty's part as he realised that this chap, whoever he was, would not be put off by tales of how harsh the winters were in these parts and how difficult it was to raise any sort of a crop without a plough-horse. If Mrs Fraser could see her way to lending them one, perhaps from one of the other farms, he was sure he could begin to pay his rent in, say, twelve months but as for the arrears . . .

Harry stopped him with a lift of his hand. They were sitting at a littered table, the family grouped about them, Evie Weaver hovering at her husband's back, bewildered by the accounts book which had printed on its cover 'Foxwell Farm', words she couldn't read, and which according to the gentleman, Mr Sinclair, he said he was, proved

34

that they had paid no rent for nearly three years. As they none of them could read or write it was double Dutch to them, and they said so, complaining bitterly, since Arty was sure he had been up to the estate office not so long ago and put the rent in Master Chris's hand, God bless him. Surely Mrs Fraser remembered it, and when Lally shook her head doubtfully Arty gave the impression that he was convinced they were all out to 'do' him.

They left Foxwell by a dilapidated gate after Harry had told the family, who collected with an air of acute misery to see them off, that the rents for the past years would be cancelled but on the first of January Mrs Fraser would expect to see one of them in the estate office with a month's rent in his hand. That they must clear their fields—after all, counting himself, Arty had six able-bodied people to help him—and in the spring a crop must be sown. Arty nodded dejectedly and when the man and Mrs Fraser had ridden off turned to his wife and told her that the good times were over and what were they to make of this chap who seemed on good terms with the new widow. It seemed indecent to him with the poor young chap scarcely cold in his grave for the missis to have taken up with someone else, didn't Evie agree with him? Despite the looseness of her own daughters' morals, Evie did!

Thickpenny Farm, rented by the Higgins family, Cowslip by the Grahams, Prospect Farm by the Archer family, Folly by the McGinleys and the Home Farm by the Jacksons, were, in comparison to Foxwell and the Weavers who rented it, in comparatively good shape. The stock was well

35

cared for, mostly pigs, sheep, poultry and an excellent herd of Friesian cows at two of the farms, the rest given over to the growing of mangolds, some wheat, potatoes, oats and rye, and all promised to keep up with their rents now they knew that Mrs Fraser, poor lass, had an agent, as they thought Harry Sinclair to be, to help her with the estate and to whom they could go in times of need. Many of their outbuildings needed repair and Polly McGinley confided that the roof of the farm leaked 'summat dreadful', so much so that she and Sean were forced to sleep in the parlour and their son Denny and his wife Kate, who lived with them, shared a pallet by the kitchen fire.

Harry promised that Mrs Fraser would see to it all the moment the rent was paid.

'How am I to mend their roof, Harry? I haven't a penny to my name,' Lally asked disconsolately. They were almost the only words she had spoken during the whole of the morning as they travelled from farm to farm. She seemed overwhelmed by the sheer magnitude of the task she proposed to take on and had Harry not been beside her, gently encouraging her, she would have put Merry to a gallop and made for home. They were riding through a great belt of timber rising from a jungle of undergrowth that covered the entire south-eastern section of the estate. It was at least two miles across and about a mile deep with a clearing in the middle which was covered with the sodden carpet of russet autumn leaves. There was a fallen log in a patch of sunlight and, reining in Piper, Harry dismounted and held out his hand to her. She took it and jumped to the ground and was for a bare moment held in his arms as he caught her.

She remembered thinking he smelled nice, a lemon scent of some sort; perhaps shaving soap. He was dressed very casually in a tweed jacket, riding breeches with well-polished, knee-high riding boots and a high-necked jumper. His ebony hair fell in a tumble of curls over his forehead and for a disturbing moment she wanted to reach out and brush them back as she might young Jamie's. His dark brown eyes, the colour of chocolate, darkened even further and a faint flush came to his amber cheeks. His lips, well cut and firm as though to proclaim he would stand no insolence or opposition from any man, lifted at the corners with a hint of humour and as she slipped to the ground their bodies were pressed against one another then he let her go and turned away.

'Perhaps we could sit here for a moment,' he said politely, getting out his snowy white handkerchief and brushing it over the fallen tree trunk so that she might sit.

'I must get back to the children. Dora is still somewhat . . .' she was about to say 'inexperienced' then she remembered that Dora, Jenny and Clara came from a family of twelve and, as Jenny had remarked when Dora was taken on, she could bring up two babies with one hand tied behind her back.

Harry sat down beside her. He wanted to take her hand, enfold it between his own, helpless beneath the wave of tenderness that swept over him but he knew it was far, far too soon for that. Let her get used to him, to having him help her, to calling often, on the estate's business, of course, and when she began to feel at ease with him and was becoming used to her loss of Chris then he

37

could perhaps . . . well, he was not sure what he would do but he *was* sure he could start to . . . to . . . court her. *Court her!* Was that his intention? This feeling he had for her had come on him so suddenly it was still unwieldy and he was not certain how he was to handle it, or her. First he must make himself indispensable to her so that she trusted him, treated him as a friend, then perhaps he might . . . Oh, to the devil with it, let's get today over before we start planning the bloody future!

'You're anxious about money, I know that, and the problem of how you are to mend the roof at Folly Farm and all the other repairs needed, which seem to be many, must appear to be insurmountable but you must allow me to help you there.'

She turned abruptly, her mouth opening on a denial but he held up his hand. 'No, just hear me out. I'm not suggesting I should lend it to you but if you were to see Anson, he's the manager at the bank in Moorend, he will give you good advice on how to raise a loan. The rents, when they start to come in, will repay it and in a year or two you will be out of debt and the farms should all be in good heart and making a profit. Most of the tenants seem to be honest and hardworking and must have money in the bank. They have been paying no rent for years as far as I can see and with a bit of encouragement'—he smiled wryly, for he knew what he meant by that—'will soon be round at the estate office. Where is it, by the way?'

She looked bewildered. 'I'm not sure. Chris didn't . . .'

'No matter,' he said, wondering what else Christopher Fraser hadn't told this lovely wife of

38

his or even if he knew himself. Years and years of neglect had run the estate into the ground and he also wondered where the money had come from, which moneylender had provided the means, the cash for Chris, and his father before him, to throw about so lavishly, and where it had gone. They had lived like princes. As a youth, he himself had been, with his own father before he died, to dine at the Priory and had been open-mouthed at the liberality and display. Champagne drunk as though it had been water and came out of the taps in the kitchen, exotic foods prepared by the French chef Joe Fraser had kept, card games for extremely high stakes which his father had smilingly refused to play, and every lamp in the house lit so that it looked like an enchanted fairyland. He had hunted from there with the rest of the county people, admiring the expensive hunters eating their heads off in the stables, the hounds kept by the Frasers, the hunt servants, the display of wealth. All gone now and this slender young woman was left to pick up the pieces.

'I'm sorry to be of so little help to you but I will find it and set it up as an office. Where did you find the accounts books for the farms?'

So she was not quite so confused as she seemed! They had been lying on the top shelf in a cupboard in the kitchen, unearthed by Mrs Stevens when he questioned her. Probably slung there heedlessly by Chris when his father died and he had found them too complicated for his careless mind to understand.

'I found them one day on the kitchen table, Mr Sinclair,' Mrs Stevens had told him, 'so I put them away for safety until Master Chris should ask

39

for them. He never did.'

'They were . . . safe with Mrs Stevens,' he answered shortly, since he did not want to blacken the name of her dead husband who had been a light-hearted fool.

'Then . . . what shall I do next, Mr Sinclair?'

He sighed, for it seemed she had not yet accepted that he was of her generation, the brother of Chris's friend and not an elderly man from that of their fathers'!

'First we'll return to the Priory and locate the estate office, look through the records for the agreements with the tenants, the leases, then, when you are free we'll ride into Moorend and see Mr Anson at the bank. When would—'

'This afternoon would suit me. You could stay to luncheon and then, if you can spare the time we could—'

'I'm sorry, Lally, but this afternoon I have an important appointment but perhaps tomorrow?'

'Of course.'

He could see she was somewhat deflated, having made up her mind that he was to be at her disposal whenever she needed him and he was sorry. But before he took her to see Fred Anson he must speak to him alone, for there was not a shadow of a doubt that the bank manager would refuse her. The estate would be heavily mortgaged, of that he was certain and there would, no doubt of it, be overdrafts, creditors and the like, and the chances of old Anson throwing good money after bad, as he would see it, were absolutely nil. *Unless he himself offered to stand the loan!* It wouldn't be a loan really, not from the bank, but he would be forced to go through this charade to convince Lally that it

40

was.

'But I would like to take you up on your offer of luncheon. My appointment isn't until three.'

They mounted their horses and rode on through the wood, Harry making silent estimates of the value of the timber, since it would be one way of putting some money into the estate. They emerged into the pale sunshine of the steeper and less dense Moor Wood that rose behind the Priory and Harry could see the back of the house lying in the valley as they crossed rough ground leading to the paddocks which had once teemed with horses. Ebony was there, peacefully cropping the grass beside Blossom, the little cob that pulled the lawn mower. They both looked up and the cob whinnied a welcome, then walked towards the fence, ears pricked forward. They entered the stable yard where Carly ran to take their bridles.

'Give them both a rub down, lad,' Harry said, with the casual authority of one who is used to giving orders and having them obeyed.

Carly looked at his little mistress, thinking she looked tired but she smiled at him as she dismounted and murmured, 'Thank you, Carly,' and if he could have got down on his knees and kissed her feet he would have done. This Sinclair chap just took everything that was done for him for granted but Miss Lally never failed to smile and thank you. He led the two animals towards the stables and watched as Mr Sinclair and Miss Lally entered the kitchen by the back door.

Biddy was for a moment confounded by the unexpected arrival of the visitor. She was at the stove adding salt to a stew she had made that morning. Scrag end of mutton, which was all they could afford, with plenty of vegetables, which Barty had sent round to the kitchen door with Froglet, to be served with a mountain of boiled potatoes. There was an appetising smell and the stew, cooking slowly in an enormous copper pan, would do them all, including the men who worked outside, for their midday meal and then this evening she would contrive something with a chicken, an old one plucked and cleaned by herself that had only yesterday clucked unconcernedly in the yard. She was good at that and managed to feed the household, though for how much longer she shuddered to think. If Miss Lally didn't get some brass from somewhere soon they would all fade away, including those babies in the nursery. She had made bread earlier on with Clara's help and several large loaves lay cooling on the table.

'Mr Sinclair is to stay for luncheon, Biddy,' Miss Lally told her as she and the gentleman, who looked somewhat astonished by the unconventionality of it all, walked through to the hallway beyond the kitchen door. Jenny and Clara stood with their mouths agape, but then Miss Lally was like that, unaware of the proprieties and if she was, not caring a jot or tittle about them. As Master Chris had been.

But Biddy Stevens was unfazed. 'Very well, Miss Lally. If you would take Mr Sinclair through to the drawing room and offer him a sherry, I will set luncheon in the breakfast room.'

'Thank you, Biddy,' and without glancing at him Lally led her visitor through the hallway and into the drawing room where a good fire was burning. 'Will you take sherry, Mr Sinclair?'

'Goddammit, Lally, will you call me Harry,' he

snapped and with raised eyebrows at his tone Lally shrugged and indicated the drinks tray. 'And if it's all the same to you I'll have a whisky. I see you have a bottle here.'

'Of course, help yourself. Chris . . . used to drink it. It's not been touched since . . . since . . .'

'Thank you and . . . let us talk about the farms.'

*   *   *

At one of the farms two of its occupants were talking about her. Jed and Ham Weaver were lounging before the fire in the kitchen of Foxwell Farm, both smoking a clay pipe. Spurred on by the sudden appearance of their landlord, or should they call her *landlady* now, both Arty and Evie Weaver were poking about at the back of the building among the nettles and docks that proliferated there. They were searching for the scythe to cut the weeds with and which, by Arty's reckoning, he had left leaning against the wall last summer.

'I were cuttin' the bluddy things when you come over badly an' I were forced ter give over an' give yer a 'and inter't kitchen,' making it sound as though had it not been for her the whole lot would have been cleared and the scythe returned to its proper place in the ramshackle barn.

'Nay, I can't remember but do us 'ave ter find it right now? An' anyroad I reckon it'll be rusty and if us—'

'Give over, woman. Did yer not see the look that man give us? If us don't get summat done 'e'll 'ave us outer 'ere and then what'll we do. We gotter mekk a start somewhere an' them two lazy sods

43

inside can gerroff their bums an' all. We gotter find next month's rent from somewhere an' it's up ter them ter earn it in the only way they know.' By which he meant poaching.

Them two sods, unconcerned by their parents' sudden anxiety, were telling each other what they would like to do to the 'widder woman' if they could get their hands on her which, though unlikely, made a pleasant discussion. They went short of women, for though they were well-set-up young men and not without looks, they were known to be rough, vicious even with the women they got their hands on, and shared. Most women in the district gave them a wide berth. They sometimes had to resort to forcing one or other of their sisters, which was all very well and certainly scratched their itch but a sweet little morsel like the 'widder woman' would make a nice change. Let her just ride up here on her own and they'd show her what real men were like, they told one another, and that was a bit different to that milk-sop she had married.

'We'd 'ave ter be careful like, our Jed. She'd 'ave the law on us if they catched us.'

Jed smirked. 'There's ways an' means, lad.'

'What d'yer mean, Jed?' Ham was what was known as a bit of a gawby, not quite all there, as clever as a clog nail as they said in Moorend, which suited Jed for it meant he was the leader in whatever mischief they got up to.

'She'll not know it's us, is wharr I mean, Ham, me lad.'

They both began to laugh and it was not until Arty entered the kitchen and gave them both what he called a 'thick ear' that they stumbled from the

44

farmhouse and into the barn where they kept their traps and lines and the old rifle they owned for the purpose of taking out the squire's deer.

*   *   *

Lally spent the rest of the day after Mr Sinclair had left, and far into the evening, sitting by the drawing-room fire poring over the estate books which, to her surprise, she found quite fascinating. She had played with Jamie for an hour under the disapproving eye of Dora who was of the opinion that Miss Lally made her son far too excited and it was Dora who had to settle him down after she had left. She was lovely with the baby though, nursing him against her empty breasts and kissing the silken curls on his head, then his rounded cheek, because by now he had accepted the milk from the bottle and was beginning to thrive, for which Dora took the credit. She had helped her mam with half a dozen bairns and, her and her mam being so busy in the smallholding her pa kept, had no time for pandering to mardy children. They should be bathed—though not a lot of that went on in their cottage—changed, fed and put down to sleep. Miss Lally swore the baby was the dead spit of Master Chris, which he was, they both were, handsome and lively, but must not be spoiled and Dora meant to make sure they weren't and with Miss Lally busy about the estate Dora had a good chance of keeping them in line.

Lally turned page after page, the books recording the events of each farm, the acreage, the tenants, the stock, the crops and the names of the farms and their occupants. Thickpenny, Cowslip,

45

Prospect, Folly, Foxwell, and then the Home Farm which belonged to the Priory. It was from there came the milk Alec drank, the eggs, bacon, cheese and butter which would be their staple diet soon if she didn't apply herself to the task of picking up where Chris had left off and it was then that the thought came to her that she had no idea what or when that might have been, for never once in their three years of marriage had she seen Chris take the slightest interest in any of them.

CHAPTER FOUR

As she rose from her chair, her face lighting up at the sight of him, he strode across the room and dragged her into his arms. Her own arms went round his back, holding on tightly, and from the doorway Harry watched, the furious darts of jealousy taking him by surprise. Six weeks after the death of Christopher Fraser, Roly Sinclair had come home from his travels!

'Lally . . . Lally darling,' he murmured, holding her close for longer than Harry thought necessary, then he held her away from him and looked deeply into her dry eyes, expecting her to be tearful, which he was ready to be if she required it, though how sincere it was Harry couldn't guess. His brother was the best salesman that was ever born, selling miles of Sinclair cloth all over Europe and America, journeys planned well in advance, carrying his cases of samples from country to country, at the same time selling himself as the charming, impish, boyish chap he showed to the world. His smile illuminated a room and drew people, especially women, to him and he had an easy assurance and a total conviction that everyone liked him, which they did. 'Harry telegraphed me but I was in Rome and couldn't leave. Dear God, poor Chris, and he was such a good horseman. I shall miss him. Come, darling,' leading her to the sofa by the fire, stepping over scattered toys, a spinning top in what had once been bright but were now faded colours, a soft rabbit, a golliwog, balls, a duck and several tattered rag books all of which had once belonged to Chris.

'Now tell me how you are. I believe old Harry has been helping you with the estate and now that I'm home I can lend a hand, at least until I'm off again. And just look at you in that frightful black. Oh, I know it's the custom; what is it, a year for a widow and you with such marvellous dress sense. You were the leader of fashion in Moorend . . . well, never mind, I insist that when I take you to the theatre next week—oh yes, I will not allow you to sit about in this great house moping—you shall wear that lovely apricot silk you had on the night you and I and Chris and . . . what was the name of that pretty little thing who came with us? Vivienne or was it Virginia? Like a hedge-rose she was without a thought in her head, though of course she couldn't compare with you. Mind you, she more than made up for it in—'

'Roly,' Harry warned, still standing in the doorway since it seemed neither of them cared where he was, but Roly merely grinned.

'Now then, why don't you go upstairs and change into something enchanting while Harry and I admire that wonderful Christmas tree you have in

47

the hall. I'm glad to see you're keeping up the new practice. Good old Prince Albert, God bless him.'

She was beginning to smile, the sheer audacity of Roly's cheerful conversation instead of the woeful, sympathetic murmurs her other callers gave her lifting her spirits. She was a widow, they told her, and should act accordingly as though they could see the devastation in her heart. Only Biddy knew of it as she held her in her arms when Chris's ghost came to haunt her. Chris had been a scamp but his heart had been good and cheerful and he had loved her.

'It's good to keep up the traditions,' he repeated. 'For the children, I suppose. Two boys you have now, Harry tells me.' He turned his affectionate smile on his brother. 'Come on, old chap, don't dither in the doorway,' making it sound as though Harry was some elderly gentleman who was not quite sure of his welcome or even of how to get to a chair. At once Lally rose from the sofa, loosening herself from Roly's arms, to his chagrin, and moved across to Harry, taking his hand, her smile warm and welcoming.

'Come and sit by the fire, Harry. It's cold today and Carly assures me it will snow. Roly,' turning to the wryly smiling man by the fire, 'ring the bell and we'll have coffee, or perhaps hot chocolate.' She held on to Harry's warm hand and led him to the sofa opposite the one on which Roly lounged. In the last month she had come to realise the worth of this rather quiet, self-contained man who was guiding her through the intricacies of estate management and had even brought her a hefty book on the care and management of stock, on the growing of cereal and grain. He came every couple of days and they had scrutinised every account book, every ledger, every lease and liability for rent, every written agreement and contract that had gathered dust for years in the estate office, getting to know the size of every farm and the tenants in them. He had taken her to see Mr Anson at the bank and had explained the loan which Mr Anson had promised her and had ridden with her once again to visit the farms where most welcomed her kindly if a little warily. The office had been scrubbed and scoured by Jenny and Clara, the books dusted and put back on their shelves, the windows cleaned, the chimney swept and a good fire lit to get rid of the slight smell of damp that hung about the room so long unused. She spent every morning at the desk, making the room her own with bright pictures on the walls and curtains purloined from rooms not used in the house.

At the end of two weeks Aunt Jane had gone back to her small house in Skircoat, having failed dismally to convince her young, widowed relative that it was not seemly for her to remain in this big house alone.

'I am not alone, Aunt Jane, I have Biddy with me.'

'That is not the same, Amalia, and you know it. I would offer you a place with me but the two boys are somewhat trying to my nerves.' Aunt Jane suffered dreadfully with her nerves and the couple of weeks she had spent with Amalia had made them worse.

'I cannot run the estate from town, Aunt Jane. I must be here.'

'And that is another thing, Amalia. It is not right

49

for a gentlewoman to run an estate. Could not a
. . . an agent be put in to see to it all?'

'I have no money to pay wages, Aunt Jane.'

And so Aunt Jane had given up, packed her bags
and returned to Skircoat, effectively washing her
hands of her rebellious relative.

But it was Harry's action on Christmas Day that
had given Lally the most pleasure. Polly McGinley
had trudged over from Folly Farm with a turkey. A
turkey with short spurs and black legs which
proved it was young and would be tender. A gift,
she said, in thanks for the work that had been
started on the roof of the farmhouse so that now
she and Sean, Denny and his wife Kate were all
sleeping in their own beds in the bedrooms
upstairs. What a relief it was to have her parlour
back and she and Kate were as happy as sandboys
in the kitchen without the pallett which had been
got out each night.

Lally had been overwhelmed and had even
hugged her, to Polly's amazement, she told Sean,
and that young landlady of theirs had a warm heart
and if there was anything Sean or Denny could do
for her they must see to it at once.

So the turkey had been stuffed with forcemeat
of Biddy's own making, fried sausages arranged
about it for garnish, the gravy made along with the
bread sauce, the bird cooking for a couple of
hours, ready to be served at one thirty, when the
front doorbell had rung. The dogs had barked
furiously and Biddy had hurried along the hallway
muttering about visitors on a day such as this what
with Miss Lally in a deep depression, the children,
sensing their mother's mood, grizzling and Clara
complaining of a pain in her belly.

It was Harry, standing at the foot of the steps holding the bridle of a large, strong pony, dark brown, and known as a dales pony from the north-east of England, used for pulling Harry's gig. 'Stand, Dancer,' he was saying, then, addressing himself to the astonished Biddy, asked her if she would send the groom round to help him. The back of the gig was loaded with parcels.

When he had been ushered in to the warm drawing room where Lally was sitting alone, her head resting on the back of the sofa, her face sad and almost plain in her sadness, there had been an immediate change in the atmosphere. Carly had staggered in with an armful of parcels, helped by an excited Clara who had totally forgotten the pain she had complained of, and Harry had asked if the children could be brought down for a moment. Dora, the baby squirming in her arms and Master Jamie leaping and falling and picking himself up in an ecstasy of joy and wonderment, entered the drawing room and for the next half-hour a brand-new railway engine, a bright blue rabbit, a clockwork mouse, a small wooden horse on wheels and pulled on a string, several books and a set of coloured bricks were revealed, over which Jamie said his new word, which was 'minc, mine'. He allowed Alec to reach with wandering infant fingers for the pretty paper in which they had been wrapped. There was the usual upset when he and the baby were removed at last by Dora and Clara, Jamie howling his displeasure which could be heard all the way up the stairs.

'And now it's the turn of the grown-ups,' Harry said, smiling his slow, infrequent smile, for it was the only way to hide his real feelings. 'Can the

51

maids be spared from the kitchen for a minute or two?' And when they were brought in by Biddy, the two girls and Dora, of course, were overwhelmed by the lovely rolls of dress fabric in the prettiest colours with which he presented them. There was a silver bracelet for Biddy, plain and simple, and Biddy, beginning to see what was in this cool, unruffled man, thanked him and ushered the girls away to the kitchen.

'Now it's your turn, Lally,' reaching into his pocket for a small, beautifully wrapped parcel and handing it to her with a stiff, almost reverent bow.

'Harry,' she whispered, holding the gift in her hand. 'You know I can't . . .'

'Why, who is to know? We are friends, are we not? I am alone on this day when families are supposed to come together, and so are you, though you have your boys. Will you not allow me to be, just for a day, an uncle, or a . . . distant relative to give them a Christmas gift and having done so how could I leave you out? It's getting on for six weeks since Chris . . . I'm sorry, forgive me, I should not have mentioned him.'

He stood irresolute in front of her, looking down at her bowed head, dismayed when she raised her head and he saw the sparkle of tears in her eyes. He had never seen her cry but now, when there was no need, it seemed she was about to do so. He sat down beside her, longing to reach out and touch her, even if it was no more than her hand, the one that held his unwrapped gift but he knew, as he had known before, that it was too soon to show his feelings for her.

'Please, give me the pleasure of giving *you* a Christmas gift.'

She said nothing but slowly, her fingers inclined to tremble, she opened the small parcel which contained a velvet box. Opening the box she gasped, for lying on another nest of velvet was the prettiest bracelet, a fine gold chain linked every half-inch with a tiny turquoise the exact colour of her eyes.

'I couldn't resist it, Lally. It was made for you and I knew it the moment I clapped eyes on it in the jeweller's window. Will you let me put it on your wrist?'

'Harry, it's much too—'

'No, it's not. Perhaps it's . . . not quite the thing to give a young widow so soon after her husband's death but if you don't take it I shall be forced to present it to . . . to Biddy so that she has one for each wrist.'

Wordlessly she held out her hand and carefully, slowly, so that she would not see his own hands trembling, he fastened it against the deep black of her sleeve.

'There, now not another word and since it is almost one o'clock I must—'

She had been fingering the lovely bracelet and looking down at it with pleasure, for it was a long time since she had received anything so beautiful and yet so exactly right, but she sprang up at once and took hold of his hand.

'No, you will not go, Harry, not to that empty house; it is empty, isn't it, for you have just told me so. You shall stay and keep me company while I eat my Christmas turkey, plum pudding and . . . and whatever other Christmas fare Biddy has put together. I shall ring the bell and tell her to set another place at the table. Oh, Harry, I can't tell

53

you how wonderful this is. I was expecting to eat by myself. Biddy is a stickler for the conventions and says she is a servant and could not sit down to luncheon with me though I'm sure I could have persuaded her. Now reach for the bell and then you can tell me all the news before we eat. I wonder if there is any champagne in the cellar . . .' Then she began to laugh when he reached into another bag and triumphantly produced a large bottle of the sparkling wine.

They talked of everything under the sun from the children and Jamie's amusing antics with his new presents, to the possibility of snow; the gossip his visit would cause should it be known in Moorend, Harry doing his best to mimic Mrs Frederick Anson, the banker's wife, making her laugh as once she had done with her cheerful young husband. He spoke to her of the state of the army in the Crimea after the Battle of Inkerman and the appalling inefficiency on the part of the government in providing the soldiers with proper clothing and shelter to meet the winter. All this had been reported in *The Times* during November by Mr W. H. Russell, correspondent for the newspaper in the Crimea, he told her, but then Lally had been so deep in her grieving she had not heard of it.

Biddy heard their voices and her laughter from the kitchen and though she knew the conventional folk of Moorend would be scandalised by the behaviour of the newly widowed Mrs Amalia Fraser, she didn't care, for it was the first time her lass had enjoyed herself for months. Even before his death, Master Chris had gone out alone, to hunt, to gamble, to drink with his friends, leaving

54

Lally alone since she could not accompany him on account of her condition. She had moped about the place, cursing the bulge that prevented her from doing all the things he did, but now it seemed Mr Sinclair was entertaining her, making her laugh, and on the very day they had all dreaded. When he finally left it was dark and he would have the devil's own job to find his way across the moors with the gig but it seemed he did not care, for the expression on his face told Biddy all she had hoped for. Miss Lally needed someone to look after her!

Now on the day Master Roly returned Lally had Jenny bring in a pot of hot chocolate on a silver tray which Biddy had found in what had once been the butler's pantry, cleaning and polishing it to mirror brightness. There was plum cake and hot mince pies left over from Christmas, for though she knew her lass still grieved badly for the loss of her young husband, Mr Sinclair had given her something to fill her days, to occupy her mind and a hope for the future. The Priory was her sons' inheritance and must be nurtured and from a flighty, thoughtless young wife she must now become the protector of that inheritance. With Mr Sinclair to help her she would succeed.

'Now tell us where you have been, Roly,' she was saying, the pretty bracelet Mr Sinclair had given her twinkling on her wrist. 'Do you know I have never been abroad, even with Chris. I wanted to go to Italy for our honeymoon but . . .' Her voice tapered off and Harry longed to reach out to her, hold her hand, kiss the back of it and tell her she had only to say the word and he would take her to the ends of the earth if she wished it, but it was Roly who took her hand, looking strangely like

55

Chris, perhaps not in his features but in his manner, his disarmingly frank smile.

He spoke about Rome and its splendours, its architecture, its weather, its food, giving the impression that all he did apart from sell Sinclair cloth, which he did superbly, was visit museums and art galleries, bringing a smile to Harry's strong face and lifting the corners of his stubborn mouth. Harry knew his brother was a complete hedonist, consorting with actresses, courtesans, the bored young wives of wealthy old gentlemen, giving pleasure to women, and himself, dining in the best restaurants, staying in the best hotels, but at the same time not neglecting the business which took him to many parts of Europe and North America. He would be home for a few weeks, studying the latest designs that came off the Sinclair looms, knowing as much as Harry about the many processes that wool went through, sorting and scouring, blending, carding, spinning and weaving. He might give the impression that he drifted from one pleasure to the next with no thought in his head but where to obtain the best champagne and the prettiest women and the fanciest waistcoats, but he was an astute businessman.

Lally had colour in her face when at last they stood up to leave. She had not run upstairs as Roly had exhorted her to change into one of the lovely gowns he remembered but had promised to think about his invitation to take her to the theatre in Ward's End in Halifax.

Roly held her hand and kissed her cheek as they left. Harry took her hand and turned away as Roly ran down the steps to where Carly held the two fine horses, Roly's chestnut gelding, Foxfire, and

56

Harry's bay, Piper.

She watched them walk, then break into a gallop down the drive which Barty and Froglet did their best to keep raked and clear of weeds, but as she watched them go she suddenly felt tired, for it was all so hard. There seemed to be no joy in her life. Roly's call had rejuvenated her for an hour, as had the Christmas Day she had spent with Harry, taking her back to those magical days of their childhood and later when she and Roly and Chris had ridden and played and laughed their way through their days of golden youth—which was a strange thing to say when she was twenty years old and Roly only twenty-three—but now, with him gone, it was bleak again. She did not for a moment consider the man who, though she was not aware of it, loved her with a growing strength and passion that would have astounded her. It was not the love of a young and eager man, which was how Chris had loved her, but with the depth, the immutability of the stones that scattered the great stretches of moorland, which was Harry Sinclair's world.

She trailed up the staircase, her hand touching the banister, turning at the bend in the stairs, her black gown dragging on the wide and shallow steps. A past Fraser had taken a fancy to a cast-iron statue of a full-sized stag which stood at the turn of the stairs and on which she and Chris and Roly had often sat as they played games the two boys made up. All part of those days when . . . when she . . .

Suddenly she stood still just as she was about to pass it. There was an enormous gilt-framed mirror, old and flaking, just above the stag and as she caught sight of the dreary figure in black she

57

wondered for a moment who she was. Dear God, it was Lally Fraser, pale, listless, *dull and graceless* and as she stared she came to a sudden decision. She was *twenty years old* for God's sake and though she would love Chris for the rest of her days was she to drift about looking as dead as he was? Was she to have no joy in her life again? She had her children, her two boys who must be cared for and this house and the estate which Harry Sinclair was doing his best to help her run but need she look like a crow while she did it?

Picking up her skirts, she ran up the rest of the stairs and along the wide hallway to her room. Inside she tore off the black gown and corset— Lord, why did she need a corset with a waist that measured no more than nineteen inches?—and stood in her chemise and petticoats while she rummaged through her wardrobe. Her clothes had been much talked about when she was young Chris Fraser's bride and she had not enquired where the money had come from to buy them. Chris loved to see her well dressed and that was enough for her. She was seventeen, attractive and in love! She had plain, pastel-tinted afternoon gowns, delicate creams, near whites. Richly patterned crimson and emerald-green silk shawls. A walking dress of coffee-coloured *foulard des Indes* trimmed with velvet. Light summer dresses with sleeves of puffed muslin and tulle with wrist bands of ribbon and pearl and a dozen sparkling butterflies to choose from to fasten in the dark curls of her short hair. She had once been a butterfly herself in colours ranging from ecru, tawny brown, crimson, flame, apricot, honey gold to sea green and duck-egg blue!

58

She found a lovely rose-pink woollen gown, tight-waisted and with a full skirt. The bodice had buttons from waist to neck, each one covered in rose-pink satin and around the waist was a broad sash to match. It was plain, simple and very becoming and the moment she put it on she felt better. The colour put a flush in her cheeks and her eyes sparkled with that particular blue-green which Chris had called turquoise, the whites clear, her long lashes, dark and thick, outlining them as though with ink. She looked quite . . . quite lovely, she thought, and more like the woman she had been before Chris died. There, she had allowed the thought—the word—into her head and she must get used to it. *Died*. That was the word she had been unable to say, even to herself, but now she had said it and must get on with life and she would start right now with the rose-pink dress and she would accept Roly's invitation to go to the theatre. She would take the estate management into her hands, learn all that Harry Sinclair could teach her and . . . and . . .

She bent her head and stared at the threadbare carpet, despair doing its best to enslave her again, then she lifted it, lifted it high and, turning on her heel, moved to the door of her bedroom. Slowly she descended the stairs knowing she would get 'what-for' from Biddy and she did!

Clara was scrubbing the massive wooden table which had been scrubbed so often over the years the wood was almost white. Jenny was in the scullery washing vegetables and Biddy was poring over the household accounts book, doing her best to make a halfpenny do the work of a penny. A rich aroma of beef broth assailed Lally's nostrils,

59

while coals glowed red beneath the simmering stew pot. A kettle emitted a puff of steam and the blackleaded range gleamed beneath the hanging utensils. The tabby cat which was stretched before the fire opened one eye to study her then closed it again and the two dogs rose, their tails waving lazily as they ambled across the kitchen to greet her.

All three woman looked up as she entered and utter silence followed, a silence so dense the sound of the simmering broth was quite deafening. The two maids stood as though petrified, their hands stilled.

Biddy rose to her feet and over her face rippled a look Lally knew well. She had seen it a hundred times over the years whenever she had done, or was about to do, something of which Biddy disapproved. Biddy, though Lally was not aware of it, cared nothing for convention, nor the rules of society as applied to herself. Before she had worked for Mrs Atkins, Lally's mama, she had done many jobs Miss Lally knew nothing about, though Delphine Atkins had. It was Delphine Atkins who had rescued her one evening from the clutches of a drunken soldier who had dragged her into a doorway and had her skirt up around her waist. It wasn't the poor chap's fault really because she had been working the streets for several months when she lost her job as a scullery maid. But for some reason she had objected to him and had screamed out for help and it was Miss Lally's mam, passing by in her carriage, who had rescued her.

But Miss Lally had been brought up as a lady. She *was* a lady and ladies did not discard their mourning and change into a rose-pink gown six weeks after the death of a husband. Miss Lally, if she was to retain her position in society, must not deviate an inch from the path that society demanded.

'What do you think you're doing?' she asked, her voice icy, her face rigid with displeasure.

Lally swung the full skirt of her gown. 'I can't think what you mean . . .'

'Don't try to cod me, lady. Go upstairs immediately and take off that dress and put on the black.'

Lally hesitated for a minute, the habit of listening to Biddy strong in her, then, quietly, for she was her own mistress and was about to start on a new phase in her life, she answered her.

'I don't think I will, Biddy. Now, I would be glad of tea if Jenny could bring it through to the drawing room,' and turning gracefully she left the kitchen, leaving all three women open-mouthed in astonishment.

CHAPTER FIVE

He paid her a great deal of attention and gradually the people of Moorend began to notice and not only to notice but to disapprove.

The first time she accompanied him to the theatre in Ward's End, a play by Shakespeare was being performed. In the audience, three rows from the front where they had a good view of the boxes, were Mr and Mrs Frederick Anson with their friends, Mr and Mrs George Bracken, and all four were shocked into stunned silence when they saw the widow and Roly Sinclair, who was known as a ladies' man, enter one of them. The play was *The Merry Wives of Windsor*, described as a romantic comedy, but the two upright and leading citizens and their wives, especially their wives, could hardly have told you a word of its content, since their whole concentration was centred on Amalia Fraser, a widow of no more than ten weeks, positively *flirting* with her companion. Alone, the pair of them, in a private box which must have cost the earth but then the Sinclairs were probably the wealthiest family in the Halifax area and could afford it. She was dressed in a gown in a pale shade of what Mrs Anson would call duck-egg blue, with a low-cut décolletage and in her dark hair nestled a glittering jewelled butterfly, and who had bought her that, they whispered among themselves? On her wrist they could distinctly see the sparkle of what looked like an expensive bracelet! He was, of course, in full evening dress, handsome in black and white.

Harry Sinclair, from a seat in the back row of the auditorium, watched Lally and his brother but, unlike them, he also noticed the reaction of the audience, many of whom knew Lally Fraser and Roly Sinclair, and had known Chris Fraser. They were horrified that one of their own should be guilty of such an atrocious error of judgement, a wicked deviation from the accepted code of conduct. It was not a crime for a widow to remarry, of course, but only after a decent period of mourning and that had certainly not passed in the case of Lally Fraser. Indeed she should not even have been seen in a theatre and absolutely not alone in the company of a young, unmarried gentleman. Even with a relative it would have been unthinkable!

He felt the pain in his chest where his heart lay, the bitter pain caused by the malevolent pangs of jealousy, and yet at the same time a sadness that Lally had so easily succumbed to his brother's pleading. But could you expect her to be wise at her age? She was young, twenty years old and could not be expected to suffer the living death of widowhood for twelve months or even, as in some cases, a lifetime. Many widows, in fact most of them, had been married for years when their husbands passed on and had lived in their shadow in all that time. They had brought up children who were probably themselves married if daughters, and their sons were out in the world. These elderly widows were content to live in some seclusion, paying calls and receiving them, going about with friends, women friends and relatives, virtually retired from life and certainly not pushing themselves forward, for they had been taught to believe they had none!

But Lally Fraser was not one of them. Certainly she was widowed but her life was hardly begun and when the time was right and her period of mourning was over or even a little before, Harry meant to step in and make his intentions known. He could give her what she had had with Chris Fraser and a lot more besides: his love, his protection, expensive clothes, jewellery, her own carriage, a good education for her boys, a life of ease and luxury free from worry. He would employ an agent to run her estate so that she could fulfil her duties as his wife and the mother not only to

Chris's children, but to his own which she would start to bear him within twelve months of marriage. He would surround her with the devotion, the caring, the love she deserved and which he had in abundance.

He was at the end of the row and in the darkened auditorium he could watch her without being noticed himself. He had opera glasses trained on the box and her lovely face was animated, the expressions chasing one another across it as she became absorbed in the play. Roly spoke to her several times but Harry saw her put up her hand as though to silence him as she became enthralled in the action and words from the stage. She was obviously enjoying every minute and he made a small vow to himself that when they were married he would take her to the theatre, here, in London, in New York, or wherever they travelled. Then he pulled himself up and called himself every kind of fool, for it was clear that Harry Sinclair was not, and had never been in her thoughts except as an acquaintance who was helping her to pull the estate together. *London! New York! Marriage!* He must be a bloody fool, he brooded, as he set his opera glasses back in their case, stood up and strode from the theatre. He collected his bay from the stables at the White Horse Inn further up Ward's End, and with a ferocity that startled the stable lad, as Mr Sinclair was known for his love of horses and his politeness to servants, he galloped full tilt into the street and headed off towards Trinity Road which led to the edge of the town and Mill House where he lived.

*　　　*　　　*

Lally, knowing she had already broken every rule of society by not only leaving off her mourning but by appearing in public alone with an unmarried gentleman, refused absolutely to take up Roly's offer of a bit of supper at the White Horse Inn where the food was good and the wine even better.

'I can't, Roly, you know I can't. Biddy has already told me my reputation is torn to shreds by—'

'Then if that's the case, my pet, you can hardly damage it any more. You know you are absolutely safe with me. It's a shame to end the evening so early and, anyway, what has Biddy to do with it? She's a servant and has no right—'

Lally's face closed up. 'Roly, I will have nothing said against Biddy. I don't know what I would do without her.'

'I bet she's had enough to say about me.' His hand was at her elbow as he guided her from the box, along the carpeted corridor towards the steps leading down to the street. There were well-dressed ladies and gentlemen moving in the same direction, many of them known to her. There were a few frozen-faced nods in their direction but she noticed that most of them kept their faces averted to make it clear that they disapproved of her behaviour. She knew she had broken every rule of her own class but she had been unable to resist the temptation to wear the last evening gown that Chris had bought her, the duck-egg blue satin trimmed with guipure lace with a crinoline which had filled the carriage. The neckline was extremely low, showing the tops of her small white breasts. She had lost weight since Chris's death and Biddy had been cajoled into helping her take the bodice in, grumbling the whole time. Well, hardly grumbling, for the tirade that followed her announcement that she was to attend the theatre with Roly had been loud and long and furious.

'You realise, I suppose, that your reputation will be totally ruined. That not one of your friends will have anything to do with you in the future. No one will receive you or call on you.' All the time she spoke, or rather ranted, her hands were busy with the seams at the side of the bodice. 'I know that at the moment you are not yourself—'

'What *is* myself, Biddy?' Lally asked passionately. 'I'm twenty years old and I might as well be dead. Oh, I know I have the boys and I love them more than life but I can't *make* them my life. I must do something.'

'Mr Sinclair has given you something to do. You are to look after your sons' inheritance. Learn to manage the estate. You know he will help you. He already has with the loan you have from the bank and you know the tenants are already glad to have their farm buildings put in order. Polly McGinley at Folly Farm is most grateful.'

'I know, Biddy, but that isn't *fun*. I want to laugh and enjoy myself as I used to do with Chris. Roly Sinclair makes me laugh. He makes me feel young again and as I was before . . . before Chris died. Do you know Chris wanted to join some regiment or other and go out to the Crimea to fight the Russians and I wouldn't let him because I was afraid he might be killed.' Her tone was bitter. 'Dear God, I might as well have given him my blessing since he died anyway. Oh, God, Biddy, I can't bear being a widow, expected to dress in

66

black from head to toe and never have anything that might be called enjoyment. I mourn him, of course I do and I will never forget him and how much I loved him, but why is it considered wrong for me to have a perfectly innocent trip to the theatre with a man I've known since childhood? We are almost brother and sister, for heaven's sake. He and Chris were like brothers and he would never do anything to harm me.'

'No, I don't suppose he would but we're talking about your reputation, lass.' Biddy bent her head to bite off the thread with which she was sewing. The lovely gown slithered on her lap and the light from the window fell across its folds, rippling them from the palest blue that was almost white to a deep aquamarine and in each fold was the exact colour of the eggs laid by the ducks on the lake at the front of the house.

Lally was roaming about the bedroom, picking up ornaments and putting them down again, stopping to look in the mirror and thrusting her fingers through her short hair. She was restless, bored, and she knew the reason why. It was all very well to talk about managing the estate which she was determined to do but it was not the days that bore her down but the nights in the big, lavender-scented bed she had shared with Chris. She had been married for three years and during that time she had learned the joy, the passion, the repletion of physical love and her body was a jangle of nerves without it. She had loved her husband and she had loved the act of love. Her body had sparkled with pleasure wherever he touched it and no part of it had been deprived of his caress. She had adored it, and him. She had loved his nudity

67

and her own, the sensation of bare flesh against bare flesh, the emotion it stirred in him and in her. When he had entered her body, which he had done every night and sometimes morning too since the day of their marriage, it had closed about him, holding him fast, fusing them together with love and self-abandonment. That was all gone now and she missed it, her body throbbing with loss. She might only be twenty years old but she was a mature woman in the ways of the flesh. She would marry again, she knew she would, but until she did she must subdue these urges that came on her and drove her to a mad restlessness that nothing could assuage. But she could see no harm in her friendship with Roly who was, as she had said to Biddy, in all but name, her brother. She was aware that society deeply disapproved. But she was beginning to find out that she did not much care. The return of Roly had brought a small amount of merriment into her life, since he himself cared for nothing that was considered *proper* in society and the pursuit of enjoyment was second nature to him. She refused to consider that the double standards that were the measure of their class allowed gentlemen to do as they pleased, discreetly if possible, but the same rule did not apply to its womenfolk.

It was the beginning of February, mild, spring-like almost, and each week she rode out to visit her tenants, usually astride having discarded her riding skirt, much to the embarrassment of the men in the fields and farmyards, for they were not used to seeing the shape of a female leg, even those who were married. They made love to their wives in the dark and most had scarce seen them without a layer of petticoats and a sensible, workaday dress since the day they had wed.

Carly had averted his eyes the first time she strode across the stable yard to where he had Merry waiting for her. Automatically he had bent, his hands linked to give her a lift into the side-saddle, not really looking at her, but he had been astounded when she told him to change it.

'I can get about more easily if I ride astride, Carly. I have to get down to open gates and it's easier dressed like this.'

'Mrs Fraser . . .' he had mumbled, but then it was not up to the likes of a groom to lecture his young mistress on the correct way to dress. He had done as he was told, changed the saddle and helped her into it, opened the gate and watched her break into a trot across the park, her two setters at her heels, turning to the house where three dumbfounded faces peered out of the kitchen window. He shrugged his shoulders at them, then, removing his cap, he had scratched his head in bemusement and returned to the job of mucking out. His young mistress seemed determined not to conform to the practices of her own kind. Just look at the frequency with which young Roly Sinclair had been out here in the last weeks. He'd lost count of the times he had run out to hold Foxfire, Mr Roly's chestnut gelding, while the young man had visited Miss Lally, and in the evening sometimes which wasn't proper!

Polly McGinley was in her hen-house when Lally shouted at the gate. She came running to open it and her face bore the same expression of astonishment when the mistress jumped down from her horse with what looked like, for a

69

moment of horror, naked legs. Even when she realised that Mrs Fraser actually had on a pair of beige kid riding breeches she was still startled. Mrs Fraser wore a warm, chocolate-coloured riding coat reaching down almost to her knees and the tops of her polished riding boots, which made the outfit somewhat more decent. Polly was not to know that the coat had once belonged to Chris Fraser though she could see it was far too big for his young widow. A scarf was wound round her neck and she wore no hat so that with her short hair she looked like a schoolboy.

'Morning, Mrs McGinley,' she called out cheerfully and Polly was glad to see her young landlord, or rather landlady, was recovering.

'Mornin', ma'am. Lovely day fer February. Sean an' Denny's down in't field seein' ter't 'taters but me an' Kate was just about ter 'ave us a brew. Will yer come inside, but I've just done't kitchen floor so I'd be obliged if yer'd keep them dogs outside.' Mrs Fraser might be her landlord but Polly believed in speaking her mind. She and Sean had paid up the rent owing and as far as they were concerned that entitled them to do as they pleased in the farmhouse and in the fields. She and Kate were doing well with their poultry, the money Mrs Fraser had put into the property allowing them to experiment with different strains of hens and what they didn't eat themselves was sent each week to the market-place in Halifax. Eggs, butter, trussed chickens, fancy cheeses and they were making steady progress. She had a lot of time for Mrs Fraser who was, at least, unlike her charming, but sadly dead husband, doing her best with the farms on her estate.

Despite her warning about the dogs, which Polly had implied might fetch muck into her kitchen, the yard was as neat as a parlour surrounded on two sides by farm buildings whitewashed and in good repair. The pig pen in which several pigs rooted looked as if it had been freshly cleaned out and the great horse which was used to pull the plough poked its head enquiringly over the stable door, whickering a welcome to Merry. There was a well-tended, well-fenced vegetable garden to the side of the kitchen door with a gate leading into it and, tethering Merry to the fence, Lally followed Polly into the kitchen. Kate McGinley, Polly's daughter-in-law, was up to her elbows in flour and, like her mother-in-law, did not believe in submissiveness to her betters. Respectful, yes, humble, no, so though she bobbed a small smiling curtsey she went on with making her bread. Tea was poured into great mugs, strong and sweet as *they* liked it and without stopping her task Kate gulped hers down while Lally and Polly sat before the enormous fire in the comfortable rocking-chairs, which had come from Polly's mam when she died, and drank their tea. Lally felt at ease, comfortable as she listened to Polly's plans for their future which, it seemed, were to include a grandchild by the summer. Polly was made up, she said, giving their Kate an affectionate look and if Mrs Fraser didn't mind she and Sean and their Denny meant to make the small cottage at the back of the farmhouse into a cosy home for the new family.

'Mrs McGinley . . .'

'Polly, please, ma'am.'

'Well, Polly, I'm absolutely delighted. The baby will be the first to be born to the estate since I . . . I took over.'

'If it be a lass . . . well, we was 'opin' yer might be godmother.' Polly beamed and when Lally said again she would be delighted Polly McGinley told their Kate afterwards she'd do owt fer the new landlord and whatever it was, she'd only to ask.

When Lally finally returned home she told the girls in the kitchen that she was awash with tea and she had even been forced to use the privy at the back of Cowslip Farm where Elsie Graham had pressed her third or was it her fourth mug of tea into her hand. Thankfully it had been spotlessly clean, which was a good sign for the Grahams had not been expecting her. They were all so welcoming, she told Biddy, she felt as though she had been visiting old friends. After all she had only met them recently, for in all their married life Chris had never done the rounds, with or without her. She had been with Harry Sinclair but the tenants had been somewhat constrained in his presence since he was the sort of man who did not easily thaw to others. He was proud and wealthy, used to giving orders and his rather arrogant, stiff manner did not put them at their ease.

But today, on her own, she had felt a sense of well-being. Except at one farm, though she said nothing of this to Biddy because if she had Biddy would have insisted that Carly accompany her and she did not want that. Her tenants evidently liked and even trusted her and Carly's presence might impede the progress she was making. The exception, of course, had been at Foxwell Farm where the Weavers appeared to have nothing to do but sit about in their cramped and sour kitchen, the men smoking their pipes, the women staring at a heap of rushes which, as she entered, they fell on with an air of great urgency, stating that they were busy with their baskets which they were to sell at the market!

It was the two sons who made her uneasy. They were big, handsome lads, as their father must once have been and the way they eyed her with easy familiarity from the tip of her boots to the windblown curls on her head was nothing short of insulting. They took great interest in her legs, nudging each other and grinning and she supposed she should not have come here dressed as she was. Her other tenants treated her with respect and though they might not approve of her outfit they would not dream of letting her see it. She had refused drab Evie Weaver's offer of a cup of tea and, addressing her remarks to Arty, who at least had the goodness to stand up when she entered the farmhouse, asked if there was anything he required in the running of his farm. It was February and his hedges needed trimming and she had noticed there were repairs required to his dry-stone walls, she said politely. Mr Sinclair had mentioned that spring corn should be sowed so should not his field be ploughed by now and what about early potatoes?

Clearly taken aback by her knowledge of farming, which she had learned from the dozens of agricultural books she had found in the estate office, Arty began to babble, bowing and scraping and rubbing his hands as he did so, that he needed the 'lend' of a plough-horse since he and his family could not afford to buy or even hire one. This bitch, as he privately called her to his family, had caught them all on the hop. They had lived a life of lazy ease for years since the young squire and his father before him had paid scant heed to such things as ploughing and planting. They had hens and one skinny cow, pigs and with what Evie and the girls earned with their baskets and the fruits of his sons' poaching, without doing a hand's turn they had lived a comfortable life.

'Us needs all manner o' things ter make a proper start 'ereabouts,' he whined.

'Come up to the house and see me and we'll discuss it,' Lally told him, wanting to get away from the sly grins and narrowed eyes of his two sons who had not stirred from their positions before the fire since she arrived. She would make sure Harry was with her when Arty Weaver presented himself. 'Perhaps the day after tomorrow would suit you,' she added, 'in the morning. I'm usually there between ten and twelve.'

'Well, yer see, ma'am . . .' Arty began but, slapping her boot with her riding crop and calling to her two dogs who leaned close to her, their muzzles slightly lifted in disapproval of the atmosphere in the kitchen, she turned on her heel and walked out into the yard. She was conscious of the male laughter that erupted as she lifted herself somewhat awkwardly into the saddle but nothing on God's earth would allow her to ask Arty Weaver to give her a hand.

She had crossed the stream, a tributary of the River Calder, and was just entering Priory Wood when she heard her name called and the sound of horse's hooves snapping the fallen twigs in the undergrowth. She turned her head, disorientated for a moment, since her head had been filled with how she was to deal with the family at Foxwell as it seemed to her that they would never become decent tenants on what could be a small, but profitable farm. Riding along the edge of the wood came the familiar and handsome bay on which Harry Sinclair rode and on his back was Harry.

She was ready to smile but his face was thunderous, scowling with what looked like murderous rage and so alarmed was she, she hauled at Merry's reins, causing the mare to throw up her head and jink sideways. Harry trotted towards her and even before he had reined in Piper he raised his voice and demanded to know what the hell she thought she was doing.

'I beg your pardon?' Her face fell into frozen lines of annoyance.

'What the devil are you doing riding about by yourself and in that bloody get-up? Are you determined to do not only yourself but your reputation even further damage? I gave strict instructions to Carly that whenever you rode out to the farms he was to go with you and when he said he was the only groom and who would look after the others while—'

'What right have you to order my servants about, may I ask? And he has other duties to perform besides—'

'I know that so I offered to send over one of my grooms to take over while he accompanied—'

'Dear God! I am on my own land with my own tenants all within shouting distance so what harm could possibly—'

'That is not the point. You might have a fall—'

'I have been riding since I could walk and am hardly likely to—'

'And then there are those two ruffians at

75

Foxwell. I don't like the look of them.'

No, neither did she. They made her feel extremely uncomfortable with their sly looks and grins, the way they licked their lips when they stared at her, but she was not having this man order her around, who, though he had been inordinately helpful when she had been at her lowest ebb, did not own her.

'And what is wrong with what I'm wearing, pray? I am modestly covered from head to foot and, besides, it is not your place to say what I should wear. This coat was Chris's and is warm and . . . and I like wearing it. It is comfortable for riding and really, why should a woman be trammelled by wide skirts and hoops and . . . and all the paraphernalia she is forced to wear to please society. No one can see me so—'

'The tenants can see you including those rogues at Foxwell. That outfit is not the attire of a lady, as you are, and what's more you have been seen at the theatre in a gown that was not suitable wear for a widow. Really, Lally, I thought—'

'Do you know, Harry Sinclair,' she spat out, 'it is a matter of supreme indifference to me what you think. I am a free woman and I shall do as I please. Now I would be obliged if you would get out of my way as I have things to do and no time to waste. I bid you good-day.'

Harry stared in sinking despair as he watched her break into a furious gallop, her dogs at her heels, and disappear into the woodland.

CHAPTER SIX

Moorend was a quiet town in an obscure setting of moorland and fast-flowing streams surrounded by other towns such as Halifax and Bradford and Huddersfield, these three coming into their own with the invention of steam engines, spinning machines and mechanical looms. They had transformed the cottage craft of weaving into what was increasingly known as the industrial revolution. They had all, with the exception of Moorend, doubled their size annually, filling up with smoke-blackened factories and to accommodate the growing population hundreds of cramped, terraced houses had been built clustered around the woollen mills.

But Moorend, which was a small township south of Halifax on the outskirts of the more dignified Skircoats, had somehow escaped this grand tidal wave of progress and it was here, spilling over from Skircoats, that the owners of the factories and mills lived in smart villas and even mansions, depending on their status and bank balance. There was a park and recreation ground with a small ornamental lake and regimented flower gardens, a great favourite with Sunday strollers who came to listen to the brass band. There was a market square in which was situated the elegant shop, or salon as she liked to call it, of Miss Violet Hockley, a clever young dressmaker and milliner who catered to the gentry. She worked hard, supervised her workroom and kept her girls in order and was well thought of in the town, for not only was she respectable as were her staff, she was imaginative, creative and the soul of discretion. There was Jewsbury & Brown, Pharmaceutical Chemists, whose shelves contained row upon row of exquisitely coloured jars in which the mysteries of medicines were displayed, a high-class grocer, a perfumer and wig-maker by the name of William Roberts, Mr Walter Jupp who created hats for gentlemen, a baby linen warehouse where the new mothers of the town fitted out their children, and on each Saturday an open-air market where one might purchase cheese, butter, poultry and eggs straight from the surrounding farms.

A People's Park was to open the following year in Halifax which was, so it was said, to be an even greater affair than the Crystal Palace at Sydenham, designed in fact by Sir Joseph Paxton and was to cost £50,000. It was to have a terrace providing views over the park to the moors beyond, while pavilions in the form of an Italian loggia would give shelter from inclement weather. In the central pavilion was to be a large seated statue of the donor of the park, Sir Francis Crossley, though of course many other wealthy men of Halifax and its surrounds had given generously to provide what was to be, or so they thought, the most splendid park in the north.

One of those benefactors was Harry Sinclair who, along with his younger brother, owned High Clough, West Heath and South Royd Mills and who was at the moment seated in what his housekeeper called the 'drawing room' but which his grandmother, a down-to-earth Yorkshire woman, had known as the parlour at Mill House. Mill House was situated on a shelf of landscaped greenery overlooking his woollen mill High Clough, a vast six-storey building capable of housing 500 looms. The gardens in which the house stood were cut from the bare hillside, surrounded by beds of fragrant lavender and carnations and other flowers with which Harry did not concern himself, leaving it all to the gardeners he employed. There were stables behind leading off a cobbled yard where a couple of grooms looked after his horses and the gig he used when necessary. The house had high ceilings to its airy rooms which were still stuffed with the sturdy furniture his grandmother had thought appropriate to the sturdy men who lived in it, among them her husband and those of her sons who had survived the afflictions that were visited on young children. Nothing had been changed since those days and Harry and Roly were comfortable enough, well fed and cared for by Mrs Cannon and her staff of three girls.

He had a glass of after-dinner brandy in his hand and a cigar between his lips when his brother strolled into the room. They had dined together on vermicelli soup, crimped cod and oyster sauce, roast beef with horseradish sauce, with meringues and whipped cream to follow. They had eaten a prime Stilton cheese with a decent claret followed by port and cigars. They had chatted in a desultory fashion about the ratification of the peace treaty between Great Britain, the Allies and Russia, and the possibility of increased trade in the woollen industry which the ending of the Crimean War would bring about and then, after drinking coffee brought into the parlour by Ivy, the housemaid, Roly, who was once more home from his travels, had excused himself, saying he had an appointment in Moorend.

'With Lally Fraser, one presumes?' Harry could have kicked himself as the words burst from between his lips. It was weeks since he had seen Lally as she rode back to the Priory and he had remonstrated with her for going about the estate alone. He had had his head bitten off for his trouble and had decided to stay away from her for a while to give her and himself time to cool off, but at the same time he had been worried that his desertion of her, at *her* command, might perhaps have left her rudderless. His feelings for her were his undoing, he was aware of that. His anxiety for her safety, though he supposed she was perfectly safe on her own land with her own people about her, had led him to say more than he meant. To let her see his concern was unwise, he knew that, but somehow he could not always help himself. She was so vulnerable, so fragile in her widowhood and he was desperate to help her, to get her through the pain and sorrow she must be suffering. Or so he had thought until he realised that his own brother was the one who was doing what he longed to do. It was common knowledge that Roly visited her at the Priory whenever he was home though there had been no more visits to the theatre or indeed anywhere; even so there had been a decided falling-off of callers to the Priory, he had heard, and who could be to blame for that, Harry asked himself bitterly, but his own brother. Roly was a good-natured, gregarious sort of chap with no thought of causing damage to Lally Fraser, but she was a beautiful young woman, the widow of his best friend and if he could make her life a little more cheerful then why not? He had a way with women, with everybody come to that, even Harry himself, but could he not see he was doing Lally Fraser no good?

'Well, yes, as a matter of fact,' Roly answered, surprised. 'I'm to be off again soon as you well know, and she has little enough company besides that woman who insists on sitting with us whenever I call.'

'I'm glad to hear it,' Harry pronounced sharply, drawing deeply on his cigar. 'You know the ways of our society as well as the next man and your attention to Lally, who has been a widow for some five months, has not gone unnoticed by the—'

'Oh, for God's sake, Harry, are we to take heed of a lot of old cats when poor Lally is so much in the doldrums over Chris? I'm only—'

'I don't know what you are only doing. I only know you are giving a decent woman a bad name, or so those old cats are saying. I had Albert Watson at West Heath the other day to look at that wall—you know, the one with the crack in it, and he had the effrontery to suggest . . . well, I won't tell you what he suggested with his innuendos but . . .'

Roly sat down and reached for a cigar from the silver box on the small occasional table beside the chair. He lit it and drew in the smoke then turned to Harry, a sneer on his handsome face. 'No, Harry, do tell me what that old buffoon implied and then I will go over to Skircoats and knock his bloody block off.'

'Very well, he was winking and nudging me with the implication that you were doing well for yourself with the widow . . .'

'And you let him say it!'

'No, I didn't, as a matter of fact. I told him to sod off and I would take my business elsewhere. When he began to argue I . . . I chased him to his carriage to the amusement of several hands who were unloading a wagon.'

'Good for you, old chap.'

'And I'll do the same to you if you continue to destroy Lally's reputation. If you hurt her you'll have me to answer to. She is very young and though she has been brought up in the best society and knows the rules she is at her lowest ebb and cannot judge—'

'Are you saying I'm taking advantage of her?'

'Yes, I bloody am and you should be ashamed to—' Harry bit off his words abruptly, aware that he sounded mean and petty and yet what he was saying was the truth. Lally was exposing herself to the disapproval of her own class who would drop her should the slightest taint of scandal touch her. And Roly knew this. He was off to America in a week where he would no doubt wine and dine many pretty women without a thought for the young woman whose position in life he was endangering. He would be away for a month or two selling the cloth from the looms of the Sinclair mills, which he did superbly and would come back with enough orders to keep the workforce busy for the whole of the following year, 1856. But Roly was not only a first-rate salesman, he also had a full working knowledge of how to run the business. He was as capable as Harry himself of taking off his expensive jacket and tackling a piece of machinery, of spinning and weaving and all the processes of turning raw wool into a 'piece'. He gave the impression that he drifted through life, smiling his

82

lazy smile, charming, a likeable, witty young rascal. He was never defeated, never dismayed, a young man for whom life seemed a carefree, cloudless summer day. He meant no harm but he did it just the same.

He was smiling now, that irrepressible smile of pure mischief which Harry knew he must be wary of if he were not to reveal his true feelings for Lally.

'Why, brother, I do believe you have a soft spot for the little widow yourself,' he said.

'Don't be so bloody ridiculous. I am merely trying to protect an innocent woman from the attentions of . . . of . . . the devil take it, you *are* supposed to be Chris Fraser's oldest friend and one would think that if that is so you would leave Lally alone at least until she is out of mourning.' He knew he sounded like an utter prig.

Roly stood up and threw his cigar into the fire, still smiling that insufferably smug smile, and Harry felt a great desire to knock his teeth down his throat. Jealousy sank its poisonous fangs into his heart, for he knew that Roly had this way with women which he himself had never learned. He wanted to be able to meet Lally Fraser with a smile as Roly did, to put her at her ease, to make her laugh, as he had done at Christmas but all he had done since was to antagonise her and he hadn't the bloody courage to get on Piper's back, ride up to the Priory and engage her in the light conversation at which his brother was so superb. And he was worried that she might be having a hard time working with the tenants. She was determined to achieve what previous Frasers had failed to do. She meant to keep the estate in perfect order and had made it plain to him that she would not overlook a decaying stone, a sagging gate, a loose tile or a choked ditch. But to do that she must have the cooperation of those who rented her farms. The Weavers would certainly diddle her if they could though the others were decent enough. Had they paid her the quarter's rents that he knew were due, having seen the account books at the beginning of this month? He could hardly ask Roly to question her, could he, so he must grit his teeth, swallow his pride and ride over to see her.

Roly was adjusting his neck cloth in the mirror above the fireplace. He bent down to stroke the large heads of the Labradors who sprawled at Harry's feet and was rewarded by a thump of two black tails.

'Well, brother, I'm off. Don't wait up for me,' he added flippantly as Harry reached for the decanter. 'And don't drink too much of that stuff, at least not alone.'

'Bugger off,' Harry said mildly, raising his glass to Roly's retreating back.

*   *   *

She rose from the sofa where she had been drooping by the fire, her face lighting up at the sight of him. Biddy, on the other side of the fireplace, sighed and put down the pillowcase she was darning. When visitors called it was considered bad manners to be sewing on such a domestic item and scraps of fine embroidery were kept for the purpose, but Roly Sinclair was not considered by Biddy Stevens to be worthy of such consideration.

'Roly,' Lally cried, 'how good to see you. Biddy

and I are badly in need of entertaining, aren't we, Biddy?' She held out both her hands to him and he bent his head to kiss them. Lally felt herself ready to blush, something she had never done in her life, for she was not and never had been the sort of girl who did such things. She was pleased with Roly's gesture though and her delighted smile said so.

Biddy said nothing. She had picked up her sewing again and continued to put in the neat stitches to the worn place in the pillowcase, something that was becoming increasingly necessary as the good linen purchased when Chris Fraser's grandmother was a bride was beginning to wear out. She sniffed disparagingly in reply to Lally's question, her head bent, and when both Roly and Lally studied her with an expression on each face that told her she was expected to leave the room, she ignored it. She did not trust Roly Sinclair. She, like his brother, did not believe he would deliberately hurt her lovely lass, but his thoughtless commandeering of her young mistress when he was home was downright wicked. She was a young widow with two small children and until her period of mourning was over should keep to the seclusion of her own home and should she venture out in her carriage it should be in the company of another woman, preferably a relative, or with a family retainer. Such as herself.

Lally was looking exceptionally lovely this evening. Her gown was of a blue so pale that it merged into smoke-grey. It was a muslin, soft and fine with flounces rippling down her body and flowing behind her in a train, totally unsuitable for a widow, as Biddy had told her as she helped her to dress but the girl had pleaded passionately.

'Biddy, let me wear it, there's a dear. There's only you and me to see it and I'm sick and tired of this terrible black.'

'But black suits you, my lamb. With your colouring and—'

'Rubbish, I'm not fair enough. Only those with golden curls can look good in black. Anyway, I shall wear it this evening whatever you say and tomorrow I'm going to ride over to Harry's mill and beg him to come and do the rounds with me on the estate. I'm sure with the money that is being put into the farms the tenants will prosper but I need Harry to—'

'Let Carly ride over there and fetch him, lass. There's no need for you to go gallivanting about the moors . . .'

The argument had continued until Lally sat down to her evening meal, alone, for there was one thing that Biddy would not do and that was sit down with her at table as though they were equals. Miss Lally was the mistress of this house and the estate, and servants did not dine with their masters or mistresses.

But she was prepared to dismiss this rule when it came to the period after dinner when she and her young mistress spent the hours before bedtime in a companionable 'chin-wag' as Biddy put it. Not that Miss Lally had much to say, for as she told Biddy you had to have been somewhere, or spoken to someone during the day and she went nowhere and spoke to no one other than the children and the servants from one week's end to the next.

'That Roly Sinclair had enough to say when he was here t'other day,' Biddy began, but Lally interrupted her coldly, telling her it was nothing to do with her when Roly came or how many times and it was at that moment that the man himself was shown into the room.

Lally had been playing with the boys before dinner, or rather having a rough and tumble with Jamie watched by a vastly disapproving Alec who could not see why he should be excluded from the fun. There had been a great deal of squealing, some of it coming from herself as Jamie dragged her under the red plush cloth that covered the nursery table, while Alec, who at five months was just beginning to wobble to a sitting position, fell over with a roar of rage. One of the flounces on her lovely dress was torn and her hair stood out in a halo of dark curls as a plump baby hand sank into it.

'Oh, madam,' Dora kept reiterating, 'mind yer frock an' watch bairn or 'e'll get trodden on . . . oh, madam . . . now, Master Jamie, don't pull yer mama's frock . . .' and soon all four were engaged in a glorious free-for-all which Dora described later to the other servants as a 'right bit o' fun' but what that there Mr Sinclair would think to it, him bein' a bit of a dried-up old stick, didn't bear thinking about. They all knew what she meant, for though Mr Sinclair was only a few years older than Mr Roly you'd think he was his pa the way he acted!

The outcome of this interlude was that when Roly entered the drawing room Lally had that delightfully rumpled look he associated with a man and a woman and a dark, secluded corner where a kiss, or even more, might be had.

'Lally, you look good enough to eat,' he told her unwisely, tipping his head in Biddy's direction in

87

the hope that Lally would dismiss the servant, but Lally grimaced and shrugged her shoulders, since she knew that no matter what she said Biddy would not leave her alone with Roly. They sat down side by side and sighed.

'It's quite mild out,' Roly said innocently. 'I noticed the daffodils and wood sorrel were thick under the trees as I came through the wood. The sycamores are in full flower and leaf and—'

'You saw this in the dark?' Biddy heard herself saying then bent her head to her stitching for it was not her place to question Mr Roly. They could not force her to leave the room but she should not join in the conversation. She was amazed when Miss Lally sprang to her feet and at once Roly did the same.

'I must see them, Roly,' Lally declared. 'Ring for Jenny, will you, Biddy, to fetch my cloak.' She did not look at Biddy as she spoke and neither did Roly, though he was hard put to suppress a smile.

'What?' Biddy gasped.

'My cloak and perhaps a lantern. I want to take a walk; oh yes, I know it's almost full dark but—'

'You can't go out at this time of night, lady. It might be April but—'

'Biddy, I think you forget yourself,' Lally told her imperiously. 'Oh, never mind, I'll get my own cloak. Wait for me in the hall, Roly.' And she ran out of the room, her face flushed and excited, leaving Biddy with her mouth open. It quickly snapped shut into a grim line of disapproval as Roly followed Lally into the hallway. He picked up his caped greatcoat and when she ran down the stairs took her arm and guided her to the front door and out into the cool night.

They strolled arm in arm, which seemed quite natural to Lally. It was as though Roly were Chris; was taking over Chris's role in a strange way and when he reached into his pocket and produced his cigar case, lighting a cigar and blowing the fragrant smoke into the equally fragrant April night air, she sniffed its familiarity, for the cigars were the same brand as those smoked by her dead husband.

He took her arm again as soon as the cigar was lit, drawing it through his. The two setters could be heard howling in the stable where they were shut up each night, for they could sense that their mistress was outside.

The couple did not speak as they sauntered down the slope of the springy grass to the lake where a sleepy twitter of birds could still be heard among the burgeoning branches of the trees that surrounded it. There was a full moon and they had no need of the lantern Lally had suggested. Its rays shone in a straight line across the lake, a lovely silver path which drew a breath of sheer delight from Lally, especially when a pair of swans sailed silently across it on their way to their nesting place.

On the far side of the lake they entered the woodland which soon would be dense with summer growth. Wood sorrel grew thickly, and in what seemed carefully placed arrangements in the roots of the trees there were cowslips, pale and colourless in the moonlight. As they stepped across the carpet of the woodland floor there rose faintly the smell of spring which they both unconsciously drew deep into their lungs. The ash trees were all in flower and some of the young sycamores, and through them shone the light of the moon. The dark was creeping across the sky and Lally knew

89

that Biddy would be standing anxiously at the window watching for her to return, for Biddy did not trust young Roly Sinclair, Lally was well aware. Which made him all the more exciting to be with. It was so long, almost six months since Chris had died and it was exhilarating to see the admiration in Roly's eyes, she who had known none all these months. She did not count the sly and acquisitive look that lingered in the eyes of the Weaver boys which she treated with contempt when she visited Foxwell Farm on her rounds, and since her widowhood and especially her ill-advised visit to the theatre with Roly, she had received no visitors. She was lonely, she supposed, which was why she did so enjoy Roly's company.

'I shall be off on my travels again soon, my pet,' he told her lazily, stopping to gaze up into the branches of an enormous horse chestnut tree. It was already thick with the fat, sticky buds which were opening to reveal their downy green leaves. With its wide spreading branches it presented a towering mass of the luxuriant growth that was to come in the summer, its branches almost touching the ground. It was so low it scraped Roly's head and when he guided her to its centre and leaned her against its massive trunk she made no protest. She was appalled to think he was to go away once again, for though she saw him no more than once or twice a week she looked forward to his visits and his cheerful, insouciant humour which made her laugh.

'Oh, Roly, no! When?' she questioned him.

'Next week, I'm afraid. To New York to find further outlets for the cloth which my admirable brother turns out by the mile each week.'

90

'How long will you be gone?' Her distress was so strong she barely noticed the bark of the tree trunk against her back, nor his arms which stretched on either side of her, the palms of his hands flat on the trunk, effectively capturing her, should she take it into her head to escape, which she didn't.

'A few weeks, perhaps a month or two. It depends on the customers I am to call on, those who have shown an interest in Sinclair cloth.' His light grey eyes were sharp, speculative, almost colourless in the pale light beneath the tree as they looked down into her face.

Speechlessly she returned his look and a sudden tension in his tall figure woke her senses, her female senses to the danger, no, not danger for Roly would never do anything to hurt her, but the hazards she was allowing herself to be led into by this familiar but suddenly fascinating man who had been her husband's closest friend.

She made a movement as though to break away but he leaned forward so that his breath fanned her cheek.

'Will you miss me?' he murmured.

She made one last effort to move away from this perilous moment, for she finally knew that this should not be happening—surely?—so soon . . . so soon but when his mouth came to rest on hers she felt her lips parting. His caressed hers, folding them ever so gently into his, nothing fierce or even passionate, so that she was able to pretend to herself it was no more than a friend kissing a friend.

'Lally, sweet Lally, it won't be long before I'm home again,' he told her and as he led her, bemused, out of the woodland and up the slope of

91

the lawn to the house she wondered what he meant.

CHAPTER SEVEN

She had spent the morning discussing spring sowing with John Graham at Cowslip and pigs with Henry Higgins at Thickpenny, understanding not a word of what they told her and worse still, *knowing* that they were well aware that she was out of her depth. It made her all the more determined to ride over to High Clough to see Harry and if he was not there to try one of his other mills until she found him. She had prided herself that she could manage without him, foolishly believing that the scant bits of information she had picked up from John Graham, from Bob Archer at Prospect and from Polly McGinley at Folly, from the estate books in the office, had provided her with all she needed to know as 'squire' of the estate. She had ridden astride Merry from farm to farm, dressed still in her kid breeches but with her riding-habit skirt decently draped over them, having realised she had shocked many of the tenants in her bold outfit. The skirt had a slit up the side which made mounting and dismounting easier and it meant she had no need to ride side-saddle. She also took Fred and Ally with her wherever she went, for she was wary of the Weaver boys who always seemed to appear, grinning like idiots, slipping out from behind a group of trees or rising from the very ground whenever she rode through Moor Wood or Tangle Wood at the back of the house and where, she presumed, they were poaching her game, or even a deer. They did not try to accost her but they made her uneasy and she felt the need to have someone, even if it was only Carly, at her side. But then Carly had duties to perform, if not with the horses and the stables then giving a helping hand to Barty and Froglet who had their work cut out maintaining the extensive gardens and the grounds about the house.

Those who farmed Thickpenny, Cowslip, Prospect, Folly and the Home Farm were all doing their best to help her 'play herself in' but she was aware that they saw her as a lady, a member of the gentry who was incapable of running an estate such as this and that soon she would lose interest and they could slip back into their old ways. At least some of them! She had learned many things such as how much fallow land Bob Archer had at any one time, how many acres supported his Friesians and how many were devoted to wheat or barley or root crops. She knew because she had recorded it in the estate books and then memorised it. Henry Higgins had given over his twelve-acre field to kale. Folly Farm was principally a dairy farm sending twenty-eight dozen eggs to market each week, along with dozens of baskets of butter shells, which Polly was an expert at making, neatly trussed chickens and specially ripened cheeses, while the Home Farm was the principal source of market garden produce which also went to the market in Moorend. She knew all that but in the six months since Chris's death none was as yet showing a profit. She fed money into the estate, and the farmhouses and their outbuildings had been renovated, implements replaced, stock on the

93

farms had improved, the lambing season had been a success and the moorland beyond the woods was white with skipping bleating lambs and their anxious mothers, all due to the money provided by the bank, but she knew she was falling behind since she had so much else to do. There was the household to be supervised, with the help of Biddy, of course, and the children to whom she must give some of her time, but with Harry's invaluable guidance and encouragement, and company, she admitted, since she missed Roly, she knew she could do so much more.

She had taken her midday meal with the children in the nursery, the dogs following her up the stairs and nosing their way into the cheerful room. Alec was rolling about on the floor and at once the dogs, since they were still young, began to play with him as though he were a puppy himself. They pushed their big heads against him and trapped him with their paws, being gentle but making him shriek with laughter and delight. They licked every patch of bare skin they could get at and when Jamie fell on them, determined to have his share of the fun Nanny Dora, as she had begun calling herself, lamented that they would become over-excited. But it did no good, for the mistress was as bad as them and, taking off her riding skirt, joined them on the floor, rolling over and over with the two little lads in her arms, protecting them from the hard floor but making them squeal with delight. The dogs barked and the noise was heard downstairs where Biddy tutted as she set the nursery tray.

'Take this up, Jenny, and tell Miss Lally not to get those lads in a state for it'll be us that has to calm them down after she's gone off wherever it is she's going this afternoon. Her animal is waiting in the yard and Carly has things to do other than walk the thing up and down. I don't know, you'd think she was a child herself the way she is with those lads . . .' but she was smiling, for it did them all good to hear Miss Lally laugh again.

'Where you off to, lass?' Biddy asked her suspiciously as she passed through the kitchen, longing to beg her to take Carly with her but knowing it would do no good. The lass had a mind of her own these days and did as she pleased since there was no one to gainsay her. At least she had on her decent riding skirt over those brazen breeches.

'To see Harry Sinclair,' Lally replied, which answer pleased Biddy inordinately.

She set Merry to a wild canter across the springy moorland towards the lane leading into and through Moorend. High Clough and Mill House which overlooked it were reached by what had once been a rutted lane but Harry had made it into a firm cobbled highway to accommodate the dozens of wagons that trundled up to the mill a dozen times a day. They brought the bales of raw wool to the sheds to be sorted and scoured and carded, proceeding through the many processes until they reached the finished product, the lengths of fine woollen cloth which were then transported to their destinations, either to different parts of the country or to the ships that conveyed them to the four corners of the earth or at least to the buyers Roly had found for them. Once, in his grandfather's time, it had been sturdy calamanco which would last a woman all her married life but

Harry had seen that though this was all very well in the old days women today did not wish to wear the same garment so long, preferring the fancy lightweights that had become the fashion. He had experimented with lightweight worsteds and within two years had doubled the mills' profits.

She clattered into the frantically busy yard where brawny men, hot and sweating, were unloading the fleeces from a wagon, their muscles rippling in the spring sunshine. They stopped to stare at her, for it was seldom lasses of her kind were seen in this yard, only the beshawled women who worked in the sheds for twelve hours a day with their children beside them!

She dismounted at what she supposed to be the outside stairs to the offices, turning to smile at a young lad who ran eagerly to take the reins.

'Is this the way to Mr Sinclair's office?' she asked him and, delighted and speechless, the lad nodded, turning to look at the men to make sure they were witnessing his glory.

Harry sprang to his feet as she side-stepped the clerk who was determined to announce her, his face breaking into a revealing smile before he had himself in hand.

'Lally, what are you doing here?' he stammered, ready to kick himself, for he sounded like a foolish schoolboy confronted with a female for the first time. He had not seen her since the awkward day when he had come across her out alone on her mare and before he had had time to curb his tongue had given her the length of it in his dismay. She had told him in no uncertain terms that she considered him to be an interfering old fuddy-duddy, or so it had seemed to him and since then

96

he had had no news of her except through Roly. Now, with Roly out of the country, he had pondered on whether he might ride over, casually, of course, and enquire into her health and that of her boys. Now here she was in his office and he felt the joy of it enter his heart. He knew he would cut a ludicrous figure if he showed his feelings and so his voice became gruff to hide them.

'Can I give you . . . er . . . tea . . . coffee, perhaps . . .' turning imperiously to the hovering clerk. 'Hawkins, is there such a thing available?' causing the clerk to raise his eyebrows, for Mr Sinclair well knew that there was a woman in a small kitchen at the back of the offices whose job it was to cater to Mr Sinclair's every culinary need.

'Of course, sir, which is it to be?'

Harry turned politely to Lally and was quite astounded when she began to laugh. 'Oh, Harry, I don't care. I didn't come here to drink your tea but to ask you to . . . well, would you like to dine with me one evening? I have so much to tell you . . . to ask you and we can hardly do it here . . .' with this man goggling at us, her words implied. 'We could make it a celebration for Her Majesty's birthday. We're only a few days late and I'm sure Her Majesty won't mind. What d'you say?'

Suddenly conscious of the clerk still vacillating in the doorway, Harry made an impatient gesture for him to leave, the moment giving him a chance to hide his gratification at what seemed to him to be her genuine desire to heal the breach that had developed between them. He wished she had not made mention of the Queen's birthday and the country's celebrations, for it would have pleased him much more if her invitation had been solely to

97

dine with *him* but nevertheless it was a beginning. She looked so lovely, her cheeks glowing with health and the enjoyment of her ride over, her eyes gleaming a turquoise blue between her thick lashes, her lips parted in a wide smile so that he felt a most foolish need to jump over his desk and sweep her into his arms. What would she do, he mused, if he gave in to the desire, but as was his nature he hid his feelings though his mouth twitched ready to break into a most unusual broad grin.

'Why, I should be delighted,' he said gravely, wishing he had his younger brother's charming aptitude for spontaneity. Never at a loss for words, was Roly, and always ready to meet any situation with exactly the right manner. And yet at Christmas, before Roly came home, he and Lally had seemed to get on and be at ease in one another's company. Well, whatever it was that she had in mind he was fully prepared to take advantage of it. Dear God, he brooded, even his own thoughts were stilted!

'Shall we say tomorrow evening then, unless you have something else . . .'

'No, no, I've nothing . . . planned . . .' and even if I had I would gladly cancel it. 'But won't you have that cup of tea or . . .'

'No, I must get back or Biddy will be sending out a search party.'

'You don't mean you've ridden over here . . .' he began, then stopped himself, for it was over the same subject they had quarrelled last time.

'Now then, Harry,' but she was smiling as she moved towards the office door.

He strode across the rich carpet and held it

open for her, breathing the fragrance of her as she passed him. Good sweet Lord, he loved her . . . he loved her . . .

'Until tomorrow then, Harry.'

'Until tomorrow.' His face was at one and the same time boyish in his gladness and yet remote, as was his nature. His eyes were their usual deep impenetrable brown, with seemingly no warmth to them and his hair, which she had seen tumbled in thick curls over his forehead, was brushed smoothly back. His voice was so cool in his effort to conceal his feelings she turned for a moment to look at him as though to say what the devil have I done wrong now, but his eyes, reflecting his emotions though he was not aware of it, became warm and she smiled at him as she made for the staircase. The boy still held the reins of her horse and the tail end of the smile caught him a stunning blow.

'Thank you . . . er . . .'

'Sam, missis.'

'Thank you, Sam.'

Sam was enchanted. What a tale he would have to tell his mam when he got home. She was confined to the tiny room they shared, her emaciated, frail and bone-weary body keeping her in bed for the most part. She saw no one because all the other women and their families who lived in the tall and tottering house were in their loom gates from five thirty in the morning when the gates were closed against latecomers until dark fell and she looked forward to his homecoming and the things he had to tell her. Mostly it was nothing much except what had happened in the sheds and yard about them and the hour he had spent at his sums, but today he could describe the lovely young lady and the words she had spoken to him. She had asked him his name and thanked him for holding her horse. She had smiled at him and was ready to allow him to help her on to her glossy horse until the maister got there before him.

But she had hesitated, ready to hoist herself into the saddle and the maister was at her back and, to Sam's disappointment, helped her up. She looked down at him, looked into his blue-green eyes and at his wavy ginger hair, just as though she were about to say something else but instead she put her heels gently into the mare's side and urged her into a trot.

'Goodbye, Harry, until tomorrow.'

'Goodbye, Lally.'

'Goodbye, Sam.' Then she was gone leaving the men in the yard staring after her, including Harry and Sam.

*   *   *

The following evening the pair of them were smiling at something Lally had said when the front doorbell rang. It had been nothing extraordinary, something about the lad who had held her horse when she had visited Harry's offices the day before.

'How can I possibly know personally all the people I employ, Lally? Hundreds of them. I might perhaps recognise many of them by sight but their names, no. The boy you mention probably works in one of the sheds as a "piecener" or "scavenger", twisting together the broken threads or retrieving the waste that collects beneath the machines and

100

what he was doing in the yard I cannot imagine. You seem to have a strange interest in the scamp.'

He leaned forward, the light from the lamp falling on his amber-skinned face and she wondered how his flesh came to have such a healthy colour when he worked indoors all day. He was dressed meticulously in the black and white evening dress that was the fashion, a black dress coat, a white waistcoat with embroidered borders, black trousers, silk stockings and black pumps. His stock was an immaculate white but his black bow tie was endearingly crooked. In fact she wanted to lean over and straighten it for him but something held her back. He looked his best though he would never be as extraordinarily handsome as his brother. He was too serious, his chin too square, his mouth too big, his expression too arrogant. But he was an interesting dinner guest. He described to her the growth of the woollen industry, and to her surprise she was quite fascinated. How he and his father had competed with other firms to produce goods, particularly in the ladies' dress trade by anticipating the 'frock fashion' and acquiring in advance the colour and designs of the forthcoming season's fashions. How wool must be bought at the right time to determine the price of the end product and the overall profitability of the firm. He described the coming of the factory system and of machinery and steam power, the thousands who had poured into the textile towns from the countryside looking for work and his own efforts to alleviate the suffering of children employed by mill-owners, the little ones, some no more than six or seven who were beaten to keep them awake. He did not approve of child labour but many families

101

relied on the wage these children brought in so he set the age limit at ten years of age and had even started a school in the yard at the back of High Clough where for an hour a day the children learned to read, write and do simple sums. Some of the factory owners insisted on strict factory discipline and lateness, drunkenness, talking and sleeping on the job were punished by fines. Harry was not one of these but he was strict.

'That boy who held my horse looked as though something could be made of him,' she was saying and it was at that moment that the bell rang.

'Who on earth . . .' she began, standing up, her napkin in her hand and at once Harry rose to his feet, ready to curse whoever it was who had come to disturb this wonderfully pleasant evening. She had seemed pleased to be in his company, ready to listen to him describe the mill, what was done there and by whom, which was how they had come to be discussing the boy. They had talked at length about the farms and the progress that was being made and he had brought the conversation round to an exhibition of art which was to be shown in the Town Hall to which he said he hoped she might like to accompany him and she had appeared to be genuinely interested.

She had on a gown of the palest gold, a shimmering thing with a full skirt and a well-fitted bodice, her arms and shoulders bare, her skin flawless, translucent in the candlelight. She wore a thin gold chain about her neck and on her wrist was the bracelet he had given her for Christmas. He resolved to find her a necklace to match the bracelet, a lovely collar of gold and turquoise that he would place about her neck before kissing her just beneath her soft chin. Sweet Jesus . . . if only he could tell her how he felt! He liked to think she had dressed this evening for his benefit and though he hardly dared bring himself to hope, surely this was a promising beginning to a relationship—a friendship that could develop into something stronger. He castigated himself silently for his inability even to *think* in warmer terms but her smile was a lovely, encouraging thing to see and, encouraged, he was able to convince himself that at last she was looking at him, not as an elderly brother, or cousin, or even friend, but as a . . . Dear God, he dared not think further than that.

When his brother was announced he swore savagely under his breath and when Roly walked into the room, pretending astonishment at finding Lally entertaining, ready to apologise in his charming way, Harry could have hit him. As Lally hurried forward to greet him, her smile wide and eager, he could have *killed* him.

'Harry, old fellow,' he drawled, his arms still about Lally's waist. 'I had no idea . . .'

'Naturally.' Harry did not smile. 'When did you get back? I did not expect you for weeks.'

'This evening. I had finished my trip earlier than usual and as Mrs Cannon had nothing I fancied to eat I thought I would come over to Lally's and see if she could offer me something.' He looked down at himself ruefully. 'I do apologise for not being dressed correctly but . . .'

'Roly, think no more about it. We don't mind, do we, Harry? Now you must join us. I'll ring for Jenny to set another place.'

Harry's face had closed up at the sight of his brother and his mouth had clamped tight over his even white teeth but neither Roly nor Lally seemed to notice. There was a great deal of running about as Jenny, who thought Mr Roly the handsomest man she had ever come across, rustled about with cutlery and napkins, setting a place for him, bringing soup and what was left of the curried chicken which Biddy had contrived from the remains of two cold fowls from the Home Farm. There was a delicious apple pie with cinnamon and thick cream, cheese and fruit, a simple meal but filling and cheap, and all the time he ate Roly entertained Lally with descriptions of what he had seen and where he had been in Amercia, turning now and again with great politeness to his brother. He did not speak of business or of how many orders he had brought back, for that would wait until tomorrow at the mill and besides would not interest Lally. She sat at the end of the table, her chin in her hand, her eyes fastened on his mobile face, laughing at his accounts of his travels and it seemed neither of them noticed Harry Sinclair who sat silently at the other end of the table.

He rose abruptly, startling them both. It was as though they had forgotten his presence in their absorption in one another. He felt as though there were a stone in his chest that was rough with sharp edges and it was hurting him badly and if he did not get out of this house, away from *her* and her attentiveness to his brother, he might do or say something he would be sorry for. His disappointment was so intense—the devil take it, *disappointment* was the most laughable word to describe what he felt—he knew he must take his leave before he made a fool of himself.

'I must go, Lally,' he said harshly. 'Thank you

for your hospitality. You were . . . have been most kind. No, don't get up, Roly. I'll see you in the morning and perhaps I might suggest that you and I, Lally, make the rounds of the farms before long. Let those Weavers see an eye is being kept on them. I'll bid you goodnight, both of you.'

Turning from the expression on Lally's astonished face, he crossed the room and opened the door into the hall, wondering where the devil that maidservant had put his outdoor things. He had driven over in the gig in keeping with his evening attire and he supposed someone would bring the vehicle round to the front . . . someone . . . Dear God, his pain was depriving him of his wits but he really did not . . .

The woman—what was her name? Biddy?—emerged from the kitchen door at the end of the wide, flagged hallway and at once she had him in his overcoat, murmuring that Carly was bringing the gig round and she did hope he had enjoyed his meal. Her voice was soft, sympathetic, he thought, and he wondered why. He was not to know that Biddy Stevens had fervently hoped that her lass would take to this rather stern, quiet man, for he was just the kind of husband she needed. That Mr Roly was nothing but a scamp, a charming scamp but not reliable, not what you might call a steady sort of chap who would guard and cherish Lally Fraser. He would make her laugh, listen to them even now, the sound of their merriment drifting through the dining-room door so that it seemed they might be laughing at Mr Sinclair who was blundering towards the front door as if he thought so too.

Lally beneath her merriment felt a strange

sadness that Harry had left so suddenly and since she was not a foolish woman she knew it had something to do with Roly. They were brothers, equal owners of three prosperous mills but whereas Harry was straightforward, perhaps obstinate, grave, forbidding at times, Roly was blithe, merry as a cricket, fun-loving and ready to do all sorts of wicked things if he was allowed. And yet they worked equally hard in their positions of owners of the most prosperous mills in and around Halifax. Roly was tall, broad, dark and striking whereas Harry was lighter, finer, though both had the dark hair and eyes of the elder Sinclair.

He stayed far too long in Biddy's opinion and though she entered the dining room on some pretext or other on several occasions they lingered at the table, Mr Roly sipping the brandy, which would soon be finished, Miss Lally a glass or two of Madeira, laughing, chatting about nothing of any consequence since that was not Roly Sinclair's way, enveloped in the fragrant cigar smoke from his cigars. He was holding her hand at one point, which she did not seem to mind and both of them were apparently unaware of her entrance.

The old grandfather clock in the hall struck twelve and Biddy entered the dining room on the last stroke. Both the maidservants had been in their beds for hours and upstairs the babies slept peacefully in the care of Nanny Dora.

'Miss Lally, I'd like to lock up now, and Carly is waiting to get to his bed,' Biddy said pointedly. Roly Sinclair looked round at her, his hand still holding Miss Lally's, but at once, as though aware for the first time of the enormity of what she and Roly had done to Harry who after all had been her

106

guest, Lally stood up, her hand, it seemed to Biddy, reluctantly letting go of Mr Roly's.

'Oh, dear, is it that late? Of course, Biddy, and Roly, you must go home at once. No, don't pull a face at me. I have to be up early to be with my children.'

Biddy stood woodenly in the doorway, her stance making it quite plain to Roly Sinclair that she was not going to leave, therefore depriving him of the goodnight kiss he had hoped to get from Lally.

There was a good deal of giggling at the front door where Carly stood patiently with Roly's chestnut gelding. Both he and Biddy had faces on them that would have killed the cat, or so Roly whispered in Lally's ear, but at last he mounted the animal and with a merry wave set off up the drive at a mad gallop.

'Well!' Biddy declared, knowing that her lamb would understand exactly what she meant.

CHAPTER EIGHT

'Have you the faintest idea what you are doing to Lally Fraser? Or to her reputation? There is not a family in Moorend or anywhere for that matter in and about Halifax that is willing to have anything to do with her. I dare say she does not care at the moment while you are at home to squire her about, or perhaps it is more accurate to say she has not noticed, but when you leave again on your travels at the end of the week what is she to do then—'

'God in heaven, brother, where on earth did that

107

come from? You make it sound as though I were deliberately ruining her, or trying to seduce her, is that what you're implying? I have done nothing—'

'But destroy any chance she might have of making a decent life for herself and her children in the future. You know perfectly well what society must be saying about her. A recently widowed young woman, a gently bred woman, gadding about with a young unmarried man, *alone* and only months after her husband died. You are destroying her, Roly, treating her as though she were one of your light women who have no reputation to destroy in the first place. Oh, I realise she can refuse your offers of visits to the theatre and the other entertainments you whisk her off to, but she is a beautiful woman who is too young to be widowed, a woman who has never really conformed to the dictates of her own society but has never really done anything that might cause offence to her own class. You are what is described as 'good company', witty, amusing, entertaining and, more to the point, very like her dead husband. I presume—'

Roly Sinclair sprang from the sofa, his face suffused with rage and for a moment Harry thought he was going to strike him. Which would have suited him fine, for the mood he was in, the fury, pain and resentment he felt had him in a state that would love a good fight. He longed to knock his brother's block off, as they said in Yorkshire, smash him to the ground, and when he got up knock him down again. Roly was doing all the things he longed to do with Lally: taking her about, escorting her to balls and plays and concerts where, since she was in his company, in the company of one of the Sinclair brothers who were prominent members of society, she was not shunned; but just wait until he was gone again on his forthcoming business trip and the men and women who were forced to accept her and smile while she was in the company of a Sinclair would drop her like a hot potato and not one of the women would call on her. She should be in the deepest black, keeping to the seclusion of her own home, at least until a year's mourning was up but here she was, on Roly's arm, dressed in all the lovely colours she had favoured as a young, married woman, flaunting herself, as they would see it, in their very faces!

'I take exception to what you are saying, brother,' Roly snarled, as incensed as Harry. 'I have done Lally no harm, made no claims on her that could not be shared with the most stiff-necked matron. I treat her with respect as becomes the widow of my oldest friend and I resent your implication that I am doing my best to seduce her. She is as innocent as a . . . as a . . . schoolgirl and I have made no attempt to change that. We are friends who enjoy one another's company and—'

'Stuff and nonsense. Given half a chance and you would have her—'

'Where, *where*?' Roly's voice was dangerous and he swayed over his brother who still lounged, an after-dinner cigar between his lips, on the sofa on the other side of the fire. 'In my bed, are you saying, or in *her* bed? Goddammit, man, that woman of hers watches her like a bloody hawk.'

'So you are saying that but for "that woman" you would have . . .'

'No, confound it, I'm not . . .' But even as he

spoke Rory Sinclair knew that had it not been for Biddy Stevens, who always seemed to be hovering within earshot, he would certainly have done his best to get lovely Lally Fraser into his arms. He was half, well, not a half, but a little bit in love with her, as he had been years ago when good old Chris had married her, but he admitted that when Chris and Lally married, though he had been disappointed, smiling wryly and shrugging his shoulders since there were thousands of pretty girls in the world, he had not been broken-hearted. He doubted whether he could ever fall in love, truly deeply in love, for it was his nature to be light-hearted, *light-minded*, insouciant. He was never unkind, he believed, not deliberately but, good God, he was only twenty-four and meant not to marry for another ten years. Then it would be to a lady of unimpeachable character, young and beautiful and *monied*, who would bear him several healthy sons. Even had he loved Lally Fraser to distraction he would not have married her, for she was a poor widow with two sons. It was a shame since she was good company, as dedicated to having fun as he was himself. She made him laugh. She was intelligent and well bred but he must be the first, the only one to know in the biblical sense the woman he married. He had amused himself with Lally and she with him and had seemed to understand, in fact he knew she understood, for she had loved Chris and wanted no entanglements. Still, he would have liked to . . . to . . .

His thoughts were interrupted by his brother's bellow as he surged from the depths of the sofa, throwing his cigar into the fire.

'You bastard, if you had half a chance you

would . . .'

Roly turned on his heel and strode towards the door. 'I'm not listening to this nonsense a moment longer,' he thundered over his shoulder. 'You must be mad to think I would dishonour a lovely young woman who was once married to the best chum a chap ever had. She is my friend, just as Chris was my friend and I really don't know what worm has got into your brain.' Suddenly he stopped speaking, looking closely at his brother whose face had drained of all its healthy colour and whose eyes were narrowed to what seemed slits of madness. His hands were clenched into furious fists and it was at that point that Roly recognised what was savaging his brother. It was not, as he pretended, concern for the reputation of a friend but something much deeper and for a moment Roly felt compassion, then his young arrogance gathered force.

'You're in love with her yourself, aren't you?' he taunted, taking a step towards Harry. 'That's what's eating you up. The thought that I might get what you covet. Well, let me reassure you, brother. I am not in love with Lally and never will be. I am merely cheering up a woman who has had a bad knock. She is young and lovely and had Chris lived would have been, as she had been for three years, the toast of the society in which she moved. I . . . I realise that she is not strictly speaking keeping to the rules of that society but there is no harm in what she and I do together. She deserves a bit of—'

'*Fun*,' Harry sneered, moving a step towards his brother.

'Yes, if you must describe it as such and if you

111

imagine that a decent young woman like Lally would . . . would dally with the likes of me then you are a fool. She loved Chris Fraser, and still does.'

He turned on his heel and, leaving his brother torn with an emotion so strong he was incapable of moving, slammed the door behind him. The servants, who had listened, paralysed, to every word, for how could they not, slowly came to life. Mrs Cannon, who had been the Sinclair housekeeper for many years, began to chivvy the three maids about the kitchen, clearing up the meal the brothers had just eaten. Her voice was inclined to break, for she was deeply shocked.

'Now then, Ivy, finish sideing the table, and you, Annie, give her a hand. Tess,' who was kitchen-maid, fourteen years old and agog with what she had just heard, 'start on those pans and I want to see my face in them when you've done, d'you hear?'

'Yes, Mrs Cannon,' Tess said humbly, for she was the lowest of the low in the kitchen and at everyone's beck and call. She ran into the scullery while Ivy and Annie made their way through the kitchen door to the passage, quiet as mice since they had no wish to meet Mr Harry, glancing fearfully at the closed drawing-room door behind which Harry Sinclair was slumped on the sofa, his head in his hands.

*   *   *

Roly had been at home for six weeks. He was to be off to Europe at the end of the week, he had told Lally, a trip that would take him through France, Germany, Spain, Belgium, Austria and Italy and he would be away for several months, but during those six weeks he was in the country he had called most evenings at the Priory. They had gone about a good deal, to balls, concerts and the theatre and even to the exhibition to which he had invited her. He had made her feel alive again. He had not ridden over the previous evening and she had been disappointed, but she had eaten her solitary meal, hoping up to the time darkness fell that he might come galloping up to the front door with his usual dash and verve, scattering Barty and Froglet's carefully raked gravel. He had not come so she had gone to her bed, restless and bored, wondering how she was to manage when he had gone. He had kept her amused, if that was the word, taking her mind off her loss and the emptiness of her days, for when he was there she forgot about the estate, the farms, the problems of keeping it all in heart, and had been the girl who had ridden at the heels of Roly and Chris, who had been carefree with nothing but a bright future, the future the young are entitled to. She had not seen Harry whose guiding hand she had missed but it had not seemed to matter when Roly was there to make her feel young, pretty, *a woman* again.

He was at the door the next morning, laughing and joking and teasing Jenny who had answered the bell. He even got a twitch of a smile from Biddy who did not approve of him in the least particular, for did he not threaten her young mistress. Perhaps he meant to marry her, Biddy thought in the depths of her hopeful heart and though she would rather have given her lamb into the safe hands of Harry Sinclair who would return her to her rightful place in society, at least if she

113

wed Roly, despite their dreadful behaviour, her reputation could be salvaged.

They rode across the park, through the woods and out on to the vast moorland, moving up the track that ran from Moor Wood. Roly had a magnificent seat in the saddle, his wide, laughing mouth shouting something back to her as he urged his gelding up the steep slope that led on to the moor itself. His hair was all a-tangle in the wind, tumbling with boyish disorder above his swooping eyebrows. His grey breeches clung to his strong thighs and buttocks and Lally thought how attractive he was and how she missed him when he was away. He wore no jacket and neither did she, and her white cambric shirt could scarce contain her bouncing breasts, the nipples of which could clearly be seen. The fine fabric was taut, pulling at the buttons and her kid breeches, over which today she wore no skirt, revealed the soft curve of her booted calf, the long firm muscles of her thigh and the twin globes of her buttocks. Two handsome young animals intent on enjoying the bright and sunny day. The sky was high, placid and blue and the pale sunshine fell in a golden haze on the two riders. There was a slight breeze which was warm and soaked in the fragrance of the heather and gorse. It moved the shadows cast along the track they rode, rippling through the shoulder-high bracken.

At last they reached the summit of High Moor and with fluid grace they both sprang from their saddles and with a word to their horses and the black and white setters which had streamed behind them they sauntered across the uneven, spiky grass to stare, sighing, over the vast expanse of purple and yellow moorland that lay beneath them. For several minutes they were silent, for though they did not voice it they both loved this enchanting land. It was beautiful today, soft and mellow, kind and quiet, but they had known days, riding together with Chris, when it had been cold, wet, cruel, biting winds and fierce storms and they had all three loved it just the same. It was theirs. Their land, filled with their memories, of Chris whom they had both loved, of the bewitching past when they were children, and this place, to where they had ridden without words, had been a favourite haunt. They had roamed these moors, the three of them, ever since she had learned to sit a horse, she trailing far behind the boys since she was younger and had not had the strength nor the expertise to keep up. They had been riding since they had been old enough to sit a horse but it had not taken her long to catch up, to be as swift and as adventurous as they, guiding her mount across tumbling streams and wooden bridges and stony paths to huge outcroppings of rock like the one they had reached today.

Without a word they lowered themselves on to the soft dry grass, leaning their backs against one of the tall, grey-pitted roughcast rocks, shoulder to shoulder, their legs stretched out and crossed at the ankle. Still they did not speak, for a feeling of sadness had come over them at the thought that this would be the last time they would be up here together for a long time. It was still July but autumn would be next, to be followed shortly by the winter, a time when the weather would force them to be careful where and when they rode. God knows how long he would be away, Lally brooded and how she should keep herself from losing heart without his merry ways to keep her spirits up.

'I don't think I can bear it without you, Roly,' she whispered and at once he turned to her and took her gloved hand in his. 'You have made me feel so much better, helped me to accept Chris's death, given me a breathing space. I know I must get on for the sake of the children but it will be hard without you to make life more . . . sparkling. That is what is missing in my life. Sparkle. It's what Chris gave me, and so have you. I shall miss it, and you.'

'Don't say that, dear Lally. You will have plenty to keep you occupied with those farms of yours. You have neglected them shamefully while I have been home; no, I'm not blaming you. I have been just as much to blame by encouraging you to play truant. But there is a challenge there for you and you know how much you love a challenge. Remember that gate at the back of Mill House? Chris and I jumped it time and time again and time and time again you tried to do the same. And every time you came off. God, we thought you would break every bone in your body. We pleaded with you to give up but you wouldn't and at last you did it. But you weren't satisfied even then and had to do it again. That was a challenge you overcame and so is this. Those farms, the estate, belong to Chris's sons and it's up to you to keep them safe for them. Old Harry'll help you, like he did after Chris died.'

She hung her head and without thought he put his arm about her shoulders. She turned to him, thrusting her face against his chest and began to weep, the emptiness of the days ahead without him

116

in them to cheer her up taking away the staunch resolution to be strong that she had imposed upon herself since Chris's accident. Her body shook with her desolation, first for her young husband who had been snatched from her so cruelly and then for this man who had been his friend and was hers and was to leave her again. Not quite as Chris had left her since he would be back, but leaving her nonetheless to her sadness and the emptiness of her life.

'Oh, Roly,' she wept, putting her arm about his neck and lifting her wet face to his, and when his lips met hers he found them eager, warm, parted, moist with her tears and with something else that comes when a female is aroused by a male. Moving their heads, their lips trembled and clung and urgency overtook them, since he was a male and eager to take what seemed to be on offer and she was a female who had been deprived of physical love for many days and nights. Their breathing became ragged as his mouth moved down to her throat which she arched in need, then dipped down into her shirt to the swell of her breasts. His hands invaded her clothing, moving to cup her breasts, taking the nipples, first one then the other and rolling them between excited fingers. He was not gentle, for, spending time with her, he had been deprived of a woman ever since he came home. He moved swiftly, nailing her to the stone at her back, pulling her down in the grass so that her skin rasped against the roughness of the rock leaving bloody tracks, making her wince, his hands busy now with buttons and belts and she was the same for it had been so long . . . so long. The dogs watched, bewildered. Fred stood up and began to

117

whine, then lay down again, her head on her paws, her ears twitching at the strange sounds that were coming from her mistress but Lally did not hear her. Her head was thrown back as her body responded to the delight that had been missing from her life all these months and when he entered her, throwing his own head back as he thrust in and out, she cried out, a long-drawn-out cry that silenced Fred's whimpers and stilled the many small creatures who had their home on the rolling moorland.

They lay joined for several awkward moments, for both knew at once that what they had done was a terrible mistake, then he withdrew and sat up, adjusting his clothing, moving away from her, looking off into the distance as she did the same. Her fingers trembled as she buttoned her shirt and pulled her breeches into place. Neither spoke until Roly stood up and moved to the edge of the small plateau where they sat.

'Dear God, Lally, I'm sorry . . . that was unforgivable . . . to take advantage . . .'

'It took two of us, Roly,' she murmured. 'The blame was not all yours . . .'

'I am a man and should know better. Sweet Jesus, you are the wife of my dearest friend.'

'Widow.'

'That does not excuse what I did. I can only plead . . . you are so sweet and were . . . upset. I have never seen you cry, even when you took some terrible tumbles when we . . .'

His voice trailed away miserably. He did not know what to say or do. He had never been in such a tricky situation before, since the women he made love to were either of another class who were easily

118

rewarded, or the willing wives of gentlemen who themselves had mistresses. Lally was a woman from his own society, a lady, and therefore beyond his reach and yet he had thrown her to the ground and taken her like a common whore. Well, perhaps not that, for she had been as eager as he but nevertheless he was caught in a situation from which he did not know how wriggle. He was very fond of Lally, very fond indeed and she was fond of him but her true love had been Chris. But she was a woman, a passionate woman who had been deprived of the enchantment of physical love for many months and had been easy prey! God in heaven, how that made him feel the lowest, most base creature that could be called a man but it was done now and she seemed calm about it.

'You must not feel badly, dear Roly, I wanted it, needed it and now let us forget it ever happened. The customs of our society would have it that a woman does not share the . . . the physical feelings of a man but it is not true. I have been . . . deprived of love ever since Chris died and you . . . how can I describe it without being crude but you will know what I mean. Now then, let us forget it happened, or if we can't forget look on it as a . . . happy interlude between two friends. So, help me up on to my horse and let us get home. I think it might be wise if you were not to come to the Priory again before your trip. Biddy is . . . she might suspect there is something different about us and . . . So, when you come home I hope you will visit me, as a friend, and in the meanwhile I will set about guarding my sons' inheritance which I have sadly neglected these past weeks. Roly.' She smiled. 'Don't look so tragic. We have shared a moment that was . . . pleasing to us both. Now let's get home.'

She bade him farewell at the back of the house, just where the woods ran down to the rear of Cowslip Farm, waving to Elsie Graham who was in her yard feeding her hens. She appeared to feel nothing but a strange langour which she supposed came from Roly's lovemaking and which she remembered from what seemed a long time ago. Chris . . . oh Chris . . . !

She took the children for a walk that afternoon, Alec in the baby carriage that she and Chris had ordered from Hitchings Baby Stores in London when Jamie was born with no thought of the price or where the money was to be obtained. It was large, high-backed and had three wheels, just like the one Her Majesty the Queen had bought for the royal princes and princesses. How proud they had been of their baby son and how enthusiastically they had taken to parenthood, wheeling their son about the grounds until Chris had grown bored, since he preferred the rough and tumble of the nursery floor.

Jamie, two years old now and fast becoming the ruler of the household, demanding and getting the adoring attention of all the servants, swooped and dived about the garden, stopping every now and again to crouch down to study a leaf, a worm, something that aroused his boy's curiosity while his brother, who could crawl now and according to his devoted nanny was ready to walk, wailed his frustration at being trapped in the baby carriage. She took them to see the horses in the paddock, Blossom, the cob who pulled the gig, Merry, her own chestnut mare, Ebony, Chris's coal-black

120

gelding and Jeb, the dale pony. They all four ambled across the rough grass to greet the newcomers and Jamie, delighted with them and demanding to ride Ebony, climbed on the fence and was ready to jump into the paddock with the intention of climbing on the gelding's back.

'Me ride, Mama,' he demanded. 'Me ride Papa's horse,' for Lally had told him of his dead father and he had accepted the truth easily, since he was a child of the nursery and Chris had been a distant, exciting figure in his young life but hardly to be missed.

'Not yet, darling. Ebony's too big for you but soon Carly will put you on Jeb's back and teach you to ride. You will come with Mama up on to the moors and we will—'

'Now, Mama, ride now. Me can ride . . .'

'*I* can ride, Jamie,' she rebuked him absently, but Jamie did not understand, wriggling to reach the horses just beyond the fence. Screaming his resentment, he was removed and plonked in the baby carriage with Alec, who screamed in sympathy and Lally was glad to hand them over to Dora, who told Jenny privately that she did wish Miss Lally would not take the babies out and bring them back so excited they took her, Dora, hours to calm down.

She sat that evening beside the fire in her bedroom, the pretty bedroom she had created for her and Chris when she married him and her thoughts would not be turned away from what had happened that morning. She felt a shiver pass through her and knew it was a shiver of delight. She was fulfilled, *for the moment*, as a woman, but she knew it would not last. She missed the times

121

she and Chris had shared their loving in the lavender-scented bed in the centre of the room. They had loved in the pearly grey light of dawn, in firelight and candlelight and her heart ached for those times and for him. But today, for the space of half an hour, she had known great joy through another man's body so did that make her love for Chris any the less? She was life and warmth, vital and strong, and needed a man in her life, but that did not make her promiscuous, surely.

She sighed deeply, staring sightlessly into the flames of the fire. Roly would not come back into her life, she realised that, for it would be too much for both of them. What had happened today had parted them for ever and the sadness of it washed over her in great waves of pain.

The door opened and Biddy came into the room, her eyes taking in the desolation of her young mistress, knowing its cause, at least part of it. But she was glad he had gone. He was not to be part of Miss Lally's life after all and she was relieved, for perhaps with him gone Harry Sinclair might once more call at the Priory. Miss Lally needed his help. Roly Sinclair had made her laugh but would he be there when she wept? Biddy doubted it!

CHAPTER NINE

She knew within three weeks that she was pregnant. Her fertile womb which had quickened so effortlessly to Chris had done so again with Roly! What should have come a week ago had failed to appear and she, who was as regular as clockwork, knew the full horror of her predicament. *Predicament!* What a pathetic word to use to describe the terrible situation she was in. It was as though she were bemoaning the weather on a day when she had planned a garden party; that she had a head cold or was suffering any number of inconsequential occurrences come to plague her. *She was pregnant.* She was a woman whose husband had been dead for almost a year and she was to have a child. Roly Sinclair's child! The worst thing that could happen to a woman was happening to her and her mind was stunned with the shock of it, the dread of it and she had no one in whom she could confide. No one to say there was no need to worry as it would all come right, for it wouldn't come right. Her life would be in ruins, worse than it was now, for the tenants on her farms, who were, most of them at least, friendly and welcoming, would turn against her because even in their class it was a disgrace, for the culprit and for her family, to bear a child out of wedlock. It was not so long ago when a girl would be thrust from the family home, beaten from the village, forced into a life worse than death—prostitution— to support herself and her child. It would not happen to her, of course, since she had a home, she was mistress of her own destiny and could not be turned on to the streets but her life and the future of her sons would never be the same again.

Since Roly's disappearance from her life she had done her best to keep busy, spending hours in the estate office poring over the books on farming Harry had given her and going over the accounts and records of the farms on the estate. She had

had Merry saddled, side-saddle, as though conscious of her different state and, wearing the riding habit, top hat, gloves and boots that were the convention of her class and gender, had visited all the farms, watching the reapers swathing across the corn harvest, the sheaves standing to dry and later being collected and formed into a rick shaped at the top like a roof. It had been a warm, dry summer and the harvest had been a great success which boded well for her rents. Those who had sheep had gathered them in and the rams had been put to the ewes and in five months' time there would be lambs whitening the fields. Ploughing had been done as soon as the fields were free of the corn and winter wheat sown, and root crops, potatoes and mangold gathered in and on all the farms there was promise of greater profits. She watched the men on the farms getting ready for the hard winter ahead. They mended dry-stone walls, cut peat and wood, dug ditches, ploughed fields which next year they would plant and weed and harvest. They laid snares to catch predators and saw to their farm tackle which had to be kept in good trim. Broken wheels and ploughshares were taken to the wheelwright or the blacksmith on the edge of Moorend, for Jack Eccles and Bill Andrews kept forge and workshop side by side for convenience. Most of them did well, her tenants. Not that she took any credit for it, but when she voiced this to Biddy she was told not to be a fool.

*   *   *

'Who d'you think encouraged them to take an interest, to plant and sow and . . . and whatever else they do?' since Biddy knew nothing of farming. 'Who put money into their farm buildings, new roofs and that? Fences and such like? Who took an interest and showed it, riding round the estate and . . . well, just talking to them, showing your face, letting them see that you were there for them if they had a problem? Polly McGinley was at the back door only the other day delivering eggs, saying she had a tidy little sum put away from her poultry. Made up she was and the rest's the same. All except them layabouts at Foxwell. Polly was saying they're still after her Sean for a loan of his plough-horse and the place hardly touched since . . . since you took over. Them lads are still taking our game and what we need is a gamekeeper.'

Her voice became artless. 'Why don't you speak to Mr Sinclair about it, my lamb? He'd soon sort it out. Not that we've seen much of him recently what with Mr Roly here all the livelong day and most evenings. He'd be a great help to you if let, would Mr Sinclair, and now that Mr Roly's taken off and—'

'I can't keep running to Mr Sinclair every time I have a problem, Biddy. I must learn to work them out myself . . .' and the worst one is to come in about six months' time. She couldn't even tell Biddy at the moment since her head surged with sea waves of terror, confusion, roaming from place to place looking for an answer to her critical dilemma. She was surprised that Biddy had not yet become aware that the 'curse', which was not a curse at all, had been missed, for it was Biddy who had care of the clean and soiled clouts used each month by Lally.

125

That day she had flung on a pair of breeches and the warm jacket that had been Chris's, tied a scarf about her neck and with a shout to Carly to saddle Merry, had ridden hell for leather up the track that led to the high moorland. There were heavy, blue-black clouds hanging over the tops heralding a downpour and though the sun shone it would not be long before it vanished behind them. The track was bordered by rough, dry-stone walls, one side broken and scattered so that Merry had to pick her way delicately among the rough stones. The bracken was fading and brown with no living creature moving except the grey sheep, the ewes who had been brought down to the ram and then turned out again to await the bitter winter. No movement apart from a small dot which was coming towards her along the track and which, as it got closer turned out to be a small boy dressed in worn but neatly patched clothing. Breeches too big ending above boots that surely were third or fourth hand, so battered were they. He wore no stockings and his legs gleamed whitely between breeches and boots. His jacket was also too big, the sleeves hanging below his hands, on his head a faded cap with a badly frayed brim. A hand-knitted scarf was tied neatly and securely about his thin neck and fastened with a large safety pin at the back. Someone had put him in it and made sure it did not come loose. Someone who cared about him, and his bright eyes shone with what seemed to Lally to be well-being.

'Mornin', missis,' he chimed, doffing his cap politely as he stood to one side of the track.

'Good morning.' She smiled, quite taken out of herself by the boy's manners.

126

'Sam,' he continued, holding his cap across his chest.

'Sam?' she queried.

'Aye, tha'll not remember me, I reckon, but I mind thee.'

She reined in the mare and turned back to him. 'Oh . . .'

'It were at mill. You was there along maister. I held tha'—'

'Of course, Sam. I remember. You work for Mr Sinclair.'

'I do that.' And he said it proudly as though it were an honour to be employed by the great Mr Sinclair. 'I'm just on me way there now.'

'To the mill?'

'Nay, ter Mr Sinclair's. 'E sends me mam stuff, 'er not bein' well, like. Bairn's due soon an' she can't work. Mr Sinclair ses she's not ter trouble 'ersenn. Me pa's dead, yer see.' It was said simply with no demand for sympathy.

'I'm sorry . . .' And it was then that the decision was made. 'I'm about to visit Mr Sinclair myself. Would you mind if I walked along with you, and then, if it would be no bother to your mother, I'll ride you back to your home and have a word with her. I'd like to meet her if you think . . .'

'Eeh, missis, she'd be made up wi' it but theer's no need fer yer ter do that. It's not far an'—'

'How far is it, Sam?'

'No more'n five mile. I'm used to it.' He grinned endearingly.

She looked at his poor battered boots, at his cheerful face, his thin, ill-clad body and she felt her heart wrench. He had no complaint with the world though it treated him so poorly. He had a job, his

127

mam had a roof over her head and Mr Sinclair was a right good chap, his manner said, and she knew the latter was true and that she could go to him in her troubles. He would tell her what she must do, as he had done in the past.

When she and Sam walked into the yard at the back of Mill House, Harry's groom, Ben, was currying Harry's bay, Piper, the strong sweep of his arm smoothing the animal's satin haunches. He looked surprised but called at once to the second groom.

'Mornin', Mrs Fraser,' he said respectfully. 'Enoch, get you out 'ere ter see ter Mrs Fraser's horse. Nice day, ma'am,' he added, turning to look at the urchin beside her.

'Indeed. Is your master at home, d'you know?' She smiled the lovely radiant smile that made men want to make her laugh, for surely a smile so grand would produce an even grander laugh.

'He is,' a cool voice from the kitchen doorway said and Harry Sinclair stepped down into the yard. He was hastily throwing on an old jacket, one he probably kept behind the kitchen door, Lally suspected. He did not smile, at least at her but as his glance turned to Sam the corners of his mouth lifted.

'Harry, good morning. I just thought . . . well, I met Sam here on the moor and as he was walking to Mill House I thought I would come with him. It's been an age since I saw you and . . . well, too long, really . . .' She knew she was floundering but he made no move to help her out. The two grooms watched curiously and the boy moved from foot to foot, evidently sensing something though he was not old enough to know what.

128

'It's always a pleasure to see you, Lally. May I offer you a drink? Something to warm you before you ride home.' It was a deliberate slap in the face, telling her that he would be the courteous host but that she was not particularly welcome.

She did her best not to recoil. 'Thank you, I would like that. I wanted to . . . to speak to you.'

'You have a problem?' he asked politely.

Lord, you might say that, her anguished mind quavered inside her. Her heart turned over as fear overtook her again because she had thought, subconsciously she supposed, that as she had done in the past she could go to Harry with any problem, any troubles she might have and he would find a solution. It seemed it was not so.

He turned to the boy. 'Mrs Cannon has your parcel, Sam. Tell your mother—'

'No, don't go without me, Sam.' Lally looked up into Harry's face. 'I promised Sam a ride back to his home. I would like to meet his mother, you see . . .'

'Why?' he asked bluntly.

'Why not? If there is anything I can do for her and Sam . . . perhaps work when the . . . Sam tells me she is expecting a child . . .' And her plight is so close to my own that I feel compelled to help her. She had a husband and though he is dead she will not be ostracised as I will be. The thoughts whirled in her head and the tension in her must have reached him, for he dropped his shoulders which he had not realised he was holding so stiffly.

'Come in and Mrs Cannon will give you some hot chocolate. If you wish to talk about the farms I'll—'

'It's not the farms,' she blurted. Her hand rose

129

as though in supplication and at once the love he had for her cast out the pain, the anger, the feeling of rejection he had known since Roly came home and swept her off her feet. He opened the kitchen door wider.

'Come inside, and you, Sam, wait in the kitchen. Mrs Cannon will give you a drink or something.'

The servants watched in bemusement as their master hurried Mrs Fraser through their workplace, through the door and into the passage that led to the parlour. 'A pot of chocolate, if you please, Mrs Cannon,' he told his housekeeper as he banged the door to behind them.

They sat, one on either side of the fire which crackled cheerfully in the grate, saying nothing, for they had nothing to say, at least about mundane matters and when Ivy entered with the tray bearing a pot of chocolate with cups, saucers and a plate of Mrs Cannon's delicious almond macaroons, Harry waited until the maid had left before speaking.

'Will you pour?' he asked her politely, which she did.

Then, 'What is it, Lally?' His voice was gentle now, for he could see she was deeply troubled.

She put her cup down carefully, not looking at him as she did so.

'It seems I'm to have a baby.' The words were flat, expressionless as though she were telling him that her mare was to foal. 'I shouldn't bring this to you but I don't know who else to tell . . .' and as she spoke she wondered dazedly why this should be. Why should she turn to this one man when she was troubled, and not just troubled but *desperate*? Why could she not have confided in Biddy who might have been able to help her, perhaps with . . . well,

130

she knew of Biddy's early days and the profession she had followed so surely she might have known of some potion—something—that would get rid of the burden she carried. Why had she come here? The answer was unclear to her!

She sat with her head bent, staring at her hands and waited, and had she looked at Harry she would have been shocked. The blow hit him just below his ribs, like the blow a prize-fighter's fist might have struck. And it had the same effect. The air left his lungs and he felt himself begin to fold over, at the same time thanking God he was seated or he might have collapsed. He could not speak, nor hardly think. His brain became numb, the only thought remaining was his thanks to God again that he was not standing, for he knew he wanted to strike her, hit her flat across her face and knock her down since she had taken something from him that was the most precious thing he had known. Oh, he still loved her and always would but he hated her too.

She did not speak nor look at him, but plucked at something in her lap. Then, with a jerk of her head she looked up at him and was horrified by his expression. His face was the colour of clay, his eyes wide, flat, muddy and his mouth had become a thin line of what seemed to her to be pain. She started to rise, to go to him but he put up a trembling hand to stop her.

'Roly's?'

His voice sounded strange.

'Yes.'

'Then he shall be brought home and you must be married.' His voice was harsh, gritty, as though he had sand in his throat.

'Oh no!' She stood up jerkily and he stared at her, appalled.

'What . . .'

'I can't marry Roly. He doesn't love me and I don't love him. He won't want to marry me.'

'Bugger what he wants.'

'No . . . oh, no, Harry. I couldn't marry a man . . . force him to marry me. What sort of a life would we live? No.'

He had recovered some of his composure. 'Tell me this. If you don't love one another how did you come to be in such a bloody mess?'

'Oh, Harry . . .' She sighed and sat down disconsolately. 'It was a . . . a thing of the moment. I suppose I missed Chris and . . . what we had . . .'

'In bed, you mean?'

'Yes.'

'So you and Roly——' Here he used a word she had never heard before but she supposed it to be one men used to describe coarsely what went on between the sexes.

'It was . . . we were fond of one another; he was leaving and I was upset and . . .'

'So you—one another.' Again he used the word and his face bore such an expression of disgust and contempt she wanted to weep. Somehow she had missed what this man felt for her, though she had not realised it at the time, and the slow death she had struck him was more than he could manage.

He stood up abruptly and strode to the window, a jerky stride as though he were no longer in control of his legs. He stared out at the garden which was just beginning to lose its summer glory. Though he was not a man for such things as flowers and gardens he employed men who were clever and 'green-fingered' as they said, and it had been a picture. Dying roses still nodded in the slight breeze. A landscaped greenery had been cut from the otherwise bare hillside, fragrant with lavender and carnations and over it all the sun still shone though in his heart there was nothing but a frozen wasteland. She was to have his brother's child and he could simply not bear it. She had loved Chris Fraser and had two boys with him but she had been pure, a married woman doing what women of their day did. A home, children, a life that was virtuous, above reproach, but this with his brother, though she had already made love and borne a man a child, two children, was obscene, *dirty*!

'What will you do?' he asked her. He stood with his hands behind his back, rigidly in control now and she wanted to weep, for herself, for him, and for the child she was to bear.

'I don't know. I suppose Biddy might know of a remedy, or perhaps some woman who would—'

'Don't you dare,' he snarled, whirling to face her. 'Let some woman with a dirty knitting needle tear your insides out, perhaps kill you, and the child.'

'But I can't—'

'There is only one thing to do and you know it, or why should you come to me.'

'Harry . . . ?' she faltered.

'You must marry me.'

*   *   *

She rode with Sam as far as the house where he and his mother lived. He climbed up in front of

133

her, quiet, uneasy, for the master and Mrs Fraser seemed so . . . he didn't know how to describe it since he was only a child but their faces were turned from each other as they bade one another farewell. 'I will call on you tomorrow, Lally,' the master had said and Mrs Fraser had bowed her head in agreement. That was all.

Susan Harper was astonished when her son entered the room they rented in the tumbling old house on the edge of Moorend, leading a lady by the hand. She was a lovely young lady, though she was pale and strained and her eyes had a curiously defenceless look, which Susan recognised at once, for she saw them each day in her own face when she peered into the scrap of mirror she had on a shelf above her bed.

'Sam, lad?' she questioned softly, her hand going to caress her son's rough tumble of uncut hair. ' 'Oo'st this then?' She smiled, one of the sweetest smiles Lally had ever seen and at once the two women, two women from totally different classes, began what was to be a friendship that would last them until death.

'Oh, I beg your pardon,' Lally said. 'Forgive this intrusion but I met your son,' smiling down at the bright-faced boy, 'on the track to Mill House. I travelled with him and then gave him a ride back on Merry. It's a long way for a boy to walk . . . oh, please, I am not criticising,' for the mother looked abject with contrition. 'I know he has to work but Mr Sinclair is a kind master. He has sent you the . . . package. Sam has it. Dear me, how I do go on but I am—'

'Wilta come in, ma'am?' Sam's mother asked diffidently, for this woman would not be used to

134

the conditions in which she and her son lived. The houses had once been lived in by the rising industrialists, the woollen men who had long since built fine mansions beyond the town's boundaries. With the influx of the Irish, the workless, the homeless, the families seeking work, the houses had been split up into rooms, even the cellars housing them, but at least she and Sam had a window in their room and could look out on to the rambling lane that led into town.

'I'm Mrs Fraser. Lally Fraser. I am a . . . a friend of Mr Sinclair's.'

'Aye, our Sam told me. Me name's Susan Harper but yer welcome ter . . . sit thee down if tha've a mind.' She was obviously troubled but Lally was not to know that Susan Harper, teetering forever on the edge of poverty, had nothing to offer her in the way of refreshments and she felt it keenly. She did not really know who this lady was who had brought her lad home, nor why, but nevertheless she indicated to Lally that she should sit in the only chair the room possessed. There was a meagre fire in the ancient range as this had once been the kitchen of the old house and a kettle simmered on it but unless Mr Sinclair had sent a packet of tea she could not even offer this lady a drink.

Lally sensed Susan Harper's unease. Sam's mother was enormous, her belly swelling the clean apron she wore. She clasped her hands beneath it as though to support the weight of the child inside her, hovering at Lally's back, ushering her politely to the chair but Lally could see the circles under her eyes and the tired droop to the soft mouth and knew that Susan longed to sit down in the chair

135

from which she had just risen.

'No, Mrs Harper, I won't stay. I have to get back to my own children but I just wanted to make the acquaintance of Sam's mother.' She nearly added, 'I don't know why,' she only knew that somehow, again she didn't know why, this young woman, probably only a few years older than herself, was going to be important to her. They were both to bear a child, Susan Harper before not very long and she wished to help her. The idea that this woman who had worked in the loom gate at Harry's mill was to return there as soon as her child was born was not one she cared to contemplate. She had taken a great liking to the engaging lad who was Susan's son and she felt a strong desire to include the pair of them in her new life.

For she was to have a new life, that was certain. She had listened to Harry and the outline of his plans for them, for her sons and the child she would bear and, knowing she had no choice, she had agreed. She supposed she was in a state of shock, a vacuum through which she must step to reach a safe harbourage. For the sake of Jamie and Alec Fraser she must do as he wished, for if she tried to get through this on her own it would not be just her who would suffer but the innocent children she already had. *She had no choice!*

'I wish you well, Mrs Harper,' she murmured as she turned to go from the achingly neat but bare room. 'I will come again, if I may. Perhaps Sam will let me know when your child is born and . . . well, I will ride over.'

She took Susan Harper's thin hand between her own, smiling, then ran across the lane to where she

136

had tethered Merry. She leaped on to her back and with a wave of her hand cantered in the direction of the moorland track that would take her home.

CHAPTER TEN

They were married three weeks later, the bridegroom insisting on it and though the whole of Moorend was buzzing with it when it became known, the married couple were oblivious to the furore. The bride existed in a state of blind acceptance as she had done for the past three weeks. She felt as though she were under a glass dome, one of those that housed dried flowers and birds and which were so popular on chiffoniers in the best homes. She could see out but though it was made of glass no one could see or hear her.

She was pale and slender, her pregnancy not as yet visible, as she stood beside Harry at the altar of a small church in White Cross, a village where neither of them were known. Harry had arranged for the banns to be called and on a still, fine day at the end of October, accompanied by a bewildered Biddy, they exchanged their vows in a church empty of all but the two of them, the minister and her. A carriage awaited them at the lych gate where it had dropped them before the ceremony and the three of them, in total silence, were driven back to the Priory. There were no celebrations, no toasts, no champagne.

Though Biddy was delighted by the news that her lass was to be safe and cared for by Mr Sinclair she was aghast and suspicious of this sudden decision to marry. After all, Miss Lally had been squired around Moorend and even into Halifax by Mr Sinclair's own brother, Roly. The talk of the parish, they had been, causing such scandal not one of their previous acquaintances had called at the Priory for weeks. Hours they had spent, laughing and talking in the drawing room, even singing at the piano which Miss Lally could play by ear, 'Are You Going to Scarborough Fair', 'Early One Morning', 'Believe Me if all Those Endearing Young Charms', and many others, their voices reaching the kitchen where Jenny and Clara hummed along with them as they washed up the dinner pots. They had ridden up on to the high moors, taking paths once trodden by packhorses, coming home flushed and smiling, and only the good Lord knew what they got up to. Biddy had been worried to death and even tried to remonstrate with Miss Lally but she had taken no heed, saying that it was wonderful to be with someone who made her laugh for a change.

Now, right out of the blue and only two months after Mr Roly had gone off on his travels, and with no sight nor sound of Mr Sinclair, Mr *Harry* Sinclair, in all that time, Miss Lally comes home and casually announces that she and Harry Sinclair were to be wed.

'*What!*' Biddy had sat down heavily in the nearest chair, her hand to her heart and her face like a drift of snow.

'Harry and I are to be married . . .'

'Dear God, child, I heard you the first time but I'm so stunned I just can't believe it. Only a month or two back you were—'

'I know. Roly and I were . . . good friends but he

would not make a good husband or father to my boys so . . .'

'You're to marry Mr Harry! Just like that! And what I want to know is how has this come about?' She shook her head in bewilderment then moved across the room, dragging Lally round to face her. Lally was pacing restlessly about her pretty bedroom. It seemed she could not settle nor could she look Biddy in the eyes.

'It's something that . . . that is convenient to us.'

'*Convenient!* You talk about it as if it was a business arrangement, like . . . like one firm that is going to sell out to another or summat. There's summat be'ind this.' As she did when she was upset Biddy lapsed into the northern brogue of her early days. She turned towards the door abruptly. 'I shall 'ave a word wi' Mr Sinclair,' just as though she were to be off this very minute to the Mill House or High Clough, wherever the chap happened to be and get this silly nonsense sorted out!

'No, you will not, Biddy.' Lally whirled to face Biddy's retreating back. 'This is between Harry and myself. We have . . . have always been fond of one another and have come to believe that marriage between us would be in our best interests. My sons will have a father and a home.'

'They've got a 'ome.'

'A proper home where money isn't so damned hard to find. A decent education at a decent school. Ponies of their own to learn to ride, all the things they would have had if Chris hadn't died.'

'Mr Chris hadn't two farthings ter rub tergether.' Biddy's voice was savage with fear. 'What's be'ind this, my lass? You've never bin bothered about brass before, an' neither was

139

Mr Chris. Now, all of a sudden yer tekken up wi' the need fer ponies an' such. So tell me this. D'yer love 'im like 'e loves you?'

Lally caught Biddy's arm as she opened the door. Her face was a picture of astonishment. 'What the devil d'you mean by that?' Her hand was cruel on Biddy's flesh and Biddy winced.

'D'yer mean ter say yer don't know what that chap really feels for yer? I've sin it as clear as day though I'll grant yer he does his best to 'ide it. So 'appen he's caught yer on the rebound like, though who from I don't know. Chris Fraser or Roly Sinclair. As like as two peas in a pod they were, harum-scarum pair, and I reckon that's why yer took up wi' Mr Roly 'cos he was so like Mr Chris, but Mr Sinclair's a different kettle of fish altogether so think on. There's more to this than meets the eye, lady, an' I mean ter find out what it is. Now, let go of me arm fer I've things to attend to. Just let me know when the bridegroom's coming over to inspect his new home because if I know Mr Sinclair he'll want to change things to his own satisfaction. He's used to living in luxury is Mr Sinclair and when he moves in here he'll want the very best.'

Biddy swept from the room, closing the door quietly behind her.

And so here they were, Harry moving about the drawing room picking up objects as though debating whether to keep them or chuck them away as rubbish, evidently inspecting what was to be his new home and deciding what was to be altered while the fascinated Jenny, who was serving the hot chocolate her new master had ordered, watched closely so that she might report back to the kitchen. They had all been open-mouthed with astonishment when it had been announced that their little mistress was to wed the wealthy Mr Sinclair, Mr *Harry* Sinclair, with Mr Chris hardly cold in his grave, but then their mistress really did need looking after what with them boys and the farms and that. She looked like death, poor little thing, Jenny was to tell the others in the kitchen when Mrs Stevens had left the room, though her frock was lovely. The colour of apple blossom, floating about her with a short train and in her hair, which curled about it, was a little cap the same colour as her frock, decorated with pale pink petals. She had a small bouquet attached by satin ribbons to her wrist.

'Will that be all, madam?' Jenny bobbed a small curtsey.

'Thank you, Jenny. It *is* Jenny, I believe?' her new master said.

'Yes, sir.'

'Yes, well that will be all, thank you. We will ring if we need anything.' He was already in command. Jenny scurried from the room, eager to get back to the others, hoping that Mrs Stevens had not yet returned from wherever it was she had gone. The new Mrs Sinclair and her husband did not look like newly weds, at least not in Jenny's understanding though she had not been married herself. But one of her sisters had and the bridegroom had hardly been able to keep his hands from her and was obviously longing to get her to himself! Mr Sinclair's groom had delivered a trunk only yesterday which had been placed in the bedroom that Miss Lally had once shared with her dead husband and they were apparently to share the bed, which Jenny had made up this morning while Miss Lally was at the church.

'Perhaps we should order dinner,' Harry said when Jenny had left the room. 'You must be tired and an early meal will suit me.' He was scrupulously polite as he had been for the past three weeks ever since he had told her they must be married. His face was expressionless, as had been Biddy's when told of it just as though they were arranging some business affair.

He had ridden over to the Priory the day after his proposal and with cool dignity told Lally what he had planned for them, for her servants, her children and for the Priory itself. He would, of course, live at the Priory since there was no room at Mill House for them all, especially with two lively boys and then, naturally, a space must be made for the child who was coming. When the time came he might build a house, his own house, in which they would live, for the Priory was her sons' inheritance and would come to one of them when they were older. And, of course, Mill House must be kept for the return of Roly whose home it was.

In the meanwhile changes at the Priory must be made which he would explain to her when he had moved in. If she had any objections to anything he suggested she had only to say. She would be given an allowance to spend as she liked and naturally if there were things she needed for the boys and the child yet to be born she had only to ask. He thought it might be wise, he told her coolly, if they were to share a room though she might find it distasteful, in view of the . . . the coming child. Servants were known to gossip and after all the

142

baby was to be passed off as his! A ripple of distaste crossed his face. It would look strange if it were to get out that the newly married Mr and Mrs Sinclair were sleeping apart. Did she agree? She did.

*　　　*　　　*

They ate a silent meal, Lally still dressed in her lovely wedding gown, the one Miss Hockley in Market Square had been astonished but delighted to design and make for her. Like the rest of Moorend she had been aware of Mrs Fraser's relationship with Mr Roly Sinclair and to be told that she was to wed Mr Harry Sinclair and in three weeks' time caused a ripple of whispers to flow from floor to floor in her busy establishment, and from there to spread quickly through the parish.

At last Lally, fiddling with a butter knife, could stand the silence no longer. 'Are we never to speak, Harry?' she said abruptly. 'Are we to live in this silently polite world for ever? We once were friends. You helped me enormously after Chris died. I have made a terrible mistake and again you are protecting me but if we are to have any sort of life together . . .' Her voice trailed away and Harry felt the pain of it, *her* pain disintegrate something in the region of his heart. She looked fragile, vulnerable, defenceless against what she saw as his careless indifference to her misery. She had not wanted to marry him. She had been forced into it by circumstances, admittedly brought about by her own foolishness, but still it was not all her fault. Who better than him knew Roly's charm?

'Lally, speak, my dear. Whatever you wish to

143

say, please feel free to say it.' He leaned across the table and cut himself a piece of cheese. The table looked elegant, with bowls of flowers, fruit, cheese, wine, savoury biscuits baked by Biddy who he had ascertained was an excellent cook and for the time being, he had told Lally loftily, he would keep her on. Oh, he realised she was more than a cook to Lally and she would not be turned away. She was a decent housekeeper and with the money he was prepared to pour into the household purse would do very well. For the moment! Mrs Cannon would stay on at Mill House with her staff but the grooms would be needed here at the Priory since he meant to purchase thoroughbred stock. Ponies for the boys and the children he would have with Lally, a son of his own . . . Dear sweet Lord—a son of his own!

'I have nothing in particular that I wish to speak of but . . . well, there must be something we have in common. Once upon a time we used to . . . Oh, Harry, this is . . . we are married and I for one would like to make a success of it, a life for—'

'A success of it. Would you indeed, when you carry my brother's child.' His face twisted with what looked strangely like anguish though Lally did not recognise it.

'Yes.' Her voice was passionate. 'I came to you, not for this . . .' indicating the pair of them sitting at the table, the expensive setting of cut-crystal wine glasses, the flowers, the scented candles, 'though it is very pleasing.'

'What did you come for?' he asked her coldly.

'I don't know. You were my friend and as such I somehow found myself admitting my . . . my sin, I suppose you would call it. That's what Moorend

144

would call it. But when you offered me marriage I found myself liking the idea. We have not spoken of it during the past three weeks. I have travelled the days in a dream world, led along by some mysterious compulsion.'

'You mean you were made to marry me?' His voice was cold, that of a stranger, polite but uncaring.

'No, no. I . . . for the sake of my boys . . . the scandal would have ruined their chance of a decent life among their own kind . . . and for myself . . .'

'You would rather live a lie than be ostracised by society, you are saying?'

He smiled cruelly and Lally wondered why she had never seen this side of his nature before. He had always been kind, gentle, helpful, ready to give freely of advice. He had shown a humorous depth to his nature, making her laugh, lightening a part of her life that had been cheerless after the accident that had killed Chris. Now he was this cold stranger who seemed intent on humiliating her. And yet she remembered the strange words Biddy had spoken when she had been told that Lally was to marry Harry. She had implied that Harry loved her but that was totally ridiculous, for she had seen no sign of it. In the past he had been friendly, trustworthy and understanding, unstinting with his advice and help and certainly not at all lover-like.

She sighed deeply, catching the eye of Jenny who had just entered the room and was at the ancient sideboard ready to pour more coffee should it be needed but it seemed Harry was ready to start on something stronger. He had already drunk a full bottle of wine, Lally having merely a

145

sip or two, and turning to Jenny, smiling politely, he told her she might go.

'Shall we move to the drawing room, Harry?' Lally enquired, just as politely. 'There is brandy, whisky, port . . .' for Harry himself had replenished the meagre supply she had managed for guests. 'We could be more comfortable.' She hoped this didn't sound too inviting as though she were importuning him to some more intimate situation but she did long to get this first evening and *night* over and done with.

They had dined on vermicelli soup, breast of veal, followed by a transparent jelly inlaid with brandy cherries and topped with whipped cream. A simple meal, but well prepared and cooked and Biddy had outdone herself with the table and so far Harry had seemed well pleased. He rose and moving round the table took her hand and led her from the dining room, across the enormous slabbed hallway in which a huge fire burned— already the house was showing the results of the money he meant to put into it, and his own comfort—and into the equally warm drawing room where applewood logs burned brightly in the wide fireplace. He ceremoniously seated her before it on the worn old sofa which he had already told her he meant to replace then moved to the drinks table and poured himself a large brandy.

'May I offer you a liqueur, Lally?' he asked her courteously. She had not even known there was such a thing among the many bottles he had had placed there.

'Thank you, yes,' for it might give her courage for the ordeal to come. He poured her a pretty coloured drink into a tiny glass—she had no idea

146

what it was—and handed it to her. It tasted lovely and after he had lit a cigar and drawn the smoke deeply, satisfyingly into his lungs, she asked for another. He gave it to her and she was made aware that he too was eager to facilitate the situation, make it easier for both of them.

They did not speak, both of them gazing sightlessly into the fire. Of what *could* they speak? Current affairs? The comings and goings of the royal family? The impending wedding of Joshua and Mildred Fawcett's daughter to which he—but not Lally—had been invited? He drank brandy, glass after glass, and when the clock struck ten he stood up abruptly.

'Lally,' he said, his voice harsh with some emotion that seemed to devastate him. Lally's face was drawn suddenly into a mask and he knew she was afraid, not of what was to come for she had known a man's body before but of what was to happen between *them*. It could be disastrous. His own brother had impregnated her several months ago and now he was to attempt to go where Roly had been before him. It was intolerable, both of them knew it, but it had to be done. If they were to make any sort of a life together this night and all the ones to follow, it must be done. A terrible mistake had been made and this was the only way to rectify it.

'I'll be up in a minute.' His eyes looked directly into hers and she was made to understand that there would be no avoiding what was to come. As she obediently left the room she saw him reach once more for the brandy bottle.

Biddy had gone, saying nothing, for what was there to say to the tragic figure who sat in the centre of the bed. She had helped her to undress, put her into her demure nightgown, brushed her short hair and kissed her cheek.

'Blow the candles out, Biddy,' the small voice from the bed told her.

'Nay, lass, tha' 'usband will do that.' She shut the door quietly behind her.

He strode into the room, fortified by the enormous amount of brandy he had consumed, without which he would not have been able to do this thing. She shrank away from him for an infinitesimal moment and he almost turned away since he could not in all conscience force her to his will, then her head came up and her eyes, so blue and lovely with their flecks of green, darkened. Even in the subdued light of the candles he could see them, then they gleamed with what seemed like defiance. Her head came up and her soft mouth tightened. With one glorious movement she stood up in the bed and drew off her white frilled nightgown, tossing it to the floor. She stood, challenging him and in answer he threw off the brocade robe which was all he wore and advanced towards her. She did not shrink from him. Her body, though slender, was in perfect proportion, her breasts high and proud despite bearing two children, her waist neat, her hips soft and flaring and her legs long.

'Well then,' he heard himself murmuring, he had no idea why. His own body was bold, virile, thrusting, lean as an athlete's, but strong and the colour of amber. Quite beautiful, masculine, a manly beauty which she had time to notice before he stepped up on to the bed and drew her into his arms. His penis pressed against her belly then he

148

pulled her—not gently—down into the softness of the bed that she had once shared with Chris Fraser. He had not yet told her but he meant to change that and move them both into another room, one he would make into *their* room, a bedroom that would be made luxuriously lovely and would have no memories of her dead husband. But tonight they must make do with this and he hoped to God the ghost of Chris Fraser would not come to disturb them. Even Roly, his own brother might have shared this bed with her; he had never asked her where the event had taken place in which the child had been conceived but as soon as possible he would have the builders, decorators, designers, furnishing experts in to change not only the bedroom he and Lally would share, but the rest of this threadbare, decaying old house.

He loved her that night in a way that took her by surprise. She had expected it to be quick and not exactly brutal, for she instinctively knew Harry was not a brutal man, but not gentle. He kissed her, parting her lips, caressing them, folding them softly with his, then began to lead her along the sweet and honeyed paths which he had learned with other women but which was also his nature. She felt the beginnings of joy as his hand held her breast, moving down to her belly, the dark triangle of hair at the base of it and into the increasingly eager centre, the moist centre of her womanhood. She cried out and he hesitated but she grasped him to her, pulling him down with no thought for the child growing within her as he entered her, spilling his seed where his brother's and Chris Fraser's had once been spilled. For a moment he agonised that he was not the first but, by God, he would be the last, his triumphant cry said.

She slept then, her back against his belly, his arms cradling her, his face buried in the sweet scented tangle of her hair. He lay awake, his thoughts filling his head and his sad heart, for he loved this woman more than life itself and his love was not returned. He drew deeply into his lungs the smell of her, her soft hair tickling his nostrils and as he himself drifted off to sleep his last thought was that he would persuade her to grow it.

He woke in the night. The candles had burned down but the fire glowed orange and red in the grate. She was still in the same position in which she had gone to sleep. She murmured something and as he turned her towards him she smiled. He kissed her, moving from her mouth to her jawline, down her throat to the peak of her breast where the nipple stood in a rosy point. He took it in his mouth and sucked gently and when, still half asleep, she pressed his head to her he smiled in triumph.

'Chris . . . darling . . .' she murmured, arching her back the better to accommodate him. At once he lifted his head and turned away from her to lie on his back, devastated by the name she had uttered and when she sat up he turned away from her, his wonder and the rejoicing that had filled him at what he saw as her acceptance and even eagerness to have him in her bed become ashes in his mouth.

She lay back on her pillow, saying no more, then edged away from him so that they no longer touched. He lay for what seemed hours beside her, listening to her breathing, then fell asleep himself.

Strangely, when they both woke she was curled

up beside him again, her arm across his chest, his own holding her closely. It was still dark, five o'clock in the morning and at once he leaped from the bed and reached for his robe.

'You must excuse me, my dear,' he said in his polite, cool way, 'but I have a mill to run. Several, in fact, and I must be there at the gates when they open.'

'Of course,' she answered in the same tone as his.

'I'll be home for dinner so until then . . .'

He did not kiss her as he left and she turned over, staring blindly into the darkness wondering why she felt so foolishly disappointed.

CHAPTER ELEVEN

The woman on the bed stifled a moan, heaving herself on to her side in an effort to alleviate her own suffering. The boy crouched beside her, his pale face twisted into an anxious frown. He put out his hand and touched her sweated face and she did her best to smile as though the birth of a child was nothing more than the grazed knees he often brought home for her to bathe and to receive the kiss and cuddle that made it better, but as the pain returned, knifing her in the small of her back, she could not help the cry that escaped from between her bitten lips. The boy seemed ready to cry himself, for he was only ten years old and though he lived among the poorest of the poor, the multitude of rag-pickers, the mill workers, the under-privileged, the slum dwellers who lived cheek by jowl with one another in the tenement building he called home and had heard the cries of the downtrodden women who gave birth every year, he and his mother did not mix with them. Mam was different from the rest of them. If his father had not died in an accident in the weaving shed at High Clough, an accident that had taken not only his pa but the child he had tried to save from the lethal machinery that had trapped them both, he and his mam would not now be in this frightening situation for Pa would have seen his ma through it. The child, a scavenger like himself, had slipped on a patch of oil, put out his hands to stop himself from falling and had been dragged into the machine's clutches. His pa, working in the loom gate, had tried to save the child and in so doing had slipped in the same patch of oil and had shared the child's fate. Bled to death the two of them and ever since then the maister had looked out for Sam and Susan Harper. Mam worked two looms in the vast weaving shed at High Clough where 816 machines clacked and whirred in the 'fly'-laden air, seventeen rows of forty-eight in each row. She had carried on, grieving silently for her young husband until seen one day by the maister, struggling to reach the cord that jerked the wheeled shuttle across the loom. She was seven months gone then, hampered by her swollen belly, and without a word the maister had sent her home and with his help and Sam's small wage they had managed. Sam should have been at the mill two hours ago.

'Tha' go, lad,' Mam had told him but he could not leave her like this, could he?

'Nay, Mam, ah can't, not wi' you like this.

152

Babby'll be 'ere soon. Then ah'll go.'

Susan Harper clutched the sheet with work-worn hands and writhed through the next pain, gasping for breath and wishing she had mixed more with her slatternly neighbours who might have helped her, since it was not fair to expect a ten-year-old boy to deliver her but she and Jack had kept themselves to themselves. They had clawed their way upwards, kept a clean home, ate cheap but nourishing food and had even gone to the local evening classes, taking their baby son with them, and had learned to read and write. They would better themselves, Jack had told her confidently. He was not sure how but when they had mastered the art of it he would approach Mr Sinclair and see if there was work, perhaps as a supervisor, that could be put his way. They would teach young Sam to read and write, which they had done and with their combined wages, though it had tormented them to put Sam to scavenging, they had kept themselves decent, their room spotless and had been shunned by their slovenly neighbours who lived their lives in muddled chaos.

'Sam, love,' she gasped, clutching at his poor little hand, making him wince, 'tha'll 'ave ter go fer 'elp. Tha' can't do this on tha' own.'

''Oo shall ah fetch, Mam?' His child's face was frightened and yet set with a determination to help his mam. 'Will ah go fer Mr Sinclair? 'Appen 'e'll know o' someone . . .'

'Eeh, no, lovey,' she gasped. ''E's a busy man an'll not be bothered wi't likes—'

''E will, Mam, 'e will,' the boy said eagerly. ''E's a grand chap.' And before his mother, who was in the grip of another spasm, could stop him he was

153

out of the door and running up the slimy cobbled road that led to the track across the moorland and the mill at High Clough.

*   *   *

'I'm taking Merry out for a gallop, Biddy. The children are both taking a nap and it's more than my life's worth to wake them. Dora makes it quite plain who's in charge of the nursery and it's certainly not their mother. I won't be long.'

'Don't go far, lass.' Biddy looked compassionately at her young mistress. She had been married a week and had shared her bed and eaten her meals with her new husband—apart from breakfast, since Mr Sinclair rose and left the house so early—but anyone less like a happy bride Biddy had yet to see. She drooped about the house, only coming alive when she was with her young sons. 'Shall I get Carly to go with you? I don't think Mr Sinclair'd like you to be riding on your own,' for Mrs Harry Sinclair was a vastly different kettle of fish to Mrs Lally Fraser.

'Of course not. I've been on the moors by myself ever since I can remember. Now don't fuss, Biddy. Ask Carly to saddle Merry and I'll be down directly.'

Biddy, grumbling beneath her breath, left the room while Lally opened her wardrobe door and sorted through her outfits until she found her riding habit. Throwing off her pretty negligee she reached for her breeches, pulling them up about her waist but was dismayed to find that since she had last worn them, which wasn't all that long ago, they had become very tight. They clung to her hips and were like a second skin across her distended belly wherein Roly's child lay. She could hear Biddy coming back up the stairs, still muttering on the inappropriateness of Mrs Harry Sinclair riding out alone and woe betide them all when he came home and heard of it, so hastily Lally shrugged into her riding jacket which she was still able to fasten and which covered her almost to her knees. She draped her full riding skirt about her. Jamming her tall beaver hat on her head, since she knew that would please Biddy and might distract her from looking too closely at the rest of her, she picked up her crop, pulled on her gloves and strode from the room.

'Where do you intend to ride?' Biddy asked her anxiously as they passed on the landing, running her eye approvingly over Lally's outfit.

'Oh, not far.' Lally's voice floated airily up the stairs.

She found she needed a helping hand to get on Merry's back, which surprised Carly, for normally she leaped into the saddle as lightly as thistledown.

At last she was away galloping and for several minutes she went at full pelt up the grassy slope, past Cowslip Farm through Moor Wood and out on to the wild, open moorland beyond. She found the dogs had slipped through the gate as Carly opened it, two black and white streaks racing one on either side of her mare who was so used to them she took no notice.

'Keep up, Fred, and watch out for Merry's hooves, Ally. I do wish you wouldn't run so close to us, you rascals,' but she knew from past rides that the dogs were well used to keeping their distance.

She kept going but at a canter now, up and up

155

above the deep, tree-covered valley below her. There were several isolated farmhouses down there, smoke from their chimneys going straight up into the sky, while huddled against the skyline a small village was almost hidden beneath the pall of smoke that told her there were woollen mills nearby. Dry-stone walls cobwebbed the swathes of green and brown, grey and the purple of the dying heather and against the wall to her left was a splash of white where cotton sedge still bloomed. She could hear the singing tumble of many mountain streams falling from a dozen hidden places and was just about to dismount and hitch Merry to a stone at the top of the wall when a small, running figure came over a dip in the track. He did not see her for a minute but when he did he recognised her at once, almost tumbling over his own clogged feet in an effort to reach her. His face was scarlet and she thought there were tearstains on his thin cheeks. She could tell at once that there was something badly wrong. The boy was Sam whose mother was to have a baby.

'Oh, miss . . . miss . . . it's me mam. 'Er time's come an' theer's only me ter 'elp 'er. Ah sed ah'd run fer t'maister but me mam sed no but ah don't know what ter do. Theer's no one ter 'elp 'er an' she's in a right pickle. Oh, miss, ah can't stop . . . ah must get on . . .' and he began to run in the direction in which he had been heading.

For a moment she was taken aback then she ran after him, calling his name.

'Wait, Sam, wait. You run back to your mother and stay with her. I'll ride to High Clough . . . No, no . . . *you* run on and tell Mr Sinclair what is happening while I ride to your mother and see if I

156

can help her. Tell Mr Sinclair where I am and that he is to send for a doctor to come to your home.' She took his anguished face between her hands, resisting the desire to plant a comforting kiss on his cheek as she would her own boys. 'Don't worry, Sam. Your mother will be fine. I shall ride as fast as I can and you *run* as fast as you can. Mr Sinclair will help you.' And as she spoke she knew it to be true. Harry Sinclair, beneath his present stiff exterior, was one of the kindest men she had ever met. He was keen to hide the fact but she was well aware that he would go out of his way to make life easier for anyone who asked for his help.

Without another word, though relief shone in his eyes, the boy set off at a run and with help from no one she clambered on to Merry's back and put her to the gallop. She remembered the row of tottering houses in which Sam and his mother had a room and within five minutes she was reining in before the one at the end where a broken wooden fence provided somewhere to tether Merry. The smell about the place was as bad as she remembered and she averted her gaze from the channel that ran down between the cobbles in front of the houses. Several children were splashing in the sluggish water running down the channel, their bare feet and legs coated with dirt and some nasty substance which she was loth to inspect more closely. Several women, slatternly, thin, some with scabby faces and who stood in rotting open doorways, stared at her open-mouthed and she wondered at the advisability of leaving her gentle mare out in the open where any of these appalling creatures might not only go near her but damage her, but she could hardly take the animal inside, could she. Tying the nervous mare to the fence she walked up what passed for a pathway and, knocking on the door, walked inside. There was another door to her left which she remembered from the last time and again knocking she gently opened it and ventured inside.

The woman on the bed lifted her head. 'Sam?' she enquired weakly.

'No, Mrs Harper. Sam has gone for help. It's Mrs Fraser . . . Sinclair, I mean. I came to see you a few weeks ago, with Sam and I'm here to help you. Sam has gone for Mr Sinclair but I said I would help . . . stay with you until help came. I've had two babies of my own and you have had Sam so I'm sure between us we can manage. What d'you say?' She moved over to the bed and looked down at the pain-racked face on the stained pillow.

Susan Harper did her best but water was not always available from the standpipe at the end of the row of houses, which meant she could not always keep up the standard of cleanliness that was bred in her. Sam did his best too but he was a growing lad and since the death of her Jack she had not been able to feed him as she liked. She went hungry herself to keep his belly filled which, in her condition, was not good for her or the child she carried. She was weakening fast as her pains became more intense and her labour continued and now here was this ladylike being cheerfully informing her that now that she was here everything would be all right.

Lally, firmly believing she could, if pushed, deliver the baby herself, since she had been through it twice, forgot that she had had Biddy and a doctor, clean water, hot and constant, towels,

158

nourishing broth, cups of tea and was a healthy, well-fed young woman at both her confinements. You pushed when told to, gave birth, the cord was cut and a child was placed in your arms. That was all there was to it and if Lally Fraser . . . Sinclair could not manage that then God help her.

Susan Harper did her best not to cry out in the presence of this well-bred lady who, before very long, began to look as dishevelled and soiled as the women who had stared at her in the lane. She held Mrs Harper's hand until her fingers were swollen and clumsy; she wiped her face and even attempted to give her a kind of bed-bath, for the woman began to smell. She ran to the end of the street as Mrs Harper directed her, her skirts trailing in the muck that abounded, and filled an old bucket which seemed in danger of springing a leak and when Mrs Harper shouted at her that the child was coming, stuck her head between the labouring woman's legs and watched the crown of the baby begin its journey, followed by a screwed-up face and then, with a suddenness that startled her, the rest of the infant sprang forth and, with it, a wave of blood.

'Dear God,' she whispered, terrified, appalled and delighted all at the same time, then, under Mrs Harper's directions, packed a wad of old cloth to the place from where the child had come. The child wailed, still attached to his mother, but in the disordered confusion Lally had seen that it was a boy and at that moment the room seemed to be filled with people. Harry was there, drawing her away from the bed and with him the doctor, it seemed, who Harry had forced to come with him, for Doctor Channing was not accustomed to

159

tending to patients at this end of town. Sam was there, struggling to get to his mam, and with surprising ease it was all done. The cord cut, the child placed in Susan Harper's right arm, the left about Sam, and Harry was positively dragging his bedraggled wife out into the open air.

She struggled with him, doing her best to get back to the woman who she considered to be *her* responsibility, but Harry continued to drag her towards an open carriage which apparently belonged to Doctor Channing.

'There is nothing more you can do for her, darling,' he was saying, the endearment slipping out in his fear for her. She did not appear to hear it. God only knew what fevers hung about in this godawful place and, but for the lad, for Sam whom he had made a pledge to help when his father had died in one of Harry's machines, he would probably have sent one of the women from the weaving shed. But for Sam and Lally! His beloved wife was helping to deliver the child of one of the hands from his own sheds and must be brought away at once and he was doing just that even though she was making it just as plain that she was not about to be brought away!

'Leave go of me, Harry,' she shrieked. 'I must make sure Sam's mother is all right. She has just had a little boy and . . .'

'I am aware of that, Lally, but the doctor will do all that is necessary and—'

'And then what, Harry? Who is to care for her while she is confined to her bed, and what about Sam? He is—'

'I will send someone to see that—'

'Oh, no.' She managed to get her arms free.

160

'Who does that carriage belong to?'

'It's Doctor Channing's. I left my horse at—'

'Right, you take Merry and then ride to the Priory and bring our carriage. Carly can ride over and fetch your horse. Mrs Harper and Sam cannot stay in this frightful place,' looking about her in lip-curling disdain. 'They and the baby must be brought back with us until they are all well. I will not have them left here in this . . . this muck-heap where there is no clean water unless brought from the standpipe which I am told is turned off for most of the day. I am amazed that anyone can survive . . .'

'But survive they do, Lally, and your plans for Mrs Harper and her family are absolutely out of the question. She must stay here and—'

'Then I will stay with them. I am strong and will carry water.'

Harry looked appalled then his face tightened. 'Damnation, Lally, you will do no such thing. What in God's name are you thinking of?'

He was white-lipped with anger, a fierce, knife-edged anger that made her take a step away from him but she would not give up. He himself had begun this sequence of events when he had felt compelled to help this small family and no matter what he said, she *had* delivered the baby and she meant to keep an eye on him. There was plenty of room at home and with Dora's help and even another nursemaid Jamie, Alec, the child born this day and the one to come would be very comfortable in the large nursery. She might have it decorated and perhaps a wall knocked down and a schoolroom added, for Jamie was ready for simple lessons. A . . . a governess, perhaps, and then there

161

was Sam who was not meant to crawl about under those lethal machines in Harry's mill. A decent education, maybe at the local grammar school where Chris, Harry and Roly had been taught . . .

The two dogs were milling about their feet, alarmed at the raised voices and the tension that strained the air. They were used to Harry but he was still a stranger in their mistress's home and they were inclined to be somewhat wary of him.

Lally was quite carried away, even excited at the thought of this new project, for there was no doubt in her mind that Harry would take over the management of the estate and the farms, perhaps putting in a steward of some sort and then what would Lally Fraser . . . Sinclair do with her time? She had taken a great liking even in two short meetings to Sam Harper's mother, who seemed to Lally to be struggling against all odds to bring up her small family in a decent way and, after all, they had both lost a husband in dreadful accidents. Surely it would be fitting to try to make Mrs Harper's life more tolerable but first she must get her away from this nasty place.

Harry was standing just outside the doorway. He had a way of wiping all expression from his face when he wished and as she looked at him, her own filled with anticipation, she had not the slightest idea what he was thinking. She soon found out. He had been angry a moment ago but now he was inscrutable.

'Get on your mare and ride home, Lally,' he told her quietly. 'I will accompany Doctor Channing in his carriage and retrieve Piper. I will arrange for a decent woman to come in and look after Mrs Harper and the baby but—'

'I don't think so, Harry. I want Mrs Harper to come to *my* home where she will be cared for by my servants. This place is not fit for a dog let alone a woman who has just given birth and Sam needs a good feed by the look of him. I *will* ride back to the Priory but only to bring back the carriage and pick up Mrs Harper and her two sons. I have known you a long time, Harry, not well, perhaps, but I know you for an honourable man with integrity. You are a gentleman in the true sense of the word and though you are about to deny it you cannot. You hate to see people in pain and distress, which has been proved by your kindness and care for Mrs Harper and her son. Please return to your mill and let me deal with this. Let me do it, Harry. Let me do it with your blessing, for you must know me well enough by now to know that I will do it anyway. You have been a true friend to me and recently'—she glanced away with a bright flush to her cheek—'more than that in . . . in our marriage. You have saved me, which is not my only concern, but my children, from disgrace and though I deserve it Jamie and Alec do not, nor the . . . the child to come. I'm sorry . . .' as he turned away in what seemed to be distress. 'So let me help this woman and her children. We can give her and Sam work that is not beyond their strength.'

'Would you save the rest then?' he asked harshly.

'The rest?'

'All the other women and children who work in my mills?'

'If I could . . .'

'They would not thank you.'

'Probably not.' She sighed and turned away to

stare unseeingly across the cobbled lane and the dry-stone wall that edged it to the far, rolling wilds of the moorland. It was a pleasant day, the sky a streaky blue and shades of pale grey. The sun tried to shine, a ray of it catching a tiny group of buildings on the far side of the valley. A white farmhouse and, in the foreground, sheep grazing. An even smaller figure of a man crossed towards the flock and on the clear air a piercing whistle was carried towards them. A dog at his side began to chivvy the sheep towards a gate. Nearer to them was a patch of rough grass, taller than the rest and a sheep suddenly popped its head up and stared at them then disappeared again as though it were hiding from the dog.

Harry, as if he could stand no more and wished only to escape her, turned sharply away and began to walk towards the carriage. Doctor Channing emerged from the rotting doorway, wiping his hands on a bit of cloth which he then stuck in his bag. It was bloodstained and Lally knew that what she proposed to do was right. This man cared nothing for the rough working folk in this place, or indeed any place, and had it not been for Harry and his power he would not have deigned to come out to Susan Harper.

'I've stitched her up,' he said carelessly in Harry's general direction as though to say he had earned his fee but Harry stared away from him and from Lally towards the distant horizon.

'Thank you, Doctor,' Lally said to him. 'Is she all right to leave for half an hour or so? I must get—'

'Of course, Mrs Sinclair.' He smiled pompously. 'These women are up and out of childbed before the child is barely wiped round. She's probably—'

'Thank you, Doctor.' She interrupted his smugness quite rudely, making a mental note to look for a decent man to doctor to her own household's needs should it be necessary which, naturally, it would when her child was born. She watched him climb into his carriage, saying something to Harry and nodding courteously but Harry did not respond, then with a click of his tongue and a slap of the reins on the horse's rump they were off and bowling along the road, followed by a screaming group of half-naked children. The women in their doorways watched Lally as she turned towards the doorway of the woman they called a 'stuck-up cow' and went inside.

'I'm off home now, Mrs Harper.'

'Susan, please, Mrs Sinclair.' Mrs Harper, or Susan as she had asked to be called, had the baby at her small breast which, to Lally's inexperienced eye did not appear to have enough milk for even this little mite but the infant was sucking heartily while Sam sat and watched with great thankfulness.

'Us'll be all right now, thank you, Mrs Sinclair. Sam can get up ter't mill fer—'

'Oh, no, Susan. Sam will do no such thing. I shall go for the carriage and I shall take both you and Sam and the baby . . .'

'Jack.' Susan looked with great fondness at the infant.

'Pardon?'

'Ah'm to call 'im Jack after me 'usband.'

'Oh, of course. That is just right, but let us talk of your move to my home where—'

'Oh, no, Mrs Sinclair. This is our 'ome an' as

165

soon as ah've 'ad me a bit of a rest I'll tekk meself back ter work. Mr Sinclair's bin right good to us but ah can manage on me own now.'

Susan Harper, like her husband had been and the Yorkshire family from which she came, was fiercely independent and had it not been for the baby in her womb would not have accepted Harry Sinclair's help. But now she was delivered she would see to herself and her family. This lovely young woman who had appeared so magically to help her and Sam had been a blessing but Susan would strap her baby on her back, take young Sam's hand and within a day or two be back at her loom.

Lally, who argued with her for the best part of an hour, was forced to admit defeat for the time being but as she moved slowly out into the fitful sunshine she made up her mind that she would keep her eye on this little family and at the first sign of it faltering she would make it her business to make their lives better. After all, she had delivered young Jack!

CHAPTER TWELVE

Within weeks of their marriage Harry began the renovations to the Priory but though there was warmth, comfort, luxury even, apart from the new *bathroom* which was a miracle to the maidservants who had the task of cleaning it, somehow he managed not to change the nature of the beautiful old house. The original medieval great hall, stone-flagged, oak-ceilinged. The long gallery lined with an impressive array of Fraser ancestral portraits. An old wing with plasterwork and paintwork so obviously nearing the end of its life that it reminded Harry of the musky beauty of rose petals approaching decay. The carved oak staircase rising majestically from the hall, the dining room, the drawing room, all in sad need of repair and the ancient and dilapidated winter garden. All had a frail beauty, the baroque plaster moulding mellowed from the original white to delicate cream in places and all of which would need a master craftsman to put right. The chimneys which smoked would be cleaned and repaired and, in short, Harry Sinclair meant to make this his own magnificent establishment until he decided the time had come for him and his growing family to move on.

Even outside where Harry liked to stroll with an after-dinner cigar was scarcely touched; the wych-elms, the sycamores, the gnarled and knotted oaks from generations ago seemed to please the new tenant and he spent many hours with Barty and Froglet discussing their care. He inspected the stables and outbuildings, assessing what needed to be done to restore their crumbling walls and leaking roofs, the coach house which had the small gig for Lally's use and soon would have a new and splendid coach with its own coachman. There would be quarters above the stables and coach house for the outdoor servants and their families.

Inside the house the hall was furnished with deep and comfortable armchairs grouped round the enormous fireplace in which a great leaping fire was kept burning night and day and at one side of the hall a big refectory table of heavy oak was

167

installed on which estate maps were laid out along with newspapers and sporting magazines. The bedroom where he and Lally were to sleep, since he did not care to use the same bed she had once shared with Chris, was transformed into what looked like a bridal posy in peach silk and white lace with a dressing room knocked through to a somewhat more spartan bedroom where, should he be late back from a meeting or at the mill, Harry would spend the night. Their bedroom had an enormous bed, its curtains drawn up into a gleaming brass crown, the curtains at the windows of the finest, lightest silk, exquisitely draped and tied back with lace ribbon. There were crystal chandeliers with flickering candles in the main rooms downstairs, their floors covered in pale Chinese carpets in lovely shades of apple green and pink, their texture like velvet.

The winter garden was given over to Barty who could scarcely believe the amount of brass he was allowed to spend. It was completely stripped of its wilting plants and re-stocked with a huge pot containing bird-of-paradise flower, tubs of bleeding heart vine, orchid cactus in hanging baskets plus a vividly colourful display of trailing ivy in all shades of green and geraniums of every hue from the palest pink to a startling red with white mock orange blossom to set it all off. There were water hyacinth in a small pool and even cages in which singing birds poured out their hearts. There were crimson climbing hibiscus and perfumed jasmine, a wax plant with flowers that perfumed the night and passion flowers with edible fruit, and here and there a magnificent palm tree. The floor was re-tiled in terracotta and in the centre stood a round table covered with a green, floor-length cloth topped with a lace throw. Four wicker chairs heaped with cushions surrounded it and, usually drowsing in a companionable heap, Ally and Fred and the kitchen cat found they liked its warmth. Even in the winter when the sun was absent it was warm with some hidden heating system Harry had had installed.

Extra servants were employed, two gardeners named Wilf and Evan, a groom, Ben, come from Mill House to care for Harry's bay, Piper, Ebony, whom Chris had once ridden, Jeb, the moor pony, Blossom the cob who pulled the gig and the lawn mower, Lally's mare, Merry, and the two ponies Harry was to acquire for Jamie and Alec when they were old enough to ride. There were two more housemaids, one for the kitchen named Dulcie and another called Tansy who was to help Jenny and Clara as a parlour-maid. Biddy was in charge of the kitchen and housekeeping but Harry confided to Lally that he was seriously considering employing someone to do all the cooking, for Mrs Stevens, as he called her, had enough to do with the general supervising of the house. A steward was hired, a man by the name of Cameron with a broad Scots accent, stern and dour with a wife and three silent children and they were housed in what had once been a tumbledown cottage at the back of the stables, but with money spent on it was transformed into a cosy home for the five of them.

Lally often wondered what the Weavers of Foxwell Farm made of Cameron but as she grew bigger and more ponderous and it was realised that the new Mrs Sinclair was already pregnant with her third child, Mr Sinclair's child, it was no longer considered circumspect to move about the estate and the tenants scarcely saw her. She sauntered about the increasingly well-kept gardens, her two sons tumbling about her skirts for Alec, now over a year old, was already floundering perilously on sturdy legs, constantly and good-humouredly falling over and picking himself up. The two dogs raced about and knocked the boys' legs from under them and the garden was filled with laughter. Even the kitchen cat deigned to walk in a dignified manner at Lally's back! It was winter now, and cold, with Christmas come and gone, but she wrapped them up warmly in their brand-new outfits and to Dora's disapproval she took them out of the nursery and down the back stairs, out into the garden and across the meadow to the paddocks where Jamie as usual did his best to nip under the fence rails to get to the horses. There were six of them and Jamie wanted to ride them all!

She lived in a luxury she had never before known. Harry had given her carte blanche to spend whatever she wanted for the children and the rooms they occupied at the top of the house and with the help of a builder and a decorator provided by Harry, who seemed always able to call on men to do his bidding, she had walls knocked through so that there was a night nursery, a day nursery, a bedroom for Dora and a room planned for a schoolroom. It was all painted in a delicate cream with scores of highly coloured pictures in bright rows where small people could most easily see them. There were toys, for with money to spend without thought she bought her sons trains and boats and stuffed animals, books and games all piled on to white painted shelves and Dora again tutted disapprovingly because her charges were in distinct danger of being ruined!

When it was delivered she often took the gig over the moor—with Carly on the sturdy moor pony beside her since Harry would not hear of her going alone—to visit Susan Harper who, though she was glad to see her and thanked her politely for the huge basket of food she brought over, was not best pleased to be the recipient of charity. But Lally knew, being a sensible and responsible mother, that Susan was deeply glad of the extra food, since it kept her Sam healthy and made it possible for her to nurse Jack with a plentiful supply of milk and though the three of them set off each weekday to tramp to the mill, the exercise did them no harm. Her room was kept spotless and her fire was never allowed to go out for she could afford the extra coal. Susan knew, as did many of the nursing mothers who worked at High Clough Mill, that Mr Sinclair was a fair employer. He expected a decent day's work from them all, men, women and children, but he was resented in many parts of the woollen trade for what was considered his laxity with those who worked at his spinning machines and power looms. It was well known that women who were forced to take their newborn babies to work with them were allowed time to stop and feed them and it was a bloody wonder to them how he managed to make a profit with his soft ways. There was a sort of a crèche where a woman was kept to tend to these infants and a schoolroom where, for an hour a day, the older children were taught their lessons. Those who scorned him did not realise that Harry Sinclair,

171

instead of being 'soft' was in fact a shrewd businessman, for the women he employed were the most efficient in the industry. Susan Harper knew that, for wasn't she one of them? He had even sent across one of his men to put sturdy locks on her door in the tenement building where she and her children lived and though she was not on intimate terms with Mrs Sinclair she was deeply grateful for the better life her friendship—if she could call it that—with the maister's wife afforded her.

*   *   *

It was March when Roly Sinclair came home from his travels!

She was dressed in a warm and luxurious bottle-green cloak, its hood and hem edged with pale grey fur and on her hands she wore pale grey kid gloves. She was in the garden in deep conversation with Barty who, with no children or grandchildren of his own, and with the extra help had a bit of time to spare, asked her hesitantly whether she might fancy a tree house for the lads, as he called them. There was a grand old oak with branches that would lend themselves to such a thing, not far from the house and with a ladder, which he, of course, would build with the help of Froglet and the handyman. Master Jamie and Master Alec, when they were a bit older, would be made up with it, in his opinion. It would be safe and sturdy, he would see to that, and Lally was made to realise that he and Froglet, who hung about at his side, were quite excited at the idea. They kept their eyes averted from the burgeoning bulge of her pregnancy as Barty walked her down the grassy slope towards

172

the tree he had in mind, his arm at the ready should Mrs Sinclair need it in her cumbersome state. They were all surprised by the speed at which she and the new master had started a bairn and at the size of her already but they were simple folk and accepted her condition without question.

Not so Biddy! She had watched her mistress almost from the first days of her marriage, for the speed with which it had happened had startled her. Of course with Mr Sinclair about she and Miss Lally had not been as close as once they had been. She could no longer wander in and out of her little mistress's bedroom as she had been wont to do and when she did, after the master had left for the mill, Miss Lally was often still in bed. But one day, a few weeks after the wedding, she had taken up a pile of freshly laundered underwear and with barely a tap on the door had entered the bedroom to find Miss Lally about to shrug herself into her shift. For a moment the girl had stood with her arms above her head, the shift in her hands, and the swelling of her belly, the growing fullness of her breasts were fully revealed.

Biddy hissed unbelievingly then the clothing dropped from her suddenly nerveless hands.

'So that's why . . .' Her mouth dropped open and her face lost its colour and for a moment she thought she would faint and it was only the small distressed sound that came from the back of Lally's throat that kept her upright.

'Biddy . . . Biddy, please . . . What else could I do?' she pleaded, knowing that Biddy would understand exactly what she meant.

Biddy sank on to the unmade bed and Lally knelt at her feet, taking her hands in her own and

173

so they remained for several long moments until Biddy regained her senses.

'Whose?'

'Roly.'

'Does Mr Harry know?'

'Oh, yes. I told him and at once he offered—'

'Marriage.' The word was harsh but at the same time Biddy knew a vast relief, for who cared who the father was as long as her lamb was safe.

'Yes.'

All Biddy said was, 'Thank God,' and from that moment Biddy Stevens was Harry Sinclair's 'man' and would have died for him. She could not do enough for him, in an unobtrusive way, of course, and would have no word spoken against him. Not that any of the servants would do so and in every way she could, should anything have been whispered, she kept up the pretence that Miss Lally and her new husband had, perhaps, anticipated their wedding night and the servants, forgetting the way Mr Roly had haunted the place before the wedding, accepted it.

'Now tha' see't way them branches mekk a sorter platform, Miss Lally,' Barty was saying, pointing with his hoe into the crown of the oak while Froglet nodded his head enthusiastically. 'Well, that's steady as a rock up there an' when us've—'

He was interrupted by the sound of horse's hooves on the now smoothly raked gravel of the drive. The children and the dogs began a surge towards the horseman and the three adults, if you could call Froglet such, turned to look up the drive in the direction of the approaching animal and the man on his back.

It was Roly Sinclair!

She had often pondered on how it would be when they met again, the unthinkable moment when they would come face to face but now that it had actually arrived it was not at all as she had imagined it to be. How had she imagined it to be? He would know, naturally, that she had married his brother and that she was pregnant but he would not be aware that the child she carried was his. When the baby was born he might speculate, as many would on its early arrival, but she was a respectably married woman with a wealthy and influential husband and nothing could change that. But somehow the circumstances did not unduly worry her. She was heavy not only in her body but in the senses, her emotions lulled, half dormant, pulse beat and heartbeat sluggish, submerged in her role of breeding female, too placid and patient to arouse any kind of anxiety.

Nevertheless she turned away, ready to go as fast as she could towards the house and the safety of Biddy who was the only one who knew the truth. Biddy would see to him. Biddy would get rid of him. Biddy would explain that Mrs Sinclair was not up to visitors, but it was too late as Roly covered the last couple of yards to where they stood, skilfully avoiding the boisterous group of children and animals. He leaped gracefully from the saddle and handed the reins to the open-mouthed Froglet and took Lally's limp hand in his. His eyes swept the bulging line of her stomach as he bent to kiss her hand.

'Lally, my dear, how well you look. Positively thriving, I must say, and it all seems to have happened so quickly. I had no idea you and Harry

175

were . . . well, never mind, you are now my sister-in-law and I must say I couldn't be more pleased. I said so to Harry when I arrived this morning but he had something tricky on the loom and he was in a temper so I left him to ride over here to congratulate you.'

Without turning he indicated to Barty and Froglet that they were to leave and take his gelding with them, then, putting Lally's lifeless hand through his arm, he began to lead her towards the house. 'Come, are you not going to offer me a drink?'

'Of course,' she answered, falling automatically into the role of welcoming hostess which had been bred in her. They walked side by side up the slope, Lally still in the state of startled shock which the sight of him had produced. Suddenly realising she had, in her bewilderment, totally forgotten her children, she wrenched her hand from his arm and turned back but Barty and Froglet had them securely in hand, informing them sternly that if they did not do as they were told, which was follow their mam, Barty would not build them the promised tree house. They had been enjoying the freedom their mama allowed them, for everyone knew her to be an indulgent mother, away from the stricter rules of Dora, and they did not want to return to the nursery but they *did* want a tree house even if the baby Alec was not at all sure what it was.

It was the gentleman who persuaded them.

'Come along now,' ordered in a way they were both aware he meant. Not in five minutes or even five seconds but *now*. Recognising the voice of authority they plodded up the slope after their mama and the gentleman.

'It's as well you have married Harry,' Roly remarked pleasantly, taking Lally's arm again. 'They need a man behind them, I'm thinking, and Harry will stand no nonsense. Where is their nursemaid hiding, would you say? I do believe in children being restrained in the nursery, don't you?'

Again she pulled her arm away from his hand. 'No, I do not,' she snapped and perhaps for the first time she realised that of the two brothers she had married the right one. Harry was inclined to be sharp with the boys at times, but he did it in a way that let them know he meant what he said. At the same time he was always fair, and already her sons, though still so young, understood that he was a tolerant, kind-hearted man. She herself had come to recognise that kindness could easily be confused with weakness but this was not the case with Harry. He was a man of many layers, unpredictable, deep, keeping the private part of himself, which he allowed no one to see, well concealed, but as the weeks passed and she grew accustomed to his presence she had felt herself drawn to his masculine virility. He had at first taken her every night in their bed but as she grew bigger and more clumsy he had taken to sleeping in the bedroom on the far side of the dressing room and, strangely, she had missed him. She would forever be grateful to him for what he had done, for her, for Chris's boys, for Susan Harper even, and soon, for his brother's child who was doing a fandango in her belly at this very moment.

Biddy's face was a picture as Lally and Roly entered the hallway. She was directing Tansy, the

177

new housemaid, in mixing furniture polish, following a new recipe she had found in a magazine and was eager to try, which included linseed-oil, turpentine, vinegar and spirits of wine. She supposed Mr Sinclair's housekeeper must already have taught the girl the rudiments of being a parlour-maid but Biddy liked her own ways and was busy teaching the lass what they were.

'Shake the mixture well and rub it on with a clean piece of linen then polish with a dry duster. It will produce a lovely shine,' she was saying while Tansy watched somewhat mutinously, for hadn't she been housemaid at Mill House for years and knew all about cleaning. They both turned towards the door as their mistress and Mr Roly entered and for some reason unknown to Tansy, Mrs Stevens muttered something under her breath, something Tansy could not catch.

'Beg pardon?' she said, but Mrs Stevens, with a twitch of her head, indicated that Tansy should return to the kitchen. Mrs Stevens's face had lost all its colour and Tansy wondered why.

Lally knew, of course. She smiled or rather grimaced in what was meant to be a smile, turning brightly to Roly. 'Would you care for coffee, Roly?' she asked.

'That would be most welcome, Lally.' He nodded at the frozen figure of the housekeeper, probably wondering why the woman looked so strange but Lally distracted him as she removed her cloak and tossed it carelessly in Biddy's direction. If he was surprised, and he was, at the fullness of her figure, he did not show it, though it seemed to him, having been married for no more than five months, she was remarkably plump. Not

178

that he knew much about women who were pregnant since those of his own class kept to their homes during pregnancy and only took exercise in their closed carriages and even after giving birth remained secluded for at least six weeks.

He followed Lally into the drawing room. Everywhere was warm, even the huge stone-floored hall where a crackling log fire blazed. As he entered the drawing room he was quite amazed as his feet sank into the thick velvet of a carpet and his gaze encountered the comfort and luxury that had been added to the room which he remembered as rather threadbare and only warm about the fireplace and that only *luke*warm! It was filled with flowers, pictures hung on the freshly papered walls and ornaments of what he recognised as highly valuable porcelain stood on dainty-legged tables. He also recognised that his brother must have spent a great deal of money to transform this house, for he supposed the bedrooms had had the same treatment, into one in which he could live comfortably and entertain his business friends and acquaintances. He wondered if Lally was up to such a thing, for she and Chris had been careless as host and hostess to their many, equally careless, friends of whom he had been one. It had not mattered to them who had turned up, or when, and the glorious romps in which Lally had been included were not the sort of thing his rather staid brother would expect.

'And how long are you to be home this time, Roly?' Lally asked politely after he had seated her rather heavily on the sofa to the side of the roaring fire and had sat opposite her in the matching and extremely comfortable sofa on the other side of the

179

fireplace. She had pulled her . . . well, he could only call them *draperies* about her thickening figure, fine woollen garments, but full and ingeniously constructed to hide her belly, in a light rose, the colour flattering and he had to admit she looked very lovely. Her skin was flawless, her dark, curly hair tumbling about her head in a glossy cap. Her eyes were a clear blue-green and the lashes surrounding them seemed thicker and darker than he remembered. It was as though her pregnancy had enhanced the natural beauty that had been hers the last time they met.

'Well, as I have been away for eight months, travelling the length and breadth of America and then on to Russia and Europe I feel I might stay at home for a month or two. Harry has plans for an extension to High Clough and I believe I should be here when he starts. After all I am an equal partner in the business and he is inclined to go hell for leather at things without consulting me. I go away and when I come back he has altered something I'm not sure I agree with. He intends to turn the carding of the wool entirely over to West Heath which seems, on the face of it, to be a good idea but I would like the chance to consider it.' He smiled, as polite as Lally, brooding on why he was talking to her, to Lally, who was as fun-loving as himself, about business. Something in her demeanour was burrowing into his alert mind and though he could not have said what it was he felt himself wondering at his own sudden unease. Well, not exactly unease but a feeling that there was something in the air, in Lally herself, that disturbed him.

'What a shame you missed Christmas at home.'

180

He grinned impishly. 'Oh, I enjoyed Christmas in America so I did not exactly miss it. They are very hospitable, the Americans. I brought some presents back, Christmas presents and though it's now March I hope you will accept them. I have them here.'

He stood up and from his pocket produced a small, beautifully wrapped parcel. To her astonishment he handed it to her with a bow.

'Oh, Roly, really, you should not have . . .'

'Rubbish. I saw this and at once thought of you. It is nothing . . . well, I say it is nothing but the jeweller told me it once belonged to a European princess.' He stood over her, though at the same time he did his best to assume a casual air.

When she unwrapped the parcel she found it to contain an exquisitely hand-made box covered with fine tooled leather, slightly worn. She opened it slowly. The box was lined with silk and lying snugly on the silk was the most beautiful necklace and bracelet she had ever seen. It was a combination of pearls, gold and enamel set off by a dazzling selection of diamonds. It was made of multiple strands of small pearls, the focal point of the necklace the diamonds which were set like a heart hanging from the pearls. The bracelet which nestled at the centre of the box matched it in miniature.

'I thought it would match all the evening gowns I have seen you wear though I'm sure by now my brother has bought you many more. Or will when your confinement is over.'

She could not speak, since she knew as well as she knew that the sun rose in the east and set in the west that there was nothing more certain than

181

that Harry Sinclair would not allow her to wear this beautiful jewellery bought for her by the father of her child!

CHAPTER THIRTEEN

Caterina Sinclair, to be called Cat to the end of her days, was born on a gentle April day, a soft day filled with bright sunshine and nodding daffodils, those that Barty had planted at back end, adding to those that had already pushed through the earth and the grass about the house for the past century and which made a magical golden carpet as far as the eye could see. There were golden catkins on the graceful weeping willows hanging over the lake and in their shade the ducks glided and dived for something tasty to eat. Marsh marigolds were in bloom mixing with primroses and wood anemones, clustered by the lake and under the great trees which had stood there when the monks had worked and prayed beneath them in the time of Henry V. The sky was a cloudless blue and the first swallow was spotted by Barty as he and Froglet hung about in the stable yard, since it had been reported that the mistress had started in labour and they were eager to hear how she did, for they were fond of her. A bit early, they whispered to one another, the servants, who had been taken by surprise since the child had not been due for several more weeks but still it was a lovely, healthy little girl, Dulcie reported to them importantly just as though she had been present at her mistress's bedside during the infant's birth, helping out Miss

Lally's new doctor. Doctor Burton was a young, recently qualified medical man direct from London and the great teaching hospital of St Thomas's, very up to date in his method of delivering babies and not at all like the old-fashioned Doctor Channing who had ministered to the Fraser family for many years. Brought from High Clough at Miss Lally's first pang, Mr Sinclair had moved restlessly about the house and even into the garden, smoking cigars one after the other, but could you blame him for worrying since it was his first. Pity it wasn't a lad though since the maister had a splendid business to hand on but, still, Miss Lally was young and there was plenty of time for many more.

Lally lay in her nest of pillows, washed and changed into her clean nightdress, her hair brushed and a bright blue ribbon tied in her curls. The birth, her third, had been relatively easy and Doctor Burton was pleased with her and the child. He was obsessed with cleanliness, hygiene, he called it, finding favour with Biddy who had helped him at the last, offending the nurse who had been employed by Mr Sinclair to look after his wife. Not that, in Biddy's opinion, she had been needed at all, for wasn't Biddy there to see to Miss Lally, before and after the birth and was the one who put the baby, even before she was properly cleaned up, into Lally's arms. The doctor was engrossed in sterilising his instruments because after he had made a small cut to ease the passage of the child a stitch or two had been needed. Better a clean cut than a tear, he had told her, and Mrs Sinclair would heal more easily; and if the father would like to come in and see his child, and his wife, of

183

course, he had no objection.

Harry had done no more than eye the child politely, seeming to recoil from the lustily bawling red-faced kicking scrap who gave the impression she would like to box his ears!

'The doctor tells me you have done well, Lally, and that the . . . the infant is healthy.' He smiled or at least showed his teeth for the benefit of the nurse and the doctor. The doctor knew quite well that this was a full-term child, as did the nurse, both assuming that Mr and Mrs Sinclair had anticipated their wedding night, for it was known in the district they had been married in October of the previous year.

'A fine child, and what are you to call her?' Mr Sinclair asked politely, surprising the doctor who was wrapping his instruments carefully away in a spotless piece of linen, placing them in his leather bag and making ready to avail himself of the steaming hot water brought up by the maidservant. Surely a man and his wife would discuss the naming of their first child—together—before the child's birth but from Mr Sinclair's manner one would think it was really nothing to do with him.

'I don't know, Harry,' Mrs Sinclair answered just as politely. 'Have you any preference?'

'No, not really. Perhaps a family name?'

'Your mother . . . ?'

'She was called Agnes.'

'Well, no, I think not but there is plenty of time.'

'Of course, well, I will let you rest.' Harry turned to the doctor who, being young and rather pleased with himself, was waiting for a word of approval but none came. The new father merely nodded and walked stiffly from the room and there was none to

184

see or hear him as, in the privacy of his own spartan bedroom he sat down abruptly on his bed, his face in his hands and groaned aloud.

Oh, dear God, how am I to bear this? he agonised silently. I took it on willingly. I knew it was coming, but she looked so beautiful, like a Madonna with her baby in her arms and the child . . . the child is . . . is *his*. I am to pretend a joy which is a bitter thing to me but I must . . . it's hard just now, for it is new to me but I cannot let them see . . . it was a shock, my brother's child at her breast . . . Dear sweet Jesus, give me the bloody strength . . . they must not know, any of them. The child must be kept to the nursery so that I can avoid . . . I must get out, go to the mill. Jesus, if I did not love her as I do I might be able to manage it. If I could view her dispassionately as a woman who will be useful to me—entertaining, a hostess for my table, a woman in my bed to serve my needs. What will she be like when Roly comes home? Please God he does not recognise . . . it is supposed to be a premature child but even I, who know nothing of such things, can see it is not.

Savagely he stood up and strode about the room, twitching back the curtains to look out on the daffodil-carpeted slope, watching the nursemaid Dora following Jamie and Alec and the two boisterous dogs as they made unerringly for the lake which, as children will, they would do their utmost to fall into. Why did water fascinate them, he mused, taken out of himself for a moment as he watched them tumble down the slope, the dogs leaping round them, doing their best to elude the harassed nursemaid. His thoughts jumped from one thing to another, unable to land firmly on any

185

particular one. Thank God it was a girl, a girl who could be fitted into the household without too much trouble. A girl who would have no claim on the Sinclair inheritance, a girl who he would not be expected to notice since it was well known that a gentleman only valued and was interested in a son to inherit and continue the family name.

He reached for his jacket and made for the back stairs, since he had no desire to run into the doctor whose small gig was still standing at the front door, fetching up in the kitchen. It was a big room with a massive table in its centre which had stood up to years of pounding, chopping and scrubbing and from its ceiling, thanks to the expertise of Biddy Stevens, hams were suspended. The walls were whitewashed and beside the pots and pans standing in neat rows on the well-scrubbed shelves, was a vast array of highly polished copper utensils hanging on the walls. A leg of pork was being spit-roasted over the open fire and set in the wall was a huge enclosed range, blackleaded, glowing and dark, and cleaned every morning by Dulcie. Everywhere they could be handy were all the implements of a good kitchen, trivets and skillets, toasters and grills, and on the enormous dresser jelly moulds of copper and earthenware jostled with a tea set and dinner service in a delicate blue willow pattern from which the servants ate and drank. Everything was spotless, for Mrs Stevens was a devil for tidiness and cleanliness and was behind them all the livelong day. There were several beautifully carved and well-proportioned Windsor chairs, old and well cared for and at the end of the day, when everything was to Mrs Steven's satisfaction, the maids were allowed to

186

rest in them and drink the cocoa that set them up for bed. Not that they needed a sedative of any kind, for they worked hard and slept the sleep of the just!

To the astonishment of the servants who were clustered in the kitchen 'wetting' the baby's head, the master strode through them without a word and out into the yard, shouting for one of the grooms to fetch his horse and be quick about it. Ben, who had been celebrating the birth of the master's first child with the rest of them, ran after him, slapping his glass of ale on to the kitchen table.

'Well, wouldn't yer think 'e'd be up there wi' Miss Lally? 'Is first bairn, an' all,' Tansy said, quite astounded as they all were. With Mrs Stevens still up with Miss Lally they felt free to express their amazement.

'Aye, now if it 'ad bin a lad,' Dulcie offered knowingly, smacking her lips over the small glass of port Mrs Stevens had allowed the maids. The men were drinking ale and all of them agreed that if it had been a lad they would have been tipping back a glass of champagne. Mr Chris, God bless him, had pressed them to champagne on the birth of both his sons but then Mr Chris had been free-handed. Not that Mr Sinclair was a bad employer. He wasn't, for weren't they all well fed and housed, fairly treated and counted themselves lucky to be in such a household.

'Still, yer'd think 'e'd be up there wi't missis, wouldn't yer?' Clara added, wide-eyed and slack-jawed. For a moment they were all silent as they considered this last remark then the door to the front of the house opened and Mrs Stevens

187

entered. At once, even though they had been given permission to do what they were doing, they all scattered, Barty and Froglet and the outside men darting to the back door, with Carly elbowing them to be the first through it. Mrs Stevens could be a bugger at times. She was in charge of them—well, not Ben, Alfie, Clancy and Seth who were really Mr Sinclair's men, having come with him from Mill House, but all the women servants. Ben had run out to saddle Piper who he had just unsaddled and given a rub down, not expecting the master to return to the mill this day, the day his first child was born but Mr Sinclair could be seen racing off down the lane leading to the moorland track that led to High Clough just as though the devil were after him.

*　　　*　　　*

Lally was alone with her child. The nurse had gone off to the nursery to make suitable arrangements for the baby, telling Lally she would be back soon, for the baby must be bathed and the wet nurse, the one thought appropriate by all ladies in society, got ready. The baby would need to be fed and if Mrs Sinclair would hand her over Nurse would take her . . .

'No, Nurse will not,' Mrs Sinclair told her imperiously. 'Go and do what you have to do and then come back for her. I wish to be alone with my daughter.'

'But, Mrs Sinclair, she still has birth blood on her . . .' The nurse was appalled.

'I don't care and therefore neither should you. Leave her with me, if you please.' Lally looked

188

down into the face that rested against her breast, searching for signs of Roly Sinclair but she could see none. The Sinclair brothers were alike in their colouring apart from their eyes, Roly's being a cat-like grey and Harry's a deep brown and the screwed-up eyes of the infant did not reveal their colour. They were both dark with smooth amber skins, tall, lean, wiry, only their nature being vastly different. Roly was good-natured, light-hearted, with a firm belief in his own ability to get what he wanted from any woman, or man for that matter who crossed his path, which was why he was such a good salesman. Harry was the steady one, firm, fair, shrewd, and with no inclination towards the charming ways of his brother. But he was also kind, reliable, so why was she staring into this child's face looking for something that, even if it was to come, would scarcely show itself on the day of her birth. The baby was yawning now, having worn herself out with her own birth and the hullabaloo she had set up in the minutes after it. She rested her tiny, starfish hand against Lally's breast and Lally waited for that glow of maternal pride, that bond she had formed with her sons in their first meeting. For that soft wonder and the awed need to touch her child's cheek, to put a finger in the curled shell of the child's hand but none came. The baby might have been another woman's and she wished that the nurse would hurry up and come back. She had needed this moment to contemplate the child, Roly's child, to be alone with her, waiting for that precious moment in a mother's life, but it had not come and when the nurse returned she handed her the baby without protest.

'I'd like a bath, please, Nurse. Will you ask

189

Mrs Stevens to come to me and tell the maids to bring the tub in here. A further clean nightdress and the bed changed then I'll have some of her broth. I feel remarkably hungry. Oh, and tell my husband to come in, would you, after I have had my bath and—'

'I'm afraid he's not here, madam,' Nurse said with what seemed to be relish in her voice. She was not used to being ordered about like a parlour-maid, nor to have her orders defied by 'mother'.

'Not here?'

'I believe he has gone to his mill, the housemaid told me. Shall I ask one of the men to fetch him, madam?'

Lally, for some reason she couldn't fathom, felt totally let down. Gone to the mill! The child no more than an hour old and already he had left the house. Dear God . . . but then, this was not his child, her rational mind reminded her. He had done what all fathers are supposed to do and that was to be there at the child's birth and should this one have been a boy, to lead the wild celebrations that would follow. Not only was the child in her arms *not* a boy but it was not even *his* child so what else could she expect of him?

Biddy bustled in to the room, summoned by the nurse and by her own need to see how her lamb fared. She of them all knew exactly what was in the master's mind and could you blame him, poor chap. He had protected Miss Lally against what would have been her fate as an unmarried mother and probably thought that was enough for any man. Was he expected to stay and gloat over the child got on his wife by his own brother? Hardly, but she could and so, presumably, would Miss

190

Lally, but it seemed the baby was already in the nursery, being bathed and fed by the woman brought in to see to her needs. The boys were still gallivanting about the garden with Dora who had been told to keep them out for as long as possible so that their sister, *half*-sister, could be dealt with before they were introduced to her.

But she had not expected Miss Lally to part with her new daughter so abruptly!

'Where is she?' she demanded to know, longing to get her hands on the girl child just born. 'You've never let that woman take her already. I thought you'd have been having a hold and I've come up for my turn. A little girl and right bonny.' She stopped speaking abruptly. 'What's up?' she asked, moving towards the bed, her eyes suspicious.

Lally shrugged disconsolately. 'I don't know. I can't . . .' Her voice trailed away.

'You can't what and be quick and tell me because the bath and the hot water are on the way up though why you can't use that lovely bathroom Mr Harry put in, I don't know.'

If Lally noticed that Biddy was now calling Mr Sinclair, *Mr Harry*, she did not remark on it. She felt edgy, unsettled, not at all in the contented frame of mind she had known when Jamie and Alec were born. Perhaps it was because she didn't love Harry and he had only married her to save her reputation, *and his brother's, she supposed*, since she might have named him as the father of her illegitimate child.

'Come on, lass, out with it. What's up? There's only you and me know . . . know the truth and it's safe with me.'

Lally sighed, because really she didn't know

191

what was the matter with her except the uneasy fact that she did not quite love her new daughter. Perhaps in a day or two, when the child had become . . . *part* of the family. If Dora and the wet nurse were to bring her in here with her brothers . . . Dear God! Her brothers!

'Anyroad,' Biddy said cheerfully, seeing that what Miss Lally needed was taking out of herself. 'What are you to call her?'

'I don't know, Biddy. I can't seem to . . .' She had been about to say 'become interested' but she hastily changed it to 'think straight about it'.

'My mam had a pretty name. At least I thought so,' Biddy said almost shyly.

'What was it?' she asked, without much interest.

'Caterina. *Her* mam was a bit fanciful, they say. My great-granddad, her pa, came from Italy, don't ask me why since it's a long time ago but it was said Caterina was Italian for Katherine. He was a sailor, so it was told to me.'

'Caterina.' For some reason the name pleased her and she realised that it would save her the trouble of talking it over with Harry if the name was already decided upon. Besides, would he care? 'Caterina, that's nice. Caterina Sinclair.' She twisted in the bed and stretched out to grasp Biddy's hand. 'Oh God, Biddy, what if she looks like him?'

'Does it matter, lamb? They are blood, after all, and there's bound to be a family likeness.'

'But their eyes . . . Roly and Harry . . .'

Biddy knew just what she meant but was not to be discomposed. 'And there's always you, lass. Your colouring. Anyroad, let's wait and see when she opens her eyes, bless her. Now, here's your bath . . .' as someone tapped on the door and in a flurry of hot water and clean towels, fragrant-smelling soap, even her hair washed and fluffed about her head by Biddy, Caterina Sinclair was temporarily forgotten. She was herself being bathed and fed by the competent woman who, having lost her own baby at birth several days ago, was glad to be rid of the unending flow of milk that filled her painful breasts. Kitty Morgan had been distraught when Doctor Burton tended her, sent by Mr Sinclair in whose loom gate she worked and had at first refused, but the money could not be ignored and from the first moment Cat Sinclair was put in her arms she had filled the yawning gap left by the death of her own little lad. After all, her young husband said, they could have another and Mr Sinclair would be eternally grateful, wouldn't he. He did not use such words for he was an illiterate weaver in Mr Sinclair's weaving shed but both knew it might put them on the road to something that might not otherwise come their way.

And Biddy's prediction proved correct, for when Cat Sinclair, fed, peaceful, washed and dressed in one of the little lawn nightgowns Biddy had made, was put once more in Lally's arms and opened her eyes and looked up with what seemed like keen interest into her mother's eyes they were the exact shade of her own. Her hair was dark in soft flat curls about her skull, the top of which pulsed, and her skin was like buttermilk, not white nor even cream, and at her rounded cheeks was a flush of good health. Her eyes were a pale blue with a shade of green in them, unfocused yet and almost milky, surrounded by lashes so thick and long it looked as though some finger had smudged coal dust about them. She was a replica of her mother and as Harry Sinclair bent over her dutifully he felt a great thankfulness enter his sorely tried heart. A thankfulness directed at God, or nature, or whatever it was that made up the construction of the human form and had produced this tiny scrap in the exact likeness of the beloved woman who held her. He felt something move inside his chest, his heart, he supposed, a place where he kept his secret hidden and which no one knew about and the twinge of interest that the baby's face awoke in him startled him.

'What d'you think, Harry?' Lally managed to say, for she had sensed something in him and, strangely, in herself. The tiny hand that rested companionably on her breast twitched, as it seemed the baby dreamed, though what of Lally could not guess. She had only had a few hours on this earth so what could she possibly know to dream about? She smiled and put her finger inside the tiny fist and though she slept the child immediately gripped it and then it happened. A great wave of loving tenderness, a great drowning in which she and the child were swept along together, deeply floating in perfect harmony until they reached the surface. Harry was kneeling now at her bedside and Biddy silently slipped away from her corner of the room, leaving the parents with their new child, for that was how she felt it to be. It was all right. What had not happened—to either of them—at once, had happened now. 'Caterina,' Lally murmured, looking up to smile into Harry's face. The look on it startled her for it was soft with some emotion she could not decipher.

'What?'

'How do you like Caterina?'

'Caterina.' He frowned, then the frown became a smile. He looked from the child to her. 'Where did that come from? It sounds a bit foreign.'

'Italian, so Biddy says.'

'I might have known that woman would have something to do with it,' but it was said with good humour. 'Where did she acquire the knowledge of Italian names, for God's sake?' his eyes still on the baby's sleeping face.

'Her grandmother, apparently. Her great-grandfather was Italian. In English it would be Katherine.'

She was watching him closely, for she was amazed at his sudden interest in his brother's child but like him she sensed it was something to do with the baby's likeness to herself. Thank the good Lord, for she believed if there had been even the slightest resemblance to Roly, or even himself as the child's uncle, he would have dismissed her from his life and their own would not go forward as she hoped. She *liked* Harry. He did not stir her in their bed which they had shared when they were first married, probably because she had believed he was making love to her not because he wanted to but for the sake of appearances. She did not love him. She did not love Roly. Sweet and loving in her heart remained the memory of her young husband where he would always be but she believed, given a fair chance, she and Harry might have a contented future together. Her sons were fast getting out of hand with only herself and Dora to discipline them and a stern, masculine hand

195

would do them good. This lovely little girl in her arms might bring him, Harry, some female influence that would warm his heart and if the shadow of Roly could be dispersed perhaps they would have a chance. She would give him children of his own, sons, perhaps another girl to make their family, *his* family complete. She would be forever thankful to him for what he had done for her and her sons. He had given her a second chance, not just of respectability for her children, which now included Caterina Sinclair, but for her to mature and develop a life that would please them both.

She put her hand on his and he looked at it in bewilderment. 'I think it might be time for you to hold . . .'—dare she say 'your daughter'?—'the baby. Would you like—' But at that moment a great hammering at the door caused him to jump to his feet as though he believed whoever knocked might think him a bit soft in the head but when Biddy burst in he could see that there was something badly wrong.

'Sir . . . oh, sir . . . please . . .'

'What the hell is it?' He sounded annoyed, which he was, for he had found he had begun to enjoy the intimacy he, his wife and the baby shared but Biddy crossed the room in two strides and took hold of his arm.

'An accident at mill, Mr Harry. A lad, the chap said. In a right state he was an' he said you was ter come at once . . . please . . .'

It was six o'clock and the day shift would nearly be over which was why Harry had come home to check, not on the child but his wife who was beloved by him, but within two minutes of his

196

leaving her Lally heard his horse's hooves rattle on the gravel as he put him to the gallop in the direction of his mill.

CHAPTER FOURTEEN

The coming of steam power, which in the woollen trade had brought prosperity to the mill-owners and poverty to the small independent hand weavers, also brought the factory system to the West Riding of Yorkshire and to the textile towns of Halifax, Leeds and Huddersfield among others. The spinning mule, as it was called, produced a thread firm enough for weaving, the loose slivers of wool being drawn out and twisted. The cotton industry gave the lead in the introduction of steam power but the woollen trade soon followed and the lethal machines had been installed at High Clough where the owners, Harry Sinclair and his younger brother Roly, were at the forefront of their trade. They aimed at the fine worsted ladies' dress trade. As times grew harder on the land thousands poured into the textile towns in search of employment from their urban living. Long hours, anything up to thirteen a day, even for young children, was quite normal as was the custom of beating children to keep them awake at their jobs which was as 'pieceners', fastening broken threads, and 'scavengers', clearing away the waste, the oil, the fluff that gathered under the flying machinery. These children, some of them brought from London workhouses and supposedly 'apprenticed' to factory owners, were treated as virtual slaves by the unscrupulous.

Easing the workforce into the new work ethos was a management responsibility which some took seriously, among them the Sinclair brothers' grandfather. Attendance at the mills in the early days was very irregular. Men still felt they could take time off work to do the autumn harvest, or on the first day of the working week, called by them, 'St Mondays'! Wakes Week also brought the usual toll of absenteeism and truancy. Consequently factory owners came to insist on a strict factory discipline, often introducing fines for being late, for drunkenness, talking and sleeping on the job. A man, woman or child needed to be absolutely alert when working the mule, or, in the case of children, *under* it.

The small boy understood this. He was barefoot, dressed in a shabby but neatly darned shirt and drawers. He was on all fours, keeping his head well down to avoid the moving carriage of the mule. His hair was a bright ginger, curly and coated with a sort of dust, as was the rest of him. He was pushing a great bundle of woollen waste and oily dust under and between the rows of machinery. Finding the bundle too awkward to push he crept behind it and put his childish strength to dragging the filthy mass, moving backwards towards the corner where he shoved and heaved the pile on to a heap already begun. On his hands and knees he retraced his movements back to the further end of the row of clacking, whirring, lethally moving machinery, the flying shafts and straps of the spinning mule, nimbly avoiding the carriage as it glided on its wheeled tracks towards the women in charge of each machine and the threads above his head as he

198

prepared to sweep another pile of waste towards the one that he and other scavengers had deposited at the further end of the room.

Someone shouted and thinking he heard his name he stopped his sweeping and lifted a bright face to the woman at whose feet he knelt. He smiled at her as she glanced down at him and she smiled back, the carriage still resting against the roller beam.

'What did tha' say?' he shouted to her, for the din was ear-splitting and before she could tell him that it was not she who had spoken the carriage began its inevitable journey back towards her. For a moment she panicked, because she could see the boy's head was higher than it should be and knew what was about to happen if he did not watch out. She stepped back, her hands held up beseechingly as though to warn him but it was too late. The carriage continued towards her and the boys' head with a horrible crunch was caught between the roller beam and the carriage as the latter was putting up. His small skull, so fragile in a child, was smashed into an obscene shape, elongating somehow and his bright little face, still smiling, was forced into a grimace of death. The woman, though well used to accidents in the thirty years she had worked in a woollen mill, particularly in the early days, began to scream as the carriage, carrying the child's blood and some matter hard to describe, returned to the roller beam, leaving the crumpled body in the mess he had been about to clear up.

The long room was filled in every conceivable space with humming machinery and despite the time of the year it was hot and humid. The women

199

at the mules were drenched in sweat and all along every row children crept on all fours from one machine to another but as the screams of the woman rang out their shrill voices were stilled though the machinery which cared nought for death and disaster rolled inexorably on.

'Dear Christ . . . dear Christ . . .' one woman whose own children worked in Mr Sinclair's mill kept saying over and over again and the spinner beneath whose mule lay the body of Susan Harper's son stood as if paralysed though it had not been her fault. It was no one's fault really, for Mr Sinclair was a good man to work for and did his utmost to prevent accidents. The child had just been distracted for that fraction of a second and had paid the horrifying price. Mr Sinclair would be devastated. He was good to all his hands but especially to the women who had young children to see to and had been one of the first to open a school for an hour a day for the younger children and made arrangements for the care of infants while their mothers worked in their gates.

Susan Harper, who had heard the screams, had run like a chased hare to where she knew her Sam was working. She had cried out like a wounded animal when she saw him, a sound that had the women weeping in sympathy, then a wordless moan of pain escaped from between her lips, on and on and on. She was on the filthy floor, her son's misshapen head in her lap, his blood on her apron, her face like granite as she cradled him to her when Harry Sinclair ran panting between the silent looms and the equally silent workforce. His own face was as though it had been cut from marble and when he knelt beside her he reared

200

back, for she hissed at him like a snake as he did his best to take the boy gently from her.

'Leave 'im . . . 'e's mine . . .'

'Susan, let me help you. Come, you can't stay here. Give me the boy.'

' 'Is name's Sam . . .'

'Yes, I know. Let me have Sam and you and I will . . . See . . .' He turned distractedly to the nearest woman under whose machine the boy had been injured. 'Send a man for the doctor. Doctor Burton. Run, woman, run, for God's sake . . .' though Harry knew it would be useless. If he could get his hands on the lad he might be able to determine if he had a pulse, or a heartbeat but Susan held him to her in a grip of iron.

Though it was but half an hour since the word had come of the accident at the mill, the name of the one who had suffered it was whispered at the back door of the Priory and within thirty seconds of that the news had reached Lally.

Tansy, who had been about to take up a pot of hot chocolate to her new young mistress, listened avidly to the garbled tale until Mrs Stevens sent her on her way.

'It's nothing to do with you, Tansy Beesley. Take up the mistress's chocolate before it gets cold.'

But with the vicarious pleasure some take in being the imparter of bad news Tansy poured the whole story into Mrs Sinclair's ear.

'Who was it, Tansy?' Lally asked anxiously, taking the tall cup of chocolate from the maid's hand.

'A lad by't name o' Sam is all ah know, ma'am,' Tansy said importantly, trying to look sad but as she didn't know the boy it was a bit tricky. Well!

201

she was to say later, tearfully, to Dulcie, how was she to know the mistress knew him? You could have knocked her down with a feather when the new mother leaped—yes, she leaped, there was no other word for it—from her bed, chucking the chocolate all over her lovely carpet and she knew who would have to clean that up, didn't she? She demanded that Tansy help her into her outdoor clothes.

'Eeh, no, ma'am,' Tansy gasped. 'Wi't bairn not yet a day old tha's confined ter tha' bed an' maister'd be—'

'If you won't help me, Tansy, then I shall have to manage on my own,' the mistress said, her pale face, which had drained of all colour when Tansy had told her the name of the boy, turned a bright pink as the blood ran under her fine skin.

'Eeh, ma'am, ah'll fetch Mrs Stevens.'

'You'll do no such thing, Tansy. Now, look in that wardrobe and bring me a gown . . . no, no, any will do and . . . and some drawers and a towel to pad . . . well, you will know what I mean . . .' though Tansy hadn't the faintest idea, never having had a child, until she saw Mrs Sinclair stuff the towel between her legs! 'My warm fur cape and a pair of boots then run down and tell Carly to bring the carriage to the side door and if you so much as breathe a word to Mrs Stevens or that damn nurse I swear I'll fire you. Go by the back stairs and out of the side door.'

'Eeh, ma'am . . .' Tansy began to cry, for it was all too much for her who was only a housemaid. Mrs Stevens would kill her!

*   *   *

Harry had Susan, her son still in her arms, in his office when Lally, helped by the appalled Carly, almost crawled up the stairs that led to it. Carly was ready to carry her, for surely she should not be out of her bed yet or if she was, since she was known to be a wilful young woman, should still be confined to her bedroom. She had walked steadily enough from the side door but had allowed him to help her into her carriage. He had done his best, since they had known one another ever since she had come as Mr Chris's bride, to argue with her, telling her he would gallop to the mill to find out what he could about the little lad but she would have none of it.

'Do as I ask you, Carly. I don't know why such a fuss is made just because a woman has given birth to a child. In the fields of India I believe the women give birth and a few minutes later are picking tea or whatever it is that grows—'

'Wi' respect, Miss Lally, this ain't India an' Mr Sinclair'll—'

'Mr Sinclair is my business, Carly, and I will deal with him. Now, are you to drive me to the mill or must I take the reins myself?' Which was sheer bravado since she could only stand with great difficulty, let alone drive a carriage. The pad between her legs was chafing her where Doctor Burton had sewn her up and blood was seeping out of her but as long as she could sit, in the carriage and back again, with Susan beside her, she would manage.

Doctor Burton was there, doing his best to get Susan to relinquish her pitiful burden, but she merely sat, her gaze focused on her dead son's

203

face, saying nothing. One hand was tenderly brushing back his ginger curls which were stained with blood and though she spoke no words the sound of her agony rustled through the office.

Lally managed to walk quite steadily across the deep pile carpet of Harry's office. Doctor Burton turned an appalled face towards her, springing to his feet, his hands outstretched to her, but she took no notice of his cries of admonishment, sinking to her knees before the ravaged figure of Susan Harper and the child she cradled to her. Sam seemed to be no more than a baby, his thin little body, undernourished and overworked as it was, making him appear a lot younger than his ten years. Harry, speechless for the moment at the sight of his wife, reared back in his chair which he had drawn up to the one in which Susan huddled. He had been struggling with the problem of what he was to do with her, with her baby which lay on a couple of cushions beside her, and with her dead son who must be got ready for the undertaker and the sight of his wife who had given birth only hours ago rendered him not only speechless, but senseless.

'Lally . . .'

'Mrs Sinclair,' both men croaked but Lally ignored them. She put gentle hands on Susan's arm, stroking it, then took Sam's lifeless hand which dangled down over his mother's arm, holding it with one of hers. She said nothing then leaned forward and in a lovely gesture kissed Sam's cheek, his misshapen cheek, and her hand went to the bit of bright hair that rested on his mother's breast.

'You shall come with me, Susan, you and Sam

and Jack. I have a room where you can be with them, with Sam and your baby. I will help you to . . . do what is necessary and you will have peace and quiet, privacy to be with your children. My carriage is waiting. Come with me, darling. I will take care of you until you are . . . more yourself. You must not be alone in this. You will *not* be alone in this. We will help each other in any way that is needed. My husband will help you. Come, dearest, stand up. Will you let Mr Sinclair or Doctor Burton carry your . . . carry Sam? No . . . then of course, you will take him to the carriage and hold him for as long as you want to. There is a clean bed for him and a cradle for Jack . . .'

Susan stood up and the rigid expression on her face relaxed a little and Harry felt the wonder of his love for Lally expand and creep more incredibly into his heart. Incredibly because he had believed that he could not love her more than he did. She had drawn this grieving woman into her own heart, taken from her the formidable decision on what she was to do, at least for the next few days. They could hardly have sent her and her sons, one dead and one very visibly and loudly alive, to that hovel in which she lived and what was she to live on while she recovered from this hellish blow? Lally had risen from her childbed and come to rescue her. She looked pale, her pallor worsening with every moment but she was strong, courageous for this suffering woman whom she hardly knew.

Susan allowed them to lead her to the carriage. Harry carried the baby who was beginning to bellow even louder his displeasure at missing a feed, Lally with her arm about his mother, herself looking as though she might fall at any minute, with the good doctor nearly carrying them both. Carly, thinking the same, hovered at her side, his arms ready to catch either or both women.

The lights of the Priory were gleaming in every window as though to light a group of weary travellers who might have lost their way and at the door Biddy waited with a trio of maidservants at her back, for by this time she had been told by the almost hysterical Tansy what had happened in her mistress's bedroom. She had landed the girl such a clout poor Tansy sported a black eye the next day but Biddy, knowing her young mistress as she did, was quite prepared for what happened. What else would Lally Sinclair do but bring the poor woman back here, but it must be admitted they had not bargained for the sight of the dead boy in her arms. The three maids, Dulcie, Jenny and Clara, had tears rolling down their cheeks though they knew better than to cry openly before Mrs Stevens.

'Room's ready, Miss Lally,' she said steadily. 'I've put the bath in there and . . . now Jenny will get you back to bed.'

'I'll see to Susan first, Biddy, but I'd be glad of your help.'

'I really think you should go back to bed, Mrs Sinclair,' Doctor Burton was saying, doing his best to separate Lally from Susan but Lally's arm was still gently holding Susan as she led her up the stairs. Biddy, like a shepherd directing his flock, arms spread wide as though to encompass them all, followed on Lally's heels, determined at the first possible moment to get Susan Harper and her two sons into the comfortable bedroom that had been prepared for her.

'Dulcie, take the baby from the master, if you please, and put him in the nursery where—'

'*No! No!*' shrieked Susan. 'Babby comes wi' me . . .' and Tansy began to cry in earnest.

'Stop that, lass, and help Mrs Sinclair to—'

'Leave us alone, Biddy. I will get Susan—'

'Mrs Sinclair, you must get to your bed. I do not wish to alarm you but I really must insist.' The doctor might have addressed his worry to the banister rail for all the notice Mrs Sinclair took of him.

'Lally, listen to what Doctor Burton is saying.' Harry was beside himself and the maids fell back, for it seemed as though he might lift Mrs Sinclair by force and take her to her bedroom where warmth, comfort and rest, which is what she needed, were waiting for her. Fancy going out to help this ordinary working woman, a spinner in her own husband's mill, only hours after giving birth and it was becoming very evident that the mistress was at the end of her strength. Suddenly her knees buckled and with a soft sigh she swayed against the very woman she was determined to help. Susan Harper, just as though she were abruptly aware of what was happening, looked down on the young woman who was sprawled by her side on the staircase.

'Mrs Sinclair . . .' Her voice was low but it was evident that she was in her right mind. 'Lass, tha' mun get ter tha' bed. These . . . folk'—looking around her at the maidservants—'' ll get me ter me room.' She waited expectantly and at once Biddy, with a great sigh of relief, directed Dulcie, who still clasped the screaming baby, to show Susan to the room which, like Miss Lally's, was warm, comfortable and quiet and where she could be peaceful with her children. She could nurse her bairn and with the help of the compassionate maidservants prepare her boy for his burial.

With a nod at the doctor Harry lifted his wife's inert body and, taking the stairs two at a time, carried her to her bedroom where he laid her tenderly on the bed. He knelt at her side and even as the doctor watched him, he brushed her hair back from her forehead, kissing her and murmuring her name with such a wealth of love John Burton wanted to turn away, for it seemed to him he should not be spying on such an intimate moment.

But this was not the time for sentiment. 'Mr Sinclair, I beg you, let me attend to your wife. I must examine her at once, for who knows what damage she may have done to herself. I had to stitch her and I'm afraid . . . Ask the nurse to come.' But before Harry could move towards the door with the intention of obeying the doctor, it opened and Biddy moved quickly into the room.

'There's no need for that, Doctor. Tell me what to do.'

'Clean towels, madam, hot water . . . ah, yes, it's as I feared, she is haemorrhaging . . . Quickly, woman. Why she was ever allowed to get out of her bed so soon after childbirth is a mystery to me and not only that but to gallivant about the mill and—'

'Doctor Burton, my wife is the most courageous, compassionate woman I, and you, have ever known. She helped Susan Harper and . . . but sweet Christ, do something . . . don't let her die . . .' His voice broke and he fell to his knees beside the doctor.

'I have no intention of letting her die, sir, and if you will get out of my way . . . ah, here is . . . whatever your name is, come here and help me,' as Biddy returned to the room with Jenny, the most sensible of her servants, behind her carrying all that the doctor needed. 'And my bag, if you please . . .'

*   *   *

Lally awoke to a feeling of great tranquillity as though her dreaming mind was aware that all was well. That everything she had set out to do was done. She was not yet certain what that might be, for she felt so drowsy, so peaceful, so rested she wanted nothing more than to stretch and sigh and settle herself down in her warm and comfortable bed once more and drift off to sleep. A slight noise from the fireside brought her back again and when she turned her head there was Harry in his shirt sleeves asleep in a chair before the fire. He was unshaven, his hair standing in spikes about his head as though he had pushed his hand through it a score of times. He looked rumpled, crumpled, not at all like his usual immaculate self; there was even what looked like blood on his sleeve. His head lolled to one side of the wing chair and he was pale, drawn, with deep smudges under his eyes. She watched him for several minutes, smiling, then all of a sudden it all came back to her and she sat up and was ready to swing her feet to the floor. Her movement woke him at once and in a second he was across the carpet and pushing her quite roughly back beneath the covers.

'What in hell's name d'you think *you're* doing?

209

Get back in that bed at once and until Doctor Burton says you may get up, you'll stay there, even if I have to sit here and watch you twenty-four hours a day. D'you hear me? After that bloody performance yesterday . . .'

Her mind, astonished by his outburst, suddenly returned to yesterday. Struggling against his restraining hands she did her best to sit up.

'Susan . . . I must go to Susan . . . that poor woman . . .'

'That poor woman . . . and yes, I am as sorry as you, but she is being cared for by every maidservant in the house. They are all terribly sorry for her, sweetheart, and can't do enough for her. She is in bed where the doctor put her and the baby is in a cradle next to your . . . to our daughter.' The endearment went unnoticed by both of them.

'Oh, Harry.' She fell against him and began to weep. His arms went round her and she felt the comfort of them, the strength and warmth and was thankful for him, and for his arms. She wept softly and he let her, then he began to talk quietly.

'She has Sam with her. She wanted it that way and though the servants were uneasy at first to have a dead child in the room, they let her have her way. They have bathed him and put him in a nightgown that was once Chris's when he was a child. He is on a small trestle bed with candles about him and she seems to find comfort from it so who are we to deny her. The baby is sharing the breast of . . . of the woman who is nursing . . . our child and is content, or so it seems. He has been taken in to Susan and . . . and all that you wanted to do for her has been done. Now, will you rest, or must I carry you in to see her? Yes, I see I must. Very well, let me wrap you in that shawl.'

Harry picked up his wife, holding her against his chest where she felt his strong, sweet, kind heart beating beneath her cheek. She nestled against him and though he smelled of masculine sweat which was unusual for him she realised he had been fully occupied in helping others and she found it did not repulse her. She was safe with this man, wondering as the thought occurred to her, *safe from what*? And did it really matter?

He knocked on the door of the guest room then entered, still carrying her. For a moment she was dismayed, for it was as though she were entering a church in which a service was about to take place: a service of committal for the small figure on the trestle bed. Sam, whose head had been crushed by the spinning mule but whose face had barely been disfigured, seemed to have a small smile about his mouth. His once impish face looked quite angelic. His vivid ginger hair had been washed and brushed and his curls glowed in the light of the candles that had been placed at the head and the foot of the narrow bed. Susan sat beside him, rocking slowly in the old rocker which someone—Lally for some reason suspected Harry—had placed there for her. It was the sort of chair that would be found in a cottage or the kind of home a woman of Susan's class would feel comfortable in. Not grand as was most of the furniture at the Priory and Lally wondered where it had been found. Susan was nursing her baby who slept peacefully in her arms. She made no attempt to rise to her feet when her master entered the room.

'You can put me down now, Harry,' Lally told

him, which he did. He pulled up a small velvet-covered chair, putting it close to the grieving mother, then left the room when he saw Lally comfortably settled. 'Ring for me when you are ready to leave,' he said quietly before he closed the door.

They sat there together, the two young mothers, not speaking, but Susan was made aware that Lally Sinclair grieved with her, sorrowed for her and was here, an arm's length away should Susan need anything it was in Lally's power to give her.

Then, 'Tha little lass were born on't same day my lad died.'

'Yes.'

It was as though some bond was forged between them with those words. Lally sat for half an hour, studying the face of the dead boy until Susan spoke again. 'Tha'd best get ter tha' bed, lass. 'Appen I'll come an' see thi' when . . .'

'I'd like that, Susan. Bring Jack and I'll introduce you to my babe. She is called Caterina. Cat for short.'

CHAPTER FIFTEEN

The small funeral service was held at the local chapel of St George's near Sowerby Bridge, Susan having come from a family who were of the Methodist persuasion. Mr Sinclair gave permission for women, and men if they cared to, to have an hour off from their mules, for the lad's death had deeply distressed those who worked beside Susan Harper and particularly those who had witnessed

212

the horrifying accident. Those who attended, and there were many of the be-shawled women from the mill at High Clough, were astounded when the maister entered the chapel carrying his wife in his arms. Of course, it was not many days since she had herself given birth to a daughter and it was said that she had done herself some harm when she came hot-foot to the mill when the little lad was killed. Maister had nearly gone out of his mind, those who were there to see it told others, and since Mrs Sinclair had insisted she would attend the committal, even if she had to walk to Sowerby Bridge, he had no choice but to carry her. Both of them seemed not to mind the experience!

The day, as though to mock the sadness of the occasion, was one of those sunshine-filled late April days which seemed to give the promise of the summer to come. The sky was like blue silk stretching above the roof of the plain chapel. The bit of woodland in which the chapel stood contained hawthorn trees that were freckled with green and some firs which stood here and there along the edge. Beyond the dry-stone wall that surrounded the small graveyard the trees seemed to swim in a purple-pink haze as the swollen buds shone in the sunlight and there was a pale tide of shimmering primrose spreading across the rough grass and about the gravestones. The primroses were huge and fragrant, every stem seeming to be about four inches long and some of the women who must have been there early had gathered small bunches which they were ready to put on the child's grave when he was under ground. The widow stood straight as a lance, her head up, staring into the soft sky as though she could see

213

her lad being carried up to heaven where his pa was waiting for him and was saying goodbye to him. She did not weep, though many of the women did. She had been what they called a bit 'stand-offish'. She could read and write and kept herself, her home and her little family clean and decent against all odds and had not really been one of them, but the lass had lost her husband and her child to the mill and you could not help feeling her sorrow. Mrs Sinclair held her arm, supporting her, though it seemed to them she was the one who could do with a bit of support. Still, the maister was there ready to catch her if she faltered. Heads bowed, they watched the bereaved mother throw a handful of soil into the grave, then a lovely flower, a rose they thought, come from the garden of their master, before being led away by the doctor who had attended her boy. The rose had actually been grown in the newly refurbished hothouse at the back of the Priory and was the pride and joy of Barty and Froglet.

To their amazement Mrs Sinclair made a great deal of fuss until Susan Harper agreed to return in Mrs Sinclair's carriage to the Priory, where it was said her baby crowed in the nursery with Mrs Sinclair's children. Was she to stay there and if so what were they to make of that? they wondered among themselves, watching as the maister swung his wife up into his arms the moment the committal was over and carried her to their carriage, settling her next to Susan Harper and the doctor.

The argument began the moment Susan walked in through the front door of the Priory. She nodded politely at Biddy who stood in the entrance hall waiting for the four of them to come inside. Harry wanted to carry Lally up to her room at once but she waved him away impatiently.

'I can walk from here to the sofa in the drawing room, Harry. I allowed it at the chapel because I didn't want a scene . . . well, it was hard enough, but I shall remain down here with you and Susan, and Doctor Burton, of course,' turning to smile warmly at the doctor who, she could sense, wondered what he was doing here at all, but as she had said to Harry in the privacy of their bedroom, he had been inordinately kind and attentive, seeming to care, not just in the medical way but as a friend would, about Susan and Sam. He had been and would continue to be a great support to them all and she felt he should be present.

'It might be a good idea if you were to rest, Mrs Sinclair,' the doctor advised her.

'I shall do. On the sofa. Now then, Biddy, would you ask Jenny to bring in tea and cakes and . . . well, I feel hungry so would it be too much trouble to ask for hot buttered toast, for us all, I think.' She turned towards the drawing-room door, beckoning to Susan to come with her but Susan had turned towards the stairs, ready, it appeared, to go up them and collect her child.

'Where are you going, Susan?' Lally's voice was soft and one could even say affectionate. The two men hovered by the door waiting for some sort of development, as it was certain one was to come.

'Ah'm goin' fer Jack, Mrs Sinclair. 'Tis time ah were away 'ome so if tha' would . . .' Her face mirrored the expression of fondness on Lally's. 'Tha's bin so kind ter me, got me through these last days an' I'll never be able ter thank yer but I

215

got ter—'

'Come and sit down with me, Susan. Have a cup of tea at least before we decide what you are to do.'

Susan's face became wary. 'Ter do—what should I do but get 'ome? I've me life ter get on wi'. I mun earn me livin'.'

'And you shall, Susan. But you will stay here to do it.'

But already Susan was shaking her head in denial. Biddy watched, her eyes going from Lally to Susan and back again. She was not awfully sure she liked what was happening here. This Susan . . . well, you could only feel sorry for the poor lass but what on earth was Miss Lally planning and when it was revealed would Biddy Stevens, who was Miss Lally's only friend and confidante and had been for many years, would she like it? She had acted as a mother to her lass since Miss Delphine, Miss Lally's mother, had died and felt uneasy at the way things appeared to be going.

'Susan, don't shake your head before you have heard what I have to say. Come into the drawing room and we shall have some tea and I shall tell you what I have in mind.'

Both men looked mystified. Susan stood with her foot on the bottom step but Lally, wanting to sit down all of a sudden, moved into the drawing room and sank into the depths of the sofa before the fire which crackled cheerfully in the grate. Biddy watched Susan Harper battle with herself and her damned independence, knowing exactly how she felt. A proud woman was Susan Harper who did not want to be beholden to any living soul. She had been terribly weakened by the loss of her

216

little lad and had allowed herself to be guided, cherished, supported by the kindness and full heart of Lally Sinclair but now all she wanted was to be off back to her life and the work that would keep her and her baby fed, clothed and housed.

'You'd best go, lass,' she said softly to her, beginning to shepherd her towards the drawing-room door. Susan hesitated, her bemused eyes looking round her at the splendid comfort of the room. The lovely pictures which Harry had chosen, the deep-piled carpet, the flowers, the delicate ornaments, for in the months since his marriage and with an endless supply of money at his disposal, the house and gardens had been transformed. Outside the undergrowth of years had been cleared, hedges clipped, unnecessary trees cut down, specimen trees planted, the lake cleaned, flower borders laid out and fresh gravel laid on the drive from the gate to the house. Barty and Froglet, with the help of the two men employed by Mr Sinclair, had been in their element, for at last they could display their special horticultural talents.

The young woman who sat, dressed in the black of mourning for Susan's little lad, last worn for the death of her husband, was patting the sofa, urging Susan to sit beside her.

'Mrs Sinclair, me babby . . .'

'Shall be brought down to you.' She smiled at Biddy. 'And will you ask Dora and the nurse to bring Caterina as well,' for with two babies to take Susan's mind off what must be positively overwhelming her, Lally's own drawing room and its contents, surely it would be easier to speak to her about the future.

'Harry, do give Doctor Burton a whisky or whatever he wants,' she told her husband, 'or perhaps he would prefer tea and hot buttered toast.' Her brilliant smile was turned on the doctor.

'Tea and toast for me, Mrs Sinclair,' he said boyishly. 'I love tea and toast.'

Susan smiled for the first time and John Burton was quite bowled over by its sweetness and luminosity. He could not remember ever having seen her smile before.

A large pot of tea, the pot of fine bone china decorated with birds and flowers, accompanied by four cups and saucers, milk jug and sugar bowl, was brought in by Jenny, all set out on a white lace cloth and placed within reach of her mistress. Harry stood with his back to the wide door that led to the conservatory from where the fragrance of the newly planted and lovingly tended blooms floated, watching as his wife poured tea which the doctor leaped to hand round, then passed him the toast which with a boyish appetite he seemed to enjoy hugely. He was twenty-six years old, only a couple of years younger than himself, a clever and dedicated doctor as he had proved when attending Lally, but he was youthful, engaging and one could not help but like him. Even now, though he was tucking in to the toast as though he hadn't eaten a square meal for days—which perhaps he hadn't, for he lived in lodgings—Harry could tell he was watching Lally for any signs that she might be overtaxing her strength.

The two babies were brought down by Dora and the starched nurse who had been brought in for Lally's confinement. Susan held out her arms for her Jack, that lovely winsome smile lighting her face again and Lally nursed the infant Cat for a moment or two before the doctor suggested mildly that Nurse should take her back to the nursery. Cat was a lovely child with none of that crumpled, red-faced, snuffling appearance that newborn babies seem to possess. But young Jack, now six months old, was delighted with the attention he received, sitting on his mother's knee and beaming round at the company. His hair was the same bright copper as his brother's and father's had been, standing in a thick cloud about his head. He had two teeth which gleamed in the pinkness of his gums and he clapped his hands, showing off a new trick he had learned in the last day or two. He was dressed in a little gown that had once belonged to Alec. It had a broad sash and pretty smocking on the bodice. He wore knee-high white socks and little slippers of the softest leather and might have been taken for a girl but his nature was not at all girlish. Within minutes he began to squirm, doing his best to get off his mother's lap and reach the floor where he was already able to make the motions of a fish on dry land.

Dora took him, kissing his cheek, which was not as rounded as Doctor Burton would have liked, for these children of mill folk did not get enough of the nourishing food they needed to encourage healthy growth.

The two babies were taken away, Jack howling his displeasure and as his voice faded up the stairs Lally at once began to talk.

'Now, Susan, you can see how we are placed here.' Her voice was crisp, revealing nothing of her true feelings. She wanted Susan to believe that Lally could not manage without her. Susan's pride would not allow her to be given charity, Lally had already found that out, and so she must be made to believe that her help and support for Lally were vital. But that was not the whole truth. She really *did* need help for Dora, since two growing toddlers and one new baby was too much for the young girl to cope with. She had done well with Jamie and Alec but they were already strong-willed little boys, taking after their father who had always got his own way, and needed a firm hand and Susan could provide that. Besides which, this would give Susan stability in her life for herself and her remaining son. She was still deep in shock, still grieving not only for Sam but for her young husband, and a home and respectable, worthwhile employment, plus a friend, which Lally felt herself to be, would make her life easier to bear.

'I badly need a nursemaid for Jamie, Alec and Cat. Now Dora is good and kind but she needs help. She is so young herself and needs a steadying influence such as yourself. You would be doing me a big favour if you would consider taking on this job. And would it not be better for you and Jack not only to be together all the time but to have a good home, decent worthwhile work and to be with people who value what you are doing? I'm not saying that your present employment is not worthwhile,' she added hastily, flashing a smile at her husband, 'but with your qualifications—'

'Qualifications?' Susan interrupted in amazement.

'I believe you can read and write.'

'Yes, but—'

'You will be able to teach the children, including your own boy, the rudiments of reading and writing until they have a governess or go to school. Susan, do you not see how invaluable you would be to me, to our children, to this household? Tell her, Harry.'

Harry Sinclair let out his breath on a long-drawn-out sigh. Lally was racing far ahead of him in her plans for Susan Harper. He had intended to give the widow a helping hand over the next few months while she came to terms with her loss, with her need for employment and for the care and upbringing of her boy, but it seemed his wife had, and probably even before the death of Sam Harper, a scheme worked out whereby she helped Susan to a new and better life. At the same time she had worded it so that Susan believed *she* was helping Lally.

But neither of them had bargained for Susan Harper and her sense of what was proper.

'Eeh, no, Mrs Sinclair, that'll not do. Ah'm a spinner, 'ave bin since I were ten year old, like our Sam.' A spasm of pain crossed her face. 'Ah don't know owt else,' she went on. 'Ah'll see ter mesenn as soon as ah pick up a bit. Me an' our Jack kep' oursenn decent and owed nowt ter nobody an' I don't mean ter start now. Lass, ah know nowt about teachin'.'

Lally leaned forward eagerly to look directly into Susan's face. 'But you know about children, Susan. I have to have someone I can trust to look after my babies and who else would I choose but you? Did I not say we could help each other and in this way do we not make it possible?'

'Ah'm right sorry, Mrs Sinclair, but ah'll not tekk advantage any longer o' yer kindness. Ah've a job at mill'—turning to Harry—'an ah reckon . . .'

221

'Please, Susan, do this for me and let me do this for you. I cannot bear to see you go back to that horrid place,' again with a brief apologetic look at Harry, for the horrid place was, after all, one of the mills which provided him, and her and the children with the lifestyle they had. 'I shall be busy in the future since Harry and I have sadly neglected our social duties. We wish to entertain. I shall be busy with the supervision of the estate, helped by Mr Cameron who is Harry's steward, of course, for this is my sons' inheritance and must not be neglected. I shall need to visit friends, afternoon calls and such like . . .' for if her sons, Chris's sons, and her baby daughter were to take their place in the society to which they belonged—and what mother was not conscious of the importance of that—they must mix with their own kind. They must be accepted, young as they were, for this was when it began. Children's parties, birthdays, Christmas parties to which they would be invited and the hospitality they received would be reciprocated. It was strange really, she thought, with one part of her mind not occupied with Susan, that though she herself did not care very much, and neither had Chris, about that sort of thing somehow it seemed important that her children at least had the chance. Harry and Roly both moved, or could if they cared for it which Harry didn't seem to, in the society of the millocracy which was only one rank lower than the landed gentry and because of who they were, their wealth and their connections, mixed quite easily with both. Her children must be allowed to do the same. So she must spend some of her time cultivating the people who dwelled in that world. She could not leave her

222

children, and any more she might have, for she was pretty certain Harry would soon claim his conjugal rights, in the hands of a country girl who herself could not read or write. Dora was a sensible lass and while the boys had been no more than babies had coped admirably but they needed more and Susan was the answer.

'I can't manage without you, Susan,' she said simply and the truth of the statement was written in her brimming eyes. Dear God, I must not cry, she told herself, gulping, for the last thing she wanted was pity. It must be the emotions a woman feels when she has just given birth, she thought, but it seemed it was to influence the young widow, for she was looking undecided, biting her lip, her own eyes beginning to fill up and Harry and the doctor exchanged glances.

Harry was quite amazed by Lally's behaviour because if there was one thing Lally could not abide it was women who got their own way with tears. She had been strong in all things. Chris's tragic death, tackling the enormous problem of running the estate, even her pregnancy which, had he not stepped in gallantly—smiling inwardly at the word—she would have survived somehow, for that was what she was, a survivor. But it seemed she was about to do the very thing he had hoped for and that was to mix again with their social equals, with his business acquaintances which, of course, would do him no harm. There were still many renovations to the house he meant to put in hand. If they were to entertain, perhaps weekend parties which the gentry might be tempted to sample, there would be shooting on the grouse moor, hunting for which he would need good

223

horses and, naturally, Lally must have a wardrobe that would be unequalled in Moorend.

The smile inside him widened into a grin, for the very idea was absurd. He was Harry Sinclair, not a bloody aristocrat. A mill-owner, a man of business who meant to make the Priory into the sort of home a man would be comfortable in, the building itself sound, the gardens, the park, the moorland in good heart until the day when he would build his own house, a monument to the power of machines and his own courage and ability to use them. He was already hugely successful but he had dreams like any man and he meant to make them all come true and at their heart was the frail-looking woman who drooped on the sofa.

Susan stood up abruptly as though she meant to leave at once before she was persuaded into something she did not care for, but within her where no one could see was a small beating gladness, not for herself, but for her lad. She had lost so much to the mill. She had no one but her little Jack and surely she did not want him to go back to the place that had killed his father and brother. She had—what was it Mrs Sinclair had called them?—qualifications, she could read and write and somehow, though he had not known in what way, her Jack had always said that one day the skill would take them to something better than they had now. *Jack had been right!* So could she refuse the chance she was being offered, which Jack's son was being offered? He would be brought up with Mrs Sinclair's children. He would have an education but not the simple one she and Jack had wrought for themselves but a *proper* one, school, perhaps even university, not just a spinner, or even

224

an overlooker in Mr Sinclair's mills but a profession, for both she and Jack had had brains, intelligence, determination and surely their little lad would inherit some of that. Their Sam had but he had never had a chance to go further, poor lamb, poor little lamb. They would be decently clothed, fed, housed and she would be doing a worthwhile job in caring for Mrs Sinclair's children. How could she refuse?

She sat down again, just as abruptly, and in his chair beside her John Burton felt his heart beat with the same gladness that had moved Susan's, but not for the same reason. He had tended to the poor woman in her tragic loss, had done what he could for her boy, which had been really no more than tidy him up, make him look . . . well, he could hardly call it *presentable*, for the child's skull had been crushed like an eggshell but when laid out in the clean nightshirt Mrs Sinclair had offered, his head on the soft white pillow in the coffin, his face had been peaceful and as bonny as John Burton could make it. It had barely a mark on it when John had finished with him. The boy's mother had sat beside him, her eyes on his waxen face and John had felt she was grateful to him for what he had done for her poor, disfigured child. She had looked at him, her gaze soft and warm as though to thank him, her blue eyes, though swollen with her grief, surrounded by long, thick, brown lashes tipped with gold. They would be beautiful eyes when back to normal, he thought. She was a bonny woman, not pretty like Mrs Sinclair, but pleasant-faced. Her hair was tightly confined in a black scarf, hidden away apart from one endearing curl that had escaped at the back, lying on the white

225

skin of her neck. It was a pure rich chestnut but it seemed to him it had a glint of gold in it. She was painfully thin, frail, her black skirt and bodice, which he was not to know were all she possessed, hanging on her. She wore clogs and knitted socks and round her shoulders was a thin shawl which she had draped over her head at the graveside but was now pushed back.

They all focused on Susan but she seemed to be unaware of them as she gazed into the fire. They all held their breath, though they were not aware of it, and at last she spoke.

'Wheer would ah sleep?'

Lally leaned forward eagerly, almost springing to her feet in anticipation. She was beginning to smile, ready to hold out her hands to Susan Harper. Harry wondered as he watched the whole thing in silence why it was that Lally had taken such a liking to this woman. Not that there was anything to *dislike* about the young widow but she was so obviously a working-class woman; you only had to hear the way she spoke and would that be allowable with young children who would possibly mimic her, or at least pick up her broad Yorkshire way of speaking.

'There is a spare room next to the nursery, Susan. The nursery is made up of three rooms, a day nursery where the children play and . . . well, where they spend their time during the day and a night nursery where they have their little beds and now, of course, a cot. Dora has a room of her own and on the far side of that I mean to make a schoolroom and a bedroom for the governess they will have. The whole of the top floor will be given over to the children while they are babies but you

226

will have your own place where you and Jack can be alone should you want to. You would spend your day with the children and Jack, of course, would share everything with them. You would earn a decent wage, I promise you, and would have the run of the gardens and the park. A day off, say once a week, when you and Jack could go wherever you pleased. Oh, do say yes, Susan . . . please.' Lally's face was coloured with her excitement and again Harry brooded over what Lally was about to do, or hoped to do.

Susan stood up again and so, for some reason, did John Burton.

'Right, I'll do it,' she said, her face firm with her sudden resolve, 'but ah'll not work wi' that nurse, choose how.'

CHAPTER SIXTEEN

She stood at their bedroom window and watched her husband, mounted on his bay, Piper, canter down the drive towards the gate, his two dogs behind him. The drive curved and the gate was hidden by the line of trees that edged it and as he passed out of sight she drew in a deep breath, letting it out on a long sigh. She remained at the window for several minutes, the palms of her hands flat on the sill, looking out over the long sloping lawn that stretched on both sides of the drive, the grass as smooth and even as green velvet. With the extra help, Barty and Froglet were now free to care for the grounds as Barty, who had been gardener at the Priory since the days of Chris's

227

grandfather, liked. He could be seen pottering, for he was no longer young, down the drive, his acolyte in the shape of young Froglet following at his heels, both with a pair of shears in their hands. It was not quite seven o'clock but at this time of the year the sun was well up and it promised to be a warm, bright day. Two other men, probably Wilf and Evan, could be seen on the far side of the small lake, cleaning out the weeds and scattering the ducks who swam away in a great swathe of annoyance. It all looked so lovely, so graceful, so peaceful, restored as it was to its former glory and she found it in her heart to hope that Harry would not be too hasty in building the new house he was promising himself.

She had found, to her surprise, a great contentment in her situation since their hastily contrived marriage, and it was all due to him, to his enormous wealth which he spent so lavishly and to his excellent taste. The house itself was beautiful, of course, standing as it did alone on a slight hill set in its acres of gardens and terraces dug out of the sloping land generations ago, though it was Harry who had perfected it. The gardens surrounding the house were full of old-fashioned flowers, sweetbriar roses, cabbage roses, white damask and maiden's blush, sweet william, iris by the lake, peonies, carnations, wallflowers and Canterbury bells, discussed and chosen at great length by Harry and Barty. Clipped hedges and paved walks were sheltered from the cold winds that blew for six months of the year, for the house was exposed to fierce winter storms that swept over the wild, black and rugged moorland, by a woodland of oak and birch that encircled the gardens and challenged the fury of the tempestuous gales. Below her window and stretching along the front of the house were terraces crammed with lovely Grecian urns in which the gardeners had planted vivid geraniums of every shade of pink and red and beyond were the rolling hills of West Riding, a perfect setting for it all.

She turned away from the window and moved to sit in front of her mirror, studying her own face, then picked up a silver-backed brush and began to brush the mass of short curls that flared about her head. Despite Harry's urging to let it grow, for like all men he thought that long hair was more feminine, she had continued to have it cut as she had always done. She didn't know why really. Perhaps it was a throwback to the days before she had been Chris's wife, since then she had longed to do nothing but be as he and Roly were, young, free, unencumbered, flouting convention, almost as boyish as they were. She had worn breeches as they did when they rode, and had been as they were until the day she and Chris had fallen in love. But now she was married to Harry and could really find no fault with that. She did not love him as she had loved Chris but she was fond of him, she supposed, and grateful, for he had made her life one of ease and comfort. He was a diverse, complex man with many shades and nuances to his nature which she had at first done her best to understand but he allowed no one, least of all her, to penetrate. He was a man who was accustomed to having his own way but he was not arrogant about it, but perhaps the strangest thing about him, at least to her who knew the truth, was his fondness for the girl child she had borne. A pretty little girl now four months old on whom, or so it was said in the kitchen, he doted. Dora, who was inclined to gossip, told them of his visits to the nursery where he held the little girl—and why not since she was his daughter—in his arms before the nursery fire. He was attentive to the other children too, rolling on the floor with the boys, putting them on his back and pretending to be a savage tiger, scooping even Susan Harper's little lad, who was really too young for it, up with the rest.

She did not tell them, perhaps since she had not really noticed, that the moment the mistress entered the room he sprang to his feet and despite the protestations of the excited children became the rather stiff, polite master they all knew. But he did favour that baby!

That baby! How strange, Lally brooded as she still gazed at the curve in the drive where Harry had disappeared, that he should take to the child who was not his but the outcome of her and Roly's one small indiscretion. One moment of madness up on the moorland. He had made love to her last night which had been pleasant, she supposed she would call it, and he had seemed satisfied, turning from her to fall asleep at once, his breathing deep and soft.

She started as a tap on the door sounded and Biddy entered carrying a tray with a pot of hot chocolate of which Lally was inordinately fond.

'Oh, you're up then,' Biddy said. 'Mr Harry said not to disturb you but I knew a morning like this would have you out of your bed. Where are you off to today? I've just come from the nursery and those lads are asking for you. Nice day for a walk

230

up to Folly. Polly McGinley was asking after you t'other day, wanting to know when you were bringing Miss Cat up to see them. Their Kate's about ready to present them with a second grandchild. Eeh, babies don't half bring happiness.'

She put the tray down on the small table beside the fireplace, plumping up the cushions on Lally's chair, watching as her young mistress pulled her diaphanous negligee about her and strolled across to the chair. She wasn't awfully sure she liked these wisps of bedroom wear Miss Lally had taken to donning in the privacy of the room she shared with Mr Harry but then she was a newly married woman and if her husband—of whom Biddy thought the world—liked them who was she to disagree. She began to pick up items of clothing, Mr Harry's velvet dressing gown, a pillow thrown from the bed—what had they been up to?—a discarded slipper of Miss Lally's and a fine silk stocking, among other items, some of which surprised her. Miss Lally was not the tidiest of women and it seemed Mr Harry was picking up her habits!

Lally sipped her chocolate, staring into the empty firegrate in which an enormous vase of mixed roses from the garden had been placed. She hadn't made any plans for today as since Susan had taken over the nursery and Cameron was in full charge of the farmland, under Harry's instructions, she found she was a lady of leisure. She, after much persuading by Harry, had taken to calling on the wives of men who could perhaps be of use to him in his business. Mrs Fred Anson, the banker's wife, Mrs George Bracken whose husband was in cotton and Mrs Albert Watson, wife of the builder

231

who was at the moment in discussion with Harry over the proposed extension of one of his mills. She was bored to extinction, she told Biddy but she owed it to Harry after all. They had given a dinner party or two, inviting not only those who might help Harry in a commercial way, but younger members of the millocracy and always included was Doctor John Burton. One day, if she could prevail upon Harry and, not least, Susan herself, she meant to include her in one of their more informal gatherings, for already Susan, who was quick and intelligent, was taking on a certain gloss which would not look amiss among the down-to-earth members of Harry's acquaintances.

For an hour each morning Susan sat Alec and Jamie round the nursery table, books spread out on it and was attempting to teach the boys their letters and with a rather surprising talent had managed to gain and keep their attention by some clever trick with crayons, big books which they coloured in the letters of the alphabet, each one an animal or an object of interest to two small boys, and without them realising it they had already learned to spell simple words connected to what they were colouring. A train, a cat, a dog, a tree, a ball, and though one hour was enough before their childish span of attention was reached it was reaping a rich reward. And somehow, just as important, it gave Susan an inordinate amount of satisfaction to know that she was doing a worthwhile job of work and was earning what she saw as a great deal of money for doing it. She loved the children and was good with them. And they loved her and though Dora had sulked for a week or two at having what she had considered her place in the household taken over by another woman, she had gradually settled down and was willing to follow Mrs Harper's lead in the working of the nursery. After all, Mrs Harper could read and write. Dora couldn't but while Mrs Harper gave the boys their daily lesson Dora was in complete charge of dear little Jack who was walking now and the baby Cat who was doing her best to crawl. All in all a very satisfactory arrangement.

They were drinking their milk, which Doctor Burton insisted on every morning though he was the first to admit that it was mainly for Jack that he had prescribed it since the Sinclair children were well nourished and healthy but it did them no harm to share with Jack, when Miss Lally marched in to the nursery, moving in turn to each child round the table and giving them a hearty kiss. Jack was not left out. Already he loved the sweet-smelling lady who was always ready for a cuddle, though not like his mam, of course. His mam who he was learning to call *Mama* as it would not do for the Sinclair children to pick up the Yorkshire speech of the working class. Even Susan Harper was smoothing out her broad Yorkshire accent!

'Right, who's for a walk up to see Mrs McGinley?' cried Lally, swinging her daughter up into her arms, holding her high and making her squeal with excitement. Cat was not sure where they were off to but with her young mother it was always somewhere fun.

'Can we feed the hens, Mama,' Jamie beseeched, 'and the piglets? Mrs Polly says there are some 'ittle tiny new ones. I'm going to hold one,' he said importantly, looking round at the others. 'In fac' I might bring one home with me to

233

keep in the nursery.'

'Me too . . . me too . . . Hens, Mama, and 'ickle pigs.'

'You can all feed them if Mrs McGinley says you may. Now then, Susan, do we have your permission to have an adventure? We can put Cat in the perambulator and then if anyone gets tired,' meaning Jack, 'they can be popped in with her.'

The excitement was intense, for Polly McGinley was a great lover of children and very indulgent of their inquisitive, if sometimes chaotic ways. Even the two big dogs were not unwelcome though they were still not allowed into her spotless kitchen. Polly McGinley would never forget Mrs Sinclair's wonderful kindness in respect of the repairs to their farmhouse and the renovations to the cottage at the back where their Denny and Kate awaited the birth of Polly's new grandchild.

Barty and Froglet, Wilf and Evan watched with indulgent smiles as the erratic procession burst from the side door of the house and spread itself across the side lawn, Jamie in the lead followed by Alec and, tottering unsteadily on increasingly plump legs, Jack in the rear. Dora, like an anxious sheepdog, did her best to contain them, begging Master Jamie to wait for the others but to no avail. Following behind came Lally and Susan, Susan pushing the perambulator in which Cat was propped, yelling her disapproval, for it seemed to her the others were having all the fun. Susan passed her a favourite soft toy, an unrecognisable object with arms and legs, two ears, two eyes and a vacant stitched-on grin, which went by the name of Pinky. At once Cat quietened, for Pinky was much loved.

234

Susan had put on weight since she had come to live in the Sinclair household which was not a bad thing for she had been painfully thin when she was employed at High Clough, giving what food she had to her Sam and only eating barely enough to keep herself alive. She was still dressed in the black of mourning but she had allowed herself to be taken to Miss Hockley's, protesting that it was far too grand and expensive but giving in just the same, since she could hardly move about the impressive establishment of the Sinclairs in the threadbare garment she had worn for years in the home she had shared with Jack. Now she wore a neat well-fitted gown of good black cotton which showed off her pretty figure. Lally longed to get her in a dress of blue or yellow or rose like Dora's, for she did like bright colours about her and she knew Susan would suit any of them. She was bonny, not as lovely as Lally but her hair and eyes shone and her cheeks were rosy and rounded with health and it had not gone unnoticed by Lally nor Harry that John Burton missed no opportunity to call at the Priory to, as he said, check on the progress of her small son. And as he had told her sternly, she needed to regain her strength by eating the good food supplied by her employers. Which she did and it showed.

Lally sauntered beside her in a gown of azure-blue muslin, with a wide blue satin sash around the waist. It showed off her neat waist, her well-rounded breasts which were fuller since the birth of her three children and the curve of her slender hips. Her hair tumbled about her head in glossy curls in which the brilliant sunshine put a touch of chestnut and her amazing blue-green eyes

235

reflected the brightness of the day. Dora would have liked to wear a neat uniform to denote the importance of her job as a nursemaid but Mrs Sinclair did not care for it in the nursery where she wished her children to be brought up in a more informal manner. She had on instead a dress in a shade of pale rose, plain but very becoming and her hair, the colour of a new penny, was arranged in a curly bun at the back of her head. She was not pretty but then neither was she plain and her mam had high hopes for her in the marriage market. Not with a labourer as her pa was but perhaps a small farmer or a man in a respectable trade. Her sisters, Jenny and Clara, who were older, seemed very set in their employment at the Priory and Mrs Akroyd had more or less resigned herself to the pair of them remaining spinsters. Still, they did have decent positions.

The scattered group strolled round to the back of the house, making as usual for the paddock where the horses were placidly cropping the grass. Ebony and Jeb, the moor pony, stood nose to tail beneath the shelter of an enormous oak tree, their tails swishing lazily to keep off the flies, but the rest, Merry, Blossom, and the two sturdy ponies, named Snowy and Teddy, that Jamie and Alec were to learn to ride, all wandered over to the fence, poking their noses over the top bar to be fondled by the enthusiastic boys. As usual Jamie set up a wailing to be allowed to climb over, or under, the fence to get at his papa's ebony gelding which he told them he would ride one day but Susan, who had let it be known that she required obedience right from the first, not the obedience that their stepfather demanded which made them

236

jump to obey, but serious nonetheless, moved them on firmly in the direction of the farm. Lally, as though she were a child too, trailed after them.

'I believe there's kittings at Folly,' Susan told them and at once they began to run with Dora in full pursuit. The dogs chased round them in a surge of enchanted joy and the baby was moved over to make room for Jack who was beginning to tire. He fell over so many times his mother told him he looked like a ragamuffin in his grass-stained outfit and he made no objection to being put in with the baby who clutched him with delight though she would not allow him to hold Pinky. Their heads nodded together as the perambulator, pushed by the two women, since the slope was steeper now, waded through a field of poppies and buttercups until they reached Folly Farm.

*   *   *

The buck stood in the clearing deep in the woods at the back of Folly Farm, almost invisible in the undergrowth and closely growing oaks, hawthorn and larch. His head was up, his antlers proud and strong and his ears twitched. His nostrils quivered, searching for signs of danger, of some threatening aroma that would alert him to the presence of his enemy, of man, of those who, for many months now, he had managed to avoid. He knew they were about but his cunning was greater than theirs. Hearing and scenting nothing to alarm him, he bent his strong neck and sank his teeth into the juicy leaves of the tree under which he stood. The breeze blew away from him towards the east and the two men who froze in the bushes in that direction both lifted their guns, barely breathing, fingers on the triggers, their caps dragged with the peaks at the back so as not to impede their view. They had been after this stag for months now and there it was in their sights, unaware of their presence, waiting for the death shot and its final arrival on the counter of a local butcher who would pay dearly for its carcass.

A sound lifted the magnificent animal's head, a sound from some way off but enough to explode him into a leap and a run which carried him through the woodland and out of sight of the two men who lay on their stomachs, their guns still at the ready but with nothing to aim at other than the quivering leaves of the trees and shrubs that had been disturbed by the buck's passage.

'Bugger it! . . . bugger it! . . . bugger it!' one of the men said, rolling over on to his back, his face a mask of fury, while the second man swore even more obscenely, lifting his fist into the air and hitting out as though he would dearly love to murder whoever it was who had disturbed their quarry.

Then they heard the sound again but this time more clearly. Children's laughter, children shouting, a dog barking in excitement and the faint cry of a woman. Slowly they got to their feet and without a word moved silently through the wood until they reached its edge, and the field in which Sean McGinley had planted hay that was ripening luxuriantly in the summer sunshine. It would be ready for harvesting in a few weeks and when it was cut would be stored for winter feed for Sean's milk herd. The growing crop waved gently in the tiny breeze and sighed as though in great contentment at the care Sean and his son Denny had lavished upon it. Proud they were of their continuing success with their farm, thanks to Mr and Mrs Sinclair, but mostly to Mrs Sinclair, once Mrs Fraser, for it was she who had provided them with the brass and the encouragement to work all the hours God and daylight allowed.

The two men watched as the squealing boys, Mrs Sinclair's boys, not even waiting to open the gate but climbing over it, hurled themselves into the arms of Polly McGinley at her front porch, yelling to see the 'kittings', the piglets, the chicks but first could they have one of Mrs Polly's gingerbread men of which they were inordinately fond and which they knew she made especially for them, or so they imagined. The baby was lifted out of the perambulator and cuddled by Polly, behind her Kate, who was enormous with her second child but wanted a 'hold' as soon as her mother-in-law would allow it. Jack had clambered from the perambulator and was making a valiant attempt to follow Jamie and Alec who could not make up their minds whether to run into Mrs Polly's kitchen for the gingerbread men, or make for the enclosure where the chicks and the hens clucked and pecked, the pig pen and the new piglets, or the small barn where the new mother cleaned her family of week-old kittens in an ecstasy of purring. There was so much, so many delights, it was hard to know where to start.

Mrs Polly made the decision for them.

'Inter't kitchen wi' the lot o' yer. Gingerbread men first an' a glass o' milk and when yer've got that down yer Sean'll tekk yer ter see't animals. No, Master Jamie, not on yer own. Them animals

239

is valuable, that means they're worth money. Yer know what money is, don't yer? Yes, well, I'm not 'avin' 'em all excited wi' you playin' wi' 'em so yer'll do as yer told. See, Master Jamie, run ter't bottom field an' fetch Sean,' with a glance at Lally to see if she would allow her precious son to do such a thing but it was not far and Sean could be seen from the window. With a nod from his mama, Jamie darted from the door and ran across the yard, jumped the dry-stone wall, scorning the gate as usual, and ran shouting across the field.

They had drunk their milk and clutching a gingerbread man apiece the three boys, Jack carried in Sean's arms, did the rounds of the farmyard with Dora in tow while Susan and Lally, Cat held in Polly's comfortable lap, sat at the immaculate kitchen table and drank the hot, sweet, dark tea the McGinleys favoured. Kate, barely able to get about, pottered at the kitchen range, stirring a big pan of rich stew, peeping into the oven to see if the scones she had just flung together were ready and though told by her mother-in-law to sit 'ersenn down, continued in the small domestic tasks she could still manage.

'Us'll 'ave another one of our own soon,' Polly declared, looking fondly at Kate, bending to plant a smacking kiss on Cat's smiling face, unconcerned with the smears of gingerbread that covered the small face, the hands, what had been a pristine white apron, come from Cat's own squashed biscuit which she was sucking with great appreciation.

Promising to let the boys know when the kittens would be old enough to leave their mam *and* if their own mam would allow it, they might have one each providing they swore they would look after them, feed them, clean up after them and such. With kisses all round, a solemn handshake with Sean, for men did not go in for kisses, the group set off across the field towards the wood through which they intended to find their way home. The boys wanted to climb a tree, a *tall* tree, Jamie announced and was echoed, as usual, by Alec. The dogs bounded round them and it was not until they were almost at the edge of the woodland that the two animals suddenly stiffened. Their ears flattened against their heads and they began to growl softly in the backs of their throats. They moved slowly towards the first of the trees, crouched low in a most curious manner and at once the women stopped. Dora managed to catch the arm of the belligerent Jamie who struggled with her but something in the dogs' conduct had alarmed the three women and they froze. Of course they knew there was nothing in the woodland to endanger them, for hadn't they walked here dozens of times, even in the winter when the foliage was stiff and white and crackling, but there was something there that the two dogs didn't care for.

'Fred, Ally, come to me,' Lally said quietly and reluctantly the dogs obeyed her, doing their best to protect all those who they considered to be in their charge, though the group was somewhat scattered. 'Bring Jamie and Alec here, Dora,' she told the nursemaid and only when they were all huddled together did the dogs relax.

*   *   *

241

The two men silently backed away from the edge of the woodland. They knew they could not be seen in the thick summer foliage and they were adept at moving as quietly as any creature that inhabited the woodland. They knew every inch of it, every path and clearing and not just this wood but all of them on the estate. They made their living from it and had done ever since they were boys and could fire a shotgun. They had been waiting for an opportunity in some way to corner the bloody squire's widow—meaning Lally Fraser—ever since he had broken his bloody neck on the hunting field, but when she had married that other sod she had not moved about as once she had done. They did not wonder why they should want this particular woman, or even what they meant to do to her when they finally had her in their grasp but even if it was just to scare her, perhaps handle her a bit—with their faces covered, of course, since they wanted no trouble to themselves—their lust had not waned. She was a fine bit of womanflesh and, besides, it would do her good to be humiliated, though they did not in their illiterate and ignorant way use such a word.

'If them bloody dogs 'adn't bin there,' one said to the other as they strolled into the littered farmyard that surrounded their home.

' 'Tweren't dogs though they were—'

'Aye,' the second one interrupted. ' 'Twere the rest, kids an' t'other women. Ne'r mind, our turn'll come,' moving his shotgun from one shoulder to the other.

'Aye, one day.'

CHAPTER SEVENTEEN

Roly came home in October after being abroad for over six months and it was said in the kitchens of the best people in Moorend whose servants tittle-tattled with those at Mill House, which had been unoccupied except for the staff Harry had left in place as caretakers, that the recently returned young master went through the place like a whirlwind. Mrs Cannon was made to realise that Master Roly had become used to the finest cuisine in his travels and expected it to continue; that he demanded his shirts be ironed to perfection, his boots be polished to the highest standards, his home be warm and comfortable, that in short, as he was the sole master of Mill House, his every order must be seen to the moment he requested it!

He had travelled to all the main manufacturing towns in Europe and as far away as Russia, forming contacts that would keep the Sinclair mills busy for months, years even, building up connections with foreign businessmen, lavishly entertaining them and their wives, using not only his shrewd business acumen but his immense charm. Everywhere he went he was welcomed as a hell of a good fellow who knew what he was about, honest and trustworthy and could be relied upon to deliver on time the Sinclair cloth which was being produced by the mile.

From there he had moved to North America, travelling the length and breadth of that vast continent, for as he said in his weekly reports to his brother it hardly seemed worthwhile making the journey home when Harry was dealing so superbly with his side of the business which was the manufacture of the cloth. He did not word it quite like that, as it was not his way and Harry did not question it, knowing it to be true. They were to discuss building a new mill, or even *mills* on Roly's return, it was rumoured in the town, for the many activities in the manufacture of wool needed more space than they had at this time, or so Harry Sinclair intimated to his business acquaintances, particularly with the orders that were pouring in. Harry and Roly Sinclair were fast becoming the wealthiest mill-owners in Yorkshire, or so their rivals whispered.

Lally was told quite casually at the dinner table, for how else could her husband inform her, that Roly had arrived home the day before, asking her courteously if she could arrange a small dinner party to welcome him back, since it would surely be expected by their shared acquaintances in Moorend. He did not tell her that it had been Roly's idea.

Her heart had begun to beat an erratic rhythm the moment Roly's name was mentioned, for it was the first time that it had been spoken since their marriage. Harry had accepted Roly's child and treated her—astonishingly, to Lally at least—with as much affection as if he were her real father and since Roly had been absent for so long it had not appeared to be difficult for Harry. But now he was home and what problems was that going to cause? Roly, of course, did not know Cat was his but the sudden marriage of his brother to Chris Fraser's widow must have given him some moments of wonder. Fortunately he was not aware of the exact date of Cat's birth!

'Perhaps Tommy Bracken and his new wife. Ginny, is she called? They are both young and lively and it would do me no harm with his father with whom I do business.' This consideration was always in Harry's astute mind. 'And I know you like John. John Burton who has done so much for the family's health. He seems to be becoming a family friend though I do wish he could find some young marriageable lady to bring with him. I dare say Roly will let me know who *he* fancies and providing she is respectable we could invite her.'

'Susan.' The name was out of her mouth before she knew it and even as she said it her heart beat even faster, for the idea was preposterous. Or was it? Susan had altered in every way since the day she had come to live at the Priory. Her speech still had a definite trace of a Yorkshire accent in it, but then did not George Bracken, a self-made man with his 'Shoddy' Mill and his plans to extend, have an inflection of it in his voice? His wife, a kindly soul who was devoted to him and their only daughter, had never quite become accustomed to their rise in society. Agnes and Albert Watson, the builder and his wife, were second-generation tradesmen if you like and therefore had managed to gather a sheen of gentility about them, and their family of eight had all had good schooling, at least the boys, and were perfectly able to hold their own in what was called polite society. Lally herself had a somewhat better pedigree than any of them, for her mother's uncle had been a baronet and Chris had been of the landed gentry.

Harry looked mystified. 'Susan?'

'Yes, why not? She is an intelligent woman and

quick to learn and anyway, who would know that she was our children's nurse, or even governess. She would not be out of place at our dinner table and I happen to believe that John Burton is madly in love with her.' Lally spoke defiantly.

Harry's jaw dropped and the spoon which he had just been about to raise to his mouth dropped with it. Fortunately Jenny had a moment ago left the dining room to tell Mrs Stevens, who was still cook as well as housekeeper, that Mr and Mrs Sinclair would soon be ready for coffee in the drawing room so there was no one to hear what Harry called this insane idea. Lally fiddled nervously with her napkin, folding and re-folding it as she gazed anxiously at Harry's flabbergasted expression.

'Have you gone mad? Put a woman who not so long ago worked in my mill among our guests? Expect her to know which knife to use and how to converse with ladies and gentlemen who would have a fit if they knew that—'

'Who would tell them? She is a dear friend of mine, or will be when I have persuaded her to get rid of her silly pride, her *inverted* pride and become the person she is capable of becoming. Do you know the other evening when the children were asleep and you were busy in the estate office I went up to her rooms; well, I was alone and . . . and restless, and she was reading *The Times*. You had informed me of much of its contents at dinner and when I showed my amazement she told me everything that was in it and I knew it to be true for you had said so. If I can get her out of her interminable black and into—'

'She shows respect for her husband who has

been dead for no longer than—'

'Well over a year. I'm not sure of the date but Jack is twelve months old and the period of mourning for a widow is a year. There is a very pretty dove-grey silk that I never wear which would be perfectly proper with perhaps a touch of rose pink at the waist and no one would know that she was not a guest, or . . . or a distant relative who has come to stay with us.' Her enthusiasm grew. Her eyes sparkled and her cheeks flushed and she put out a hand to grasp his, for they had long discarded the habit of sitting one at each end of the long table. Harry could feel himself yearning towards her, longing to kiss her smiling mouth, to put up a hand and cup her cheek in love but apart from when they were in the bed they shared he kept displays of fondness to a perfunctory kiss on the cheek as he got home from the mill.

'Please say yes, Harry, please. I can show her the right way to . . . to go about things at the table and if she finds it hard to hold a conversation, well, does it matter? Anne Bracken is shy and if all they say about her is true, the new Mrs Bracken, Ginny Bracken, will more than compensate. When I took tea with Dorothy Bracken the new Mrs Bracken quite embarrassed her, I'm sure, since she is so lively. She's nice though and she has no what I believe is called "side" to her. Her father is a master cutler, loads of money but hardly of the upper classes. Oh Lord, I sound such a snob but you know what I mean.'

Harry sighed. He supposed there was no harm in persuading Susan Harper to dine with them and their guests. She only had to follow Lally's example and keep her mouth shut but even as he thought this he wanted to smile wryly, for in his mind was the surety that nothing on God's earth would make Susan Harper step out of what she saw as her station in life.

He paused before he spoke, doing his utmost not to grasp his wife's hand and bring it tenderly to his lips. 'Very well then, if Susan agrees we will go ahead. Send invitations to all concerned and I'll have a chat with Roly to make sure he invites some suitable young lady. Perhaps Anne Bracken, seeing that her brother—'

'Roly is hardly likely to thank you for Anne Bracken. She's two years older than he is and as plain as a mouse. Roly likes pretty, vivacious girls who—'

She suddenly stopped and bit her lip, for she had been about to describe herself and by the expression on his face she knew Harry realised it. He stood up abruptly then marched behind her chair and held it politely as she rose to her feet.

'You go ahead and take coffee in the drawing room. I have some work to do on the farm accounts. Those Weavers are giving Cameron some trouble still and I feel a harsh reminder is needed. I am seriously thinking of turning them off the farm and those lads, what are they called, Jed and Ham, have been seen skulking in Folly Wood. They are unpredictable and as for the rents . . . well, I will see you later, my dear.'

*   *   *

Harry was right. Before she sent out the invitations for the dinner party in honour of Roly's return she tackled Susan. Susan was appalled for a moment

248

then she began to laugh, so merrily and so unlike her usual self she quite startled Cat Sinclair who sat in her lap and into whose mouth she was spooning custard. The other children, who had been feeding themselves round the nursery table under Dora's supervision, looked at her in amazement. Susan was kind-hearted, good-natured, given to a chuckle or two now and again but they had never seen nor heard the absolute mirth in her voice at that moment.

Lally had sent Dora on an errand to the kitchen before she broached the matter of the dinner party and her hope that Susan would join them. After a bewildered moment Jamie, Alec and Jack continued to eat their custard mixed with stewed apple, and, as children do, barely wondered on the strangeness of their respective mothers.

'Are't mad?' Susan spluttered after she had managed to control the hilarity that Mrs Sinclair's invitation had induced. Lally was aware that Susan had deliberately used those words to highlight her Yorkshire working-class heritage. It was some time since she had run her words together. She had made a great effort for the sake of Chris Fraser's sons who were, or would be, of the landed gentry and it would not do for them to pick up the way she had once spoken. She had acquired a veneer and a quality not often found in a woman of her class and Lally was often startled by the gradual change in her.

'No, I'm not. You still insist on looking upon yourself as coming from a class lower than mine.'

'Because I do.'

'If you did would it matter? I am extremely fond of you, Susan, no, don't look like that, it's true, and it is my dearest wish that you and I be friends but you will insist on keeping your distance as though I were superior to you. Jack is . . . I am as fond of him as I am of you and if he is to be brought up with my children then you must rise with him. This is a simple dinner party with some friends who are not . . . not high and mighty. My brother-in-law has returned home from his travels and Harry thought . . . anyway John is to be invited.'

Susan made a small sound in her throat and Lally wondered if John's feelings for Susan might be reciprocated. It was eighteen months since the death of her young husband and he would hold a special place in her heart for ever but John Burton was the friendliest, kindest, most easy-going man she had met—though Mr Harry came a close second—and she could not help but be flattered. He was not particularly handsome but what did that matter? He was of medium height, barely taller than she was, with rough fair hair that always needed cutting, kind hazel eyes, cheerful and boyish, and she felt he was badly in need of a woman's care. But that did not mean she had the cheek to think it might be *her*! Nevertheless he had a balanced and tolerant mind which did not consider her to be beneath him, talking to her of many things besides the children's health, telling her of his own plans for the many men and women and their children who came to him in ever increasing numbers, medically speaking, that is.

But as for sitting down at table with him and a group of grand folk and eating a meal that would probably be totally foreign to her . . . well, it was laughable. In her black dress and her rough hands which were taking their time to become smooth,

250

even with the creams Mrs Sinclair gave her to rub in each night, it was absolutely out of the question.

But she had not taken into consideration Lally Sinclair's determination and when Dora slipped back into the nursery and Mrs Sinclair rose to leave she had no conception of what she was in for.

She soon found out! Every evening when the dinner table was set by Jenny or Tansy, Lally took her into the dining room and explained to her every piece of cutlery and its function, how it was laid out, the wine glasses. 'Of course if you don't wish to you need not drink wine, in which case all you do is put your hand over the glass as it is offered to you.'

'Don't be daft, Mrs Sinclair. I don't know why I let yer drag me inter this lovely room an' expect me ter—'

'And don't talk to me in that way, Susan. I know perfectly well that you are doing it on purpose hoping I will relent and let you cry off.'

'I've not cried *on*, Mrs Sinclair. The whole thing is ridiculous. I'm a mill girl.'

'You are not. You are my children's governess, my friend and of great value to this household.'

'I'm a servant and the other servants . . .' Susan began desperately, staring round the elegant and comfortable dining room with its enormous oval-shaped table which could be made even bigger with extra leaves when there were guests; at the dining chairs covered in a rich blue velvet, at the paler blue silk curtains and walls, at the central chandelier hanging like icicles from an acanthus leaf-strewn central rose. At the tasteful pictures, many of which seemed to be scarcely more than a blur of pale colour but which, when studied,

251

declared themselves to be figures, flowers, trees, animals.

The maids had been astonished when Mrs Sinclair had ordered the room and the table to be set as though the dinner party were to take place this very night but she had explained she wanted a *rehearsal*, which was daft since she had seen the place set out dozens of times since she had come as a bride to the Priory. But still she was the mistress and who were they to disagree. Mrs Stevens had a look about her that said *she* might, though, when she got the mistress alone! There were cherry logs burning in the huge marble fireplace and the serving table at the end of the room opposite the wide windows was ready with everything needed for a dinner for ten guests, candles lighted, flowers, hothouse roses grown by Barty's caring hands, even exquisite finger bowls.

For a moment Lally thought she had gone too far, since it seemed to frighten Susan to paralysis then her face softened and a look of such delight spread across it she looked almost beautiful.

'Oh, Miss Lally . . .' she breathed.

'Lally . . .'

'Eeh, I never saw owt ser lovely.'

'Say that again, Susan, properly.'

'I have never seen anything so lovely in my life.'

'So you'll do it for me?'

'Yes.'

'Promise.'

'Oh yes.'

'Then let's sit down and practise what will happen on the night of the party then we will go and find you something to wear.'

252

Lally said later to her husband, despite the difficult moments which had nothing whatsoever to do with Susan, that it had all been worthwhile if only to see the look on John Burton's face when, as he entered the drawing room for pre-dinner drinks, he found Susan Harper seated demurely beside their hostess on the sofa at right angles to the fireplace.

Though autumn was creeping slyly over Yorkshire it was not cold yet and the doors to the winter garden were open and at the far end the doors to the garden had been left wide. The fragrance of the roses drifted in, mixing with the scent of lavender which edged the borders, and the beautifully perfumed Arabian jasmine in the conservatory. The drawing room was bright with candles, with flowers raided from Barty's garden.

A pale pink rose bud, which exactly matched the colour of the sash about her waist, was pinned in Susan's smoothly brushed chignon. She sat rigidly beside Lally, her hands clasped tightly together and at once John knew she was terrified. Lally smiled at him as she rose to her feet, her expression saying she was relying on him to put her unexpected guest at ease.

'Sit here next to Susan, John, while I have a word with Thomas and Ginny,' who had just entered the room, and behind them stood the tall, lounging figure of Roly Sinclair. Though she had not arranged it and was not sure how she would manage it, the arrival of John Burton, the Brackens and *Roly* almost at the same time smoothed the way as though it had been planned. John sat down next to Susan and at once began to put her at her ease by telling her how lovely she looked and how pleased he was to see her here just as though she were really one of Lally's friends from what was known as polite society. Ginny and Thomas, Ginny bubbling with that vitality which at once diverted everyone's attention to her, greeted Lally with great enthusiasm and Lally began to feel that she might have found another friend, for Ginny was so fresh and innocently vivacious.

And behind them, a pretty young woman on his arm, was Roly. Ginny and Thomas turned to him after greeting Lally and in the polite geniality the moment of meeting Roly was passed over without friction.

'Lally,' he cried, after Ginny and Thomas had moved into the drawing room, 'how wonderful to see you after all this time and still as lovely as ever. It really is grand to be home among my family again. Tomorrow I must ride over and have a look at my new niece. Now then, this gorgeous creature on my arm is Miss Beth Johnson.'

Miss Johnson simpered and for an awful moment Lally thought Roly had brought one of his actress friends but he continued lightly, 'Miss Johnson's aunt and uncle are Mr and Mrs George Bracken who I know you are acquainted with . . .' so she is perfectly respectable, he was telling her. Behind Roly and Miss Johnson Harry glowered, seemingly unaware that Emily Watson and Edward Jackson, who were to be married in the spring, having handed their outer garments to Tansy, were waiting to be greeted by their host.

'I'm so pleased to meet you, Miss Johnson. Are you staying with your aunt and uncle?' Lally asked her politely. She knew she must make an effort to

254

usher Roly and Miss Johnson into the drawing room where to her great relief Susan and John were deep in conversation with Ginny and Thomas. She must get to Harry who looked as though he might smash his fist into Roly's smiling face as his brother turned towards him. Dear God, this was going to be harder than she thought. Why had she ever imagined that she could get through an evening with Roly all smiles and insouciant chatter and Harry silent and brooding on his need to do some damage to his brother.

'Harry, Oliver and Mary have arrived. Now Oliver, you must tell us all about your trip to Venice . . .' For Mary and Oliver Watson were newly married.

Surprisingly, it was quite a success. Roly seemed to be totally absorbed with his partner at table, for Lally had hastily changed the name places and put him and Miss Johnson together. John and Susan appeared to have plenty to say to one another, Susan watchfully following his use of cutlery and Mary and Oliver Watson needed no persuasion to ramble on about the beauty of Venice. At great length they described the architecture of its main square, the Piazza San Marco, preening a little at their own cleverness, the Ponte di Rialto, which was the Rialto Bridge they explained for those not as cosmopolitan as they, and Lally could see Harry, who sat at the head of the table with Emily Watson on one side of him and Edward Jackson on the other, relax enough to smile courteously at his guests. The room looked especially lovely: the light from the flames of the fire and the dozens of candles caught the shimmer of silver and glassware and the warmth of the room brought out the fragrance of the roses. The gentlemen were resplendent in the full black and white of evening dress, a background for the ladies who were in colours ranging from Susan's dove-grey silk to the poppy red of Lally's satin. Susan's gown was high-necked and long-sleeved but the neat bodice showed off her full breasts, her slender waist, the skirt falling in rippling folds to her ankles. The touch of rose pink in her hair and about her waist, the ruffle at the hem contrived a look of elegance and simple taste and there was not one around the table—apart from John who knew her place in the house—who questioned her presence as a friend of their hostess. Lally was quite magnificent, for the colour of her dress seemed to highlight the sheen of her hair and the gleaming lambency of her eyes. The other ladies wore buttercup yellow, salmon pink, emerald green—Beth Johnson!—and cornflower blue. Lally recognised the clever hand of Miss Violet Hockley in all of them, speculating on how busy the dressmaker must have been this last week or two.

Roly continued to whisper in Miss Johnson's ear, the pair of them laughing and exchanging glances which Lally knew would please Harry but wondered if Mr and Mrs George Bracken were aware of what a philanderer Roly Sinclair might turn out to be, for Miss Johnson, a relative of theirs, was what was known as a *lady*.

The gentlemen rose to their feet as the ladies left them to their port and cigars and as Lally led them to the drawing room where Jenny was waiting to serve coffee, she could not help but notice that Miss Johnson, as soon as there were no gentlemen to admire her, languished sulkily on the sofa, answering only briefly when spoken to. Lally chatted pleasantly with Ginny Bracken, doing her best to draw Susan into the conversation and it was not until the gentlemen joined them that Susan became more animated as John made straight for her and Beth began to bridle and giggle at Roly.

It seemed that Ginny could play the piano and with songs like 'Greensleeves' and 'Strawberry Fair' rippling from beneath her fingers it was not long before they were all singing, even Harry who put his arms possessively round his wife's waist and though he noticed his brother and Miss Johnson disappear for twenty minutes, what did he care? His beloved wife had passed the test of giving a successful dinner party that had included his brother and he relaxed enough to tell himself that it was all going to work out between them.

He was handing Ginny Bracken into her carriage at the end of the evening and so was not watching as his brother whispered something in Lally's ear. Beth Johnson was still bemused by the expert kisses her escort had pressed upon her willing mouth and was equally unaware of the exchange.

'Meet me tomorrow morning in the usual place. You'll know where I mean, as will my "niece" and her "father" if you don't turn up.'

CHAPTER EIGHTEEN

He was lounging against the tall boulder where last year he had made love to her. His shoulder blades were pressed against the stone, his legs crossed at the ankle, his left hand in the pocket of his well-fitting riding breeches and in his right he held a cigar. He looked casual, at ease, and his threatening words of the night before might never have been spoken. His chestnut gelding cropped peacefully, throwing up his handsome head when Fred and Ally raced up the slope, shying away from the boisterous dogs, but a word from Roly steadied all three animals and Lally remembered he had always had a way with dogs and horses—and women!

Though it was October it was mild and he wore no jacket. His sleeves were turned back and the top buttons of his shirt were undone, revealing the crisp hair of his chest. He looked extremely handsome, beautiful even with his smoothly shaved skin which was tinted a golden amber by the sun of the lands he had visited. His eyes were a clear, velvety grey, outlined by his thick black lashes and when he grinned lazily his teeth gleamed between his well-shaped lips.

Lally felt a curious shiver go through her as he turned his startling eyes to study her. She climbed down from Merry's back, carefully arranging the skirt of her riding habit for some reason, making sure that no part of her legs, which were in any case covered by her kid breeches, was visible, wondering deep within her why she felt so vulnerable, then chiding herself for a fool because what he had said to her last night was enough to frighten any woman in the circumstances.

'I've come, as you see, Roly,' she began at once, 'simply because of the incomprehensible statement you made last night—'

'Incomprehensible!' he interrupted. His grin

deepened round the cigar between his lips. 'I'm no mathematician, my love, but I can add up the months a woman is pregnant and what has happened here makes a nonsense of it. You and I . . . er . . . were together in July of last year and it seems your daughter was born nine months to the day almost after that. Yes, I winkled it out of one of your servants who, quite unintentionally, told me the date of the birth of the child. You and Harry were married in October so, unless you and he slept together on the same day, or thereabouts, that you and I . . . er . . .'

'Honestly, Roly . . .' doing her best to sound amused though dread was icing her veins. 'What a preposterous thing to say. I have never heard anything—'

'Preposterous, is it? Then how can you account for the fact that the child was born exactly nine months—'

'Perhaps Harry and I were . . . were . . . *close* at that time. Had that occurred to you? I have always been extremely . . . fond of Harry and naturally, when I realised I was pregnant I told him of it and we were married at once. Caterina was born six months later. Prematurely, or so everyone believes.' She showed her teeth in what she hoped was a reasonable smile.

Roly watched her intently, a cat watching a mouse that was trying to escape and for the first time she noticed a twist to his mouth that could only be called cruel. A lifting of one corner that turned into a disbelieving smile. He straightened his tall frame and moved towards her and she found herself backing away. His smile deepened.

'You're surely not afraid of me, dear sister-in-

259

law?'

'Don't be absurd.'

'No, of course not, but let us say that you're telling the truth. That you and Harry were . . . *close* as you so delicately put it, that does not rule out that the child could be mine. You and I made love on this very spot. No, we didn't make love because that implies we loved one another and that's not so. We—.' Here he used a word so obscene she gasped. She had heard it before, on Harry's lips. It was a word men used to describe what they did to women they did not respect. It was insulting and she was insulted. What on earth had come over Roly that he should be so coarse all of a sudden? Or perhaps he had always had it in him and she had not noticed. Caterina *was* his child. There was no doubt about that, for she had made love to no one but him since Chris died. She could not account for the puzzling fact that in the months since Cat was born she had not quickened. Both Chris and Roly had impregnated her at once and there was nothing she longed for more than that Harry should do the same. It would cement their relationship if they had a child, a son that Harry would know was his. But so far it had not happened and it seemed, watching the curious expression on Roly's face, that some disaster was about to take place. Roly, although he had not said so, appeared to be threatening her.

'What is all this, Roly?' she asked impatiently. 'What have you got in your mind? Caterina is Harry's daughter and I would swear before God—'

He laughed. 'Perhaps you would and perhaps you would be believed but there would be planted in Harry's mind a doubt, and in the minds of others. I don't know how you persuaded him to make an honest woman of you but then he has been in love with you for as long as I can remember.'

Lally was astonished and it showed in her expression, then she remembered that she and Harry were supposed to be having an affair before Cat was born. Dear God, what a web was being woven here and she was caught in the damn thing, struggling to save not only her marriage but her reputation, her life, her children's lives. She couldn't even guess what it was that Roly wanted. Surely he did not expect her to lie down and let him do to her what he had done last year? But there was no doubt he was about to blackmail her into doing something that might hurt her, or Harry, and she could not imagine what it was. She had nothing he might want. That brief moment last year when they had lain together, she could find no other word to describe it, the moment that had produced Cat, must not be repeated, besides which she had the idea that that was not in his mind. He had women and to spare who would gladly share their beds with Roly Sinclair. He was rich, handsome, charming, the catch of the district. He was *fun*. Had he not made her life more cheerful after Chris died, taking her about, encouraging her to do the things young widows were not supposed to do but persuading her it did no harm, making her the talk of Moorend? For years she and Chris and he had been inseparable, good friends who would stand together against the rest of the world, caring not a jot for what society thought, enjoying life to the full and to hell with gossip. Chris had loved Roly as he might a brother, and so had she,

261

but had there been a side to him that neither of them had seen? Even on the day when she and Roly had shared a moment of passion on this very stretch of tough grass beside the boulders he had appeared to be contrite, filled with remorse to have *dishonoured* the widow of his best friend. Had that been an act as well? Was there some secret part of Roly Sinclair that neither of them had seen?

She sighed deeply. 'I don't know what this is all about, Roly. Why you have summoned me up here to discuss this foolish notion you seem to have that—'

'Tell me that child in your nursery is mine. That is what I have *summoned* you up here for.'

'But why?' Lally had lost the dread she had felt and only knew exasperation. 'What has got into you, Roly? Do you honestly believe that an hour up here with you, which was a mistake, of course, could produce a baby? Harry and I were lovers for weeks,' she lied. 'And the daughter that I bore was his.'

'I don't believe you. Harry is not the sort of man to make love to a woman, a lady from decent society, without marriage. He is too honourable.' His voice had contempt in it and Lally felt wonder move through her that in all these years neither she nor Chris had really known this man.

'He is honourable but we . . . were carried away . . . he was carried away and I . . .'

'Yes,' he sneered, 'you were so overcome you allowed . . .'

Lally turned away and strode to the edge of the plateau on which they stood. Her dogs followed her, keeping close to her skirt. She slapped the skirt of her riding habit with her small whip, her mind in a turmoil, for this was obviously going somewhere and for the life of her she couldn't imagine where.

Was it something to do with Harry? There had always been some dissension between the brothers which was why it worked so well when Roly was abroad and Harry was left to run the mills as he liked, but perhaps Roly was no longer satisfied with this arrangement despite the fact that it had made them enormously wealthy.

She looked out at the October landscape which was wide and empty of all but a moving straggle of sheep grazing under the morning sun. A gentle wind blew the scents of the moorland into her nostrils—heather, bilberry, sedge, cowberry—and the moor was shadowed here and there as the wind moved the clouds, forming a pattern in the valley below and on the hillside opposite. There had been an early frost which had dissolved as the sun rose. It had tinged the tussocky grass with amber and the bracken with scarlet. Small flocks of migrating birds flew restlessly over the rugged hillsides, their calls high and piercing.

She turned abruptly. Roly had resumed his position against the huge boulder, which had been carried by ice from an adjacent valley thousands of years ago and in some strange manner had perched on a scatter of other, smaller, limestone boulders. Sheltering the clearing was a group of upland oaks, their leaves almost gone at this altitude and time of the year.

'Well, Roly, I haven't the faintest notion why you have brought me up here for what you have to say is all nonsense.'

'Really!' Roly's mouth twisted into a smile that was deliberately sardonic and unkind. 'You do surprise me, but never mind you will know in good time. Harry and I have been . . . at odds for a long while now and I have had no weapon to force him into what I want. Now I have and I shall depend on you to help me. That child of yours, of *ours* is illegitimate—oh yes, make no mistake about that,' for she had gasped in horror and every vestige of colour had left her face. Her hand went out to the rough surface of the boulder but Roly merely smiled. 'Her parents are not married therefore she is—'

'Harry is . . .'

'No, he is not and if he and you do not comply with my wishes I shall let the whole of Yorkshire know it. Now then, I must be off. Let Harry know, won't you, what we have discussed and that I shall be round to see both of you shortly. I shall consult with my solicitor.' He paused for a moment, then swung himself into the saddle and trotted down the slope, breaking into a canter as he reached the rough track made by the sheep.

She watched him go with death in her heart.

*   *   *

They were at dinner before she spoke, waiting until Jenny had left the room.

'I saw Roly today.' Her voice was abrupt. Harry was helping himself to a scoop of Stilton cheese and as she broke the silence, for they had barely spoken since they had sat down, his hand holding the cheese scoop stopped in mid-air and his face closed up. His brown eyes which, when he was at

264

peace, had a golden glow about them, immediately darkened, became shuttered and Lally wondered with that part of her brain that was separate from this drama whether he would ever be able to hear his brother's name on her lips without freezing up.

'Oh, yes. I wondered where he had got to this morning. He intimated that he had something on his mind but when I turned round he had disappeared. So he was here, was he?' His voice dripped ice.

'No, we met on the moor.'

'By arrangement?'

'Yes.' She was determined to be truthful.

'So it is to begin again?'

'What?' She was bewildered.

'Your . . . associating.' His face was totally without expression but in his eyes was devastation.

'Our association? Harry . . . ?'

'Why should he want to see you secretly? Why should he want to see you at all? When did you make this assignation?'

'Assignation! Don't be so damned silly. He . . . well, I don't really know what he's up to, if you must know. Except that he threatens to . . . to expose Cat if you and I don't fall in with whatever he has in mind.'

'What in hell's name are you talking about?' Harry stood up, throwing the cheese scoop to his plate where it landed with a clatter. Just at that moment Jenny entered the room but Harry glared at her, waving his arm and telling her to get out. Lally had the impression he would have liked to say 'bugger off'! Jenny scuttled out of the room, running to the kitchen with the tale that the master and mistress were having a row and really she

265

didn't know why Mr Harry had to speak so roughly to her since it was nothing to do with Jenny. She had only gone in to . . . Biddy told her to hold her tongue and the atmosphere in the kitchen was almost as tense as that in the dining room.

'Roly told me to be on the moor this morning where he wanted to talk to me about *our* daughter. Not yours and mine but *his* and mine. That's what he said.'

'Why in hell's name didn't you tell me this last night?'

'I don't know. I suppose I wanted to find out what he was after first. And he does want something, not from me but from you. He talked about solicitors and . . . and, unless we complied with whatever he has in mind he would tell the whole of Yorkshire that Cat was . . . was his child. Oh, Harry . . .' She stood up and tentatively touched his arm where he stood by the dining-room window staring out into the dark garden but seeing only his own and her reflection in the glass.

He recoiled slightly, so that her hand fell to her side. His face was composed now, his anguish well hidden. He had a hold of himself, not allowing her to see what she was doing to him. Their marriage had moved along tranquilly. They did not quarrel or disagree on anything of importance. She ran their home with Mrs Stevens in real control and the children, including the baby, were settled and happy in the nursery. Susan Harper ruled it, and them, with firm kindness and he had thought that their life together was settling down to a pleasant rhythm. His wife was the most stylish in Moorend and he was proud of her, encouraging her to spend a fortune on the plain, pastel-tinted

266

afternoon gowns in which she looked so well, the rich poppy evening gown, the black velvet against which her skin was whiter than buttermilk. He bought her a victoria to drive in, far superior to the conventional landau when it came to the fashion of wide crinolines, and he had been pleased when it seemed they were to become a fashionable couple. They gave informal dinner parties and the house functioned with a smoothness he found very satisfying. Of course, he knew she did not love him but he had known that before he married her and if he was perfectly honest with himself he had no doubt she would not have married him had she not been pregnant with his brother's child. All he prayed for, or would if he was a praying man, was that she would bear another child. *His!* And that one day she would come to love him.

But by God, he loved her! Every day his love grew, for she had become a complete woman, content in her own life, shaping their life and that of the children in a way that pleased him, obliging him every night in their bed with what he thought hopefully was real enthusiasm, and though he, as was his wont, kept his feelings to himself, he sometimes imagined she was beginning to look on him with a softness he found most encouraging.

And now this bombshell!

Lally watched his shoulders slump and wanted to go to him to . . . well, she wasn't sure what she wanted to do but his rejection of her a moment ago seemed to imply he did not want or need comfort.

'What are we to do?' she asked hesitantly. 'Would he really destroy our lives and the lives of our children if we do not do what he wants, whatever that is?'

Harry passed his hand over his face, thrusting it through his hair. He walked slowly towards the door, opening it for her to pass through then followed her into the drawing room. The dogs were there, sprawled in front of the fire, and they both thumped their tails on the thick carpet in greeting. He sat her down on the sofa, moving the dogs with his foot, then poured himself a stiff whisky before sitting down opposite her.

'It is widely known in Moorend that Roly and I are not good friends. You look surprised; well, it's true. And you must know that . . . what happened between you and my brother'—his face was grim and she turned away to stare into the fire—'does not endear him to me. But that is not all of it. They say in commercial circles that neither of us appreciates what the other contributes to the business. Our looms and frames are working to capacity and to order, though I'm beginning to see Roly's constant journeyings as self-indulgence but Roly insists that without his travels there would be no orders to fill. There has been for a while a fast-accumulating tension between us which Roly sets out quite deliberately to aggravate. He has always been ambitious but he lacks caution. He is autocratic and shrewd but he is not always fair. Perhaps this is a way for him to achieve what he wants.'

'What is that, Harry?'

'We will have to wait and see. Now, would you like some hot chocolate before we go to bed?'

He made love to her that night with a passionate abandon that surprised her, revealing more of himself and his feelings than she had ever seen before. His hands and tongue explored the whole

268

surface of her skin, the curves and crevices of her body with minute care, all scrutinised and caressed. His teeth possessed themselves of the lobes of her ears, the bursting rosy nipples of her breasts, not painfully but compellingly as though to let her know and to reassure himself that she belonged wholly to him. His penetration of her was deep and explosive and when it was done, though she did not herself climax, his body nailed itself shuddering to hers and he groaned as though in agony.

Though neither of them knew it she became pregnant that night.

The days passed and though she questioned him each evening as they dined together he had nothing to tell her. He would wait for Roly to make the first move, he said. It seemed Roly was taking a great deal of interest in the actual running of the mill, surprising the hands by being at the locked mill gate of either High Clough, West Heath or South Royd at the amazing hour of half past five every morning, obliging latecomers to stand outside until breakfast time and whereas Harry had thought the loss of three hours' earning punishment enough Roly fined them as well. When Harry remonstrated with him, he was told that he was concerned only with efficiency which improved time-keeping in the sheds.

'And what is to happen when you go off on your extensive travels again?' Harry asked him mildly.

'We will see,' Roly answered slyly.

The days moved on and became colder as October turned to November. It was becoming too raw now for the children to roam about the gardens and woodland with Lally, Susan and Dora, but on one fine day when the sun shone from a brilliantly blue sky they all wrapped up well and ventured out. The visit to Folly Farm in the summer had resulted in three kittens joining the nursery which was becoming overcrowded with four children and two big dogs. Caterina was considered too young as yet for a kitten but Jamie, Alec and Jack were given one each. Goodness knows, said Polly McGinley, who the father of the litter was, for each kitten was an entirely different colour. Coal black with a white star on its pointed little face was one, a soft and velvety grey another and a pure white little thing which was immediately appropriated by Jamie who was, as the biggest and oldest, the leader in the nursery. Within a week all interest had been lost and it was left to Dora to transfer the three waifs to the kitchen where they settled down equably with the kitchen tabby until, as children do, they carried them off back to the nursery to be played with for an hour.

The three of them were in the perambulator with the delighted baby, curled under her soft blanket, while Jamie, Alec and Jack hopped, skipped, ran, jumped about the vehicle, darting off in different directions to investigate some fascinating object they spotted.

'Have you seen anything of John recently?' Lally asked Susan, for it was accepted in the house that Doctor Burton was much taken with the widow and the gossip in the kitchen was rife.

Susan blushed, then lifted her head since it was no one's business but her own. Doctor Burton really had no need to come to the Priory in a medical capacity, for everyone in the nursery and

270

out of it was in rude health. But it was known that he was in the nursery at least once a week and on her day off she disappeared, telling no one, not even Lally, where she had been.

'I don't know what you mean,' she answered coolly.

'Oh, come on, Susan, don't go all coy on me. You know he is . . . sweet on you.'

'Sweet! Lally Sinclair, how dare you use such a word when speaking of a respectable gentleman. Besides which it is no one's business but ours.'

'So there is something. Has he spoken of . . .'

'What if he has?' Susan tossed her head, manoeuvring the perambulator between the roots of two massive oak trees, for by now they had entered the woodland known as Tangle Wood through which the rough path led to Folly Farm. Jack was doing his best to climb over a fallen tree trunk, following the other two boys. The dogs had raced off somewhere, probably following the scent of a rabbit and Dora, conscious of her responsibilities, was trailing behind the two older boys. They were intent on being the first to reach Mrs Polly, who made the best gingerbread men in the world.

For a moment the two women were distracted by Jack's efforts and when the two men stepped out from behind the gnarled and twisted trunk of an old holly tree they were taken by surprise.

It was Jed and Ham Weaver.

CHAPTER NINETEEN

The two women regarded the two men, first with surprise then with annoyance. Well, Lally was annoyed. She knew them, of course and she also knew that Harry had spoken of turning the Weavers off their land but it seemed they were still here. They studied her and Susan with some insolence and she felt her annoyance turn to anger.

'What do you think you're doing,' she asked them sharply, 'trespassing on private property? This land belongs to my husband and the tenants will not be at all pleased to know that you are wandering about, and with rifles over your shoulders,' for both men did indeed have old rifles slung across their broad shoulders.

'Eeh, will yer listen to 'er, Ham,' one of them said, turning to smile at his companion who smiled back. 'Trespassin' she ses an' us doing nowt but walk through woods on our way 'ome. Short cut it be ter Foxwell.' Which was not true, for Foxwell, where the Weavers 'farmed' was on the far side of the Priory from where Lally and Susan had just come.

'Well, I suppose that depends where you've come from, Mr Weaver. I hear there is a lot of game to be had in Tangle Wood.'

'Nay, d'yer see any game on us, missis?' the first one snickered, holding out his arms in a gesture that asked her to search him, in fact he would enjoy it if she did.

The baby in the perambulator stared with open mouth at the two men, her eyes wide with interest and a flicker of anxiety, for she could sense the disquiet in her mother and in Susan. The kittens popped their pretty faces out of their cocoon and in the far distance Lally could hear the barking of the two dogs, wishing they were here with them now.

'I shall tell my husband that I have seen you hanging about in the woodland with guns on your person—'

'Oh, on our *person*,' sneered the first man and both of them laughed. 'We wasn't doin' no 'arm, missis, as I say, tekkin a short cut.'

'You were doing no such thing. You are Jed and Ham Weaver, aren't you, and have no right to be—'

'We've as much right as you two lovely ladies ter be—'

'Get out of our way, if you please,' Lally declared stoutly, grabbing at the handle of the pcrambulator, for the two men had begun to edge towards them. 'Let us by with the perambulator.'

'The *perambulator*, is it? Well, I can see where it might be a bit awkward fer yer. Why don't us give a 'and across this little stream? Come on, Ham, don't just stand there.'

The little stream to which he alluded was almost dried up and anyone, even small boys, could easily step across it. The light in the glade was still shady despite the falling of the autumn leaves but the sun was lower in the sky. The drift of leaves had begun to litter the ground and the recent wet weather had made it slippery.

'Don't touch that perambulator,' Susan said sharply and both men stopped, then the one who must be Jed, since he had called the second man

273

Ham, smiled, a menacing sort of smile which matched his next words.

'That's a mighty pretty babby yer've got there, missis. Be a shame ter jiggle it across this bit o' stream. No, us two'll gerrit across. We wouldn't want ter 'urt babby, would we? 'Ere, Ham, ger 'old o' that end an' us'll 'ave it across in no time . . .' And before either woman could protest the equipage was wrenched from their protective hands, tossed across the narrow trench of the stream and placed carelessly on the other side. Both Lally and Susan leaped across and huddled defensively over the baby who had begun to wail in distress but the men merely laughed, shouldering their rifles and marching off down the track.

'Glad ter be of 'elp, ladies,' Jed shouted over his shoulder, then they disappeared into the trees. The man addressed as Ham had not spoken one word and Lally had time to wonder if he was half-witted.

Both women were trembling when they reached Folly, though they did their best to conceal it. The three boys were sitting round Polly's well-scrubbed table tucking into gingerbread men and a glass of milk each, though Polly was standing anxiously at the door looking out for the two women and the perambulator with the precious baby in it. Cat was still crying and though both women had longed to stop and pick her up and comfort her they were eager to get to the safety of Folly Farm. Polly plucked the infant out of the perambulator and held her in loving arms.

'Wheer yer bin?' she asked accusingly as though the pair of them had been up to no good. 'Us was wonderin' where yer'd got to. Them boys an't lass 'ave bin 'ere a good ten minutes.'

'Don't say anything, Susan,' Lally had whispered as they approached the farm, 'or she'll have Sean and Denny out after the Weavers and I don't want any trouble.'

'But, Lally, you can't mean to—'

'Harry will deal with it. He means to turn them off and I'll make sure he does it.'

She was very quiet on the way home, she and Susan almost running, with Dora in some confusion behind, but the dogs were with them, keeping close to the perambulator for, as animals do, they sensed some tension in the helter-skelter dash through the woodland. Dora carried the protesting Jamie while Alec and Jack were jammed in with Cat and the kittens and they did not stop until the familiar gate into the stable yard came into sight.

'Why, what's ter do, Miss Lally?' Carly asked her apprehensively but she did her best to smile and shake her head. What with one thing and another she did not feel that she could even answer Biddy's anxious questions. First the appalling intimidation when Roly had threatened to expose her and Harry to a scandal of terrible proportions and now this menace from the Weaver brothers who seemed to be promising trouble, for it appeared they meant actual harm to her children.

'No, it's nothing, Biddy, really. We just wanted to get home but I'd be obliged if you would ask Carly to ride up to High Clough and fetch my husband home.'

'Fetch Mr Sinclair home?' Biddy was astonished and so were the maids who were scattered about the kitchen at their various tasks. They had all stopped, of course, turning to stare at Mrs Sinclair.

275

Nobody fetched Mr Sinclair anywhere! He was the master and as such came and went as he pleased and they waited expectantly for further enlightenment.

The children were being hurried, fractious and vociferous with it, through the door to the hallway on their way to the nursery, Susan doing her best to keep them from the inevitable questions that she knew Mrs Stevens would ask. Mrs Stevens had a special place in this household, since before Susan came to reside in it and had become, or so Lally said, her friend, Mrs Stevens had been Lally's confidante. They were still close and Mrs Stevens thought it her right to treat Lally as she might a relative. She had not taken kindly to Susan's inclusion in one or two dinner parties given by Mr and Mrs Sinclair, those that had also included John Burton, and had been heard to say that some people should be careful not to get above themselves. It was none of Susan's doing, naturally, but who could stand against Lally when she made up her mind to do something?

Picking up the baby from the perambulator which had been lifted into the kitchen, she shepherded her charges before her. Jack was awkward. He wanted to be picked up too, since after all she was his mother, or his *mama* as he was being taught to call her, so with some difficulty she lifted him with her other arm and hurriedly left the room.

'Now then, lass, what's all this?' Biddy began, but Lally lifted her head imperiously, repeating her request that Mr Sinclair be brought home at once. She had been badly shaken by the confrontation with the Weaver brothers, for the implication had

276

been that they might harm her children and *that* really did frighten her.

*　　　*　　　*

'I shall have them arrested at once,' Harry shouted, for once his calm, rather remote demeanour scattered to the wind. He had been meaning to instruct Cameron to give a month's notice to the rabble who rented Foxwell Farm and had been musing whether to offer it to Denny McGinley, son of Sean and Polly. Folly Farm was well run and profitable and kept the two men, father and son, fully occupied, but now that Denny was a family man he might appreciate a farm of his own. They could help each other, he and his father, and with casual manual labour could easily manage the two farms. Foxwell was in a poor state but Denny was a hard worker, willing to do anything on his father's farm and would be exactly right to put Foxwell back to how it should be. Harry would give him some help to rebuild the farmhouse and the byres. The land was half derelict so he would ask no rent for the first four quarters and since he was not getting rent from the Weavers as he should he would not be out of pocket.

'No, Harry, don't get the police involved, please. Just turn the family out and make sure they leave the district. They . . . they made no actual threat today but Susan and I were . . . were startled. They had evidently been out with their guns, poaching, though they had nothing on them . . .' remembering Jed's brazen offer to be searched.

'They had probably hidden what they had poached but nevertheless I feel—'

277

'Please, Harry, it will only make them more . . . more . . .' She was going to say more menacing but decided it was not a word she should use to her husband. 'Just let's get them off our property and that will be enough. They did us no harm.'

'But they might do.'

'No, I promise we will not walk that way again until they are gone from the district or unless one of the men is with us.'

Harry brooded on this for several minutes then took a deep breath. 'I shall ride over with Cameron tomorrow and give them all notice,' then began to tell her of his plans for Denny McGinley of which she approved heartily.

'Now,' she said hesitantly, 'what of . . . of Roly? Did you speak to him?'

Harry's face hardened and Lally felt her heart sink. How were they to discuss this terrible dilemma if every time Roly's name was mentioned Harry turned away from her, and if they were not to talk about it how was she to know what was happening? She could hardly ask Roly himself and if her husband did not relent and well . . . she supposed *forgive* her, how would it be resolved?

'No, I did not since he did not appear at any of the mills and was not at Mill House when I called. He threatened you with a solicitor so I presume that is where he has gone.'

'Oh, Harry, what is it he can want?' she asked disconsolately, her face sad. They were sitting in their lovely drawing room drinking their after-luncheon coffee, for Harry had come like a madman on Piper when he received the news that the mistress wanted him at once. They were both unaware that Jenny had gone back to the kitchen

278

with a long face after serving them, saying that there was something badly wrong with Miss Lally and Mr Harry.

At once Biddy turned on her, her own face filled with worry. She had questioned Miss Lally this morning on the strangeness of her and Susan's entrance into the kitchen and their obvious concern over something that had happened while they were out with the children but she had got nowhere, brushed off with a vague excuse about the children being tired and now there was this. Jenny, who had been employed at the Priory for years, could exactly gauge the moods, the worries, the state of affairs—even if she did not know their cause—of the family and there was definitely something happening that she was not being told about. Biddy was the head of the female servants and was on good terms with the outside men and if there was any trouble she was usually the first to hear of it, if not from Miss Lally herself, then from the rest of the staff who might whisper about it. She did not believe in gossip and in fact firmly opposed it. Nevertheless she did like to know what was going on!

*   *   *

The scene at Foxwell Farm the next day became extremely dangerous and as Harry stood up to Jed Weaver he was glad he had not sent Cameron to evict the tenants on his own and that as an added precaution he had taken one of the finest hunting rifles money could buy, made by James Purdey, which both the Weaver boys, who were lounging by the fire, recognised at once.

279

They stood up slowly, ready to say or do anything that might put them in a good light, for they thought Mr Sinclair had come here to complain over yesterday's incident. They had only helped the ladies with the child's carriage, they would say, for the stream was wide and certainly had not meant to give offence. But they were not given the chance.

'Is your father about?' was all their landlord said. Cameron, who was not a coward, stood shoulder to shoulder with him in the debris and dirt of the farm kitchen. An appetising smell came from a pan simmering on the fire and Harry almost smiled, for in it would be one of the rabbits off the Priory estate. They did not go short of food in the Weaver household.

The question took the two big men by surprise. What had their pa to do with what happened yesterday?

'Reckon 'e's digging vegetable garden,' one of them said, doing his best to appear polite. The Weavers were not farmers but down-at-heel vagrants, living on their wits and what the girls earned on their backs, and when Arty Weaver, warned by one of the women, came in, simpering and rubbing his hands as though overjoyed to see his landlord, it was all Harry could do not to break into a laugh. There were hens perched on the filthy table and Harry declined to sit down and partake of a jug of cider.

'I'm not here on a social visit, Weaver. You have been warned time and again that if you did not pay your rent and keep this farm in good order I would evict you. As you have done neither I have no option but to do so. I am giving you a month's notice to quit. By the end of the year I shall expect you to have gone. Note I am allowing you some leeway. Have I made myself clear?' He shifted his rifle, which was broken over his arm, to another position, drawing their attention to the fact that he meant business. Cameron, who had his own rifle though not as good as the Purdey, also lifted his to his shoulder.

For a moment there was total silence then Mrs Weaver, who had dragged herself in behind her husband, began to wail but the sound of her cries of where should they go, and how should they manage and what had they done to deserve this was drowned by the furious bellows of the two boys.

'This is 'cause of them two bloody women, innit?' Jed roared. 'Just 'cause we give 'em a 'and wi' that there carriage what babby sat in she took agin us. Keep yer bloody 'ands off us who's way above the likes of you an' your kind. Well, yer can bloody well rot 'cause we're not movin from 'ere, are we, lad?' turning to his brother who, being slower than Jed, had not quite caught up with what was happening. Mrs Weaver had sat down in the moth-eaten chair, her head in her hands, for though she was not as daft as Ham or as mad as Jed she knew that this was the end and there was nothing any of them could do about it. Arty was bobbing and weaving, wringing his hands and explaining that he would have the rent in Mr Sinclair's hand this very day but as he had told him a while back he needed the loan of a plough-horse if he was to make anything of the fields about the farm and really, he did think Mr Sinclair might give them a bit of warning . . .

281

'I'm giving you warning now, Weaver. Over a month's notice for you to find somewhere else. And'—he turned suddenly on Jed who was straining to escape his brother's hand, his language foul and threatening—'if you don't curb your tongue and rein in that temper of yours I shall be forced to do it for you.'

Cameron began to look anxious. He was willing to stand beside his employer while notice was given but he was not really prepared to become involved in fisticuffs. Mr Sinclair was tall but he was not built like Jed Weaver who had been known to fell Jack Eccles, the blacksmith in Moorend who had done a bit of prize-fighting in his youth. Mr Sinclair was lean, wiry, strong, there was no doubt of it but hardly capable of taking on Jed Weaver.

Harry deliberately raised his rifle and aimed it at Jed Weaver whose vitriolic language dried up at once but Cameron still felt uneasy, for though his words had stopped, the deadly expression in his eyes had not gone away. Mr Sinclair waved the rifle and indicated that the Weaver brothers were to leave the filthy kitchen and move outside. Mrs Weaver's wails became even more hysterical and the old man dithered by her side.

'I want you all out of here today,' Harry growled. 'Not only have you failed completely to keep my property in good order, paid no rent and poached my game, you have insulted my wife and her companion. Pack up your belongings . . .' allowing his gaze to wander round the room, for what in this foetid place could possibly be worth taking? It was this that was his undoing. The moment his eyes left Jed Weaver the man leaped forward with a roar of outrage, his shoulder hitting

282

Harry in his midriff. The gun went off, the shot harmlessly entering the ceiling. Jed wrested the gun away and threw it into the corner and then with maddened care proceeded to land blow after blow about Harry's head and face, kicking him with his heavy boots as he fell. Cameron, like them all, was stunned for a moment but as Jed's boot broke Harry's nose and blood flowed across his face he lifted his own rifle and struck Jed in the head with the butt, knocking him semi-conscious. He rolled away to land at his mother's feet. She screamed. Ham stood turned to stone, for without Jed to guide him he was no more than a shambling child.

'' 'Ere . . . 'ere . . . let's 'ave no punch-ups,' Arty Weaver foolishly remonstrated, as Harry was lifted to his feet, even going as far as to hold out a helping hand, ready to brush him down if needed. Harry took the arm Cameron held out to him and without another word they shuffled from the kitchen and out into the fresh air. Their horses were tethered to the broken fence and silently Cameron helped his employer on to Piper's back, mounted his own animal, took Piper's reins and led the bay out of the clearing and on to the track that led towards the Priory. Harry was barely conscious. Blood streamed from his broken nose and he only just managed to keep his seat on the horse.

*   *   *

The maids in the kitchen had screamed as long and as piercingly as Mrs Weaver when Cameron, with Carly to help him, half carried their master across the threshold. Carly had saddled both Piper and

Jasper, Mr Cameron's mount, and had known where they were going and like the maids had felt a great desire to yell in consternation when he had spied them ambling slowly back across the field that led to the stable-yard gate. The commotion in the kitchen reminded Biddy of bedlam, she was to say afterwards, though she had never been inside one. The mistress was ready to shriek with the rest of them but, give her her due, she steadied herself and with a curt nod at Carly told him to ride like the devil for Doctor Burton and when he had done that he was to go directly to the police station in Ward's End and bring back the constable, for evidently murder had been attempted and they all knew who had attempted it.

Lally felt the pain of Harry's injuries as though they had been inflicted on her though her pain was in a different place. In her chest where her heart lay was a steady throbbing, a dull and heavy feeling of shame that she had not really recognised and acknowledged Harry's special understanding for those less fortunate than himself. He had saved Susan from a life of poverty, relieved her suffering when Sam died, and it was well known in Moorend that his school at High Clough and what might almost be called a nursery for working mothers at his mills relieved the worry of those who worked his looms. He had done what no man would do that she knew of and that was marry the woman who had dishonoured him with his own brother, accepting the resulting child as his own. This good man had done nothing to deserve what those Weaver brothers had done to him. He had given them chance after chance, leaving them for months to muddle through, to work the farm, to pay the owing rents, and turned a blind eye to their poaching. He had shown his beneficence in a hundred ways to scores of folk but if it was spoken about he would get angry and deny his good deeds as though they were something to be ashamed of. His poor battered face, hardly recognisable as the one she had kissed the night before, lay on the pillow. His blackened eyes were closed, his long eyelashes—why had she not recognised how long and thick they were?—made a fan on his bruised cheek and with a gentle movement she leaned over him and kissed them. He was deep under the sedative Doctor John had given him and did not wake but his mouth lifted at the corner in a half smile.

She was sitting by his bedside after Doctor John had left, holding his hand and her mind went back over all the quiet, unobserved acts of caring her husband had performed. He showed a face of calmness, steady and even remote, but his heart was warm, decent, generous and that warmth was beginning to percolate into her own heart where before only Chris had resided. In the last few days he had done his best to allay her fears in respect of his brother who was intimidating their calm lives and the lives of her children. He had ridden out to Foxwell, again in her defence, to rid them of the menace of the Weaver family and here he lay, battered and unconscious and still he was threatened by Roly Sinclair. Still he was to know no peace.

The police constables, two of them since the Weavers were a formidable family, had gone over to Foxwell to arrest the brothers but had reported back to say the place was empty; at least the

285

rubbish was still there but the family had gone. But what did that mean? Arty and his wife, and their innumerable daughters who had been out earning their living when Harry and Cameron had called, had been seen over towards Blackley End, begging at the crossroads and had been moved on, for though they had taken no part in Mr Sinclair's beating, begging was not allowed in the parish.

And so, until Harry was recovered, which might take a while Doctor John told her, for he thought Harry might have a couple of broken ribs beside the injuries to his face, it was up to her to find out what it was Roly wanted.

Though he did not say so John Burton thought Harry Sinclair might also have some damage to his skull.

CHAPTER TWENTY

He was sitting behind Harry's large, mahogany desk. Its embossed leather top was scattered with samples of Sinclair cloth, sheaves of paper, account books, records of sales through which he had evidently been rifling. It was a large room, richly carpeted and furnished with comfortable leather chairs, for Harry often met customers here. A big square window gave a perfect view of the mill yard and in the fireplace a cheerful blaze warmed the room. The clerk in the outer office had been ready to announce her but she had brushed past him and entered the room without knocking, seriously offending him, for it was his job to interrogate callers.

Automatically, as a gentleman should, Roly stood up as she appeared in the doorway but she could see by the expression on his face as soon as he recognised her he wished he hadn't bothered since she was beneath such considerations in his opinion.

He was smoking a cigar and the rich aroma drifted across to her. He was immaculately dressed, his shirt front crisply ironed and as white as freshly fallen snow. He wore a black dress coat cut back just below waist level as far as the side seams of his trousers, the skirt at the back reaching his knees; his trousers were striped in grey and black and his cravat was tied in a flat bow at the front. He looked the picture of an elegant and fashionable young gentleman.

'I'm sorry, Mr Sinclair,' the clerk apologised, 'she was past me before . . .'

He waved the clerk away. 'It's all right, Hawkins. Close the door after you.'

He sat down without offering her a seat.

'Well, my dear sister-in-law, this is a pleasure. What can I do for you? And may I say you look quite magnificent. You grow more beautiful every time I see you. Motherhood seems to suit you but I'm sure this is not a social call and I'm sorry I can't offer you refreshments. As you can see I'm very busy in Harry's absence but I should be glad if you would tell him I want to see him on a matter of business. You see—'

'Harry is . . . not well.' The words slipped smoothly from between her lips, for she had been determined she would not allow him to bait her into a confrontation. All she wished to do was to find out what was in his mind. What he wanted

287

from her and Harry. He was sitting in Harry's office behind Harry's desk which did not bode well. He was arrogant, sure of himself and with what he thought of as a weapon to threaten them with, his belief that Caterina was his child, he was lounging in Harry's chair, no doubt smoking Harry's cigars and giving orders to Harry's office staff.

He shifted in surprise as she spoke, his lips parting, the expression on his face changing to consternation then as quickly as it came it faded and he smiled.

'Not well! You mean he is hiding at home and sending his wife to do his dirty business? You are the one to tell him what it is I'm after?'

'What are you after, Roly?' She moved slowly across the deep carpet and seated herself in the chair beside the fire, turning it slightly so that she could see his face. She looked her best, she knew she did. She had dressed in a new gown the colour of pale sherry, the skirt wide, the sleeves tight as was the bodice, showing off the lovely curve of her breast. Over it she had on a velvet cloak the colour of dark chocolate lined with mink which she had thrown back as she sat down. It was raining and her short hair was starred with raindrops that looked like diamonds and her cheeks were pink with suppressed anger. Her blue-green eyes snapped and gleamed and though she was holding herself tight, determined not to lose control of her temper, the effort enhanced her loveliness.

'Well, I should prefer to discuss it with Harry but if he is . . . *unwell* I shall have to wait until he is recovered.' His voice was filled with contempt.

'Before you say another word against your brother let me tell you what happened the other day. My friend Susan Harper and I were walking in the woods when we were accosted by two men, sons of the tenants from one of our farms. Ham and Jed Weaver. They were . . . insolent. The farm their father works is in a poor way. They have paid no rents for months so Harry rode over there to turn the family off and to threaten the brothers with the police but . . . it was . . . they attacked him, broke a couple of ribs, so the doctor said, and his nose and . . .' She did not go on, for she had no intention of telling his brother that Harry, although he had regained consciousness, did not seem to know what had happened to him. He lay peacefully in their bed, allowing the attentions of John Burton, of herself, of Susan, of the housemaids, smiling at her when she entered the bedroom and holding out his hand for her to take and was so unlike his usual assertive self she had felt compelled to ride over and see what the devil Roly was up to. She had expected him to pay a call on the Priory and make clear what he had in mind for her and Harry but when he did not come she decided she could wait no longer.

'Tell me what you want, if you please and I will pass the message on to Harry. He is still in no state to be concerned with your sackless nonsense,' using a word that she had heard the servants use when some foolishness had occurred.

'Does he discuss his affairs with you?'

'Is it any of your business?' It surprised her how easy it was to meet him at this level of cool hostility.

'Probably not, but unless he knows what is happening, or *will* be happening, which apparently you are to discuss with him, there is no point in you

289

and me continuing. I want him to sell his part of the business to me or, if he will not then we can split it. A further mill will be built to accommodate the extra work which *my* efforts have brought in then the four mills will be divided. Two to him and two to me or I will give him a fair price for the lot if he cares to name one and I'm sure you could live very comfortably on what I'm prepared to offer.'

He leaned back in his chair and took a deep drag on his cigar, the picture of casual ease, a man with no concerns or worries, for did he not hold the upper hand.

She picked up a small object from the table beside her, a paperweight, then replaced it a further inch or two along the polished surface.

'Or you will spread it about Yorkshire that my daughter, *Harry's* daughter, is in fact not Harry's daughter at all but yours. That you and I had an affair and that Cat is the result. That Harry married me to cover up my immorality since the man is never to blame.'

'Exactly!'

'I shall put your proposition to Harry and let you know what he has to say.'

'Perhaps I shall ride up and have a word with him myself.'

'No,' she said sharply, her mind on the inert figure of her husband as she had last seen him. He was propped up in their bed drinking the draught Doctor John had mixed for him. John was of the opinion that Harry should be kept quiet. That he should stay in his bed until his ribs were healed and his face, which was a mass of half-healed contusions and multicoloured bruises, was back to normal. Until his nose on which Doctor John had moulded a rough cast was mended. And the worrying thing was that Harry allowed it. He seemed perfectly happy to be helped from the bed to the flush lavatory in the small water closet off the bedroom or to the cast-iron tub that was encased in painted tiles in the bathroom, one of the outdoor men giving him a hand. He was cheerful, lying in a contented state, or so it appeared, but turning frequently towards the door, Tansy or Jenny, who shared the task of watching over him when the mistress was not there, reported, pleased when Miss Lally entered the room.

But Roly Sinclair was shrewd. He had dealt with hundreds of men since the day he had entered the business and he was a good judge of character. Lally was hiding something. Her sharpness of tone when she had told him not to come to the Priory informed him that there was some underlying reason for keeping him from his brother and, though he said nothing then, he made up his mind that he would ride over to the Sinclair home and demand to see Harry who had never had a day's illness in his life and who would never, unless it was a matter of life and death, miss a day's work at one of his mills.

Lally stood up and smoothed out her skirt. He did not stand when she did, his insolence once more letting her know that he held her in no respect.

She shook her head in total disbelief. 'Well, I will tell Harry of your infantile suggestion, for it is infantile to believe you can run this business on your own, but I think I can say with perfect truth that you are wasting your time. You cannot be in

291

two places at the same time. If you were to do what Harry does, which is produce the cloth, going each day to the mills, who is to sell it abroad as you do now?'

'Oh, don't worry your pretty little head about that,' he interrupted her with one of those ridiculous statements men use when speaking of women. 'I have a man in mind who could do what I do. A clever man I met in the way of business. A born salesman so with him in place I shall be my own master. I shall have no need to listen to Harry.'

'You must be mad,' she said contemptuously, moving towards the door, 'thinking you can run a business without Harry. You are two of the wealthiest, most successful worsted manufacturers in the county.'

'But I have to defer to Harry before I can produce or sell a yard of cloth.' His face was twisted in some strange way and she realised that this had been burning inside him for a very long time and the strange thing was they none of them had noticed it. He had presented his smiling face, his charming manners, his cheerful exterior to them all—except perhaps Harry who was sharper than most—and now he had seized on the chance to put what he had always wanted into practice. To be in complete control!

'Well, I can tell Harry what you have just told me but, believe me, he will think as I do. That you are mad.'

He shrugged. 'Perhaps, but I mean what I say. Now, I have work to do so if you will excuse me. I shall be up to see Harry with my solicitor to—'

'You will come nowhere near Harry, Roly

292

Sinclair,' she hissed. 'He is in no fit state to discuss this nonsense and it *is* nonsense. I don't know what your financial resources are but I imagine this offer, or demand you are making, will stretch them quite considerably, if it is accepted which I seriously doubt.'

'My word, quite the little hell cat . . .'

'Oh, go to the devil!'

She marched down the stairs and flung herself into the carriage which waited in the yard. Carly glanced back at her furious face and, without a word, turned towards the gate and home. The afternoon was drawing in, late autumn shadows stretching across the lane. A bird was winging homewards across the thin, cool air and Lally felt a great void inside, a sense of futility, for what was to be done? Roly wanted the Sinclair mills and would do anything to get them. He wanted to call High Clough, West Heath and South Royd and the new mill he hoped to build, his own. If Harry refused and tried to force Roly to a split—since there was no way he would sell—what would it do to him and their lives together? To the children, especially Cat who was not even his child. Would he declare war on Roly, call his bluff and risk exposing the whole family, her boys, her precious daughter, herself, to a scandal that would rock the parish? How could she even ask him, report to him what Roly had said to her? In his present state he was not fit to deal with it, even if he understood, which she had begun to doubt. Until he was recovered she must keep this to herself. Oh, God . . . Oh, sweet Jesus, what was she to do?

*　　　*　　　*

293

Susan looked up sharply when she entered the nursery on her return. Lally had not even stopped to remove her cloak, feeling the need to immerse herself in the sweetness, the laughter, the pure innocence of the children's world after the taint of corruption from which she had just come. Susan knew at once that something was wrong. The children were eating what was known as nursery tea but Susan, having no truck with only bread and butter and plain biscuits which was what most nannies favoured, had laid out fruit—apples, oranges, bananas—with plain bread and butter, jelly and ice cream and when they had eaten their fruit they were allowed one of the delicious assortment of cakes Biddy had made that day. Lemon cake, coconut cake, snow cake, only one each, of course, but they had learned that when they had demolished what Susan considered was good for them, they might have a treat.

Dora was there and with a nod to the nursemaid, indicating that she was to take charge, Susan rose to her feet, took Lally's arm and led her from the nursery up the stairs to her own comfortable sitting room in the roof space of the house. Susan had a spirit stove, a kettle and all that was necessary to make tea, which she did, putting a cup in Lally's hand.

'Now then, what's wrong? I know you are worried about Mr Harry and no wonder but what has happened this afternoon?'

Lally began to weep, the tears running silently across her pale cheeks and dripping into her cup of tea. 'Oh, Susan, what am I to do? I can't manage this without Harry and how can I bother him with it when he is . . . not himself?' Her tears continued to flow and Susan, who was not a demonstrative woman, put out a hand to her but could not quite bring herself to put her arms about her as she longed to do. They were sitting one on either side of the bright fire that burned in her grate, the coals for which were brought up regularly by Dulcie, the kitchen-maid. Dulcie was just fourteen, a willing girl new to her job and having no idea of the hierarchy of the kitchen was happy to do jobs at which the others turned up their noses.

'I don't know where to begin,' Lally sobbed, and it was at this moment there came a knock at the door and without waiting to be invited Biddy marched in. She was aware that this was Mrs Harper's private domain but she had just been told that Miss Lally had come in from wherever it was she had been and, according to Carly who had begged a cup of tea at the back door, was 'fashed' about summat that had happened at the mill! Miss Lally at the mill! Biddy was on the warpath at once, for she had been told nothing about the mill and if her lamb had gone straight up to Susan's she wanted to know what it was all about.

'Now then,' she declared, 'what's all this about you going up to the mill and what's . . . eeh, chuck, what on earth's the matter?' She glared at Susan as though she were the one who had made Miss Lally cry then knelt down at Lally's knee and wrapped her in loving arms. There had been a great deal of resentment in Biddy when Susan first came to the Priory, for up to then Miss Lally had confided only in her but she had watched the growing friendship between the two young women and realised that Susan Harper was not trying to take her place in

295

Lally's affections. The woman had known great sorrow and Miss Lally, with that good heart of hers, had done her best to alleviate it, giving her a place in life, employment, a trust to care for her children. When Biddy saw that Susan would not usurp her, that she was extremely fond of Biddy's lass, that she in fact was good for Lally, she had accepted her. Biddy had her important part to play in this household. She was valued and, yes, loved by her young mistress and being a generous woman had even formed a tentative relationship with the woman from the nursery. Their paths rarely crossed and Susan took care not to interfere with Biddy, her duties, or her place in Miss Lally's affections.

Susan stood up and moved to the window which looked out over the garden where Barty and Froglet were busy raking leaves from the rolling lawn that led to the edge of Tangle Wood. She had done her best not to interfere with the unique relationship between Mrs Stevens and Miss Lally but Miss Lally would insist that she and Susan were friends, which pleased Susan, since she had never had a woman friend and was genuinely fond of the woman who had changed her life so dramatically. That was well enough but her other ideas were unworkable and Susan had yet to tell her that she did not wish to be included in any more dinner parties since she knew she was totally out of place but that was for another time.

'Oh, Biddy, it's about Cat . . .'

'Cat . . . Dear God, what's happened?'

'He knows, Biddy. He knows she's—'

'Aye up, watch tha' gabble,' casting a glance in Susan's direction.

296

'Oh, Biddy, she'll know soon enough. The whole of Moorend will know before long unless Harry will do as Roly demands.'

'Now then, my lass, Mrs Harper—'

'Will keep it to herself, won't you, Susan?' Lally directed a heartfelt appeal to Susan, who had turned from the window and was staring in dawning comprehension at the two women by the fire.

'Nay, less folk who know the better, I say.' Biddy rose to her feet and squared up to Susan as though they were about to engage in fisticuffs, but Lally caught her hand and then beckoned to Susan to resume her seat by the fireside. 'I trust you, Susan, as I trust Biddy so if I was to tell you . . .'

'Cat is not Mr Harry's daughter, is that it? This Mr Roly is holding it over you to get Mr Harry to do something.'

'You're sharp, I'll say that,' Biddy sniffed, 'how did you guess?' Then she drew up another chair and the three women sat almost knee to knee, Lally's tears beginning to dry up, for the old saying 'a trouble shared is a trouble halved' was certainly true, especially when it was shared with the two women in the world she trusted the most, the two women who loved her and whom she loved. The love between women can be as staunch and everlasting as between man and woman and these two had proved themselves, Biddy even more than Susan, to be her true friends.

'He wants the mills, you see.'

'What!' Biddy was aghast.

'Yes. He wants Harry out and himself in charge. I don't understand how it is to be done but unless Harry agrees he will tell the world that Cat is his

297

child. Dear God.' Lally raised her face to the ceiling in supplication. 'Once, only once after Chris died, I was lonely and missed . . . well, you are both women and know what a man can give a woman. I allowed him to . . . to make love to me and within a month I knew I was pregnant. I told Harry, I don't know why, I suppose because I had always trusted him, but, well, we were married and I had a 'premature' baby. The marriage has been . . . I thought we had a chance of happiness . . .'

'He loves you, lass. I told you that, didn't I?' Biddy's voice was sad.

'I know that now and I am . . .'

'Beginning to love him? He's a grand chap, is Mr Harry. Mrs Harper will agree, won't you?'

'I wish you'd call me Susan,' Susan said absently. 'And yes, I've seen the way he looks at you, Lally. But what are we'—none of them noticed the plural—'to do? Mr Harry's not himself yet and until he is we cannot trouble him with this. John'd have my hide if—'

'John, is it?' Biddy said wryly.

'We are friends,' Susan said defiantly.

'Really! But, still, that's not the subject here. Lally, you must dry your tears and go down to your husband and Susan must see to the children, for God only knows what those naughty boys are plaguing Dora with.' They all three stood up and with a simple gesture Lally put her arms about Susan, then Biddy, before she slipped from the room.

'She needs help,' Biddy said to Susan.

'She'll get it.'

*   *   *

298

His face was turned to the door when she entered and at once Tansy stood up and slipped from the room. He held out his hand and she took it, kneeling by his bed and placing a soft kiss on his lips. His responded and his other hand rose to cup her chin.

'I've missed you. Where have you been?'

'I've just come from the nursery. They were having tea so nothing would do but that I sit down and have a biscuit with them.'

'And Cat?' His damaged face did its best to smile, for the progress of the good-natured baby was of great interest to him. It seemed to Lally that he was genuinely beginning to believe that the child was his so how could she tell him of Roly's threats to expose the truth of Cat's paternity? Harry was coming along nicely, as Doctor John put it, and his ribs were healing so he should be able to get up out of bed before long. As long as he did not overdo it, he might even go downstairs, or upstairs to see the children in a few days providing they were not allowed to leap all over him which they were prone to do. The three boys loved him to get down on the floor and pretend to be a tiger and the shrieks of laughter could be heard in the kitchen.

So far John had not spoken of his anxiety about Harry's head injury. Not that he had one that could be seen. There was no wound visible but something in his skull had been . . . well, John did not quite know how to describe it. His memory had not been damaged. He knew them all, from Dulcie, the kitchen-maid who brought up the coals for his fire, to his beloved wife. He chafed at being bedfast, as Biddy described it, and though the sight of his face might frighten the children, in a few days it would be healed enough to visit them. But he never mentioned the mills, his brother, his confrontation with the Weaver brothers, indeed anything to do with what was an integral part of his life. He had been running the Sinclair mills since the death of his father, knowing not only how to manufacture cloth from the moment the wool left the back of the sheep but the machines that made it all possible. The wool textile industry had occupied a unique place in British history from the twelfth century and Harry Sinclair knew that history as he knew his own. Every machine invented, every innovation, from sorting and scouring of the fleeces, the blending, the carding, the preparation of the worsted yarn, the spinning to the weaving was bred in the bones of him and it was due to his knowledge and to his business acumen that the Sinclair mills were probably the most successful in Yorkshire. He could even darn his own socks, for the basic principle of weaving was the same. Threads sewn in one direction, then, at right angles, more threads passed over and under the first which was just like darning, his mother had told him and he had set to and darned the hole in his sock as a boy!

Now, in a few short days, he had lost a part of himself that *was* himself and Doctor John Burton who, like every other doctor in the world, knew little about what went on inside the skull, wondered if he would ever regain it.

300

CHAPTER TWENTY-ONE

He waited a week before he rode up to the Priory, apologising to the frozen-faced Lally for not coming earlier but business had eaten up so much of his time it had taken him until now to find an hour free.

He had caught her unprepared, entering the drawing room where Jenny had shown him, for after all he was the mistress's brother-in-law and surely needed none of the formality of announcing that callers were usually put through.

Lally had Biddy with her, thank the good God, she was to say later, and they were discussing the menus for the day, seated one on either side of the roaring fire for as December came in it had turned bitterly cold. They were drinking hot chocolate and if Roly was surprised to see Lally consorting in a familiar way with one of her servants, he quickly hid it.

'Well, this is a cosy scene,' he remarked, ready to raise a hand to Mrs Stevens to tell her not to stand, but as she merely sat there, as frozen-faced as her mistress and with no intention, it seemed, of standing for her betters, he could feel his own temper rise.

'I've come to see Harry since it seems he has no intention of coming to see me. There are legal matters to attend to and we both need to be involved, so if you would summon him I'd be obliged.' He sauntered across the room and seated himself on one of Lally's dainty new chairs, his smile fixed. He had handed his hat, his riding whip and his warm cape to the housemaid and his manner was of a guest who is perfectly sure of his welcome and waits only to be asked whether he would prefer tea, coffee or chocolate.

'I have no intention of *summoning* my husband, as you so delicately put it, Roly. He is not totally recovered from the beating he took and is resting but if you would like me to give him a message I would gladly do so.'

By now Lally had got a grip on herself and her smile was as fixed as his. She looked incredibly lovely in a velvet gown the colour of the heather on the moorland in the middle of summer. Her short hair had a ribbon of the same colour threaded through it and she wore satin slippers dyed to match her gown. She had just spent an hour with Harry, sitting beside his bed, for as yet Doctor John had decided he needed more rest. She was not to know that the doctor, mystified by his patient's apparent inability to remember the circumstances, not only of his injuries, but who he had been before them, had come to the conclusion that only bed rest, or at least to be kept to his room quietly, might do the trick. It could do no harm at least. Harry did not seem to mind which was quite frightening. It was not strictly true to say that Harry did not remember the beating he had taken, nor that he had forgotten his family and the servants, the children or who he was, but a part of him was missing and he had not even noticed!

'Do you not feel able to leave the bedroom, Harry?' Lally had asked him tentatively as she sat beside his bed. He had been reading *The Times*, leaning back among his nest of pillows, seemingly quite content. He liked her to be with him and with her arm to steady him he had begun to move about the bedroom and sit in the chair by the fire. He no longer needed the constant presence of one of the housemaids and Doctor John said he was making good progress. Lally had questioned the doctor, asking if he thought it might be a good idea to mention the mills and his daily routine before the beating but John decided it might be a little early yet. When he was physically restored, his broken ribs and nose mended, then they might try a little gentle probing but until then let him rest and—though he did not say this to Lally—his complete memory would hopefully be restored.

Harry had put the newspaper down and smiled at her, a sweet, trusting smile that told her without words that he loved her and believed in some strange way that she returned his feelings.

'Would you have me out on the moors with Piper under me?' His smile widened. 'My love, you know these ribs of mine are still painful and the good doctor seems to feel I should stay in bed so here I shall remain until given permission to rise. It also means I see more of you which is a pleasure to me.'

This was so unlike the strong-willed, hardworking, resolute man of business who was Harry Sinclair that Lally was beginning to be frightened. She had expected him to rail at his confinement, argue at every turn that he was not only fit to get out of bed, to sit in a chair but to go to the bloody mills. Who the devil was running them in his absence, he would be shouting and he was off to see for himself so would Carly kindly saddle Piper and where the hell were his clothes?

Now Roly stood up and strolled about the

303

drawing room, picking up a delicate porcelain figurine and studying it thoughtfully as if deciding whether to buy it. He was startled when Lally stood up herself, almost flinging herself from her chair and at once Biddy did the same.

'Will there be anything else, Roly?' Lally asked him coldly.

'Well, if Harry is unavailable I shall just have to go ahead with my plans without him, won't I, my sweet?'

'I am not your sweet, Roly, and I would advise you to postpone your *plans* whatever they are until I have had time to consult with *my* lawyer. I shall be at High Clough first thing tomorrow morning if that is convenient. And even if it is not! I will not have business discussed in my home. Do I make myself clear? Shall we say nine o'clock?'

Roly was so astonished he almost dropped the figurine then his face flushed up with what Lally supposed was suppressed anger.

'What the devil's going on here, Lally? I demand to see my brother and if you do not—'

Lally put up an imperious hand. 'Biddy, would you mind fetching one or two of the men from the yard. I would like Mr Sinclair to leave and if he won't go voluntarily I shall have him put out. I will not have my husband disturbed at this time.'

Biddy began to move towards the door but Roly was there before her, barring her way. 'I don't know what the hell you think you're up to, Lally, but you might be sorry if you—'

'We'll see. Now then, are you to leave or must I—'

Roly turned from her, pushing past Biddy and erupting into the hallway. Tansy was arranging some flowers in a crystal vase on the hall table but she flinched away from the tall, maddened figure of her employer's brother, almost dropping the vase.

'My cape, hat and whip, girl,' he snarled at her and when she retrieved them and held them out to him he grabbed them from her and flung open the big front door before she could get to it. His chestnut gelding was ready for him, the reins held by Ben who also recoiled slightly from the man who jumped down the steps and leaped into the saddle. The carefully raked gravel, done every day by Barty or Froglet, was thrown up beneath the horse's hooves, scattering across a neatly hoed flowerbed and from the perfection of the lawn where they were raking leaves, Barty and Froglet sighed deeply.

In the drawing room both Lally and Biddy sank tremblingly into a chair.

'Oh dear,' Biddy said, her voice inclined to tremble also.

'Yes, I think we have just declared war on my husband's brother, Biddy.'

'You might say that, my lass.'

*　　　*　　　*

Almost in the very centre of Moor Wood, which was north of Cowslip, the farm tenanted by the Graham family, was a cave hidden by a fallen beech tree on the bank of a tiny beck. The beck was shallow and into it ran a rivulet of fresh water. The cave was reached by a steep, pine-studded slope and stopped at an outcrop of rocks which hid the entrance. The cave was shallow and running right round it at waist height was a kind of shelf formed from the rock.

On the shelf sat a frying pan which had evidently never been cleaned, an old kettle, two tin cups, a jar of what looked like loose tea, another of flour and, piled carelessly along the shelf, the remains of several animals, probably rabbits. There was a ravel of string and various unidentifiable objects, bits of rusty chain, some nails and a hammer. An old bowl, chipped round the edges, held half a dozen eggs. A bucket with a ladle hanging over the edge evidently contained water. There were fire-blackened stones around a small fire in the centre of the cave and a heap of old flour sacks piled in one corner. Next to the flour sacks stood two rifles and several animal traps.

There were two men in the cave, lolling on a bed of bracken, dry and warm against the cold December day. They were unshaven and unkempt, both of them smoking a clay pipe. They were big men with matted hair and the dark skin that spoke of an outdoor life.

One of the men stood up, ladled some water into the old kettle and placed the kettle in the centre of the smouldering fire. He reached up for the two tin cups, peering into them. Finding one not to his liking he spat into it, wiped it round with the hem of his tattered shirt then heaped a spoonful of tea into each. When the kettle boiled he poured water into each cup and then handed one to the second man.

' 'Ow long d'yer reckon us'll 'ave ter stay 'ere, then?' he said, sipping his tea.

'As long as it takes,' was the answer.

'What if she don't come this way?'

'Well, someone will. If it ain't 'er, it'll be 'im or one o' them servants. I don't give a bugger 'oo it is as long as it's from that bloody family. We'll keep outer sight an' watch the tracks through't wood an' even slip across ter Tangle Wood fer they're right chummy wi' them bloody McGinleys. Jesus, I could slit that bugger's throat.'

'What bugger's that?'

'That Sean what's gettin' our farm. We saw 'im over there yesterday pokin' round as though it were 'is already.'

'Well, I suppose it is.'

'Don't you be clever wi' me, me lad.'

'I were only sayin'—'

'Well, don't. It were 'er what put us 'ere. It were 'er what sent 'er old man ter chuck us out an' someone's gonner pay. God knows what's 'appened ter Ma an' Pa but we couldn't bring 'em 'ere, could we? We'd be bound ter be noticed. No, you an' me'll stay 'ere, livin' off land, snug as two bugs in a rug an' when chance comes we'll 'ave 'em.'

*   *   *

The following morning at nine o'clock precisely a smart carriage drew up to the steps that led to the entrance of the office in the yard of High Clough. Men working in the yard, which was bustling with activity, stopped what they were doing to stare in astonishment as three ladies descended from the carriage helped by the coachman. One of the ladies was the maister's wife, they knew that and one or two of them thought they recognised the second lady, but the third none of them had seen

307

before.

Mrs Sinclair looked quite magnificent, the men would say to one another after she had disappeared, though they were rough working men and would not use such words. She was in blue, eggshell blue, though again the men would not have called it that, a full-skirted gown beneath which, as she climbed down from her carriage, was revealed a whisper of white lace above her dainty boots. Over her gown she wore a pale grey fur mantle with a wide hood, the fur being chinchilla, though they did not recognise it. The price of it would have kept one of their families for the remainder of their days. She wore no hat and her hair fell in shining curls about her head held with nothing more than a narrow ribbon to match her gown.

The second lady was equally fashionably dressed though not quite so expensively. She was also in blue but her gown and mantle were the rich blue of the sky at dusk, almost a purple blue. She wore a shallow bonnet far back on her head, the inside of the brim decorated with pale pink silk roses.

The third lady was . . . not exactly a lady. In fact the men knew instinctively that she was a servant. One of Mrs Sinclair's household but what the devil she was doing with Mrs Sinclair and her friend they could not imagine.

The whole yard came to a complete stop. There were enormous wagons ready to be pulled by the patient shire horses, the cold turning their breath to a vapour about their heads. Sinclair goods were being stowed on to the wagons which would transport them to the railway in Halifax where they would be loaded for their journey to all points of the compass, in this country and in many others; men shovelled coal on to a wagon ready to stoke the boilers. Against the far wall were stacked fleeces, each waiting to be divided by hand into its numerous qualities. Dirt, natural grease and other impurities needed to be removed before the wool would go to be scoured at the fulling mill, but not one man was concentrating on his allotted task as the three females made their dainty way towards the doorway and the steps that led up to the maister's office.

Again the clerk in the outer office was affronted when Mrs Sinclair and her companions calmly walked past his high desk and into the office where Mr Roly was working.

Roly had been waiting for Lally but as she entered with the two other women he rose slowly to his feet, pen in hand, consternation on his face.

'Good morning, Roly.'

'Good God, what's this? A deputation?'

'You might say that. We have come to discuss the strange demand you made to me last week and to decide what might be the best way to solve it.' She smiled, then turned to look at her companions. 'Shall we sit, ladies?' she asked them and they did, each choosing one of Harry Sinclair's comfortable armchairs, arranging themselves and their skirts to their own satisfaction. Roly, still standing, watched them with open-mouthed fascination.

'Chocolate would be nice, Roly, if there is someone to provide it. I'm sure Harry must have some little person tucked away to see to his needs. Or would you prefer tea, Susan, perhaps coffee? And you, Biddy?'

They both declared themselves to be satisfied

309

with hot chocolate. Roly, still somewhat in a daze, rang a bell and the clerk came in at a run as if to say what the devil did those damn women want now!

Roly gave his orders, then sank down into his chair behind the desk.

Lally smiled serenely. 'Perhaps I had better introduce you to my friends, Roly. My very good friends who are going to help with the mills while Harry is incapacitated. I know very little about the wool trade, I must admit, but Harry will tell me what to do, and Susan here, Mrs Susan Harper, has worked for many years on a loom in the weaving shed and knows a good "piece" when she sees it.' Susan had told her to say that! She wondered what it meant. 'And Mrs Stevens is my long-standing friend and companion. It was she who brought me up.' Biddy bowed her head graciously.

A little wisp of a woman timidly entered the room bearing a tray on which sat a tall silver chocolate pot and four dainty cups and saucers with matching milk jug and sugar bowl. Harry evidently liked to impress callers! The little woman hesitated, not awfully sure who was to be put in charge of pouring, Mr Harry's brother or his wife, then something directed her to Mrs Sinclair and she placed the tray on the table beside her.

Lally inclined her head to Roly who had as yet barely spoken, asking if he would care for hot chocolate and it seemed to bring him to his senses. He had been brooding on how beautiful his sister-in-law looked, on the meaning of her words about Harry and his *incapacity* and whether there was any chance that he might . . . well, that was for later. First he must deal with these three crazy

310

women who seemed to be telling him, or at least Lally was, that they intended to *help* him to run his own business.

'No chocolate for me, Lally, but you ladies, who seem to think I am open to morning calls, do get on with your drink.' He grinned broadly, running his eyes quite offensively over Susan's trim figure and pretty face. Her hair, showing beneath the brim of her bonnet, had a chestnut glow to its darkness and a pleasing wave. There was a scatter of freckles across her nose and her mouth was poppy red and full. She looked directly at him with the bluest eyes he had ever seen and though he stared quite rudely she did not drop them.

'You know a good "piece" do you? Susan, is it, then perhaps—'

'I am Mrs Harper, and yes, I do.' She stood up and moved across the room, picking a sample of cloth from his desk. She took it to the window and examined it in the daylight. He watched her, a small smile playing round his mouth. 'This has a "boardy" feel to it,' she went on. 'I believe it must be put right before you can send it out to your customer.'

'God Almighty, has anyone else anything to say about this piece or the running of the mill? This is quite laughable, Lally, and I'm amazed that my brother allows you to run round unaccompanied—'

'I am not unaccompanied, Roly. I have my friends and associates with me.'

He hooted with laughter. 'Associates! These two! A mill girl and a kitchen-maid. You must have taken leave of your senses.' Then he became serious. 'There are two ways of doing this. Harry can sell out to me or we can split the business. I

311

have already told you how we shall do it.'

'Will your financial resources run to it, Roly?' she asked him mildly.

Biddy watched the play between the two of them and though she was afraid for her lass, knowing that beneath his pleasant exterior Roly Sinclair was a hard and determined man, she sensed—no! not sensed, *knew* that he would eventually be beaten. He was standing on quaking ground was Roly Sinclair and she wondered how a man as clever as he was could imagine that Mr Harry would allow his mills to be swallowed up. Mr Harry was not quite himself as yet but soon he would be and then what a hullabaloo there would be.

Roly smiled. 'You have not perhaps heard the news. It has been a whirlwind romance. We decided to keep it secret until I was home and could give some attention to celebrations and so on. I have recently become engaged to Miss Anne Bracken. Yes, I see that surprises you'—which it did since Anne Bracken was twenty-seven and as plain as a pikestaff. *But very rich*—'and I am pleased to say that her marriage portion and the allowance her father proposes to give her will set me up very nicely in whatever the arrangement is between Harry and myself. I want the Sinclair mills, Lally, and I shall do anything to get them. Now, if you ladies'—smiling benignly round at them as he stood up—'have finished your chocolate, I beg you to excuse me.'

Though Lally was flabbergasted she did not show it, nor did she stand up. 'Well, allow me to congratulate you, Roly. You will certainly have plenty of funds at your disposal since George Bracken is one of the wealthiest mill-owners in

Yorkshire. He's in "shoddy", isn't he? I could never understand how rags could create such wealth. I drove past his mill with Harry on our way to . . . well, I can't remember our destination but in the yard were great bales chock full of filthy tatters with wagons arriving all the time to add to the heap. The walls of the mill were covered with thick, clinging dust and fibre which rose in volumes from the open doors and glassless windows and poured from the chimneys. Shall you like working in such a place, Roly, for I dare say George Bracken will expect something from you?'

'I shall do whatever is necessary to gain full control of the Sinclair mills.'

'Not if you're to produce cloth like that on the table, Mr Sinclair,' Susan told him quietly. 'I dare say it suited them in the weaving shed but it'd not suit Mr Harry, nor those he sells his cloth to. I've been in the trade since I was ten years old and I reckon to know a bit about wool. Oh, not the selling side or even the financial but I know a proper woven piece.'

'Is that so!' Roly was in a towering rage. To be spoken to by some working-class woman was bad enough, but to be told she knew as much or more about working a loom and the results of it than he did was outrageous. 'Well, let me tell you—'

'Are we to discuss this situation in a calm and reasonable manner, Roly, or are we to sit here and listen to you—'

'You'll bloody well do as you're told, madam,' he snarled at Lally. 'I presume these *friends* of yours know that the baby in your nursery was fathered by me.' He waited for some explosion, perhaps gasps of horror but when none came he continued. 'Ah, I

313

see they do but do they know that I will spread the story round Moorend and even as far as Halifax unless you go along with my plans. I will not be thwarted on this, Lally.'

'Perhaps the lady you are to marry and her wealthy father will not be too pleased to hear that you seduced your best friend's widow only months after his death, or perhaps you would prefer to hear from my lawyer on the matter of slander. Harry and I, even if we were forced to go to court and have our names whispered all over Yorkshire, would swear that we were having an affair months before we were married. Perhaps even before the death of my first husband. We might be pilloried but I don't imagine it would be for long. Harry is a person of enormous influence, well respected and with more wealth than any man in these parts. There are very few who would care to be in his bad books. We would both fight *dirty* to save our marriage, Roly, our life together, our children, one of whom happens to be called Caterina Sinclair.'

'I've had enough of this garbage,' Roly said savagely, reaching for his caped overcoat and hat which hung on the stand by the office door. 'I shall ride over and see Harry and if my visit harms his health, which seems very delicate at the moment, then that will be laid at your door. If you cannot keep out of my way and remain where gentlewomen are supposed to be, which is in their own homes, then anything that results from your unwomanliness is your own affair.'

Lally stood up and so did Biddy and Susan and it seemed to him, though he knew he was being foolish, that they posed some sort of threat to him. The other two were tall, standing protectively on

314

either side of Lally who was not. Their faces were impassive and though he hadn't the slightest idea what they could do, if anything, to stand in his way, he found himself taking a step back.

'I mean everything I say, Roly. I will not let you take what Harry has built up over all these years. I know you have had a hand in building it so surely you could be satisfied with the excellent lifestyle you enjoy. He will not sell any part of it to you, nor will he agree to splitting it. He has told me so'—which was, of course, a lie—'and I am only repeating what he said.'

'Why isn't he here then, fighting as a man should for what is his?'

'He cannot sit a horse.'

'Rubbish.' Roly began to pull on his overcoat. 'I shall ride over this minute . . .'

'If you come within a foot of the entrance gates to the Priory I shall send Carly for the constables and have you arrested. Now, get on with running the Sinclair mills, Roly, if you can, and I promise that as soon as Harry is well enough he will be up here to discuss your grievances. Oh, and give my very best wishes to your fiancée. I wish you both happy!'

CHAPTER TWENTY-TWO

'What will you do now, my clever lass?' Biddy was the first to speak as they sat in the carriage on their way back to the Priory. She had had nothing to say while the three of them were at High Clough and it was not because she was overawed by Roly

315

Sinclair, nor that she felt out of place, but that she was a strong woman who had learned the hard way how to stand up to anything life could throw at her and Roly Sinclair, in her opinion, was nowt a pound. Biddy Stevens, from a working-class background, came from Halifax and was twelve when her mother died and her father began to pester her, and she had left home for a life in some sort of decent work, perhaps as a domestic, a scullery maid, she didn't care as long as it was decent. Unfortunately she had discovered that even the most lowly housewife would not take on a girl who knocked at her back door without references asking for work. She did a stint in a mill that manufactured 'shoddy', working on a machine with revolving teeth called a 'devil' which tore the rags already sorted to pieces. She had to wear a bandage to prevent the inhalation of the foul dust from infecting her lungs, which was bad enough, but when she was raped by the overlooker and she made a fuss, an unnecessary fuss in his opinion, for it was a regular occurrence among the girls at their machines, she was put off. She took to the streets. If she was going to be abused, she decided, by any man who fancied it, she might as well get paid for it! She became friends with an ageing prostitute who took her under her wing, showing her how to protect herself, not only against aggressive men, but against becoming pregnant.

But the day when the old prostitute's training let her down and the man she had thought looked agreeable proved to be just the opposite was when her life had changed dramatically. The man, silent and menacing, would have raped her had not Delphine Atkins's carriage passed by. Delphine's

316

coachman was an ex-prize-fighter and with a shriek from his mistress to stop the carriage, he had soon seen off the pervert and Biddy was bundled into the carriage with nothing more than a black eye and the marks of the man's hands about her throat.

She had served Delphine devotedly until she died. She had brought up Lally, who had been no more than a scrap of white lace, a short cap of dark curls and eyes the colour of aquamarine when Biddy first saw her. She was as pretty as a picture and Biddy had loved her from the start which was just as well, for Delphine, well meaning but not maternally inclined, lived a strange life among what were known in Halifax as 'arty types'! They met in Delphine's drawing room where they quoted Balzac to one another and read out loud passages from Dostoyevsky. They discussed the merits of one painter against another while Biddy and the child sat comfortably in the warm kitchen and went through their letters from a child's reader. For several years after Delphine sadly passed away she and Lally lived with Aunt Jane, a distant relative who took them in until Miss Lally became Mrs Christopher Fraser of the Priory.

When Miss Lally had married Mr Chris, Biddy was ready to go down on her knees and thank the Being in whom she had never believed, for even then she had had her doubts about the other one, the dashing, charming, handsome sprig of a youth with whom her lamb and Mr Chris had shared their wild ways. Roly Sinclair, son of a rich mill-owner, spoiled rotten in Biddy's opinion, but likeable all the same.

But he had showed his true colours today and Biddy needed time to marshall her thoughts before she conferred with Miss Lally on what Miss Lally's next step was to be.

'I don't know, Biddy, but you can be certain Roly Sinclair is not going to get his hands on Harry's mills. He is a partner and I suppose he will have to remain so but I know Harry wouldn't sell out to him nor would he split the business to give Roly half. When we get home you and I and Susan will discuss what we think our next step should be.'

But when they got home the house was in uproar and for a dreadful moment Lally's heart leaped painfully in her chest, for she thought it was something to do with Harry but it turned out that Pinky had been mislaid and her daughter was refusing to be comforted. At eight months old Cat was a lovely child with her mother's colouring, her dark hair in fat, shining curls about her head, her eyes a brilliant blue-green, her cheeks round and soft with a tint of peach in them. She had her parents' strong will and at six months had been crawling, following the patient dogs and hauling herself across their smoothly brushed black and white backs. Even now, as she shrieked her displeasure at the non-appearance of her beloved Pinky she was doing her best to stand, pulling herself up against Dora's neat skirt. Dora was pathetically pleased to see them, declaring that even the master was at this moment searching his own room for the missing toy. For ten minutes Biddy, Lally and Susan joined the search until Pinky was found, of all places under the curled-up kitten in the kitchen who had taken a liking to its softness. The kitten, now five months old, was the only one left of the three from Folly Farm. The other two had been taken discreetly to live in the stable since they were both male and as Fluffy was female Susan said firmly she wanted no addition to the nursery which was already overflowing with animals.

Cat was overjoyed, hugging the threadbare toy to her chest, kissing it passionately and though Biddy, who was not a particular lover of animals, decreed that the toy should be washed before the child should be allowed it, none was prepared to separate baby and toy.

Harry was still out of bed when Lally entered the bedroom, in fact he was half under it looking for Pinky, his expression anxious and Lally was made to realise how much Cat meant to her husband even though she was not naturally his. He often sat with her on his knee in the chair by his bed, the pair of them half asleep, his face peaceful and loving, for the first recognisable word she had spoken had been 'Papa'!

He grinned now and shrugged when Lally told him the toy was found, standing up and holding out his arms to her and in their new closeness she moved into them, a closeness that seemed to have grown stealthily but naturally and she had not been displeased. He lifted her chin and gently placed a kiss on her lips.

'And where have you been while this drama was taking place? I was just about to call for Piper and ride into Moorend to see if any suitable replacement for Pinky might be had.'

It was the perfect opportunity to tell Harry what was happening at his mills. He had already been told that Roly was out to make trouble, since she had spoken to him about it before the incident with the Weavers but at that time they had no idea

319

what it was Roly was after. The beating Harry had taken from the Weaver brothers had knocked all remembrance of it from his mind.

'Harry.' She took his hand and led him to the sofa which was placed to one side of the fire so that in the evenings they might sit side by side. 'I think it is time we talked about . . . about what happened before the . . . before you were attacked. It is a month now and you are so much better. You are getting about the house and Carly tells me you have even ventured into the yard. I wouldn't be surprised to see you on Piper's back before long and so perhaps it is time to talk of the future.'

In the back of Lally's mind there was a slight but growing suspicion that Harry's subconscious spirit was doing its best to hide from something it did not care to remember. Nothing to do with the mills or his life as a businessman but *her* and the child who was not his but whom he had grown to love as though she were. He was beginning to move about the world of the household, stronger and seemingly *physically* recovered from his attack but something held him back from total recall. Should she chance sending him spiralling away beyond her reach? John advised waiting, saying let him come back to himself when his mind was ready for it, but quite honestly she did not know what to do about Roly's threat. Oh, she was prepared to suffer the scandal that would ripple through the community should Roly tell the world that Cat was his, for she could bluff it out, but could Harry? In his right mind, the strong and tenacious mind he had possessed before the Weavers attacked him, he would fight beside her to protect the children and their rightful inheritance and not only that but

320

their place in their own society. But he was *not* in his right mind and might not the truth damage him even further? She knew if she was honest with herself, that if Roly refused to run the business, let it come to a standstill, walked away from it and started up on his own with Anne Bracken's wealth behind him, there was no way on God's earth that she could step into Harry's shoes. She knew nothing about the worsted trade, not only the actual manufacture of the miles of worsted yarn the mills turned out each year but the financial side, the accounting, the buying of fleeces, the selling of the finished goods. Susan knew the inside of a weaving shed, for she had worked in the loom gate, 'minding' more than one machine at a time. She had known how to describe the piece Roly had been studying when they entered his office; 'boardy' she had called it, which had impressed Roly, but there was more to it than that. Biddy was staunch in her loyalty and resolution to help in any way she could, even to standing at a power loom herself since she knew the inside of a mill, Lally had no doubt, but without the knowledge that was in Harry's head and his years of experience, where were they to start?

'The future?' Harry echoed, drawing away from her as though already his mind was searching for a hiding place. Lally heard the sound of Jenny and Tansy laughing as they ran down the back stairs to the kitchen passage. They had come from one of the guest bedrooms changing the bed linen, for though recently they had not had guests to stay Mrs Stevens was a stickler for the correct way in which a house such as the Priory should be run, insisting the bedrooms were 'done out' and the beds changed every week. Daft, they called it, but since neither of them had the laundering to do, what was it to them?

Lally looked up into Harry's troubled face. The cast had been removed from his nose and the bruises put there by the Weaver boy's kicks had faded. He looked his old self except for the hesitant expression on his face. What was it that had altered his mind so that the most important part of his life had become hidden from him? He was an intelligent man, sharp, experienced in the ways of business, a man who from entering the mills as a youth and working next to his own father had learned the trade, absorbed every aspect of it so that it was a part of him and yet, though he was physically improving, he seemed to shy away from anything that was not involved in his life with her and the children, the house, even the gardens which he asked about. Doctor John told her to let him recover at his own pace, that the memory of his commercial life would return gradually as he recovered from the blow to his head but that had been weeks ago and still he clung to what she was beginning to believe was the place where he had chosen to hide.

She could not press him, she just couldn't. She must somehow manage to carry on without him, how she did not know, but the danger of forcing him to remember what his life's purpose was, running the mills, was something she couldn't chance.

'The . . . the future?' he repeated vaguely. 'I'm not sure . . .'

She smiled up at him and without thinking, put her arms about him and held him close to her. She marvelled at how dear this man was becoming to her. Once she had looked to him for protection, for security from the threat of scandal and he had not failed her. Now he needed her to safeguard his interests, to keep his mills running, his concerns forging ahead and she didn't know where to start. Roly would fight her every step of the way to get what he wanted and she must gather her frail, female strength to stop him. But not only had she to do this tremendous deed, she must keep her household running, her children cocooned in the childhood safety they deserved and she must bear the child that she knew was growing inside her. Harry's child!

'Harry, there is something I must tell you. To do with the future.'

He frowned anxiously but her smile deepened and she hugged him closer then she drew back, at the same time keeping hold of his hands.

'What would you like more than anything in the world?'

His own face lightened and his lips curled in that engagingly familiar way she had come to recognise.

'Oh . . .' He shrugged and grinned. 'Take off that lovely gown and whatever it is you have underneath and I'll show you.'

'Later perhaps, but . . . well, oh, Harry, I hope you will be pleased, I know I am, but we are to have a child. I am carrying your child. It will not be until July, I think, but that is what I meant when I spoke of the future.'

She thought the news had alarmed him, for his face became unnaturally still. He did not frown exactly but what seemed to be a look of alarm . . . no, not alarm, *suspicion* drew down his eyebrows.

He turned away and stared unseeingly through the window at the grey, lowering clouds that were building up across the skyline. Snow, Barty had announced in the kitchen, since he was knowledgeable about such things, and he and Froglet were busy in the greenhouses doing what was needed to protect their precious plants. From the side window they could be seen moving into the kitchen garden, retrieving the wheelbarrow that was filled with leaves gathered in the autumn and with which they would cover the celery beds and the parsnips to protect them from the cold. They had put in broccoli which needed attention and the fruit beds, peaches, nectarines and other wall trees which had been pruned earlier must be cosseted. Barty kept glancing up at the sky as though he expected to be immersed in a snowstorm at any minute.

'What . . . what is it, Harry? Are you not pleased that we are to have a child?' She moved towards him but he left her to stand at the window and she was forced to address his lean back. She wanted to put out a hand to him but he was so stiff and unbending she was afraid to touch him as though he might splinter and fall into a million pieces.

'Where have you been this morning?' His voice was harsh, crackling with some emotion she could not even guess at. It was a question she did not want to answer. What excuse could she give for visiting High Clough? Did he even remember that Roly was home from his travels? The one time Roly had called at the Priory demanding to see his brother, Harry had been in their bedroom, but who knew what might have been said by one of the housemaids or even that he might have heard

324

Roly's voice.

'I was . . . Susan, Biddy and I were out in the carriage. We—'

'And where did you go in the carriage?' His voice was ice-coated.

'What . . . what does it matter, Harry? We went for a drive and—'

'A drive? In this weather?' For the first flakes of snow were beginning their dance beyond the windows.

'Well, it wasn't . . . this morning the weather . . .' She knew she was babbling but somehow it seemed imperative to keep the whereabouts of this morning's drive from Harry.

'My brother has returned from his travels, hasn't he?' Still he did not turn to her and she racked her brains to search for the reason why he should be so distant with her.

'Yes, I believe so,' she managed to stutter.

'How long has he been back?'

'I'm not sure. Really, Harry, what is all this?' Her exasperation with this line of questioning was starting to turn to anger, for she could not even guess where it was leading.

'And the child is expected in July, you say.' He turned then and the expression on his face frightened her. Not for herself, but for him.

'That is what I calculated,' she managed to utter, 'but then women are known to be—'

'What a coincidence,' he murmured, his voice more menacing than if he had shouted. 'The moment Roly returns to Moorend, you become pregnant. How strange it is that though you and I have been married for over a year I have not been able to get you with child yet here you are

325

expecting what I believe is called a "happy event" nine months after Roly comes home.'

He turned back to the window and stared out at the gathering snow, taking a great interest, it seemed, in the flakes that were sliding down the panes of glass.

For a moment she was bewildered then, as the horror of what he had said struck her, she became appalled, ice in her veins, frozen and unable to speak. Every drop of colour drained from her face and as if a finger had smudged soot beneath her eyes, half circles of shadow appeared. Her mouth dropped open but no sound came from between her lips. Though she was dressed in a pale, eggshell blue the colour seemed too strong for her. The skin of her face was translucent, like milk that has been watered down and even her lips were colourless, as colourless as the exquisitely carved alabaster chess pieces that stood on a small table by the side window.

'Harry.' Her voice was no more than a whisper, scarcely to be heard. 'I can't believe . . . I don't believe . . . you can't be accusing me of . . . Dear God, I am carrying your child and you seem to be telling me you believe . . . you're out of your mind.' Which was true, of course. Harry Sinclair who was known for his sound judgement, his clear thinking, his business acumen, was damaged to the extent that his normally balanced mind seemed unable to grasp the horrific words he had spoken. He was implying that, since Roly had fathered Caterina, she and his brother had resumed their relationship and the child in her womb was his.

'I ask you again where have you been this morning?' he said with black, snarling anger, turning on her in his pain and she thought he was about to strike her.

She lifted her head and squared her shoulders and for a brief moment the true Harry, the *real* Harry saw the reality of what was happening here, what he was doing to her, saying to her and was in torment, then the jealousy and mistrust took over and he made a noise like an animal in a trap.

'You were with him, weren't you?'

'Yes.'

'You bitch . . . you . . .'

'And so were Susan and Biddy.' To hell with John Burton, her mind was whispering in a fever of self-defence and the need to get this over. 'We went to High Clough together. Carly took us in the carriage.' Her voice was quiet, composed, steady with truth.

He seemed to sag, his body folding little by little though he did not fall. His eyes grew unfocused, a kind of smoky brown and his words, when they emerged, were blurred.

'High Clough?'

'Yes, your mill and we intend to inspect West Heath and South Royd in the next few days. Someone must stop Roly.'

'Roly . . .' he faltered, reaching behind him for a chair. When he found it he sat down heavily. His face was quite blank but he managed to dig deep into his wounded mind for the last few words.

'From doing . . . what?'

She hurriedly crossed the room and sank to her knees before him. His hands lay flaccid in his lap and she took them between her own. She brought them to her lips, kissing them passionately then released one to brush back a lock of his thick hair that fell over his forehead. It was a gesture she might have used with Jamie or Alec when they were upset.

'Oh, my darling, come back to me, help me,' she cried. 'He is doing his best to get his hands on your mills and he must be stopped. Susan and I went to see him. I don't know why we took Biddy. For support, I suppose,' she went on distractedly, 'but he is making threats. He is determined to have your share of the mills for himself. To run them himself. He is to marry Anne Bracken who will be one of the richest women in Yorkshire when her father goes and even before that will bring Roly the cash he needs. Or he says he will split the business. Build a fourth mill then he will have two and you the same, the money for the fourth mill coming from the profits already accrued. Susan says he will, of course, take the most profitable and you will be left with . . .'

He turned his face to the window and after several dreadful, *silent* seconds she began to understand that she had lost him.

She tried one last desperate measure, one she was loth to bring up but somehow she must take it if she was to reach him.

'Harry . . . Harry, listen to me. If you refuse he threatens to tell the world that Cat is not your child, but his.'

He said nothing, nothing showed in his face. He simply sat in the chair, his lifeless hands lying in hers and it was as though a light, perhaps a feeble light but a light nevertheless, had been blown out inside him. He looked so handsome; no, that was not exactly the word since his features, unlike his brother's, were far from perfect. His mouth was

328

too hard though it lifted at one corner as if half ready to smile. His jaw was tense and uncompromising. His nose was slightly crooked, due to being broken and he had a faint white scar through one eyebrow. His eyes, which were the colour of treacle, were surrounded by luxuriant black lashes and normally glowed with life, with health and on occasion with good humour. He had strong white teeth. He was lean and hard and on the whole had an attractive appearance.

'Harry.' She shook his hands in desperation but when he turned his gaze back to her she wished she had left him alone. There was nothing there. Nothing of Harry Sinclair. Just a face that might have been painted on canvas.

She rose slowly to her feet, moved to the door and out into the hallway. She was not surprised to find Susan and Biddy waiting for her.

'He's gone,' she said simply. 'Doctor John was right. It was too soon to tell him the truth. 'There is only myself to keep it all together and I—'

Susan almost knocked her over so forceful was her embrace. Her arms clutched Lally to her fiercely and beside her Biddy hovered, longing to support her lass but willing to give her into Susan's safe keeping if that was for the best.

'Eeh . . . eeh no.' Susan reverted to the speech of her early years, so great was her emotion. 'Tha's not alone, our Lally,' again speaking as a northern woman will when confronted with one of her own. 'Me an' Biddy's 'ere. Between us we'll beat that bugger up at mill until maister's 'imself again. That's right, int'it, Biddy? Us'll study owt what goes on at that mill an' we'll beat it. I'll work in't loom gate again if I 'ave to an' Biddy knows all about account books, don't tha', Biddy?'

Biddy, who had been Mrs Stevens to Susan Harper earlier in the day, nodded her head, not even considering how the account books of a woollen mill might be different to those she was familiar with in the kitchen.

'Aye, we'll manage, lass. That lad up at the mill can't sell or buy anything without Mr Sinclair's signature, and between us we'll beat him. Now, we'd best get Doctor John up here to see to Mr Harry.'

CHAPTER TWENTY-THREE

He took to sitting in a chair facing the bedroom window, his face devoid of all expression, his two dogs at his feet. If left alone he would have remained in bed, the bed he shared each night with Lally and until the man John Burton had recommended came to get him up, bathe and dress him, Lally began to think he would moulder away there like a baby untended, since you could hardly expect the outside men to see to him and it needed a man's strength to move him. The man's name was Martin, quiet-spoken, pleasant, polite, a man of about forty with no family, who had been a porter at the infirmary and dispensary on Ferguson Street to which John gave some of his time. Martin had no nursing experience but he was strong and patient and what Lally liked about him was that he *talked* to Harry as though Harry were taking part in a proper conversation. He had attended Sunday school as a child and could read and write and as he and Harry sat by the window or before the fire he would read passages from *The Times* to him. They had all been appalled by the events in India brought about by the revolt of the sepoys though the reason for it was vague in most of their minds. Lucknow, Allahabad, Cawnpore were as familiar to those who read the newspapers as London, Manchester or Halifax, but the report of the butchering of those captured at Cawnpore by Nana Sahib, who seemed to be the leader, turned the stomach of the strongest. Descriptions of white women and children stripped and hacked to death then thrown down a well made the whole world shudder. But that was last year and a report that a memorial had been built at the Cawnpore well had been received with a quiet and steely satisfaction.

Now, eighteen months later and nearer to home, Her Majesty the Queen had been proclaimed Sovereign of India. She had created her beloved husband Albert, Prince Consort, a new princess, Beatrice, was born, and the Princess Royal, Victoria—known as Pussy to her family—had married Frederick III, German Emperor and King of Prussia. All this Martin read out to Harry along with accounts of ministerial crises in the government, grave conditions in European affairs and the domestic concerns of the country. Mr Disraeli and Lord Palmerston were quoted but Harry continued to sit where he was put, gazing into the coals of the fire or out of the window at the white, frozen world beyond. The trees of the woodland stood laden along each branch with a burden of diamond-studded new-fallen snow against a sky that was cold and clear and rosy with the pink frozen sun floating in it just above the tree line. The flowerbeds were filled with frozen stalks which in summer would be a glory of colour and the lawn was a pure unbroken carpet of dazzling white to the lake. On the water the swans appeared to be a dirty grey, so white was the world. Pink flushes dappled the snow in the windless chill but Harry was immune to the glory of it as he was to all that went on about him.

Doctor John had been appalled by his patient's sudden deterioration. Lally had called him in at once, even as she did so knowing there was nothing to be done. The news that she was to have another child, one that he believed was once again his brother's, had sent him over the brink of reason and she brooded on how a man so well balanced as Harry Sinclair could be affected as he was.

'Lally, I believe the blow to his skull must have damaged his . . . his brain even more than I first thought,' John told her worriedly. They had moved downstairs after he had examined Harry, leaving Biddy to sit beside him, and sat in the drawing room where they were drinking coffee brought in by an anxious Jenny, for they were all fond of Mr Harry who was a good master. 'I can't understand why, almost overnight, he should become as he has. Why, he didn't even know me and yet only the other day he was bright and cheerful and though not fully himself, recognised those about him. We know so little, if anything, about the human brain but I believed as he recovered physically he would have—'

Lally held up her hand and, surprised, he stopped speaking.

'John, there is something you should know, then perhaps it might give you some insight into why

332

Harry is as he is. He took a terrible beating. His skull was . . . must have been severely damaged but . . . but there is something else. I might say keep it to yourself but it will be all over Moorend before long.' Her voice was bitter. 'So I might as well tell you now.'

John leaned forward, his youthful, earnest face worried.

'Lally . . . ?'

'My daughter Cat is not Harry's child,' she told him abruptly and was not surprised when he fell back in consternation.

'I did a foolish thing after . . . after Chris died. Roly was our friend, mine and Chris's and . . . well, one thing led to another and Cat was the result. When I told Harry, who was already helping me with the estate, he offered me marriage. He is a wonderful man . . .'

'You love him.' It was a statement of fact.

'Yes, I do,' surprising herself as she answered.

'So?'

'I am with child again, John, but it seems that because Roly has just come home . . . well, a couple of months ago and I have just become pregnant, Harry's troubled mind has put the two events together and he believes the child I carry is Roly's. When I told him we, Harry and I, were to have a child he became as he is.'

'But surely—'

She held up her hand again. 'There is more. Roly wants the mills. He and Harry, naturally, have not got on well since . . . so Roly wants to buy him out, or split the business. If Harry will not agree he threatens to tell the world that Caterina is his child and not Harry's.'

'Dear sweet Christ! No wonder Harry's mind has retreated. That blow to his head . . .'

'Must have somehow interfered with his reasoning powers, for the man I knew would never have become as he is. He was aware of the strife between himself and Roly before he was attacked by the Weavers but add to that his belief that the child in my belly is not his . . . John, oh, John, what are we to do?'

And so it was that Martin came into their lives and each day they waited for Harry to be himself again and for Roly to make his next move in the acquisition of the Sinclair mills.

*   *   *

The following Sunday the Moorend Hunt met at Holestone Manor on Lord Billington's estate which lay to the south of the Priory. It had been feared that the snowstorm of the previous week might mean a cancellation of the fox hunting but the weather had turned mild and apart from pockets of snow lying here and there and in the shade of the dry-stone walls, the fields and moorlands were clear. The hunt—the one that had killed Chris Fraser—was popular with local landowners and squirearchy and not a few of the county folk who could afford a decent animal. The hunt fulfilled a number of functions besides the social focus and enjoyment. It rid the farmers of vermin and provided employment for ostlers, grooms, stable lads, and each hunt recruited its staunch regiment of whippers-in and dog-stoppers.

It was a thrilling scene that clear, bright morning, the hounds milling about the master, the sound of the horn, the brilliant red coats, the laughter as the stirrup cup was handed round by his lordship's servants. There were many ladies mounted in riding habits of black or dark blue, their tight jackets buttoned up the front, their cambric shirts immaculate. They had sleeves to their jackets with cuffs, a black, beaver top hat with a veil, riding trousers of chamois leather with black feet over which they wore a full skirt which allowed them to ride astride.

Among those flirting with the ladies was Roly Sinclair, mounted on a magnificent thoroughbred coal-black hunter, large, bold and confident, as he was himself, chosen by Roly for riding in flat open country with big jumps but also able to cross moorland terrain. Miss Anne Bracken, to whom he had recently become engaged, was not present since she came from a class that did not ride to hounds. He would not have been so sanguine had he been aware of the activity that was taking place on the premises of the Sinclair mills.

*   *   *

'There must be a desk or a large table up here somewhere, Susan. It looks as though all the Frasers throughout the ages could not bear to part with anything. Look at that monstrosity over there with all that carving. Is it a wardrobe, d'you think? Or that thing with a marble top and legs like an elephant. How on earth did they get it up here? I wonder. I've never seen such furniture in my life. And these,' indicating what looked like bow-fronted steps. 'It's got a lid.' She lifted the lid and peered inside and then began to laugh.

'What?'

'It's a chamber pot.'

'Look, Lally, if you're going to spend your time examining everything in the attic we'll never get done. Remember, there's only today to do what we must. Now cast about for something suitable. Big enough for a desk but small enough for the men to get it down the stairs and into the cart.'

For half an hour they poked about in the vast attics, dusty, dishevelled and disheartened until at last Susan exclaimed in excitement.

'This will do if the men can get it out. It's big enough and has drawers along the front. Drawers with locks on them if we can find keys. Oh, look, the keys are actually in the drawer. There's even a chair to match. Oh, do come and look, Lally.'

They studied the table from every angle and Susan even sat at it. Lally thought it might be a library table from perhaps the last century, fashioned in mahogany. It had well-turned legs and casters so that it might be moved about more easily.

'This is it, Susan,' Lally said quietly as though the seriousness of what was ahead of them had at last become reality. Her face was set in a mould of grave resolution. 'I'll call Carly and Ben. He has borrowed a cart from Sean McGinley and it's standing ready in the yard. And I have the keys to the gates and the office. Now, d'you think we should change?' She looked down ruefully at the dusty state of her gown.

Susan nodded firmly. 'Oh yes, we must start out as we mean to go on. Neat, simple, no bright colours but smart!'

The maids were agog as Carly and Ben

336

staggered through the kitchen with the table. It had been dusted and, while Lally and Susan were changing, thoroughly polished as only Jenny knew how before being covered with a blanket and hoisted on to the cart. The chair was given the same treatment. Susan and Lally did not ride in the cart since there was no room on the seat across it but followed in the carriage with Caleb, one of the grooms Harry had brought with him from Mill House, at the reins.

With the master absent, Mrs Cannon, Ivy, Annie and Tess, the domestic staff at Mill House, watched from the parlour window, their mouths agape, as the carriage bearing Mrs Sinclair, the young master's sister-in-law, with a cart behind it, drew up at the mill gates at the bottom of the drive. Enoch and Arthur, who worked in the stables, and George the gardener, come to watch the extraordinary sight, exchanged bewildered glances, wondering if they should go down and ask Mrs Sinclair what she was about, politely, of course, as she unlocked the mill gate. The carriage passed through the gate into the empty mill yard beyond.

George, after much prodding and whispered conversation, made so bold as to creep down to the mill gates, which had been left open, reporting to the others that the men with Mrs Sinclair had carried the contents of the cart up the stairs that led to the mill office. What should they do? they asked one another. The weaving sheds were nothing to do with them. They were house servants but Mrs Cannon told them not to worry, for as soon as young Mr Roly returned from the hunt he would be informed. Mrs Sinclair had gone, the office and the mill gates had been locked again and all was secure. They only had to wait for young Mr Roly who was in charge since Mr Sinclair's accident.

*   *   *

Roly Sinclair had enjoyed his day's hunting, and not just of the fox! It was over twelve months since Ebenezer Franklin had been able to sit a horse. At seventy-two one's bone and muscle refused to obey one's will and with reluctance he had given in to his doctor's orders that he no longer joined in the hunt. Not so his attractive young wife, Polly, who saw no reason at twenty-eight years of age to stay at home with him. She had been married to him for his enormous wealth and had given him three sons so her duty was well and truly done! She and Roly, without a word spoken, had conveyed to one another their mutual attraction and since she was a house guest of Lord Billington there was a bedroom readily available to them to assuage their lust and where Roly spent the night. There had been a wild party, drinking, gambling, and it was eight thirty the next day, the first day of the working week, when he rode up the steep drive to the stables at the rear of Mill House. He was still dressed in his hunting pink. Mrs Cannon's rambling tale of carriages and carts and mill gates went through his aching head like water through a sieve. His manager had evidently supervised the turning on of the looms and in his own good time he would drift down to the weaving sheds and climb the stairs to his office.
@line:

They were both sensibly dressed as they stood at
the gate at five thirty that morning, Lally in
charcoal grey lightened with touches of crisp white,
Susan in bottle green. The stream of men with
jaunty caps thrown to the backs of their heads, the
women in shawls and clogs, the children in cut-
down second- or third-hand bits and pieces of
clothing, mostly barefoot, stared in wonder at the
two finely dressed ladies as they hurried to their
looms. They longed to stop and stare as Mr
Mather, the overseer, did his best to move the
ladies away to the office or indeed anywhere they
would not be on display. One of them was Mrs
Sinclair, wife to the master and the other one
several of the women recognised as Susan Harper
who had once worked in a loom gate beside them.

'Mrs Sinclair, I beg you, come away from the
gate. Mr Roly will be here any moment and—'

'Thank you, Mr . . . er . . . Mr . . . ?'

'Mather, ma'am. But the gates will be closed
soon against latecomers and—'

'Leave them open, Mr Mather, if you please,'
for she could see anxious women hurrying down
the lane, dragging children who were still half
asleep, terrified of being shut out and losing
precious wages.

'Mr Roly will—'

'My husband is in charge, Mr Mather and as he
is—'

'But Mr Sinclair's not been here for weeks,
ma'am and young Mr Sinclair says—'

'I will discuss it with Mr Sinclair when he
arrives.' She turned to her companion whom the

overseer did not recognise. The 'hands' all looked alike to him. 'Come, Susan, let us go in. You know the way.' And to the consternation of the overseer the two women followed the rest into the weaving shed.

It was already hot in the big room despite the chill of the day and so noisy Lally felt that she was being deafened. Susan led the way, for this was an environment with which she was familiar and Lally followed her blindly, her senses numbed by the sheer tumult of it all. The overseer hovered at their backs pleading with them to return to their carriage, or at least to the office where they would be out of sight of the curious hands, but he might have been a troublesome child for all the notice they took of him. 'Mrs Sinclair, please, there is no need for this. Young Mr Sinclair will be here soon and will deal with anything that might be . . . amiss . . .'

'Amiss? What should be amiss, Mr Mather? Mrs Harper and I are merely looking at the production of the cloth. Won't you go back to whatever it was you were doing before we arrived?'

'But, ma'am, Mr Sinclair'll not be best pleased.'

'Mr Sinclair should be here and since he is not . . .' She stopped speaking abruptly as a tiny child— a girl or a boy, it was hard to tell—crept out at her feet from beneath a machine and for a moment she was appalled because the creature seemed no older than her own Jamie. Surely Harry was not aware that such young children were employed in his mill, but Susan was marching ahead, her face averted, and she hurried to keep up with her. There were dozens of men, women and children working ceaselessly at the machines they tended,

340

most of the children underneath the swiftly moving carriages of the mules. They were collecting rubbish, scrabbling through woollen waste and oily dust, shouldering the bundles to the end of the rows of the looms. She understood now why Susan was averting her eyes and hurrying away from these pathetic little lads and lasses, for it was just such a task that had killed her Sam.

Some of the women were in charge of more than one machine, darting from one to another in a fever of movement. They had no thought in their heads but their need to keep an incessant watch on the beam from where the thread unwound to form the warp of the cloth, the shuttle that delivered the crossways thread of the weft. They were aware of and fascinated by the two finely dressed ladies but they did not stop since it was of the greatest importance, not only to them but to their young master, who was not as understanding of their hardworking lives and the children they did their best to raise as the older Mr Sinclair. He had even put a stop to the small school and nursery that Mr Harry had started and they were forced to leave their babies with neighbours or in the charge of little lasses who were no more than children themselves.

She and Susan walked between the rows of machines, not speaking, for it was hard to make oneself heard but though Susan was accustomed to the workings of the machines, to the noise and the smell of sweating bodies, Lally was not and her head was aching and she felt she might faint. She meant to learn all the operations of her husband's mills, or at least to recognise them, but her chief interest would be in the office of the mills where the business, the heart of the concern, was carried out, to where the orders came and were completed, where customers spent their time and money, where the accounts were balanced, where the samples were studied and decisions made as to the suitability and quality of the woven cloth. She knew she would have a fight, to put it mildly, with Roly who would turn nasty when he realised what she meant to do but she would not be deterred. She had Susan who was courageous and loyal and who would stand shoulder to shoulder with her in this tremendous endeavour. Chances must be taken and her heart quailed at the thought of them but she had no choice.

The yard was busy with what seemed to be its normal day-to-day activities: lifting and stacking rolls of woven cloth on to the wagons, unpacking bundles of fleeces come from she knew not where—but she would find out, she told herself— the comings and goings of the wagons, the stamp of horses' hooves, shouts and whistles and curses.

The men all froze and became silent, watching them as she and Susan crossed the yard and climbed the steps on the outside of the building that led to the office. Lifting the skirts of their gowns and capes in order not to trip on them and to keep them from the dirty steps, they were surprised to see a man coming down them. A tall, well-built man about thirty years of age, not dressed as Harry or Roly, or indeed any commercial gentleman might dress, but neatly, plainly in good quality worsted. Black jacket and trousers under a fly-fronted Chesterfield coat, an immaculate shirt front and a plain black neck-tie. He wore no hat and his hair was dark as chocolate, straight and thick and needed cutting. His mouth was hard but a pleasing shape as though ready to smile. His eyes were a smoky brown with curious amber flecks in them and his face smooth, freshly shaved. He had a tiny nick in his chin where his razor had evidently gone too close.

He stopped in amazement when he saw them coming up towards him, then hurriedly backed up to allow them to pass him at the top. Not knowing what else to do or even who they were, since he had been at the Sinclair mills for no more than a fortnight, he bowed.

'Good morning, ladies?' His voice was questioning and there was no doubt that he was a Yorkshireman.

'Good morning,' they answered in unison.

'May I help you?' he asked politely, wondering who the devil they were and what they were doing at the mill office at this time of the morning. Most ladies of quality, or so he had been led to believe, were still in their beds drinking hot chocolate at this hour of the morning.

'May I ask who you are?' the exceptionally lovely one asked while the other, the one with the bluest eyes he had ever seen, watched him closely, even suspiciously, he thought, saying nothing.

'My name is Adam Elliott. I'm the mill engineer. I was hoping to see Mr Sinclair but it seems he's not in his office,' which, his expression said, he should have been at this hour.

They both, for some reason, looked relieved. He waited.

'Then we'll go in and get on, shall we, Susan? Oh, I'm Mrs Sinclair, Mr Elliott, and this is Mrs Harper.'

Adam felt a twinge of surprise, since he had no idea Mr Sinclair was married. No mention of it had been made to him. Indeed in the short time he had been here he had somehow got the impression his employer was a bachelor about to be wed to one of the wealthiest heiresses in the county.

The ladies smiled their thanks as he held the door open for them, then, for a reason he could not define since they were nothing to do with him, he followed them in. The clerk who had informed him that Mr Sinclair was not yet in his office leaped to his feet and began to stutter, but Mrs Sinclair, with a pleasant greeting, swept past him and into Mr Sinclair's office. There was a good fire burning in the grate and with what looked like an anxious smile she removed her cape and hung it on the hook behind the door as did Mrs Harper. Mrs Sinclair seated herself behind what was Mr Sinclair's desk and Mrs Harper sat down at a table that was placed next to it forming an L.

'Mrs Sinclair,' the clerk spluttered, evidently knowing her, hopping from foot to foot and clearly horrified. 'Mr Roly will be here soon and—'

'Yes, he *is* late, isn't he? While we wait Mrs Harper and I will have coffee—is there someone to make it? Oh, good—and in the meanwhile I would be glad if you would fetch—'

'What the bloody hell's going on here?' a voice thundered from the doorway. Adam Elliott stood to one side to allow Roly Sinclair to pass, preparing to be entertained.

CHAPTER TWENTY-FOUR

Adam Elliott was an extremely clever and intelligent man, not a gentleman, for his father had a small printing firm in Halifax. Adam was an only child and because Douglas and Minnie Elliott were decent, responsible parents, thrifty with their cash and great believers in education—they could both read—their clever son not only went to grammar school in Halifax but he worked hard and finished up at university with a degree in engineering and was a great help to his father in running the printing press.

Since the old days when spinners and weavers of woollen cloth worked at their own wheels and looms in their own cottages, the factory system had evolved and these same cottagers had been forced to leave their simple, self-regulated lives and turn to the mill-owner for a day's work. Water, which was plentiful in the grey peaked hills of Yorkshire, provided the power to the wheel that drove the machines until, with great secrecy and some danger, for men were smashing such things, seeing them as a threat to their livelihood, new machines were introduced by far-seeing mill-owners, power looms for which a supply of water was no longer necessary but a new breed of men were. Adam Elliott was one of these men, an engineer. The Sinclair mills had hundreds of machines engaged in producing the best worsted yarn in the world. Sorting and scouring, carding, the preparation of worsted yarn, spinning and weaving, and Adam was employed to keep these machines working. It seemed Mr Sinclair, the one they called *young* Mr Sinclair, had been involved in the selling of the cloth, travelling to many parts of the world and was not concerned in the actual workings of his carding machines, his spinning and weaving machines. What he had learned in his youth he had forgotten so he had employed Adam to supervise this side of the business for him. There was some mystery regarding the older brother in the business concern and now, as he stood in the doorway of the mill office, it seemed Adam was about to find out what it was.

'Good morning, Roly,' the lovely young woman who sat behind his desk said sweetly. 'Your day starts late, it seems, which won't please Harry when he hears about it.'

'Never mind Harry or what he wouldn't say or do since you and I are fully aware that Harry is incapable of taking—'

'That is why I am here, Roly, to speak for him. To sit at *his* desk and keep an eye on his mills.'

'My mills, damn you, or will be when he makes up his bloody mind about selling to me. Now, get out of that chair and go home where you belong and take this . . . this woman with you.'

He strode across the room, his manner threatening and Adam, who had been lounging against the door frame thinking it was time he made himself scarce since this was really nothing to do with him, straightened up slowly. The woman behind the second desk—what had been her name . . . Harper?—rose and moved to stand protectively behind Mrs Sinclair. He had heard vague gossip about the older Sinclair brother, of whom he knew nothing, but Adam had been employed by young

346

Sinclair, the brother he had assumed was in full charge of the business.

The young woman was quite lovely but there was something unique about the other one, the one called Harper, which he couldn't put his finger on. She was not as good-looking as Mrs Sinclair but she had the sweetest face in which was set a determined mouth as though she had had her share of troubles but had overcome them. He found himself strangely drawn to her.

Adam was so busy studying Susan Harper he did not notice the speculative expression on Mrs Sinclair's face. He would have been surprised if he could have read her thoughts, for Lally was suddenly struck with the notion that this young man, though she hardly knew him, would make a perfect match for her friend. Doctor John had been considered, at least by her, but Adam was a better prospect and she was not sure Susan thought of John in that way.

'Harry has made his mind up, Roly, and he will not sell his share of the mills to you, neither will he split the concern in two. The three mills work perfectly in conjunction with one another, he says, and that should not be interfered with. Someone, yourself, in fact, who has made such a magnificent job of it must continue your travels to find buyers for your goods, yours and Harry's goods and so—'

'I shall employ a man to do just that, my dear Lally, in fact I have such a person in mind to sell my cloth while I remain here to run the business. Elliott here'—nodding in Adam's direction—'is in charge of the machines and should one cause trouble he is trained to repair it.'

'Harry did that, Roly, *and* ran the business.

Mr Elliott,' smiling graciously at Adam, 'clever as he may be, would not be needed if Harry was . . . when Harry is back on his feet . . .'

Roly Sinclair sneered as he placed his hands flat on the desk, thrusting his face almost into hers.

'Really, Lally, this charade you try to keep up is pathetic. We both know Harry is, shall we say, not exactly himself and is not capable of making any sort of decision. The doctor is constantly at the Priory and rumour has it that my brother needs a minder. Oh, yes, I have my spies and I am told the beating he received from the Weaver brothers has taken a severe toll on his . . . his thinking powers. Best sell to me, my pet. I promise I will give you a good price then you and Harry can live comfortably at the Priory and play with your farms. They are your sons' inheritance and should be looked after, which you and your steward should manage comfortably.'

Lally sighed as though with irritated exasperation. She shook her head then turned to Susan, taking her hand in hers. 'What have you to say, Susan? Shall we accept my brother-in-law's offer?'

'Perhaps we might have some more details from this gentleman here.' Susan smiled in Adam's direction. She held Lally's hand with both of hers and there was no doubt of where her loyalties lay. It was the first time Adam had heard her speak and he was surprised. He had thought her to be of the same social class as Mrs Sinclair but it seemed she was not. She spoke correctly, grammatically but with a northern accent similar to his own. A *Yorkshire* accent which was the strongest in the north of England. He felt a stirring of interest that

348

surprised him, for in his thirty years no woman had ever caught his attention except in a physical sense. This was not like that!

He lifted his firm chin and took a step towards the desk, ignoring his employer's angry glare.

'I'm an engineer, Mrs Harper. It's my job to maintain every machine in the Sinclair mills, to ensure that they are in perfect working order and that if one should break down I put it right.'

'My husband can do that, Mr Elliott. He can do every job in his three mills as well as any man or woman who works for him,' Lally said proudly, still clinging to Susan's hand, and Adam felt a secret admiration for this woman's husband if what she said was true. She turned to Roly who had moved to stare furiously from the window into the yard. 'I thought you could too, Roly. Or have you lost the knack in the years you travelled Europe, America and all points of the compass? Well, Mr Elliott,' turning back to face Adam, 'you will be of great help to Mrs Harper and me until my husband is back behind this desk.'

Roly swivelled forcefully from the window, his face crimson with rage, and Adam instinctively moved forward as though to protect the two women who seemed in danger of violence.

'Have you forgotten the promise I made you if Harry should refuse to sell me his share of the mills?'

'The threat, you mean?'

'Call it what you will, Lally, but I mean it. I'll show you up for a trollop and Harry for a fool. The child, the children will be ostracised as will you and your husband.'

'Do you really want the family of your intended

bride to know the details of that sordid episode?' Lally rose and like a young queen stood before Roly Sinclair with great dignity. Her face was white, even her lips, but her eyes were as clear and steady and calm as the waters Adam had once seen lapping a stretch of golden sand on the coast of Cornwall and were the same exquisite mix of turquoise and green. He had only seen it once years ago when he had visited that county to study the pumping engines that were used in the mining industry there but he had never forgotten it.

He had longed to leave this office minutes ago, for what was happening here was not his concern but it struck him that these two brave women who outfaced Roly Sinclair might need support, or even a witness. He had no wish to intrude on what was evidently a family quarrel but something held him fast.

'Is that what it was? A sordid episode?' Roly laughed harshly. 'And the result? Is she sordid too? Decent families will think so, Lally. An illegitimate child. *Your* child fathered by your husband's brother.' In the doorway Adam was heard to gasp.

'Yer bastard, yer bullyin' bastard,' shrieked Susan, reverting, as she did in times of crisis, to her native tongue, her face contorted with contempt, but Lally put a restraining hand on her arm, gripping it fiercely.

'Don't, Susan,' she began, but Susan, usually so self-contained, was incensed by the callousness of the man she barely knew, and was sustained by her deep affection for Lally who had mended Susan's life when it had been so badly broken.

' 'Ow can yer say such a dreadful thing? The truth it might be but ter threaten nor only a woman

350

'oo 'as no one ter defend 'er bu' innocent bairns an' all is beyond me. Tha' little girl don't deserve yer foulness, nor them lads. Ruin their lives—yer nowt but scum.'

'Who is this . . . this slut who rushes to defend you, Lally?' Roly asked in an amused manner. 'Really, you have the most amazing friends and I wonder that Harry allows her into his home. She sounds like one of the hands from the weaving shed.'

'She was, Roly, but Harry and I befriended her and I don't know what I would do without her.'

'Christ! She's your *friend*! a woman from the weaving shed! Well, I wish you well of her, and what the devil the pair of you are doing here sitting in my office—'

'Harry's office, Roly.'

'Rubbish! It seems Harry is content to loll at home so someone has to run the business.'

'Susan and I intend to do that. Harry, who is not yet able to get out much, will advise us.'

Roly began to laugh, not a laugh of amusement but of derision. He shook his head and shrugged his shoulders as though at the woeful lunacy of women, especially these two, turning to face them both, the presence of Adam Elliott of no consequence. Suddenly his face showed nothing but cool hostility, his jaw muscles clenched tight, a hard shell that hid the true Roly Sinclair who, now that his chance had come, was about to snatch the prize and the authority he had always coveted. From the yard came the familiar clatter of men working, horses whinnying. A wind was rising and the sky above the roofline opposite was sketched in winter charcoal and Lally thought idly that it might

351

snow again. As she watched Roly she wondered why it was she had never before seen this side of her brother-in-law, who had been her and Chris's companion for so many years. He had always been, or seemed to have been, good-natured, easy-going, likeable, fun-loving, careless of the proprieties as they had been. When he left the school he and Chris attended, he had worked in the mill and had learned all the intricacies of worsted manufacturing but being the charming fellow he was his talents had lain in selling the cloth which he had done with great success. But it seemed he had always been ambitious and with no one to restrain him now he had involved himself in the management of the mills with what appeared to be an appetite for expansion and to become the man who commanded attention at the Piece Hall in Halifax. Harry had been known as a hard master, autocratic and shrewd, but fair. To ensure punctuality Harry had locked his gates at five thirty every morning, obliging latecomers to stand outside for an hour, considering the loss of earnings to be punishment enough. Lally had heard that Roly not only locked them out but fined them as well to make up for loss of profit. Harry had been approachable but it seemed Roly was not. He was concerned only with efficiency and profit. The only aspect of his business with which he was no longer familiar was running the machines which was why he had employed Adam Elliott.

She and Susan meant to keep the mills running as Harry had done and to that end Adam Elliott would be a godsend.

Roly turned on the engineer as though only just

352

aware of his presence. 'Right, Elliott, you and I will ride over to West Heath where I believe a carding machine is giving trouble. When I return I shall expect you two . . . ladies to have vacated my office and returned to your homes. I shall not—'

Lally's voice was as sharp as the slivers of ice that had hung from the gutters of the mill. 'Take your time, Roly. While you're away Susan and I intend to study the account books, the order books, records, delivery dates, etc., indeed everything connected to the Sinclair mills. My housekeeper is being driven over from the Priory with our luncheon so we will be here all day, at least until four o'clock. I am to interview a governess for my children, since Susan, who has been helping in the schoolroom, will accompany me here each day. Now then, on your way out ask—what's his name?—Hawkins, thank you, Mr Elliott, to fetch in the records.'

Adam fully expected her to say, 'That will be all,' to the slack-jawed Roly Sinclair but with an affectionate smile she turned to her companion who sat down and reached for some letters that lay on the desk and proceeded to open them. Adam noticed her hand was trembling.

When the door crashed to behind Roly both Susan and Lally slumped down in their chairs, their heads bowed, letting out long breaths they were scarcely aware they had been holding.

'Oh, God, Susan . . . Oh, Jesus God . . . Oh, God in heaven . . .'

'I never thought we'd get through it . . .'

'I was convinced he was going to hit us and I believe he might if Mr Elliott had not been present.'

353

'What will he do next, d'you think? He'll not take this lying down. What will he do?'

'Try to go and see Harry, I should think, since he'll have no truck with women. He doesn't know how Harry is . . . the state he's in . . . that he's not himself.' Lally was near to tears.

'Lass, lass, don't upset thissen. There's nothing he can do as things stand now. The mills belong to him and Mr Harry and until Mr Harry sells them to him or gets them legally split between the two of them, he can't move on. Mr Roly, I mean. As long as he never finds out that Mr Harry's . . . well, as he is, everything that happens will seem to come from him, Mr Harry, I mean. Now then, let's get that old fool in the office to fetch in all the books, records of transactions, details of prices, lists of customers. The whole history of the mills since old Mr Sinclair's time. And how about a cup of tea?'

It took them a moment or two to realise that Adam Elliott was still with them!

*   *   *

She sent Martin away and ordered her and Harry's evening meal to be brought up to the bedroom where Jenny set it out on a table before the fire. She knew Martin was in the habit of encouraging Harry to feed himself, teaching him to use his fork, knife and spoon as one might teach a small child. Biddy had made soup à la julienne which contained carrots, turnips, onions, leeks, celery, lettuce, sorrel and chervil, butter and stock, a good heartening soup, for Biddy was of the opinion that what Mr Harry needed for a full recovery was building up with nourishing food. The kind Biddy prepared! The soup was followed by a rich steak, kidney and mushroom pie, the crust so flaky it melted on the tongue, the gravy made from the stock of shin of beef, another 'building up' dish. It was accompanied by mixed vegetables, home grown, of course, and potatoes mashed with butter. Then came charlotte russe made from 'ladies fingers' of sponge, whipped cream, sugar and wine and if that didn't set him up nothing would, Biddy declared grimly.

He sat opposite Lally and obediently spooned the soup into his mouth. He ate delicately, carefully, prompted by Lally, then, when the soup was finished and the main dish was put in front of him by a watchful Jenny, and encouraged by his wife, he cleared his plate and to Lally's surprise wiped his lips with the damask napkin Jenny had placed across his knee. It was as though the habit of good table manners bred in him as a boy still remained. He placed his knife and fork correctly in the centre of his plate and sat back.

To both the women's amazement he smiled.

'That was delicious. My compliments to the chef,' just as though he were dining in a smart restaurant.

*   *   *

'Oh sir, Mrs Stevens'll be that pleased,' Jenny twittered, while something lurched inside Lally's breast. It was the first time he had spoken, at least in her presence and she was sure Martin would have told her if it had happened while he was in charge.

'Wilta 'ave a taste of charlotte russe, sir?' Jenny

355

went on. 'Mrs Stevens made it specially fer yer.'

She stood with the dessert ready to serve, her face in a huge beam for they were that fond of the master.

Immediately Harry looked confused. 'I'm . . . not sure . . . Charlotte . . .'

'Charlotte russe, sir. Try a bit. The bairns love it. Fer a treat, like.'

Lally held her breath.

'The . . . the bairns?'

'Aye, sir.' But even Jenny could see that Mr Harry had slipped back from that crack in the door to his mind, closing it behind him. She looked enquiringly at Lally.

'Serve it, Jenny, and then leave us, thank you.'

Jenny did as she was told then left the room to gallop down to the kitchen to tell them all that at last Mr Harry had spoken.

'What did 'e say?'

'Eeh, never . . .'

'Thank the good Lord.'

'I bet it were my soup. Put hairs on his chest that.' And Froglet, who was in the kitchen on an errand for Barty delivering vegetables, ran excitedly to spread the word outside.

Lally finished her meal, drinking the coffee Jenny brought up, watching Harry sip his, before speaking.

'Susan and I have been to High Clough today, Harry,' she remarked casually as though it were no big event, leaning forward to stir the fire with the brass poker. She looked lovely, the fire's glow enhancing the flush to her cheeks and the sapphire gleam to her eyes. 'We were not made welcome by . . .' Should she say his brother's name? she

356

agonised, then decided to plunge in, for might it not bring about some reaction which surely was better than this total breakdown of not only communication but Harry's functioning. The wound to his head where a Weaver boot had kicked him must be well on the way to healing and though she didn't know why some instinct was whispering to her that a direct confrontation might be worth chancing. It was a risk but to her it appeared that a shock, a sudden shock, might restore some of his mental reasoning.

He turned his head to look at her but his eyes were blank, clouded almost as though a mist were swirling in his head.

'Roly was there and he was furious when I told him you were not prepared to sell him your share of the mills. I really think he might have laid hands on us if Mr Elliott had not been there. Oh, you don't know of Mr Elliott, do you? He is an engineer employed by Roly to keep the machines running. He seems a decent fellow and with him and Susan to help me—she is pretty good with figures, you know, sharp and quick, and, of course, she is an experienced operative—we'll manage until you are back on your feet and can tell Roly yourself to go to the devil.'

She waited patiently, hopefully, hopelessly as it turned out for him to respond, to speak again but he looked away indifferently, his eyes on the leaping red and orange and yellow of the flames which the poker had flared up. The clock ticked, a pretty boudoir clock of gilt and pale blue enamel flanked by a pair of matching candlesticks.

Lally sighed. 'Well, I suppose I had better get to my bed if I'm to be up by five tomorrow morning.

357

Susan and I intend to be at the gates each morning when the operatives arrive. I hate to call them 'hands' as Roly does. It sounds so demeaning. I shall work just as you did and if it's all right with you, Harry, I shan't close the gates to female latecomers. They have children to see to and I believe a little leeway must be given. Oh, and I intend to reopen the school and baby-minding scheme which Roly closed. I shall employ some suitable young woman to superintend both. I have engaged a Miss Phyllis Atkinson—I saw her earlier—as governess for Jamie and Alec and to help Dora in the nursery. She starts the day after tomorrow so Jenny and Clara can prepare a room for her. She is only twenty years old but seems sensible and cheerful and if she only teaches them the rudiments of reading and writing and their numbers, which Susan started, it will do until they go to the grammar school. Susan was with me when I interviewed her and agrees she will do nicely. We shall need her when we have five children in the nursery.'

She paused for a moment, staring pensively into the fire. 'D'you know, Harry, it was a blessed day when you brought Susan into my life. I don't know how I should manage without her. Oh, by the way, this weekend I intend riding over to Foxwell to see how Denny and Kate McGinley are getting on and their babies, of course. Cameron tells me we wouldn't know the place. Denny and Sean are slowly rebuilding that ramshackle shed the Weavers called home. I often wonder what became of them all, especially those two thugs who . . . who attacked you.'

She shook herself as though throwing off old

358

memories that were not pleasing to her, then stood up and, bending over, kissed him softly on the lips, surprised and pleased when his parted a little in response. 'I'll just slip up to the nursery and see the children and have a word with Susan. We're to make a proper start in the morning on the sales records of the three mills. I won't be long but, Harry, let me help you to undress tonight. I would like to if . . . if you don't mind.'

She moved gracefully towards the bedroom door, her back to her husband and was not aware that as she opened it and went out his head turned and his eyes followed her.

CHAPTER TWENTY-FIVE

They had known from the start that Roly would be difficult but neither of them could possibly have imagined that the description of 'difficult' should have been what Harry called 'bloody-minded'. If there was a way to undermine what they tried to do he found it. He had declared his intention of buying Harry out. Both brothers had what was called 'brass' in Yorkshire, made over the years since they had run the business and, of course, what they had inherited from their father. Roly intended to divide the mills, in fact to conduct the business of manufacturing worsted yarn on his own terms, but when it came to the actual work of it somehow he was always elsewhere. He had been accustomed to the relatively glamorous task of selling the cloth, travelling in great luxury from city to city, country to country and doing so in style.

359

Staying at the very best hotels, eating the best of the country's cuisine, drinking the most expensive wines as he entertained the customers. He had never performed what anyone would consider a hard day's work in his life. He had an office at South Royd, a desk, a portrait of his father on the wall, but what he actually did there when he was not travelling, no one could say. He was restless. The workers considered him too fine a gentleman to dirty his hands in the weaving sheds, unlike his brother. He rode to hounds, shot grouse and pheasant in season, drank brandy and claret in low company, associated with loose women and Lally and Susan hoped he would continue to do so, keeping out of their way.

He now had the prospect of unlimited cash at his disposal from his marriage to Anne Bracken, to which ceremony his family were not invited since the bride's family did not wish to associate with a woman whose morals were, to say the least, lax. The rumour of her association with the bridegroom, who was not, of course, blamed, had soon got about as he had threatened, and he had begun to renew his efforts to enter the Priory to confront Harry. To *force* his way in if possible, for he was well aware—informed of the fact by his lawyer—that without his brother's signature he could neither split the business into two parts nor buy Harry's share, but Lally had warned Jenny that she was to summon Carly and Martin, who was a big strong chap, the moment Mr Roly showed himself at the front door. He was not on any account to be allowed into the master's bedroom where Harry sat staring blankly out of the window. If Roly found out his brother's true condition he would immediately take steps to have him declared incompetent, of that there was no doubt.

Roly was incensed by her absolute refusal to let him see his brother which he tried to do several times while she was at the mill, threatening to send for the constable, but Carly and Martin, with Wilf and Ben ranged behind them brandishing pitchforks as the mistress had ordered, would not allow him beyond the front door.

On one occasion he had pressed Jenny, who had answered the door, back as far as the staircase, her screams echoing round the hall as he struck her in the face, and into the kitchen where the kitchen-maids cowered and babbled their terror, but there were a dozen men working for Mrs Sinclair now, handymen, grooms, stable lads, gardeners, even a gamekeeper to assist Mr Cameron, the steward. They were all devoted to the little mistress who had so much on her plate and, it was whispered, was with child, and Mr Roly was soon sent packing. It became the job of the boot boy, who was the youngest in the household and the fastest runner of them all, to work by the entrance gates of the Priory and should he see Mr Roly approaching to run like the wind to warn the men.

'Well, madam,' Roly snarled, 'as it seems I am not to be allowed to see my brother on the future of the mills I shall do exactly as I please and you and your . . . your so-called friends can go to the devil.'

'I believe there is a problem with a "mule", Roly,' Lally told him patiently, 'and as Adam is the only engineer among us you might want to re-phrase that.'

'Adam can go to hell as far as I'm concerned.'

361

'And I believe you have overlooked the fact that the steam power that drives our machines needs coal to fuel the boilers which I see you have forgotten to order. There is a combing machine standing doing nothing.'

And so it went on. It was rumoured in Bradford's old Wool Exchange—the new building was not erected until 1864—that merchants went regularly to the other side of the globe to buy wool; others went to Belgium, or even *China* selling yarn and pieces and Lally did her best to persuade Roly, who seemed to hang about carrying on only the pursuits of gentlemen, thanks to his enormously rich wife, to be once again a seller of worsted goods at which he was so successful, but it was now so far beneath him he ignored her. If he could not run the business from a luxurious office, as he wished to do, then she must manage on her own. Or ask her husband!

She and Susan had started up the school and nursery again to accommodate the offspring of their workers. They had been over to Saltaire where Titus Salt, moving out of the unsanitary environs of Bradford, had built his model industrial village. An enormous mill in a cleaner location, a green and pleasant area, employing 3,000 men and women and around it were houses, a park, a school, a library and outdoor facilities. The houses were lined with brick and each had a parlour, a kitchen, a pantry and two, three or four bedrooms, and there were almshouses for the elderly. Lally was fired up with the idea that Harry's mills might do the same but when she put it to Roly, telling him of a huge piece of land for sale known as Penfold Meadow which was no more

362

than scrub and therefore cheap, he laughed in her face.

She took no notice and went ahead anyway!

Adam had not been present, since he spent most of his time maintaining the spinning frames, the combing machines and the looms on which the weaving of the worsted was done. She and Susan, whom Roly ignored as he would a maidservant who had spoken out of turn, did their best to persuade him to go and at least look at the land.

'If we built cottages as Titus Salt has done . . .'

'Ha! Titus Salt! He has more money than sense and anyway the hands are perfectly content to live as they do.' His voice was contemptuous.

'Have you seen where they live, Roly? They exist in appalling conditions. One privy to 200 cottages, overcrowded with many families obliged to occupy one room, terrible diseases, particularly among the children, no sewerage or drainage in the courts, alleys and lanes, and the smell is . . . Susan will tell you.'

He turned to look at Susan, pulling at his underlip, gazing at her as though she should go back there and good riddance, but raising his eyebrows, he turned back to Lally, for though he did not agree with her, she was at least of his class.

'D'you know, Lally, I don't give a damn.'

'He cracks on he's summat special but he's nowt but a feckless bugger,' Susan said in her broad northern accent after he had gone.

Lally laughed. 'I know, lass, but he'll not get the best of us. We're off to see the bank manager, the architect and whoever else is needed to build proper houses on Penfold Meadow and if Roly won't sell the cloth we must be prepared to find an

363

honest man who will.'

'Where's the money coming from for all this, Lally? Surely Mr Harry keeps his in an account in his name.'

Lally tapped her nose then produced from her reticule a very official-looking document on which Harry's signature was prominent. 'Ways and means, my lass.'

'What about Roly? He'll cause more trouble when he finds out.'

'How often does Roly ride out to Penfold Meadow or indeed go anywhere that does not afford him pleasure? Come on, lass, frame yersenn,' laughing at Susan's expression at her own endeavour with a Yorkshire accent.

It all went swimmingly, foundations laid for the new mill, a massive mill that would incorporate all the processes of worsted manufacturing, a mill that would, like that at Saltaire, have light, air, space and warmth. Brand-new houses were begun until Mr Anson called one morning to tell them that Roly Sinclair, since he was half owner of the mill, had put a stop to the whole business by refusing to sign the necessary papers, a procedure Lally had overlooked. The work was brought to an abrupt halt, and what had already been done must be paid for by Mr Harry Sinclair since Mr Roly insisted he had nothing to do with it!

When Lally and Susan were not at their desks doing their best to keep the spinning frames and weaving looms running, interviewing suitable gentlemen to go abroad and sell their cloth, ordering coal and seeing to its distribution and the hundred and one other jobs they were industriously tackling—many of which seemed to roll along on their own momentum, the momentum begun by Harry Sinclair—they visited the houses in St Margaret's Passage from where Susan herself had come.

There were thirty of them totalling almost 180 rooms in which 400 people lived. It was a constantly shifting population since the inhabitants took in lodgers or threw out wayward older children. Only one in two infants born reached the age of three years. They lived in squalor, most of them, though among them could be found shrewd, decent, down-to-earth Yorkshire folk like Susan herself. In one room lived Mrs Quinn with a sagging double bed where she slept with her husband and five children. Nevertheless she was at the gates of High Clough each morning as was her husband and two of the older children, the rest left to fend for themselves. She was eternally grateful to Mrs Sinclair for reopening the school, though their Alfie who was six years old was to start as a piecener soon in the spinning shed.

A Mrs O'Connell did not get out of bed to greet them, having given birth that morning to a wailing little scrap wrapped in a bit of old sacking. Her 'husband' had buggered off and she'd no money to pay the rent and no, she didn't know where her other children were and didn't seem to care.

Mrs Maguire had eleven children in her two rooms and three lodgers in her cellar. She kept a pig in her back yard and she was cheerful and uncomplaining. They lived at the moment on potatoes but she hoped to resume her work as soon as this one, looking down at the baby clinging to the nipple on her pendulous breast, could be fitted into the mill nursery.

365

It was when they returned to their office after one such visit that they learned that all the building work at Penfold Meadow had been suspended. Roly was nowhere to be found but Adam was waiting for them, sitting behind Susan's desk from which he immediately sprang. Seated in a visitor's chair, from which he also rose as the two ladies entered the office, was a pleasant-looking young man about Adam's age, immaculately turned out in a dove-grey morning coat which reached his knees, a cream waistcoat, darker grey trousers, tight and buttoning at the ankle with four buttons, and a pristine white cravat. He smiled and bowed politely as the two ladies looked at him enquiringly.

'Mrs Sinclair, Mrs Harper, may I introduce Brice Heaton. Brice, this is Mrs Sinclair, the wife of the owner of the mills and her friend and associate, Mrs Harper.'

Mr Heaton bowed again. 'Mrs Sinclair, Mrs Harper.' Judging by his well-bred voice Mr Heaton was a gentleman.

When they were all settled Adam spoke.

'I think I have found the answer to our problems regarding the selling of the worsted which is beginning to pile up in our sheds since Mr Sinclair, Mr Roly Sinclair, that is, has declined to go abroad to sell it and the man he himself chose to take his place is not doing his job. We are managing here in this country because our customers, knowing the quality of the yarn, are still buying. They see the samples, of course, and everything runs smoothly. But someone must go to Europe, to Russia, to America, even China, to continue to sell our cloth to existing buyers and to find new ones. They will

366

go elsewhere if we don't deliver on time.'

Both Lally and Susan turned to look at Mr Heaton.

'Yes, Mr Heaton. Brice. He is an engineer as I am and earned his degree at the same university which is where I met him. We have been friends since. He has learned all aspects of the wool trade, travelling to London, Liverpool, Norfolk and Lincolnshire to glean knowledge of different types of wool and how to buy and sell among wool traders. He has been more thorough than I have myself. No, it's true, Brice,' as Mr Heaton held up a deprecating hand. 'I propose,' Adam went on, 'that you employ him. I can vouch for him, ladies. Your brother-in-law may kick up a fuss, Mrs Sinclair, but I think the four of us can keep the mills going until your husband has recovered. I realise that you barely know me, let alone Brice, but I think I have proved myself and . . . well, what d'you say?'

Mr Heaton appeared to be completely unfazed by the silence that followed. He was a member of the class that was well used to dealing with any situation, having been brought up, probably by a nanny, to keep his feelings hidden.

'Well.' Lally cleared her throat and turned to look at Susan whose own expression was non-committal. They were both aware that *someone* had to travel to other parts of the world to sell their cloth and Mr Heaton was certainly presentable. A gentleman from the same class as Lally but one who had turned his back on the conventions of the gentry, learned his trade, earned his degree at university as Adam had and, taking off his fine coat, had dirtied his hands on

367

the factory floor, or so Adam appeared to be telling them. Besides, Adam, whom they had come to trust, was prepared to testify to his integrity.

Lally and Susan exchanged glances and so well did they know each other by now, each was aware of what the other was thinking. They were impressed and delighted at what Adam proposed.

They were suddenly startled by a strange sound which none of them could identify, the sound accompanied by a trembling of the air about them. The cup and saucer Lally had just placed on the desk shivered slightly. None of them moved for a moment until, with a violence that had the two men off their chairs and at the window, shouts, cries, even screams altered the clatter of cheerful voices usually heard to one of awesome terror.

'What is it? What's happened?' Lally quavered. She took a faltering step or two, wanting to run to the window where the men blocked out the light and elbow them aside. Susan followed and for one of those moments when time seems to stand still, leaving figures frozen and paralysed with shock, the scene beyond the window was printed on four pairs of eyes. No one spoke, for as they stared, horrified, a great snarling blast struck the window and every pane of glass shattered, falling in tiny pieces at their feet as they stood rooted to the carpet by the window. Minute shards pierced the flesh of their faces and flecks of blood bloomed but none of them moved. The men in the yard were all gaping at the six-storeyed mill, many of *them* with blood on them. Horses whinnied in terror, rearing up between the shafts of the wagons, almost tipping them backwards and still men stood.

'Sweet Jesus!' Adam whispered, for even as they

watched, the roof of the boiler house which was situated in the centre of the building rose into the air, lifting in what appeared to be slow motion, taking with it slates, stone, massive wooden beams, pieces of metal, parts of machinery and the remnants of wool. Worse than even that were objects that looked suspiciously like human torsos.

There were three boilers, two of them of twenty horsepower each and one of thirty horsepower, and for dreadful seconds, which seemed like hours, none of them stirred, rendered insensible, numbed by the horror of what they saw. Great clouds of dust and debris began to fall, pieces of masonry raining down on the men in the yard, causing the horses to panic even further so that those not injured by the falling debris were in danger of being trampled by the terrified animals.

It was then that the two men in the office leaped into life and with a bound they were at the door.

'Stay there,' Adam ordered the women curtly, but naturally they took no notice, racing past Hawkins who cowered behind his desk. Down the littered steps they blundered and into the equally littered yard, hardly able to see for the dust that hung about, drifting in a greyish-brown cloud and coating everything within a hundred yards of the weaving shed. Adam and Brice had disappeared as soon as they leaped off the last step, both racing, Lally supposed, towards the building.

'Hold my hand,' Susan shrieked into Lally's ear, for once they began to move across the yard where the men and horses panicked they would lose sight of one another. There were women screaming out a child's name, the men cursing, for they wanted to help, to get to the weaving shed, to rescue whoever was injured because surely there would be many of those.

As the dust, inches deep, settled, those who crowded the yard and the lane that led to it, for the folk who lived nearby and who had heard the great explosion had rushed to the mill gates, were appalled by what was revealed. They had, as yet, no idea what had caused it, all those, that is, except Adam Elliott, but though the walls of the building stood with every window shattered, there was simply no roof!

Lally and Susan, still hand-clasped, stood at the bottom of the steps, the dust, which was beginning to settle to below head height, covering the pair of them, coating their clothing, their colourless faces, their hair, their eyelashes and into their ears and nostrils making it hard to breathe. They were so stunned, almost blind and deaf, it is doubtful they would have noticed anyway.

As one they began to make their way across the chaos of the yard towards the shattered building. There was smoke now, billowing and black and threatening, for there was much oil and woollen waste for the fire that had taken hold to feed on. Ash floated higher and higher into the air above the stricken mill, drifting on the slight breeze across the yard and surrounding area, reaching up to Mill House where Mrs Cannon, the housemaids and the outdoor men stood with their hands to their horrified faces. Beneath Lally and Susan's feet, strewn haphazardly like pieces of a jigsaw puzzle, were dozens and dozens of unidentifiable pieces of wood, metal, stone, glass.

It was then they heard the screaming, not from the frantic mothers who zigzagged about the yard looking for children who only hours before they had been clouting for being slow to rise from their beds and get to the mill, but from *inside* the stricken weaving shed. There were many more in the lane beyond the gate trying desperately to get through. Men were converging on the building, accompanied by women who had a child, a man, some loved one who had, fifteen minutes ago, been peaceably working in their loom gates. When the boilers blew, six whole floors, along with the roof, had been raised to a great height with one huge lift and the entire mass of worsted spinning frames and weaving looms, along with the men, women and children working them, were precipitated in one deafening crash to ground level, entombed in the mass of ruins. It was difficult to conceive that one human life could have survived.

'Dear God in heaven,' Lally whispered, but even as she felt Susan tug at her hand, figures appeared, human figures, covered in dust and what was surely blood. They began to stagger from the entrance of the broken building. Eager hands took them, leading them gently away, the victims silent and in deep shock, the rescuers murmuring wordlessly, then, as those rescued emerged, others ventured inside, led by two men who were taking charge of the rescue operation. Adam and Brice had disappeared inside the wrecked building and though those in the yard could not see what was happening inside the standing walls except through the shattered windows, they could hear the shouts, the cries for help and of warning as those who were helping, scrabbling with their bare hands, did their best to lift enormous beams and blocks of stone from those who were buried. Flames licked dangerously close and from up the lane that led to Moorend, the fire brigade clattered, pulled by sweating horses. Timber and slate were passed out through the windows to make room for the rescuers to search for those buried in the wreckage.

The crowd had become immense by now, many of them no more than onlookers come for the thrill, and though Lally thought only minutes had gone by, it must have been longer, for a powerful troop of police and even a party of infantry from the local barracks began to take charge of the crowds who were impeding progress. Rubbish and fallen materials began to come out of the tottering building at a greater pace, for it was thought the whole mill might collapse, passed from hand to hand in a human chain and with it the bodies, some beyond help, others miraculously still alive.

It was Susan who began the task of tending to the injured, some merely badly bruised, some silent and smashed almost beyond recognition but living, some burned and screaming. Many of them were little girls who had not had the sense to run for it when the boilers went, as the older operatives had. Doctor John was suddenly beside them, along with others from the infirmary.

Lally worked by Susan's side, viciously biting the inside of her cheek to stop herself from fainting at the sight of some of the injuries. Doctor Channing, who had once tended her family, had one remedy for a broken limb. Take it off and had not John had violent words with him there would have been many a child minus an arm or a leg, or even both!

Carly was there with men come from the Priory and even Biddy who had galloped over in the gig,

372

though she had never driven it before, with Jenny beside her. The pair of them, with Mrs Cannon and her maids to help, began to carry the most badly injured children up to the Mill House where one of the infirmary doctors tended them as best he could with the help of the mill women.

Adam appeared for a moment, his face the colour of the underside of a mushroom, filthy, breathing hoarsely, his clothes in tatters about him, for he had crawled through many small spaces to reach a whimper or a moan and had many times shouted out for complete silence in an effort to locate some sound. Men and women, scarcely recognisable as such, dug frantically at whatever they could get their hands on, their places taken eagerly by others when they lurched out from the mountain of rubble that had once been their livelihood. Splinters of glass and shards of wood and metal caught the unwary, cutting them to the bone so that not only the victims but their rescuers needed attention.

Both he and Lally were alarmed when Susan suddenly darted away and before either of them could stop her or even shout to warn her she ran through the opening that Adam had just come from, disappearing into the haze of dust and smoke that filled the stricken building.

'Susan,' Adam shouted hoarsely, beginning to follow her, then he too vanished from Lally's appalled sight. Slowly she began to move towards the broken doorway but a hand on her arm held her back and when she turned, yelling at whoever it was to release her, she looked into the concerned face of Biddy.

'No, lamb, not you an' all. He'll fetch her

out . . .' But as she spoke there was another frightening rumble from the ruined mill as something gave way and a cloud of dust rose high into the air.

'Dear sweet Jesus,' Lally moaned, then hid her face in Biddy's comforting shoulder, for inside the ruin was her dearest friend.

*   *   *

In a patch of bare woodland where the fox had finally been caught by the hounds, Roly Sinclair winked at the pretty young thing who had been 'blooded', while about them those of the gentry and minor aristocracy who had hunted over her husband's land murmured that old Roly was up to his tricks again and him with a pregnant wife at home!

CHAPTER TWENTY-SIX

She and Adam stood in the yard, both silently contemplating the wreckage of what had once been High Clough Mill. It stood, or rather tottered in its woeful shambles, the walls ready to crumble and indeed were to be taken down the next day. Albert Watson had been and shaken his head in what Lally knew was to be a long-winded preamble of a tale of doom and disaster which would end with his estimate, his exorbitant estimate of what it would cost to put it all right. All that remained of the shed and the rubbish that had been pulled out from it would need to be carted away he had told them. The land would need to be totally cleared before he could even think of putting up another mill. It had been insured, of course, for Harry had been a prudent man when he had taken over from his father and the money would be there to rebuild, a fact Albert Watson was well aware of and if he could squeeze more cash from the owner's wife, who was after all only a woman and therefore unused to business, he meant to do so.

He did not, naturally, know that she had a man by her side who would challenge every word and movement, his every estimate, his cunning—for Albert was an astute man and cared nothing for the fact he and Harry Sinclair had been socially acquainted for years.

The funerals of those who had perished in the disaster had taken place two days ago, every one paid for by Mrs Sinclair. There were many operatives, most, in fact, who could scarce get through from one week's end to the next on what they earned so the chances of putting something by for an emergency, which was what a funeral would be, were well nigh impossible. There were thirty-one deaths, most of them women and children, some from the same family. Two Barkers, two Hoosons, five Mitchells besides the rest. There were children whose names could not be discovered and some so deep in shock they could not speak. These children had only been at work for a week and it was the practice not to put their names down until they had worked for a fortnight. It was a practice Lally had not known of and did not understand but she meant to change it, she told Adam, along with many other wrongs that had existed before the explosion. One child, a boy whose head had been severed from his body, was never identified and, remembering the indifference of some of the mothers she and Susan had talked to, Lally was not surprised. He was buried with great dignity in a small coffin with the inscription *God knows him* on his tombstone.

Several little girls were badly scalded and were being treated in the infirmary by the patience and compassion of Doctor John. Though several cabs had been ordered into the yard by the Superintendent of Police some of those extricated alive from the building and placed in the vehicles took almost an hour before they reached the infirmary. They were put in a special children's ward that John had set up, cared for by nurses he himself had approved though Doctor Channing had fought him tooth and nail, being of the old school who did not believe in 'cosseting' as he put it, be it a child or an adult. Doctor John had great faith in some of the herbal remedies he had experimented with and had ordered witch-hazel, known for its healing properties and as a balm for burns, to be applied to soothe the damaged skin of those who suffered and, being a somewhat radical doctor in Doctor Channing's opinion, had made his small patients drink plenty of liquids since he believed that it would have a beneficial effect on those who had lost bodily fluids. So far none had died.

Susan was recovering slowly. When Adam had found her she had been lying on her stomach trapped by the legs beneath a wooden beam and, single-handedly, his love and fear for her giving him strength, he lifted it from her. To his amazement she had a small boy in her arms, her body protecting his. She had been calling Adam's name as he had been calling hers and like the flight of two birds, the sounds of their voices had winged through the smoke and dirt, the dust and debris, guiding him to her. He had brought her out, the small boy speechless and staggering behind them and had been surprised and affronted when that bloody doctor, the friend of the Sinclair family, had done his best to take her from him.

Lally ran to meet him, elbowing Doctor John aside, fluttering round Adam and Susan in what she recognised later as a foolish manner, transfixed by the expression on his face, for what he felt for Susan was plainly written there. It was then it seemed to her that her past approval of a match between Susan and John was clearly a mistake.

'I've got her,' he had snarled. 'Get out of my way while I take her to the infirmary.'

'Let me examine her . . .'

'Bugger off and see to the others. This lad, for instance,' indicating the small boy who was doing his best to cling to the tatters of Adam's coat-tails. 'I'll tend Susan.'

'Adam,' Susan gasped weakly. 'John's a doctor. I need someone to . . . to look at me back . . . me legs . . .' for both Susan's legs were dangling in a most peculiar fashion over Adam's arm.

'Please, sir, let me take a look, then you can get her to the infirmary. I'd come with you but there are still many who need me here. When you get there ask for Doctor Gibbons. On no account let . . . let . . . er . . . any of the others attend her,' meaning, of course, Doctor Channing who would have her legs off before you could say knife.

John had strapped up Susan's legs with

makeshift splints, her agony making both him and Adam sweat and groan, for they both loved her and would spare her pain. Adam had carried her gently to a waiting gig, the one Biddy had driven at breakneck speed from the Priory and with the small, speechless lad beside them though they were scarcely aware of him, got her to the infirmary and into the experienced care of Doctor Gibbons. Doctor Channing had been greatly displeased by Adam's high-handed refusal to allow him to take the fainting woman under his wing but after hours of waiting, striding up and down the corridor, which was heaving with the injured and their relatives, Adam had seen Susan wheeled to a ward, still unconscious from the anaesthetic. He had refused to leave her, following her to her bedside and, sighing patiently, Doctor Gibbons had allowed it, and the small boy who he thought was a relative.

Susan was to come home when Doctor Gibbons allowed it, home being the Priory, and before her had come the small boy whose life she had saved and whom not one soul had claimed. He had not uttered a word since and was simply addressed kindly by one and all as 'boy'. He had been taken to the children's nursery where Jamie, Alec and Jack had studied him curiously, demanding of Dora who he was and what he was doing in their nursery. But as Dora philosophically put it, what was one more in a house already bursting at the seams with children. He seemed to settle after a bath and a good plate of Biddy's broth, though he had no notion how to play when the boys kindly invited him to join in. His little face was pinched and his eyes haunted but he was no trouble, poor little mite, said Dora, and when she put him on her knee, he sat quite still, looking like a trapped rabbit before he fell asleep. He had been placed in a cot beside the other boys and when he woke sat quietly in a small chair, his eyes on the door waiting for something or someone, Dora inclined to believe it was his mam, though nobody came to claim him.

Lally and Adam were concerned with replacing the mill that had perished, using the insurance money, naturally, studying the plans drawn up by Albert Watson and the devastation to the yard where he meant to build it.

Roly, who had not been seen for several days after the explosion, came cantering along the lane on his fine horse and bade them 'Good morning' just as though he were a passer-by who had stopped to stare at someone else's misfortune. He had been like that ever since he had first come from the direction of his father-in-law's house in Skircoats. He had not felt the need to leave Lord Billington's estate when news of the disaster reached him, for he could not have been expected to forgo the pleasures of Lord Billington's Hunt Ball, could he, nor the attention of the sweet young thing who had caught his eye when she was blooded. He expressed regrets at what he saw as *Lally's* adversity. After all, it was nothing to do with him. She had made her choice when she refused to sell him Harry's half of the business, for which now he was truly thankful, since it meant he must part with not one penny piece towards its rebuilding.

'When do you expect to be in business again, my dear Lally?' he enquired sweetly. 'Some time in the distant future it would seem.' He smiled, his lip curling up in his handsome face.

Lally returned his smile then drew her hood up over her short hair. There was a fine rain drifting lightly across the dismal scene and it clung to all three of them. Several men were rooting about in the ruins, given permission by Lally to glean what they could from the disaster. One man had a rickety cart which he was piling up with burned bricks and bits of timber. He was going to build a hen-house in his back yard, he was explaining to another and if the man would help him pull the cart he would give him some eggs. The man agreed.

'As a matter of fact we are already trading, Roly. I'm sure you will be pleased to hear it. I know Harry was when I discussed it with him this morning,' her heart wrenching for the silent man who sat and stared from his window at God only knew what. 'He has given me carte blanche to do whatever I think best. With Mr Elliott's help, of course.'

Roly's jaw dropped. 'What?'

'Oh yes. You may remember Mr Heaton. Brice Heaton. He has already travelled abroad to . . . where is it, Adam?' She turned enquiringly to Adam.

'New York. He has the names of several buyers there, taken, I believe, from your desk at South Royd, Mr Sinclair. While you have been . . . er . . . absent the three of us have been over there and he has a list not only of those who are interested in our yarn but how much is stored in the sheds. We mean—Mrs Sinclair and I—to continue business from South Royd and West Heath until the new mill is up and running.' He smiled then drew a case from an inside pocket. Taking a cigar from it and with an enquiring look at Lally to obtain her permission, he lit it and drew the smoke deeply into his lungs.

'Now look here, you two . . . two . . .' Roly began to bluster.

'Yes, Roly, what is it you wish to say?'

'You won't get away with this. Those mills are still legally part mine and I will not countenance you rummaging about in my office and taking it upon yourselves, without consulting me—'

'You were not here to consult. Perhaps you might like to put your hand in your pocket, or perhaps your wife's pocket to help with the rebuilding of the mill, Roly. It is to be erected on Penrose Meadow, by the way. Harry means to sell this piece of land and begin afresh. Not only with a mill but decent cottages for the workers, a library, schools, shops, somewhat in the style of Titus Salt's industrial village. The new mill will employ over 3,000 operatives and the children will work only four hours a day. The rest of the time they will spend in school. We mean to—'

'Dear Christ, philanthropists, is it, you and my dear brother,' he sneered. 'Well, I wish you well of it. Now I really must get home to my wife. We are also to build but it is to be a house, a mansion, so what Harry means to do with Mill House I don't know, or care.'

He was about to turn away but Lally stopped him with her next words.

'I'm glad to hear you say that, Roly, for it will not go to waste. Mr Elliott and Mrs Harper are to be married as soon as she is able to walk up the

381

aisle and Harry is to give it to them as a wedding present.'

It was a good job Roly was looking at her and not Adam or he would have seen the look of amazement on Adam's face.

'We'll say "good morning" then, Roly,' Lally added cheerfully, putting a hand on Adam's sleeve and drawing him away towards the gateway and the carriage that stood there. Waiting until they were both in it Adam burst out with the words he had been holding in.

'Now look here, Lally . . . er, Mrs Sinclair. What on earth possessed you to tell that idiot that Susan and I are to be married? No one knew and now it will be all over Moorend and—'

Lally laughed and on the seat where he had the reins in his hands Carly smiled.

'Oh, Adam, everyone knows how you feel about Susan and that she returns your feelings. You are waiting only—'

'But . . .' Adam's face was a picture.

'Is it not true, then?'

'Yes, but . . .'

'Well then. Mill House is empty and you and Susan and Jack will need somewhere to live so what could be more logical than that you should take it over? You will need, as the mill manager, somewhere suitable.'

'Mill manager . . .' he spluttered.

'Of course. Now then, let us talk of the need to get the operatives who worked at High Clough back in employment. Susan and I have discussed it, as I am sure she has with you, and we propose to run West Heath and South Royd round the clock. Twenty-three hours a day. Shift work, in fact. Two

382

shifts until Penfold Meadow is in production. That way we will produce twice the goods and lose none of our operatives who will lose none of their jobs.'

'Susan did say you had that in mind,' he told her wryly but she interrupted him.

'It means more hours of work for you, Adam, with a higher wage, of course, and with Brice selling whatever comes off our looms we should keep our heads above water. I was wondering if, among your university friends, you might know of a good man to be under-manager. I . . . er . . .' she paused delicately, 'I shall not be able to . . . work for much longer and you cannot do everything and with Susan laid up for the time being it all falls on your shoulders. One day Harry will be recovered,' she went on bravely, her mind returning as it frequently did to the quiet figure by the window of the bedroom. He was beginning to put on weight and though Biddy strenuously argued against it, Doctor John had put him on a diet. Martin walked him down the lawn every day but it was not the vigorous exercise to which he was accustomed.

Adam grinned boyishly. 'And we thought we had kept it quiet . . .'

'How could you with you at the infirmary every day? Now, with Susan back home soon I suggest you move into Mill House right away. Mrs Cannon will be surprised but she doesn't care who lives there as long as she gets her wages. Now, shall we get on to West Heath.'

*   *   *

To their astonishment and delight orders began to come from established customers, one of whom remarked on the efficiency of young Mr Heaton with whom he had dined several days ago. It came from New York where Brice Heaton had approached several of their customers and had been so charming, so persuasive, so free with his entertaining, not to mention the excellence of the samples he produced, it seemed they would be hard pressed to keep up with him. The plan to run the two mills round the clock had been received with great thankfulness by the operatives put out of work by the disaster at High Clough, and, with a young man of impeccable credentials come from the same university as Adam and Brice, a young man by the name of Frank Schofield, at his side, Adam had every spinning frame and loom working night and day. They needed extra care from the two men and a great deal of watching, for the machines carried an extra load in the way of producing yarn, each one examined and maintained so that no breakdowns or accidents occurred.

The month rolled on and though Lally had been struggling on with the accounts, the wages books, the work records relative to the manufacture of woollen goods, they now found that Hawkins, who had once been awkward and inclined to resent what he considered their intrusion into a man's world, was surprisingly helpful. It seemed he knew which side his bread was buttered, thankful that he was given an office at West Heath and retained his job. Lally, without Susan but with Hawkins's rather old-maidish advice, was helped to read a balance sheet, with ledgers, contracts and copies of negotiations with suppliers and customers. Adam, with Frank Schofield on the mill floor, often worked beside her, reading the weekly reports, audits and the invoices delivered at regular intervals from Albert Watson regarding the slow building of the mill at Penfold Meadow, called now by the one name, Penfold. From somewhere Hawkins, who had worked for the Sinclairs since he left school and could not bear to throw anything away, produced records that were extremely advantageous to Lally and Adam and she was heard to say that she wondered why the hell he had not shown them to her from the start!

Every evening she returned home to dine with Harry, sitting with him before their fireside, and in the hope that the familiar facts and figures—familiar to him that is—that she poured into his ears might awaken his dormant brain she talked to him of her day, and every morning she visited the infirmary to see Susan and do the same. Adam rode over to the infirmary every evening, his expression ardent, and instructing her severely to name a day for their wedding. He was living at Mill House and Mrs Cannon had proved most obliging. Susan would have nothing to do but give orders and be waited on hand and foot, he told her. No, she was not to return to the office at the mills since they were being run most efficiently by Lally and Mr Hawkins, forgetting in his ardour that Lally would soon not be able to *be* at the office.

She was getting heavy now in her body and she found she had to make a great effort not to allow her senses and her emotions to become lulled, her identity as a woman submerged in her role as breeding female, fighting to take over.

'I wish you could see what has been accomplished, Harry, and in such a short time. A

385

Mr Grassmann called today and quite took over the place, looking at every sample. He had come all the way from London, staying at the Golden Plough in Halifax. He was quite amazed at the sight of me and Adam but really Adam is a marvel. He took over and talked him through the weaving of what he wanted and before half an hour he had him eating out of his hand. They were talking of warp and weft, delivery dates, profit and loss as though Adam had been in the woollen trade all his life. I, very circumspectly'—putting a hand to her swollen belly—'stayed behind my desk. Adam took him to the sheds and carefully showed him several pieces still on the loom.'

She leaned towards him and took his hands, then clumsily knelt at his feet, looking up into his face. Since the weather had begun to turn warmer Martin and he not only took short walks down the sloping lawn but sat on the garden seat by the lake and his face had taken on a healthier colour.

'Darling, darling Harry, though we are managing to keep things ticking over we need you. We all need you. What am I to do when the baby comes?'

She put her face on their clasped hands which lay in his lap and as she spoke the word 'baby' his glance fell on her but she did not see it. She sighed and her breath moved the fine hairs on the back of his hands and the expression on his face, which was really no expression at all, changed in some way but again she did not see it. She got heavily to her feet, her swollen body barely registering that in some way Harry was helping her to rise.

'Oh well, I'd better go and have a word with Dora. That lad Susan saved, not to mention Jack,

386

should be in their beds by now. Honestly, Harry, the nursery is becoming very full and with this one soon to be added to it we shall have to think about extending the rooms. And Dora really needs some assistance though she does very well. Of course, Philly is a great help and plays nursery maid as much as governess. She is even attempting to teach Boy his letters, poor little lad. I wonder where his family is, or even if he had one.'

She kissed Harry, her hand smoothing the thick riot of his dark hair, her mind registering that it really did need cutting, then with another loving kiss she left him.

CHAPTER TWENTY-SEVEN

Spring came in with such surprising vigour Barty was to say again and again to Froglet he didn't know how the devil they were to keep up with the jobs that were ready for doing. You only had to look at the massed heads of the wild daffodils, which normally at this time of the year would just be thrusting their spears through the grass and were already flaunting their magnificent golden trumpets, to realise that winter had truly gone. And would you look at them wallflowers, like a flame they were against the front wall of the house. A proper picture, didn't Froglet agree and he couldn't remember ever having seen a finer show of honesty in the corner of the stable yard with their white and purple flowers already attracting early butterflies. The geraniums he and the lad had planted in pots along the terrace were almost in flower. The magnolia trees were that lovely he wished they would flower all year round. The sweet bay needed a good pruning and the grass already needed mowing. Aye, this was the busiest month of the year. Straw was needed to protect the magnolias, delicate roses and hardy plants growing up the walls, but the later in the season the tender plants could be kept in a dormant state the better, he explained to his acolyte. The gladioli must be planted along with the chrysanthemums, lupins and other annuals. The dahlias should be increased by cutting and the rhododendron beds should be dressed with cow dung brought from the farms, and with leaf mould. The sweeping and rolling of turf and gravel must be seen to and all this before they started on the kitchen garden. And everything was so far forward would they ever catch up? he asked gloomily. Froglet shook his head as though in despair.

Together they had inspected the woodland where the children played on fine days, with Dora in charge, of course, and found the floor beneath the trees an azure carpet of massed bluebells. It fair took your breath away. Talk about early, but what a glorious picture they made beneath the branches and round the trunks of the budding oak trees. As they stepped through their delicate loveliness, careful of where they put their heavy boots, he remarked sadly to Froglet that he'd best get the master to give them some extra help or they'd be at sixes and sevens for the rest of the gardening year. Then he and Froglet would exchange glances, for the mistress was master of this estate and had been for the last five months or so and any orders to be given came from her. And hadn't she enough to contend with without them plaguing her? Not only was she doing her best to run Mr Harry's mills with the help of that gentleman she employed, which was not the same as Mr Harry, was it, she was getting heavy with the babby. And that there tragedy up at the mill hadn't helped, neither.

They all admired what she was trying to do. Them lads, along with Mrs Harper's Jack and the strange little scrap Mrs Harper had rescued from the mill, were settled in to what was called the schoolroom next to the nursery. Never too young to start learning their letters, their governess had been heard to say. The whole top floor of the Priory was now made over to the children and their needs, and Mrs Harper and her Jack still had their own private room. With the governess the bairns called Philly, they scampered outside on every fine day across the lawn, down to the lake, across the park ending up, as always, over at the paddock where the horses sauntered over to greet them and take the apples Dora had in her basket. Mrs Harper's lad, Jack, at eighteen months got into all sorts of mischief but then so did they all except the one they called Boy who clung to the hand of either Dora or Miss Philly. Mrs Sinclair's little lass who would be in her perambulator, Caterina, called Cat by everyone, was doted on by Dora who had turned out to be a champion nursemaid, while Master Jamie and Master Alec, with the boy, learned their ABCs with Miss Philly and good luck to her they all said for those lads were . . . well, what you might call spirited without a pa to discipline them. Mrs Harper, when she first came to the Priory, had given them a good start, the servants heard, and now they were on their way to being clever lads like their pa.

They had pause to reflect that Mr Sinclair was not really their pa though they called him Father and that Master Chris, God rest him, their real father, had not been endowed with a sharp brain but he'd been a lovely lad, ready for a laugh or a chat with any of them. No side to him at all. Perhaps his sons had inherited their brightness from their ma, for she had certainly picked up the rudiments of worsted manufacturing and was hanging on to her husband's business by the skin of her teeth, helped by those chaps she had employed, not to mention Mrs Harper before her accident. Eeh, said Barty to Froglet as they bent over their task, what a to-do-ment life was. Froglet, not always sure what Barty meant, saying what he did right out of the blue, nodded amiably.

*   *   *

The pair of them were in the kitchen garden sowing cabbage seeds of the quick-hearted sort which would be ready for harvesting in July when the door opened and their mistress stepped out. She raised her pretty face to the sun which shone in spring-like warmth from a cloudless blue sky and smiled with pleasure. Her dark hair gleamed with a touch of chestnut in its depths and her rounded cheeks were flushed and smooth as a child's. A voice from the back of her admonished her not to go far and where was her bonnet, but she set off towards the gate that led to the paddock.

'You off to feed them 'orses, Miss Lally?' Barty

called out to her.

'I am, Barty. You know how they love their apples,' indicating the basket on her arm. She had on a light woollen cloak under which could be seen the gleam of silk the colour of bluebells.

'Well, don't you go too fast, ma'm,' Barty answered with the familiarity of an old and trusted retainer. He smiled a warning. 'And don't go too far neither, now think on.'

'I won't, Barty.'

' 'Ow's the new lass gerrin' on wi' them bairns? Governess, is it?'

'Oh yes, she's got them sitting at their books at the schoolroom table then she and Dora will take them for their walk. Well, I must be off or it will be dark before I get to the paddock.'

They watched her for a moment or two until she had crossed the yard and, opening the gate, disappeared in the direction of the paddock.

The animals all plodded over to her, pushing and shoving against one another to get to the juicy apples she held out to them, slobbering greedily, then following her as she moved along the fence line. What a wonderful day it was. The sun was warm on her bare head and though she had a dozen things to do, going over papers that she had brought from the mill office, she felt a great need to remain for a precious moment in the peace of the outdoors. Perhaps a short walk towards the greening of the woods. It was quite safe now that the Weavers had vanished and it would be grand to empty her head of accounts, figures, profits, yardage for a blessed half-hour.

Sighing with pleasure, she began to saunter along the narrow path that cut right through the wood, enjoying the freedom and the soft warmth of the sun. She was in an ancient oak wood, the enormous trunks of the trees standing in a glorious sea of bluebells. Since Barty and Froglet had inspected it the wild flowers had become even more thickly spread and Lally could not help but stop and gloat over the beauty of it all. She threw back the folds of her cloak to compare the colour of her gown with the bluebells, smiling, for they were the same shade. A shaft of dappled sunlight fell on her hair and touched the silk of her skirt but Lally saw no more as a rough bag made from sacking came down over her head and strong arms lifted her from her feet.

*   *   *

The Weaver brothers had wintered quite comfortably in their concealed cave deep in the wood. Even the smoke from their fire, had it been seen, would have gone unremarked, since Barty, Froglet and Mr Cameron, the steward, often burned old wood and fallen leaves as the forest was cleared. Not all the leaves, naturally, since as the trees shed them they were needed, as they rotted, to feed and enrich the ground and the plants that grew there.

The brothers were clever with traps and fishing lines and never went hungry. The elder, the one with the more cunning, sometimes slipped to one of the many villages away from the area, where they were not known, to buy tobacco, bread, tea, stuff they could not glean from the woods that they roamed. They poached on Lord Billington's estate and fished his trout stream, avoiding his gamekeepers, slipping like shadows through the dense undergrowth, and to make a few bob they sold what they caught to butchers and fishmongers in different villages. A haunch of venison, rabbits, grouse in season, trout or anything they could not eat themselves. They had lived on the Priory estate all their lives and were reluctant to leave what was familiar but one day they would be forced to, for this life they led and the need for concealment could not go unnoticed for ever. But the main reason they stayed, at least in Jed's mind, must be completed first.

Today it seemed it was. Lally was as still as an animal caught in an open glade by a predator. She was so paralysed with terror, not only for herself but for the child in her womb, she made no sound. When she was placed on her feet and the hood removed she backed away from the men as far as she could until her shoulder blades pressed against the wall at the back of the cave and vaguely wondered why, if they wanted to keep her in ignorance of who they were, they had removed the hood. She was not to know that Jed, despite the danger to himself and his brother, needed to see the fear in her eyes, the dread on her face and so threw all caution to the wind. Her face was like putty and her eyes, enormous in her face, were wide and unfocused. Tears poured from them and dripped from her chin to her cloak. The two men were dirty, unshaven, their beards reaching across their broad chests and their wild, uncombed hair fell below their shoulders, but she knew them at once.

The two men stared at her transfixed. She was a lovely woman, even in her present state, and Jed

Weaver had not had a woman for a long time. His hatred of the Sinclairs who had turned his family off the land that had supported them for years was deep and ferocious. When they had had their way with this one there'd be such a hue and cry he and Ham would at last be forced to flee and he'd never see his home again. These woods on which he and his brother had lived so freely, so easily, would be finished for them. But on the other hand they had managed to outwit gamekeepers and stewards for years now and even if they had to run for it they could always come back. It was a risk, for she had seen their faces but he told himself she was so petrified with fear she'd not remember.

'Oh bugger it,' he cried to his brother, 'us've waited a long time fer this.' He moved purposefully towards the cowering woman in the dark at the back of the cave. She slapped at his hands as they reached for her and began to scream like a hare caught in a trap but with an oath he clenched his fist and hit her on the chin, rendering her senseless. She fell limply into his arms and he liked it.

'Come on, lad,' he said thickly to Ham as he began to strip her of her cloak and the lovely blue silk dress, tearing them from her flaccid body, but Ham seemed, at the last moment, to be strangely reluctant. Jed had her down to her pretty lace bodice and drawers, both articles of clothing fine and clinging and it was then Ham spoke.

'Eeh, our Jed, lass is 'avin' a bairn. Us can't—'

'Gie over! What's that got ter do wi' owt?' Jed was ready to tear the undergarments from her but it seemed Ham, always backward, always the follower of his brother, had something in him his

394

brother lacked. He took hold of Jed's arm and did his best to pull him away from the semi-conscious woman whose rounded belly proclaimed her condition.

' 'Ere, what's up wi' yer?' Jed snarled as Ham tugged at his arm.

'Yer can't, our Jed. She's 'avin' a babby. Yer can't . . .'

'Don't be ser daft. She'll never know't difference then.'

'No, I say, Jed. Leave 'er be. Babby . . .'

'Bugger babby. I'm 'avin' a go an' so are you. It's what us always wanted.'

'No, Jed, I say no.' Ham, the bigger and stronger of the two, began to pull his cleverer brother away from Lally, forcing him to leave go of her. She fell at once to the floor of the cave and lay still but Jed, ferocious in his lust and fury, turned on his brother, grunting like a wild animal, aiming a blow at his brother's face.

'Leave off, our Ham,' he yelled, swaying in his need to get away to his prey but Ham, reluctant to hurt him, pushed him instead. Jed lost his balance, falling clumsily, his arms flailing, and as he went down his head hit one of the stones that encircled the fire. There was a horrid crack and at once blood began to flow across the rocky floor. Ham sank to his knees, crying his brother's name, dragging his body into his arms, cradling him against his chest. The woman on the ground was forgotten.

* * *

They did not miss her for two hours, each member

395

of the household getting on with whatever they were meant to be doing and each thinking she was with someone else. It was a Sunday and it wasn't until the carriage drew up at the front steps and the smiling face of Susan appeared at the window that they realised that their mistress was not here to greet her as she was brought home from hospital. Carly jumped down from his seat, opening the door to Mr Elliott who had gone to fetch her from the infirmary, and who lifted her carefully through the open door of the carriage, her splinted legs sticking out straight before her, and placed her in the long wheelchair that Doctor John had ordered for her. It had an extension at the front so that she was able to stretch out her injured legs and rest her badly bruised back against the padded seat.

They were all there to greet her, even the children, for she held a very special place in the household. Jack was shy, as he had not seen his mother since the day of the explosion, not awfully sure he cared to see her in what he thought of as a perambulator. He stuck his thumb in his mouth and hung back but the others, Jamie, Alec and Cat, who was held in Dora's arms, shouted and clamoured to greet her. Boy, barely recognisable as the draggled child who had been pulled out of the devastated mill, moved towards her, his face creased in a tentative smile. He was dressed in one of Jamie's outfits, for though he was obviously older than Lally's elder son, he was very small, emaciated, rickety. He had put on some weight with the good food Biddy stuffed down him and was clean, his hair, which had proved to be blond and curly, rioting about his small head. A handsome lad whom they all did their best to bring out of his withdrawn shell.

He moved slowly towards Susan and with a simple gesture took her hand, then stroked her face. For a moment there was silence and they all wanted to weep but Susan drew him into her arms and held him for a moment, a lovely, emotional moment, and at once all the children, including Jack, were all over her. Who did he think he was, this boy who had been thrust on them? This was *their* Susan who had been in an accident but Adam was having none of it. 'That's enough,' he roared. 'Susan is . . . has hurt her legs and you must be very gentle with her. She will be glad of a . . . a kiss . . . and a hug but one at a time and *gently*.'

At once they stood back respectfully while Adam and Carly carried the wheelchair up the steps and into the hall. A silent stream of sympathisers followed her. Biddy, Jenny, Clara, Tansy and even Dulcie who was the lowest of the low in the kitchen, and at the bottom of the steps, watching her go up, were Barty and Froglet who called out their good wishes since Mrs Harper was a heroine in their eyes. At the kitchen door Wilf and Evan, Caleb and Ben waited for news and on the stairs, leaving his patient for a moment, was Martin.

It was Susan who looked round for Lally who, though she was slower than usual on account of her condition, was mysteriously missing.

'Just a minute, Adam,' she said. 'Where's Lally? Everyone is here to welcome me but not Lally. Is she with Mr Sinclair?' She turned enquiringly to Martin who took a step down, puzzled as they all were.

'No, no, she's . . . she's not.'

'Then where is she? Biddy?'

They all exchanged glances, their faces reflecting their sudden anxiety, for Miss Lally had known very well that Mrs Harper was due home this morning and there was no way she would miss being here.

'Well, she was with Mr Harry earlier,' Martin faltered, for the tension was palpable among the servants, extending even to Susan herself. Biddy, who had been on her way to the drawing room ready to place Susan comfortably next to the sofa where Mr Elliott could sit beside her and hold her hand as he so obviously wanted to do and where Miss Lally could talk to her friend, whirled about, her face, for some reason, losing its colour. The children were still jumping about, doing their best to behave because Mr Elliott had ordered it, and the servants huddled together, their hands to their mouths.

'Jenny, run and ask Barty if he's seen the mistress. See, before they get far,' for both Barty and Froglet were making their way back to cutting the edges of the lawn which they had interupted when the carriage drew up.

Their bewildered reply to her shouted question made Jenny leap back up the steps and she burst into the hall where, since Mrs Stevens had said nothing to them, the maidservants still stood, waiting for news, or orders, or whatever was to happen next.

'She went . . . to the paddock . . . three hours ago and . . . oh, Jesus, she must have fell or . . . Mrs Stevens, what shall us do? She went out three hours ago,' she repeated.

398

In the drama that was taking place, the hullabaloo that reached every corner of the great house, no one noticed Harry Sinclair and his increasing agitation. Every man in the place took off to search Miss Lally's route to the paddock, and beyond when she was found not to be there, calling her name which could be heard clearly through Harry's open window.

The nearest farm was Folly where Sean and Polly McGinley were alerted and from where Sean and his son Denny began their systematic search of all the outbuildings—though why she should be in one of those they did not stop to think—and along the dry-stone walls that bisected their fields. Barty and Froglet, since they knew the grounds in which they worked every day better than any of the other outside staff, quartered the flower gardens, the kitchen garden, the fruit orchards and all the places a body could be hidden, sheds, glasshouses, the dovecote, hen coops, though why the lass should be in any of them was a mystery to them, unless she had fallen. Wilf, Evan, Caleb, Carly and Ben from the stables split up and spread out towards Moor Wood, though again they could not think what their pregnant mistress would be doing there.

Carly took charge in Tangle Wood and he and the others shouted her name and beat the undergrowth with sticks until it occurred to Carly that the lass, should she be injured and unconscious under a clump of bushes, might be hurt even more by their thrashing about. 'Carefully

399

lads, carefully,' he cautioned, shouting the mistress's name once more, as they all did, the sound echoing across the woodland, the farmland, the park and the heather moor near Lord Billington's river.

*   *   *

The woman who cowered on the floor of a cave lifted her head when she heard her name being called but *they* still crouched in the entrance to the cave, one of them making the most peculiar sounds and she was afraid to draw attention to herself. She curled herself up into a ball as well as she could in her pregnant state, and lay perfectly still. Her child was kicking and she cautiously put her arms about it and at once it quietened as though soothed by the pressure of her arms.

The Higgins lads from Thickpenny Farm passed close by but she made no sound. John Graham from Cowslip, Robert Archer and his two sons from Prospect, Bert Jackson and the labourers from the Home Farm and even Mr Cameron, the steward, astride his horse Jasper, ranged the whole of the estate through the rest of the day and into the night, which had turned cold, and in the house Tansy and Dulcie wept for their little mistress who was out in what they thought of as the wilds of the woodland and it so dark.

No one thought to look in on Harry Sinclair. Martin was out with the men, accompanied by Adam, believing Mrs Stevens was seeing to her employer, and Susan, tucked up now in her bed, though she did not sleep, thought only of Lally.

Philly and Dora had been hard put to calm the

children who were all upset, the boys Jamie and Alec ready to cry at the absence of their mama. Her name, which they knew was Lally, carried to them from the gardens surrounding the house as the men shouted for her and though Philly, who was calmer than Dora, ordered the nursery window to be closed they could still hear her name being called.

'Why is Barty shouting for Mama, Philly?' Jamie asked anxiously, doing his best to keep his hand in hers lest she vanish like Mama.

'Well, sweetheart, Mama went to see Mrs Polly and got herself lost in Tangle Wood so the men have gone to bring her home.'

'It's dark in Tangle Wood, Philly. I wouldn't like to be lost there. Will Mama be home before we go to bed? I'll need my bath soon.'

'An' Mama's got my book 'bout the five little kittings and was going to say it to me,' Alec cut in.

'Well, Dora will give you your bath with the others, Jamie, and I shall find your book and will say it to you, darling, and all of you can listen. As soon as Mama comes home I'll send her up to say goodnight.'

It was hard to settle them, the two women doing their best to calm their fears but their own were so strong it was difficult not to transfer them to the children. Jamie, Alec, Boy and even young Jack, sensing there was something wrong, continued to put uneasy questions to them.

When at last they fell asleep, Dora stayed with them, dozing in the chair before the fire and still, faint on the night air, she could hear the occasional male voice and still there was no sign of the woman they had all come to hold in great affection. The

401

men returned now and again to snatch a hot drink and to warm themselves, since as night came the mild spring day had turned increasingly colder. Biddy, surprisingly, had a violent fit of hysterics, swearing she would leather Miss Lally when they finally found her for worrying them all like this, but the others calmed her, understanding the strong bond that held her to Miss Lally. None of the maidservants could bring themselves to go to their beds, sitting about the kitchen, constantly making cups of tea and reassuring themselves that their mistress would soon be home. They all looked increasingly drawn, for what could have happened to her on the short walk from the house to the paddock and her pregnant? Every belt of trees had been gone over a dozen times and even the dogs, Fred and Ally, snuffled through Tangle Wood and Moor Wood and out on to the moor but they were house pets not tracker dogs; though they sensed something was wrong and that something was expected of them, they treated the whole thing as an unexpected outing.

The long night ended and the outside servants shuffled back from their search, for they all had work to do, with the horses and other daily jobs about the yard. The tenants returned to their farms and the milking, the ploughing, the planting, the care of their stock which was their livelihood. They were very subdued, drawn and haggard, weary and worried, for what could have happened to their young mistress for whom they had searched for getting on for twenty-four hours?

Martin was mortified, as was Mrs Stevens, when he returned to find that his master had been left alone all night. They both rushed upstairs, Martin

402

still dressed as he had been the day before, unshaven and unwashed.

They were both relieved to find Mr Harry sitting fully dressed in the same chair where he had been left, apparently none the worse for it.

'You go to your bed, Mrs Stevens,' Martin said kindly, for the housekeeper, who was not as young as she once was, looked done in. 'Have a rest for an hour or two while I see to Mr Sinclair.'

But to their astonishment Mr Sinclair fought for the first time ever against being 'seen to'!

CHAPTER TWENTY-EIGHT

No matter how Martin and Mrs Stevens coaxed, persuaded, pleaded, Mr Sinclair refused absolutely to get out of his chair from where he stared fixedly at the garden and the stand of wood beyond it. His hands gripped the arms of his chair and his face was rigid with some tension. He needed shaving and the casual suit that Martin had put him in the day before was crumpled as though he had slept in it.

'Mr Sinclair, sir,' Martin murmured, for his employer's frozen state and intent eyes alarmed the man who cared for him and he had no wish to startle him. Mr Sinclair did not respond but continued to gaze at some spot in the distance as though he were waiting for something to happen. He even shook off Martin's concerned hand. Martin circled him while Biddy watched, for if Mr Sinclair had been alone for almost twenty-four hours how had he attended to his personal needs, the bodily functions that it was Martin's job to supervise?

'Leave him, Martin,' Biddy whispered, wondering why the pair of them were being so hushed in their speech. There was no reason for it, since Mr Harry had sat through the children's racket, the maids gossiping, conversations between herself and Lally and had not even turned his head. It was just that he was being so . . . well, the only word she could think of was peculiar . . . odd . . . not himself.

'Yes, we'll leave him for a minute, Mrs Stevens,' Martin said in a low voice. They stood in a state of uncertainty, watching Mr Harry, undecided what they should do. The bairns needed checking, Biddy was thinking, although Dora and Miss Atkinson were quite capable of seeing to them in the ordinary sense but they had been so upset yesterday she wanted to see for herself and this was not an ordinary day, was it? Their mam was missing and the first thing they would ask was where she was, especially Master Jamie who at four years old was as sharp as a tack and would remember the events of yesterday, and young Master Alec at two and a half would be looking for his mother who came in every day to see them all, to take them for walks, to play and read to them. Aye, where was she they *all* wanted to know.

*   *   *

The little figure struggled through the undergrowth, falling constantly to her knees, tearing her flesh on the thorns of the bramble bushes that grew in profusion, tripping on fallen

404

branches, clutching her belly to protect what it contained. The beech trees, hornbeams and oak which had been bare all winter were now bright green with new leaf, throwing dappling, translucent shadows across the glade where she rested for a moment, the sunlight falling on wood sorrel, wood anemone, sweet violet and hellebore nestling in the roots of the trees. She lay so still, crumpled against the trunk of an oak tree, that a wood mouse darted out from its thick cover and above her a woodcock fluttered among the budding leaves.

After a moment's rest she rose to her feet, grasping at the trunk of the tree to help her up, staggering on towards her goal. A holly bush caught at her cloak, snatching it from her shoulders but she did not stop to retrieve it despite the state of her gown which was ripped down the bodice revealing her dainty lawn camisole and the edging of lace. She stumbled on, mindlcss, blind, an automaton that has been set on its course and will not deviate, resting now and then on a fallen log or a cushion of springy grass but keeping in an almost straight line from where she had been to where she was going.

*   *   *

Knowing he could not stand about all day waiting for Mr Sinclair to allow his daily ablutions, Martin was busy in the adjoining bathroom, sorting out clean towels and fresh soap when a great shout from the bedroom made him nearly jump out of his skin, he was to say later, and he dropped the soap which skidded across the black and white tiles. Mrs Stevens had gone and Tansy had made up the fire which had gone out during the night. She was just leaving the bedroom with the ashes when the shout made her drop the ash pan, its contents scattering all over the lovely carpet.

Martin shot out of the bathroom and both he and Tansy rushed towards their master, their faces agape with astonishment, as Mr Harry bellowed, his face to the glass, over and over again the name of his wife.

'Lally . . . Lally . . . Dear God in heaven . . . sweetheart . . . what in hell's name are you doing? Where have you been, for Christ's sake? What d'you think you're doing out there in . . . Lally . . . Lally . . .'

Together they stood beside him and watched in amazement, as he was doing, the little figure in her blue silk gown stagger from the woodland and make her way, step by painful step, across the lawn towards the house. She had both arms wrapped about her belly.

' 'Tis the mistress,' Tansy whispered. ' 'Tis Miss Lally. Oh, God be thanked, but what's 'appened to 'er? I'd best run fer Mrs Stevens. Oh, Martin . . . Martin, 'tis the mistress.'

The master and Martin stood side by side, the master continuing to shout his wife's name while Martin did his best to calm him down, for who knew what damage he might be doing to his poor head with all this commotion. He made the mistake of catching Mr Sinclair's arm and was thrown off for his trouble.

'Let go of me, you fool,' he roared. 'It's Lally, my wife. She wore that gown only the other day,' then, pushing Martin aside so violently that he fell

406

across the bed, he strode purposefully towards the bedroom door as though whoever was responsible for this would be in serious trouble. 'Where in damnation has she been,' he shouted over his shoulder, 'and without her bloody cloak?'

*   *   *

Barty brought her in, his old man's arms made strong and sure as he carried her up the slope, Froglet circling him like a devoted dog, determined to help if he was needed. By this time, having heard Tansy's gabbled tale, they were all crowded into the hallway and at the top of the steps, maidservants and even some of the outside men who had been in the yard as Barty staggered with her up the front steps, but he would not allow any of them to take her from him.

'Give 'er ter me, yer old fool,' Carly demanded, his face crumpled as though he would cry, but the old man was having none of it.

'Lally . . . Lally . . .' Biddy was moaning, tears pouring down her cheeks, walking backwards along the broad hallway towards the kitchen, the rest following like a lot of young chicks in the wake of the mother hen. 'Where yer bin, lass? Wharr 'appened ter yer?' lapsing into her native tongue in her distress.

They sat her by the range, longing to put their arms round her, asking her again and again what had happened to her, for something obviously had, to comfort and console, to fetch water and soft towels, bathe her wounds for she was bleeding in many small places. To beg her to tell them where she had been and what had been done to her to get

407

her in such a state. You'd only to look at the state of her frock which was torn right down the front so that you could see the whiteness, the pure ivory of the swell of her breasts to know that some . . . some beast had been at her. She was deep in shock, that was very evident, but apart from the cuts and scratches on her arms and a deep bruise on her jawline she did not appear to be hurt. She was, of course, and when her husband burst in with Martin hot on his heels they all turned in consternation. Tansy had told them that the master had spoken but Miss Lally's return had driven the news right out of their minds.

'Dearest . . . my dearest girl,' the master ventured, then with a groan that tore all their hearts, even the hovering men who crowded at the kitchen door, he flew across the room, banging his hip viciously on the corner of the big table and sank to his knees at the mistress's feet. His arms went round her, gathering her to his chest, his cheek rested on her tangled curls and he wept like a babby, his tears mingling with hers.

Then, as though just becoming aware of it, Harry clicked his fingers. 'A shawl . . . a shawl,' for even in his distraught state he was conscious of his wife's near nakedness and the men, though they averted their eyes, could see it. When Biddy's old shawl was tucked about Lally's shoulders he had her tight in his arms again, her face pressed beneath his chin.

They were totally oblivious to anyone but each other and with a soft clicking of her tongue against her teeth, Biddy cleared all the men out, murmuring as she did so, since they were reluctant to leave, that she would let them know soon how

408

Miss Lally was. God help any man who had interfered with her, the men were thinking, for they would cut his bloody balls off and stuff them down his throat. They trooped out but would go no further than the stable yard.

The master, God bless him, seemed incapable of speech so it was Biddy who knelt beside them again while the rest of the maids hovered discreetly on the far side of the room, all except Jenny who slipped up the stairs to tell Dora, Miss Philly and Mrs Harper that the mistress was safe home.

'Your mama's been found, children,' she said to Master Jamie and Master Alec, 'and will be up to see you soon,' hoping to God she was right.

'Was she in Tangle Wood, Jenny?' piped up Master Jamie.

Jenny blinked. 'Aye, that's right, my lad, but she's safe and sound now.'

But was she?

'Where've yer bin, my lass?' Biddy whispered, doing her best to get hold of her lass's hand but the master had her in his loving, frantic grip and was not about to let go.

Lally found her voice at last. She was safe now, safe not only from the Weavers but safe with her beloved husband who had miraculously been here just when she needed him most. She had struggled for months to protect not only her family, Harry's mills, their life together, but Harry himself. To defend her unborn child, to defend this great estate which would one day be her sons' but now, at exactly the moment she knew she could go on no longer, not without Harry, not without Susan whom she was going lose to Adam Elliott anyway, Harry was here to take the terrible burden from her.

'Darling . . .' he was whispering. 'My darling . . .'

His darling! That's what she was to her husband and as she peeped over his shoulders at all the concerned faces that surrounded her she knew she was valued, loved even, by them all. What had she to be afraid of?

'I was walking through the woods—'

'On your own and in your condition,' Harry began, ready to rant and rave now that she was safe in his arms.

'Let me finish, Harry, for someone will have to go to—'

'Where . . . where have you been?' he interrupted again, beginning to work himself up into what Martin would call a 'state'. Martin slipped to the back door, beckoning to Carly who was leaning against the stable yard waiting for news.

'Ride over to the infirmary and fetch Doctor John. If he's not there find him—' And before he had finished the sentence Carly was in the stable, saddling up Master Chris's Ebony who was the fastest animal in the county.

In the kitchen Clara was making a pot of tea for the mistress, since Mrs Stevens who always thought of everything was totally absorbed with Miss Lally. They were all listening avidly to what Miss Lally had to say.

'They were waiting for me.' A sigh went round the kitchen and the master seemed to groan as he crushed the mistress even closer.

'Oh, dear sweet Christ . . .' At once Lally reared back and took his face in her hands. She kissed it tenderly and they were all horribly embarrassed, for it seemed to them they should not be watching this but they had no choice, had they?

'Let me finish, dear Harry. I am not . . . hurt. They did not hurt me . . .'

'But your gown,' he moaned.

'He tried . . .'

'Who . . . who the devil?'

'Jed Weaver, but—'

Harry Sinclair threw back his head, his throat arching in pain but Lally drew him to her, comforting him as though he had been the victim. 'I'll kill him . . . I'll bloody kill him. I should have done it . . . before when . . .'

'You can't—kill him, Harry, even had I wanted it. He is already dead.'

They all froze. Clara had the old teapot in her hand, the one they used themselves when the kitchen-maids were having a 'cuppa' and for a moment she thought she might drop it. She placed it carefully on the table just in case. Surely . . . *surely* the mistress did not mean she herself had killed him? In self-defence, of course . . . but how, what with? They could hear the clatter of Ebony's hooves beating out a tattoo on the cobbles as Carly set him to the gallop but inside the silence was total.

Then Biddy, the first to recover her senses, cleared her throat. 'Dead, lass?' Her voice was still a croak. 'Who . . . ?'

'Ham killed him . . . pushed him. He fell and hit his head on a stone. Jed was ready to . . . to rape me, I think. He has always hated us ever since Harry turned the family off the farm. I was barely conscious . . . he hit me. No, no, Harry, there's nothing to be done'—as Harry once more threw

411

back his head in what appeared to be agony—'he is already dead. I heard Ham telling him I was with child, wanting him to stop what . . . what he was doing.' She shrugged the shawl more closely about her as the memory of those rapacious hands at her breast came back to her, then with a resolute movement Biddy rose to her feet.

'Right, Mr Harry, fetch the mistress upstairs. Oh, very well, give her a cup of tea first, Clara,' as Clara indicated the cup she was just filling with hot, strong tea and into which she meant to heap lots of sugar. 'Then she must come upstairs and be bathed. Now don't argue with me, Mr Harry, you shall come as well,' just as though he were a child who was afraid he was being left out of a treat. 'In fact you can carry her,' which he did, out of the kitchen and up the stairs, through their bedroom and into the bathroom which Martin had been preparing for Harry's bath.

Biddy bustled after him, ready to take the torn gown from her mistress, to fill the bath with hot water, to wash her cuts and bruises tenderly and see to all the ministration Miss Lally needed, but to her amazement Mr Harry, his wife still in his arms, smilingly shut the door in her face.

'I'll bathe her,' he said simply. At once Biddy was affronted then she drew back. He was Miss Lally's husband after all. Harry Sinclair was back.

*　　　*　　　*

She was dozing in her bed when Doctor John was admitted. He was prepared to tend not only to Lally, whose ordeal had been recounted to him by Biddy, but to Harry whom he had last seen in a near comatose state. Harry was not there!

'Well, it seems my patient is recovered,' he said cheerfully, then was filled with consternation when Lally burst into tears. At once he knelt at her bedside while she wept noisily like a child who has been severely punished and cannot understand why.

'Lally . . . oh, my dear, what is it? What is it?' then could have bitten his insensitive tongue for what else could it be but the release of months of pain, worry, confusion, a release from the burden she had carried ever since Harry had been brought home after his beating by Jed Weaver.

'Oh, John, he is returned to us,' she cried between wrenching sobs, 'but what is more important . . . well, perhaps not more important but *as* important, he appears to accept that the child I carry is his. Has he forgotten his belief that this is Roly's child? Will his full memory return and things be as they were before he accused me of . . . of taking up with Roly? Is he to return to the mill where he is bound to meet Roly? Oh, John, this is marvellous that he is himself again despite what happened to me in the cave or perhaps *because* of it. He is himself again but what is to happen when he meets his brother?'

John was suddenly made aware that far from throwing off her worries she was exchanging them for others. Only the future would tell. She and Susan, and this new fellow Adam Elliott had laboured and fought with Roly Sinclair for the past five months to keep it all going. None of them had been familiar with the commercial world but somehow, and with some degree of skill, they had deluded those with whom they dealt into believing

413

they knew what they were about. Their combined skills, which included a great deal of charm on the part of the ladies, had outmanoeuvred customers who bought their yarn, those who supplied the raw fleeces and everyone in between the two processes, and the business had not only floundered on but had achieved some measure of success. Their operatives were the best, especially the women, since they knew their infants were in safe hands while they laboured and their older children were learning to read and write and add up a simple column of figures. They had all been given a small rise in pay to encourage their endeavours so the men were satisfied. In fact he had heard that other mill-owners grumbled that since Harry Sinclair had been incapacitated and that daft wife of his had taken his place, the best 'hands' were being enticed away by the promise of better wages and were spoiling it for them.

But now Harry was back to take up the reins, please God, and just at the right time, for the destruction of his mill, High Clough, and the building of a new mill at Penfold Meadow would be a terrible challenge to this woman who, with a child in her womb and just when she needed more rest and care, would be hard pressed to keep it all going. Susan, who had been her mainstay, was crippled and might never regain the full use of her legs and that left only the engineer, Adam Elliott, to continue with the business.

But Harry Sinclair was back and pray God he would take control and not slip away again into the dark abyss in which he had dwelled for all these months.

'The men have gone to find the cave I

described.' She continued, 'Jed Weaver is there and so, I presume, is Ham. He was—Ham, I mean—after he had . . . had killed Jed, not in his right mind which is how I managed to get past him. Oh, John, it was sad to see. He just sat there holding his brother in his arms, rocking him, calling his name and will never, I shouldn't think, be the man he was. Jed was the ringleader and I hope it goes in Ham's favour that he saved me from . . . from . . . If there is a trial I shall speak up for him, John.'

John was holding Lally's hand, patting it soothingly until there was a tap on the door and Biddy entered, smoothing the snowy white apron she wore. John sprang to his feet, for though Biddy was really no more than a servant he always treated females as though they were ladies.

'How is she?' she whispered.

'I'm not ill, Biddy,' the voice from the bed said sharply.

'I know, my lamb, none better than me who's seen you go through many a . . . many a . . . well, it'd take more than a . . . But you must admit it's been a bit of a shock, not just to you but to all of us, worrying about you, then Mr Harry coming back to us like that . . . Oh, happy we are, happy as can be.'

* * *

Several days later in a smart establishment in Halifax which catered for the sometimes erotic tastes of wealthy gentlemen a casual conversation was taking place in its plush, exotically lighted entrance hall. As one gentleman was leaving

415

another was being helped off with his cape.

'Evening, Sinclair, or should I say Good morning since it's midnight gone.'

'Ah, Anson, how are you?'

'Feeling in need of some female attention, old boy. I believe Madame has a new, very young but talented girl and I wish to . . . well, you will know what I mean.' He winked.

'Indeed I do. I have just . . . tasted her. You'll like her, I'm sure or I can recommend that black and white pair. *Very* appetising! I've been here for two nights *and* a day so great was their appeal and my appetite. Good luck to you, old chap.'

They smiled knowingly at one another, then, as Anson moved towards the foot of the stairs, he turned.

'Good news about your brother, Sinclair. I was told he has been seen at the mill. He must have had a serious illness, or was it an accident? It's been so long I forget.'

Anson went on his way but Roly Sinclair stood rooted to the spot, on his face an expression that frightened the young maid who opened the door to see him out.

CHAPTER TWENTY-NINE

He was in thrall to her, listening to every word she said to him, though it was not very clear whether he was actually taking it in and believing it or whether it was her voice, her earnest face, her lovely beseeching eyes that had his fixed attention.

'. . . so you see, we cannot ignore what this

doctor—I forget his name but John will tell you, the one who has written the report, along with many others. The figures are indisputable, relating to Halifax where many of our operatives live. There are 16 deaths during the year—these are for one year, you understand—in the upper classes and the average age at which they die is 55; there are 137 deaths among the middle classes whose ages at death, taken one with another, give a mean figure of 24 years; but among the artisans, the workers in your mills and others, there are 434 persons who die at the average of 22 years of age. Doesn't that tell us something, Harry?' Her eyes were bright with hope, wide and the loveliest shade of green and blue and as he looked into them, mesmerised, Harry swore to himself that he would, the moment that bloody doctor agreed to his going into town, buy her the biggest, the most expensive turquoise he could find. Earrings, with a bracelet and necklace to match those magnificent eyes of hers, something so special she would know what she meant to him, how he valued her. She was the most precious thing in his life, his treasure and what he had longed for more than anything in the world had at last happened. She loved him as he loved her.

'What would you have me do, my darling?' wanting her to ask for something nigh impossible to obtain but it seemed she was talking of the mill again and he sighed, for he wanted to . . . to give her the moon—isn't that what all men in love said—the stars strewn across the midnight velvet sky: some vast thing that was beyond all men's reach but which he, Harry Sinclair, would get for her.

They had not then been beyond the gardens that lay in front of the house, sauntering hand in hand, or arm in arm, along the well-tended paths bordered by the rainbow beds that Barty and Froglet, with some help from Wilf or Evan since Barty was feeling his years, had brought to life. The rhododendrons were bursting into bloom, pink and white and vivid purple creating a magnificent background to the low hummocks of yellow alyssum and the vivid blue of lobelia. White arabis edged the borders of the beds, spilling out on to the paths, and aubretia in leafy cushions smothered in mauve and purple flowers. Wallflowers, Barty's favourite, which made such a splendid show from March to July, exploded against the sun-warmed wall where he had placed a wooden bench and sure enough he and the others were elated when Mr and Mrs Sinclair sat down on it, their heads together. They even kissed lovingly which made the men look away guiltily as though caught spying, but it was so grand to see them, like a couple of love birds and didn't they deserve it, after what the pair of them had gone through.

Harry had been told, of course, of the disaster at the mill and had had to be forcibly restrained from climbing on to Piper's back and galloping over there to see the scale of the calamity. He had been somewhat appeased by the man who came at once to the Priory when he was summoned by Lally. He was inclined to distrust Adam Elliott, since he didn't know him or his qualifications, but the man's quiet, dignified manner, his very obvious experience, his devotion to Lally and Susan, which showed in his determination to keep it all going despite neither lady being there, and his confidence in himself went a long way to calming Harry's fears. After all, the man whom Lally and Susan trusted so implicity had been helping to keep the business going for some five months while he, Harry, had been . . . well, he was not sure how to describe his own condition: not in his right mind, he supposed and it was all still ticking over nicely, with, apparently, another chap selling their goods abroad, for heaven's sake. He had been appalled not only by the loss of his mill but by the loss of life, but John Burton was a shrewd man who told no one what was in his mind although Biddy had her suspicions and thoroughly approved of them. He was well aware that these two needed the healing peace, not only of one another, but from the hurly-burly of commerce which the mills would throw at them and neither was ready for that yet, he was positive. So, drawing Harry aside, he told him that his wife needed at least a week of rest before she could even think of visiting the mills with him and that the only way to keep her at home was if Harry stayed there too. Though she was very calm, serene even, the experience with the Weaver brothers must have affected her and she needed time to recover.

Privately, he did the same with Lally, not alluding to the brothers, of course, swearing that Harry could not be thrown in at the deep end, so to speak, despite having Adam Elliott to help. So, both believing that they were doing the best for the other, they had taken a week to recover, to regain their strength, to be at peace with one another and with the children who, seeing their mother and father walking down the lawn, shouted that they must go too.

'Let them come,' Harry told Dora and Philly, taking the little girl, his brother's child, throwing her into the air and catching her, when he kissed her thoroughly, kissing Pinky as well when the soft toy was held up to him, pleasing the little girl enormously. She was not sure she cared for this stranger tossing her about but he made her laugh, and kissed her beloved Pinky and when he put her down on the grass and held out his hands to her she staggered from her mother to him, falling into his arms. He lifted her on to his shoulders where she clung to his hair as they all trooped down to the lake to feed the ducks. Lally held Boy's hand, for he was still withdrawn and easily frightened but the others, meaning her two sons and Jack, had become used to him by now and sped away to the fascination of the lake, bags of crusts begged from Biddy clutched in their hands. They had fun with this big man Jamie and Alec vaguely remembered and, as children do, became accustomed to his presence with their mama.

The men who had gone out to find the Weaver brothers, and there were a dozen of them, all ready to kill them with their bare hands, or at least the one their mistress had said was still alive, fell silent when they entered the cave, for the sight that met their eyes was pitiful. The brothers were there as their mistress had told them they would be. Ham leaned against the wall at the back of the cave which was filled with spring sunshine. He held the limp form of his dead brother lovingly in his arms, cradling him to his chest. The place stank and the men hung back, for it was obvious that the pathetic man who had clearly lost his mind, posed a threat to no one. He fought like a savage when they tried to take his brother from him, felling Carly and Denny McGinley with one sweep of his muscular arm and it was not until Bert Jackson and Ben from the stables clung to his arms and forced him to his knees that they managed to lift the body of Jed Weaver on to a stretcher.

'Don't let the master go with you,' Biddy had whispered to Carly. 'Wait till he's down the front garden with Miss Lally. You never know what he might do, how it might affect him.' And so Jed Weaver, with a blanket thrown over him, and his brother Ham, like a child now with his hands tied securely at his back, were taken to the police station in Halifax.

Of Roly Sinclair there was no sign and Harry did not ask about him!

*　　　*　　　*

It was a strange sight when the carriage drew up to the gates of what had once been High Clough and the men who were clearing the yard and removing the rubbish of the devastated mill asked one another what the hell was going on. They had heard, of course, that the master had recovered from his strange illness but when he and the mistress descended from the vehicle, the mistress helped not only by him but by the coachman, they all fell silent and still. They were labourers who were employed by Albert Watson who was at this moment drawing up plans for a new mill at Penfold Meadow. Lally had sat in Susan's room, Susan lying on a chaise-longue brought up for her from the drawing room, Lally in a deep and comfortable chair, so deep and comfortable she had serious

421

doubts she would ever be able to heave herself out of it. They had discussed the possibility of building *two* mills, one on the site of High Clough once it was cleared and one at Penfold Meadow and now that Harry was recovered she meant to put it to him.

He stood at the spot where the steps had once led up to the office, looking up to the empty blue sky that stretched serenely over what had been the building. The men watched them curiously, the man and the woman who were leaning against one another, the fascinated men not sure who was supporting who though the missus was big with child. It was April and it was rumoured the child was due in July. Three months to go but many of them who were fathers several times over and were familiar with the shape of a woman 'up the spout', as they called it in their class, shook their heads in disbelief. They were not even sure who had told them that Mrs Sinclair's bairn was due in July, probably their foreman who had the ear of Albert Watson who employed them.

'Was the office building destroyed with the sheds, my love?' Harry asked musingly.

'No, but Mr Watson thought that while he was building a new mill, a large mill, the office might as well be incorporated in the same building so, after consulting with Adam and myself, the office building was pulled down with the rest. Adam suggested a new wool carding mill which would house the process of carding and slubbing under one roof. Condensers would draw off the wool in continuous rolls and would then wind them straight on to large bobbins ready to be taken over to West Heath for spinning.'

422

'You seem to know a lot about it, my darling,' he said smilingly. 'You will have to take me in hand to catch up.'

She put her hand to her mouth in dismay. 'Oh, Harry, I'm so sorry. I'm afraid I have become so used to . . . to doing things, making decisions with Susan and Adam I quite forgot. Dearest, you must, of course, order everything as you would wish it. This is all yours and has been for . . . for . . .'

'Sixteen years. Ever since the death of my father but how can I deny that you have kept it all in order, made decisions that were the right ones and coped admirably with . . . Dear sweet Christ . . .' He dragged her into his arms under the awed gaze of the men, kissing her with such tenderness they all, without exception, looked away. They were rough working men, labourers, most of them accustomed to taking their wives, or any female who was handy to them, every Saturday night and would not dream of showing affection, especially in public, but these two, the master and his missus, seemed oblivious to them all.

'After what you have been through it is only a marvel that you are not in the local lunatic asylum.'

'I nearly was a couple of times, Harry. Only Susan, and Biddy, of course, kept me sane.'

'Those two bloody men . . .' His face became strained and his eyes bleak but she pulled away from him and took his hands in hers.

'Harry, darling, it's all over. You are back with us, with me and the children and soon you will be returned to your desk at . . . well, wherever you feel is the best place to run things but first I want to show you something.'

'Show me something?'

423

'Yes.' She took his hand and under the silent gaze of the men in the yard who were doing their best to make a half-hearted attempt to resume work, for even the foreman had stopped to gape at the man and woman, led him to the carriage where Carly was waiting. They both lifted her tenderly into the carriage, Harry fussing with rugs and cushions until she told him briskly to climb in and, as Susan would say, 'give over'. She felt that she should be the one fussing over Harry for she was having a baby which was a natural thing to do while he had been desperately ill for five months.

John had seen him only yesterday. 'Have you a headache, Harry?' he had asked casually, noting the way Harry kept his face turned from the window. At once Lally threw a worried look at her husband, for surely John was not telling them there could be further cause for anxiety?

'Yes, I have as a matter of fact. They came on me suddenly, just this last week, but what's that got to do with my returning to work as you know I am eager to do?' Harry began to look irritable, for he was not a man to sit about while there was work to be seen to, a lot of work, a lot of catching up. He was at home for one reason only and she sat beside him. Had it not been for the doctor and what he had said to Harry about Lally, he would have yelled for his horse and gone thundering up to his destroyed mill and started the process of putting it together again the moment he was in his right senses.

Dear God, his head began to throb so badly he had put his hand to his forehead but suddenly she was behind him, one hand soothing his brow, her cheek resting on top of his head, one arm about his

424

shoulders and, wonder of wonders, the child in her belly, *his* child, kicked against his shoulder blades with such vigour it was as though it were speaking to him, reassuring him, telling him it would soon be with him and not to despair.

'Dearest Harry,' Lally murmured into the tumble of his dark hair, 'I'm sure John would tell us if there was something . . . something wrong. John?' She turned to John, her gaze steady as though to say whatever it might be she was strong enough, *they were both strong enough* to go on.

'There is nothing, Lally. It is only to be expected after the blow to his head that he would have some after-effects. He must be careful not to overdo things. Oh, I know you well enough, Harry, and the minute—'

'No, I will not let him do anything that might . . . might take him away from me again. I am here, Harry, we are all here to tell you how much we love you and need you. We, Susan, Adam and Brice have held it together for you, awaiting your return ready for you to pick up again. We love you, Harry. I love you, your children upstairs love you and here'—turning him towards her and putting his hand on her swollen belly—'is your son or daughter waiting to be born and love you too. We thought we had lost you but you're back again . . . oh, thank God, thank God.'

Inside them both something had lurched rapturously as, for the first time Harry and Lally looked into each other's eyes with equal love. Neither of them could say with any certainty when it had begun. Harry first, of course, but she had been another man's wife and he had pushed the ridiculous notion to the back of his busy mind.

When Chris was killed he had begun to hope that perhaps this time, when the mourning period was over, he would approach her. But he had waited too long and she had turned to his brother, becoming pregnant with Roly's child. But it was not from Roly that she had sought refuge in her despair but Harry Sinclair. She had agreed to become his wife. She had not loved him but they had made a pleasant enough life for themselves and the children. But even Lally could not tell him with any accuracy when it was that the fondness she had always felt for the rather forbidding Harry Sinclair had stealthily crept, like sunshine breaking through the early morning mist, into love. The love a woman has for one special man. Not pity when he was hurt, nor compassion as she had first thought it to be when he lay wounded in his bed, but a possessive, passionate love, a tender love, a closeness she had never known before, an understanding of who he really was, what he really was and what he meant to her.

It was all there, the strength of that love, for anyone to see, a love that silenced them both, that filled them with wonder, that glowed and flamed with passion, a passion that took their breath away in its sudden spontaneity.

Cupping his face in her hands she had placed her mouth carefully on his and breathed his name and said something so quietly only he heard her.

'Harry, my love for you is endless.'

And so here they were, sitting close together in the carriage on their way to what she told him was to be a surprise. It was spring and the hawthorn hedges exploded with blossom, the meadows beyond the hedges were vivid with the brightness

426

of new grass and the yellow of cowslips. There were marsh marigolds and lady's-smock hanging over the small trickles of water that ran in the ditch beside the lane. They both lifted their heads to listen to the sound of a cuckoo, their hands clasped in shared delight just as though they had never heard nor seen such things before.

It was not far from High Clough, in fact the land was slightly nearer to Halifax than to Moorend, a perfect square bordered on four sides by country lanes, with good, unpolluted water from a river close by. There was a railway station within half a mile at Craven Edge which ran directly in to Halifax where it connected with lines to Keighley, Manchester, Bradford, Rochdale, and in the east joined up with lines to Sheffield and on to ports on the coast. Not only would their goods be transported at a far greater speed than they were at present but the raw fleeces and the coal from the Lancashire collieries would be more readily available. Lally was excited about her project, not for a moment suspecting that her husband had already had ideas along the same lines as herself before his illness. She would have been amazed if she had known; that what she thought of as a brilliant and *new* idea had been in Harry's head long before she had heard of Titus Salt, including the new opportunities held out by the growth of the railway. He did not tell her so since he knew she was enchanted with what she thought of as *hers*!

Penfold Meadow. The foundations for the mill had been laid months ago until Roly put a stop to it, the massive mill which, like Titus Salt's mill at the village he had named Saltaire, would employ

427

3,000 workers, ready, as his was, to produce eighteen miles of worsted cloth each day. They would have a celebration, as Salt had done, in the mill's combing shed, on the day the mill opened, a celebration for the 3,000 people they would employ. No children under the age of twelve and they to work for only four hours a day. There would be a community of housing, the architect telling her that if adjoining fields were purchased there was room for at least 700 houses, well-built houses in which those who were stuffed together in St Margaret's Passage and similar alleyways would live decently.

Helped by Carly and Harry, she alighted from the carriage. She wanted to tell them both that she was perfectly able to get down by herself; this constant cherishing of her was not needed. She was a healthy young woman who had already given birth to three children but they seemed to feel that she could barely move from one place to another without someone constantly at her elbow.

Opening the gate that led into the enormous meadow, they both ushered her through. She gritted her teeth and let them, then asked Carly sweetly to wait by the carriage, for he seemed intent on carrying her, along with her husband, across the scrubby grass in the direction of a hut that stood to one side, a hut that sported a hefty lock and, without waiting for help from either her husband or Carly who still stood by the gate, she moved towards it, the hem of her full skirt trailing in the dust.

'Lally . . . Madam . . .' the men said at the same time, their faces showing their masculine disapproval. Lally was fumbling in her reticule

428

from which she produced a key and without waiting for either of them she unlocked the door of the hut and flung it open, slipping inside. There was a table littered with dusty drawings and plans at which Harry, standing behind her, stared in bewilderment. It was evident from his expression that he had no idea that things had progressed so far.

'Besides the site of the new mill, this is what I wanted to show you,' Lally declared. 'I want to pull down all the terrible hovels in which our people now live, operatives from the three mills, two now that High Clough has gone. The houses will have two or three bedrooms. Do you know, according to that doctor I was telling you about, that in Union Street there are twelve persons occupying three beds consisting of two stumps and a shakedown. The family consists of six boys aged eighteen, sixteen, thirteen, eleven, eight and five, three girls aged fifteen, thirteen, nine and the youngest child of seventeen weeks. In a cellar he found a widow and her eight children, three girls aged twenty-four, sixteen and seven and five boys aged twenty-two, nineteen, sixteen, eleven and eight and in the street there was one privy for 221 persons. It cannot go on, Harry.' Her voice was passionate. 'It is said that the . . . the older boys interfere with . . . with their sisters. With three bedrooms, a dry cellar, decent sculleries, a privy to each house, not back to back but with a back passage wide enough to drive the night soil cart through, this could all be stopped. A bit of land to grow their own vegetables. It's no more than five minutes' walk to the mill if we buy this other land,' with a sweeping gesture of her arm. 'As you can see the foundations are laid out but . . . well, when Roly became aware of . . .'

'He put a stop to it.' His voice was like ice and for a moment, since it was the first time his brother's name had been mentioned, she thought she had gone too far, then he smiled down at her and her heart rose in relief. 'But what I want to know is where the money came from for this.'

'I forged your signature, Harry,' she said simply. 'No one knew of your . . . your condition, not even Roly. He thought you were . . . physically handicapped but I pretended you were directing operations from home. Did I do right, Harry?'

'My love, you are worth all the wool men in the county.'

*   *   *

The wonder of Mr Sinclair's recovery affected everyone in the house. They had all, those who had served him in his rooms, making up the fire, the bed, fetching his meals, become used to his silent presence. Clara, making up his bed with Jenny one morning, had even gone into details of how Wilf had tried it on with her behind the stable block, not mentioning how she came to be behind the stable block, before she remembered the still figure of the master in his chair by the fire.

But now he was everywhere, stamping round the house, inspecting the kitchens, for heaven's sake, as though the work that went on there was anything to interest him. He was forever in the stables, looking over the horses, lifting their legs to inspect their hooves, smoothing their coats, checking their teeth as though deciding whether to

430

buy them and Carly was of the opinion that he had
been in another world for so long he could not get
enough of being in this one again and must touch
and feel, look and listen, blessing his return from
that dark place he had been in for so long. He
roamed about the paddock, taking young Master
Jamie, Alec and Jack with him to pat and stroke
the enquiring noses of Teddy and Blossom, Merry
and Snowy and to feed them with an apple each.
He tried to encourage Boy to come too but the lad
was still timid and wanted nothing more than to
remain with the women. The two daft dogs raced
round them in an ecstasy of excitement and the
whole house seemed to come alive with his vibrant
presence. After that first week when he and the
mistress never left each other's side, he refused
absolutely to follow Doctor John's orders to rest,
to get plenty of sleep—though they noticed he
spent a great deal of time in the bed he shared with
the mistress! If she hadn't already been pregnant,
Biddy murmured to Jenny . . . well, Jenny would
know what she meant!

CHAPTER THIRTY

Roly Sinclair thundered along the wide corridor of
his father-in-law's house, his riding boots making a
great deal of noise even on the velvet luxury of the
carpet beneath his feet. He slapped his riding whip
against his boots and was evidently in a vicious
temper. The groom in his father-in-law's stables
could testify to that, as could the terrified
maidservant who had happened to be in the

hallway as he pushed past her and made for the stairs. She had flattened herself against the wall, as they all did when he was about, plain or pretty, for if you were plain he nearly knocked you over and if you were pretty you had to turn your face to the wall lest he took it into his head to interfere with you. Those who saw him gaped at the bruise about his eye which, the stable lad told the groom knowingly, would be a right shiner by morning.

Entering his mother-in-law's private sitting room he threw the door back with such a clatter that his wife Anne, who was seated on a low chair by the window, jabbed herself with the needle with which she had been placidly sewing on some small garment for the baby she was expecting and the blood from her finger dripped on to the white long-cloth, a very fine, soft material. Her mother sat opposite her embroidering a dress in which the baby would be christened. Mrs Bracken was known to embroider with such exquisite delicacy it was admired enormously in her circle of friends. White on white the embroidery was to be, as was considered suitable, for the gender of the child was unknown as yet.

'My dear Roly,' Mrs Bracken began, ready to do battle with her son-in-law, since her daughter who was quiet, timid and dutiful was ever reluctant to reproach her handsome husband. 'Can you not see we . . . ?' It was then she saw the state of his face and her hand went to her own. 'My dear Roly, what on earth has happened to your face?' she gasped

'Never mind that, Mother-in-law,' he ranted, beside himself in what seemed a temper of enormous proportions. 'I have just come—'

'Roly, I must ask you to—'

'That bloody fool of a brother of mine—'

'*Roly*, please, we are two ladies who do not care to be—'

'For God's sake,' he roared, for it was all he could do not to smash the old fool in the face but just in time he remembered who she was and who her husband was. The house that was being built for him and his new wife and the baby she carried was almost ready for them to move into and though he was not himself short of money he was not about to put in jeopardy the splendid mansion in which he meant to entertain his friends.

'I beg your pardon, Mother-in-law, but that blo ... brother of mine has just had the effrontery ... In the name of God who the hell does he think he is ...'

'*ROLY*! I will not have such language, such blasphemy in my own sitting room.'

'For Christ's sake ...' Roly Sinclair had been living beneath the same roof as his mother- and father-in-law since his marriage to Anne Bracken. They had considered it unsuitable to expect their well-brought-up daughter, used to every luxury her wealthy father could give her, to live in a small mill house next to a busy, noisy mill. Their daughter's new house was set in the countryside south of Halifax, placed on a slight rise of land off Briar Lane and indeed was to be called Briar House. The grounds fell away from it like a wide, tiered skirt, comprising lawns, flowerbeds and elaborately clipped box hedges. There was to be a summer house where Mrs Sinclair might sit with her new baby, a covered trellis walk festooned with hanging baskets of ferns and blossom and at the bottom of the slope a quiet, lily-studded lake on which swans would glide. The inside of the house was said to be richly furnished with carpets so thick one's feet would sink into the pile, drawing rooms, dining rooms, a billiard room for the master, bedrooms galore since the newly married couple would entertain sumptuously, great fireplaces in which fires would burn night and day in the winter and tall, wide windows open to the sun in the summer. No expense spared, in fact, and Roly Sinclair could not wait to move in and remove himself from the constant nagging presence of Anne's parents. It was a slight drawback that he must take his wife with him but she would be no trouble as long as she kept out of his affairs.

He had just come from South Royd and *his* office where his brother, sitting behind Roly's desk, had informed him of his plans for the future of the mills. The mills of which Roly was part owner. His engineer Adam Elliott had been with him, the pair of them poring over some papers on the desk. The sight infuriated him. He had, of course, heard of his brother's miraculous recovery from whatever it was that had ailed him but he had decided to leave it for a few days more before confronting him on the future of the mills, particularly after the destruction of High Clough.

'Well, brother,' he had said as he strolled into his own office, totally ignoring the damned impertinent bugger who had had the effrontery to think he was as good as Roly Sinclair in the wool trade, keeping his thoughts and his temper in check. 'You are fully recovered, I see, but what I would like to know is why you are seated in *my* office when you could perfectly well—'

'I am here because you are not, Roly,' Harry answered mildly. 'My engineer . . .'

'*Your* engineer?' Roly drew out his cigar case, selected a cigar, lit it and blew smoke across the desk into his brother's face.

'Well, he certainly isn't *yours*, brother. I believe my wife employed Mr Elliott here to do your job and since I have been told that you declined to go abroad and sell our cloth there is another gentleman who is doing just that, and very successfully too, by the look of the orders that are here on my desk.'

'Now look here, Harry, I have had enough of this tarradiddle. Now that you are back to oversee the mills I can see no reason why we—'

'*We*, Roly? There is no we about it. Without your help, Lally and Susan Harper, and Adam here, have kept this business running and now that you are married to the richest young heiress in the county I suggest you go home to her and get on with . . . with whatever it is you have been doing for the past five months. You will, naturally, receive your share, or what I consider to be your share of the profit made but as you will never know what that is, since the accounts will be under my supervision, you will just have to accept what you receive. I hardly think you will go hungry, lad, not with George Bracken as a father-in-law and now, if you don't mind, we have something on a loom we must look at. By the way, all the operatives who lost their jobs at High Clough have been employed at West Heath and South Royd. We are to run the mills twenty-three hours a day. A shift system, you see, until the new mill is opened.'

'*What bloody new mill?*' Roly could barely speak

435

he was so incensed.

'At Penfold Meadow. Haven't you heard? The footings went in months ago but you, in your wisdom, stopped it. But it seems with the foundations already laid we are to go ahead at once. Albert Watson is putting all his available labourers on the building. It is to be massive, Roly, in the Italianate style, something on the lines of Titus Salt's place, and will employ 3,000 workers. I have made an offer on the land surrounding the site and intend, as Salt has done, to build an entire village of houses, a park, a school, a library, a learning institute, recreational and outdoor sport facilities. It will cost a great deal of money but my wife—'

'So your bloody wife is at the bottom of all this, is she? I might have known. She did nothing but interfere with my work—'

'Your work! What work? I hear from every quarter that you spent your days, and nights, gambling, racing, hunting, shooting and leaving that poor wife of yours—'

'You leave my wife out of this,' snarled Roly, ready to leap across the desk and throttle his brother, not because of mention of his wife, who concerned him not at all, but at the reference to his activities.

'Gladly, if you will leave out mine.'

'That slut. You do realise that the child in your nursery—' It was then that Harry leaped over the desk and hit his brother. Harry had done nothing during the past five months but sit in his chair and, apart from some gentle exercise with Martin at his side, had barely moved. He had put on weight and was out of condition which he meant to put right

436

and had already charged Carly, who was well known for his sporting prowess in the boxing ring and on the football field in a team from Moorend, to help him get fit. Nevertheless he managed to get a blow in before Roly, younger and fitter, knocked him down, kicked him in the ribs and stormed out of the office, threatening to go at once to see his lawyer, Alfred Hardcastle, and put a stop to the whole bloody thing. Adam Elliott did his best to get between the brothers and had he not been there Roly might have done more damage to the man who was only just recovering from his past injuries. Roly was shouting, to the enormous entertainment of the men in the mill yard, that if Harry thought he, Roly, was about to part with a bloody farthing for this mad scheme he was out of his mind.

He said as much to his mother-in-law and when his father-in-law, who had heard the commotion from the comfort of his own study where he had been reading *The Times*, came storming upstairs to see what the hell was going on, the whole incident was related again, while in her low chair by the window his wife sobbed pitiably.

George listened—he had no choice—since Roly was so maddened he would not be stopped and George began to wonder if he had perhaps been mistaken in allowing this unstable, as he saw it, young man to take possession of his precious only daughter. At the time Roly had been in joint charge of the Sinclair mills and had seemed a fair prospect but in George's opinion, who had mills of his own, Roly Sinclair had paid no proper attention to them while his brother was incapacitated. Now the elder Sinclair was in charge and from what his

437

son-in-law was telling him, was doing the only thing possible and that was to get the whole bloody business going again. Of course he had to build a new mill to replace the one that had been destroyed in the explosion, the cost of which would be covered to some extent by the insurance which any responsible man of commerce would have put in place. He had done so himself, so what was Roly Sinclair so incensed about?

'See, Dorothy,' to his wife, 'take Anne to her room. We don't want her to be upset at a time like this,' for his girl was pregnant by this . . . this husband of hers and must be protected.

'Now then, lad,' he said placatingly when his wife and daughter had left the room. 'Let's get this thing in its proper prospective. Those mills of yours—'

'Don't call me "lad". I'm not your lad or anybody's, come to that, and if I wish to object to what my brother is doing to the mills, *my* mills, as you reminded me, then that is my business and nobody else's.'

'Of course, of course, but if Harry believes he is doing the right thing, and I'm inclined to agree with him, then you must abide by what he advises. He's an astute businessman and knows what he is about. Surely even you can see that what he proposes is the best way to get the mills working as they were before his accident.'

The 'even you' was a mistake and George realised it too late.

'Oh, for Christ's sweet sake. I can't take this.' Roly was beyond reason and with another oath made for the door. 'I'm not standing for it a moment longer. Until our house at Briar Lane is ready for us my wife and I will move back to Mill House.'

'Nay.' George Bracken was appalled. His girl could not possibly live in that poky little house where the Sinclairs had resided for generations. For God's sake, there was no bathroom, no proper kitchen, a poky parlour and dining room and three, most probably only two bedrooms and the mill . . . well, the mill had gone but it was said that another was to be built in its place and could you expect a delicate lass like his Anne to live in such a place, even if it was only until Briar House was ready for them. But Roly Sinclair was his daughter's husband and George knew that she belonged to him and that he, George, had no power to put a stop to this.

Roly was already out of the door and on the way along the landing to the room he occasionally shared with Anne. As he had done at the sitting-room door, he flung it open, George at his heels, and strode inside. Dorothy Bracken was just about to loosen her daughter's stays and help her on to the bed as Roly and her husband erupted into the room, but before she had time to speak Roly was at the bell ringing for a servant.

'What . . . what . . .' she stuttered, looking for guidance to her husband but Roly spoke before her.

'Get up, Anne, and get your maid to pack your things. Enough for one night will do. We will send for the rest tomorrow.'

'Roly . . . Roly, darling . . .' Anne began to weep again and Mrs Bracken fell back from her son-in-law's fury which she had never seen before.

'Where . . . where . . . ?'

'We're going to Mill House, my wife and I, until

439

Briar House is ready for us. I will not stay here to be insulted. Come along, Anne, get yourself packed and be ready in the hour.'

*   *   *

It was Adam's practice, since it was no more than a ten-minute easy canter, to go home for his midday meal, his home which he hoped one day would include Susan Harper and her lad. He had been 'made up' as they said in the north when Lally had told him it was his, and she hoped he did not mind if she was being a bit presumptuous but he was to consider it a wedding present from herself and Harry. He had been overcome, as had Susan when he told her but he had been out of his digs like a shot and had settled into Mill House at once. He and Susan had thought they were being most discreet in their strange courtship but it seemed his actions on the day of the explosion had given their feelings for one another away and so they were only waiting until Susan could walk again and they were to be married.

Mrs Cannon, whom he had asked to stay on, for Susan would need help for a while, seemed only too pleased to have someone to cook for and always put a tasty, light meal in front of him. Something cold, meat and pickles, cheese, newly baked meat pies and fresh bread with a tankard of ale if he fancied it and usually to finish off one of her own fruit pies. Since Mr Harry had married and gone to live at the Priory and Mr Roly had moved to the Brackens' sumptuous mansion on his own marriage, she and the maidservants had rattled about Mill House, doing the work they were paid for, naturally, keeping the place as immaculate as she had always done. The gardens were tended as they had always been and were a picture of spring colour thanks to George who, although he was getting on in years, took a great pride in his work. The stable lad and groom, Enoch and Arthur, since there were no longer horses to care for, had been taken up to the Priory but now that Mr Elliott had moved in there was talk of one of them being brought back to look after Mr Elliott's animal and the gig that was to be purchased for . . . well, it was no secret that Mr Elliott was courting that friend of the older Mrs Sinclair and they were somewhat apprehensive at the thought of having a mistress after all this time. Looking after two bachelors was a vastly different thing to being ordered about by a mistress!

George was pottering about the rose beds when the carriage came rattling up the track, pulling up at the front of the house. He stared in astonishment when Mr Roly leaped out, his face like thunder, and made at once for the front door. The coachman, whose own face was stiff with outrage, was left to help a half-fainting lady, who George supposed was Mr Roly's wife, from the carriage where she wavered, a handkerchief to her face, leaning on the coachman who had his arm about her. Without waiting to be let in Mr Roly barged through the door, almost knocking Mrs Cannon, who had also seen the carriage come up the track, to the floor and from the small dining room where the housekeeper had just been about to put a fruit pie in front of him, Mr Elliott came into the flagged hallway, a napkin still in his hand.

On his face was a look of utter astonishment, one that matched that of Mr Roly. George edged nearer, not wanting to miss what was going on.

It was a contest as to who was more amazed, Adam Elliott or Roly Sinclair as they faced one another in the hallway, their mouths agape. It was no more than two hours since they had almost come to blows over what Roly considered to be *his* desk in his office and from where Harry Sinclair had been driven home by his frantic wife to await the arrival of the doctor. Harry had not seemed to be badly hurt but that kick to his ribs had been a vicious one and Adam had felt it needed looking into, especially to a man with Harry's medical history.

'Sinclair, what the devil are you doing here?'

'I might ask you the same thing, you impudent dog. This is my house, a Sinclair house and I demand to know—'

'Not any longer! This house has been given to me by my employer, Mr Harry Sinclair, and since it is his to do with—'

'You bloody impertinent dog. How dare you move into my house and take over my servants . . .'

'This is not your house, nor are they your servants. If you would care to see the deeds which I have in—'

'Sod your deeds and sod you. I'll have you thrown out.' He strode back to the door and turned to where George hovered, the gardener wishing now he'd fled to the safety of the yard at the back of the house. He had heard the exchange between Mr Elliott and Mr Roly and was as flabbergasted as Mrs Cannon who stood dithering in the dining-room doorway, the fruit pie still in

442

her hands.

'You,' Roly snarled at the old man. 'Fetch the yard man, what's-his-name, and be quick about it. I want this . . . this intruder removed from my house at once, d'you hear. And you'—addressing his snivelling wife—'stop that immediately and come into the house.' He whirled back to George who stood rooted to the spot, his fear so great he thought he might fall over.

'There ain't no one else, sir . . .' he managed to stammer bravely, while the coachman, who had been with the Bracken family since Miss Anne was a small girl, gently put her back in the carriage, for a lady in her condition should not be treated like this. He was taking her home to her ma and pa and bugger that bully-boy she had married.

Roly beckoned to him imperiously. 'You, what's your name, leave my wife . . . yes, she can stay for the moment in the carriage but come here at once and help me to eject this intruder from my house. Come along, don't stand there with your mouth open. What the devil d'you think you're doing? Bloody hell,' for the coachman, just as though his young mistress's husband had not spoken, indeed did not even exist, had closed the carriage door, climbed up on his box and was prepared to drive away.

Roly stood there, his mouth open, his face scarlet with unbelieving rage, then turned as though he were about to attack Adam. Adam pushed Mrs Cannon behind him, indicating that she must make for the door to the kitchen, then prepared himself for the lunge he thought the maddened Roly was about to make. It was as well he did. Roly half crouched then threw himself

443

forward so that his shoulder hit Adam in his midriff, carrying them both along the hallway, through the kitchen door and into the kitchen where Ivy the housemaid and Mrs Cannon screamed out loud in shock. Tess, the kitchen-maid, at Mrs Cannon's directions, had run round to the front of the house to fetch George and his pitchfork but the old man was trembling in the flowerbeds and so, shrieking at the top of her voice, she caught the attention of the men who were at work in the yard of the destroyed mill, one of whom happened to be her mam's brother's wife's nephew.

For several long seconds the men simply stared at her in consternation, their tools in their hands, their jaws dropped then her mam's brother's wife's nephew, recognising her from some family function, dropped his pickaxe and began to move towards the gate that led from the millyard to the garden of Mill House.

'Fer God's sake, our Freddy,' she shrieked, 'theer's bloody murder bein' done 'ere.'

At once half a dozen of them began to run towards the gate, delighted to be interrupted despite the foreman's shout. Tess was a right pretty lass and they elbowed each other aside to be the first to help her.

Adam was giving as much, in fact more than he got from Roly Sinclair and would have managed without the assistance of the men who crowded at the back door of Mrs Cannon's kitchen. Roly was a drinker, a man who stayed up half the night gambling or wenching and though he had got the better of his injured brother several hours ago, he was no match for Adam Elliott.

The workmen were quite disappointed to find there was nothing much to do, for Adam, bruised and bloodied about the face where Roly's head had split his lip, had him on the floor with his arms behind his back. The language was quite foul, since Roly Sinclair was no respecter of ladies when his temper was roused and, besides, the women who worked in the kitchen were not, of course, ladies. All three of them, Mrs Cannon, Ivy and Tess, had heard worse in their working-class lives but they were still shocked that a gentleman like Mr Roly should see fit to use it in front of them.

'Your language is disgusting, Sinclair, as is your behaviour,' Adam said calmly, 'so I shall ask one of these gentlemen to assist me in removing you from the kitchen of my house and from the company of these ladies.'

He hauled Roly to his feet but Roly had not yet learned his lesson.

'You can — off, you . . . you blackguard. You'll rue the day you ever came into Yorkshire and as for these bitches I shall make it my business to—'

'Now Roly, I will not have you call my servants by such foul names.' Adam began to frogmarch Roly towards the back door into the yard, the men jostling one another in their efforts to give him a hand.

Roly began to scream, high and demented, like a woman, his fury so great he was like half a dozen madmen in Adam's hands and those at his back leaped forward.

They literally threw him down the steps and on to the garden path. It had rained in the night and there were pools of water about into which one of the men directed him. They all stood back and hooted with laughter, for he was a sorry sight but Adam, more closely involved and with more reason, knew he had made an enemy this day. Roly Sinclair had been humiliated beyond his limits. He had no way to reach his father-in-law's house except on foot and when he did he would have some explaining to do to the man to whose daughter Roly had caused such distress. It would not be forgotten and he would not be forgiven. Roly Sinclair was a dangerous animal at that moment!

CHAPTER THIRTY-ONE

'I'm afraid we haven't heard the last of Roly, my love,' Harry Sinclair said to his wife a few days after the incident at the mill from which he still bore the bruises, though he had not been seriously injured thanks to Adam. He had gone up to South Royd the following day, allowing Lally to persuade him to let Carly drive him instead of riding in on Piper. The commotion was the talk of the parish, spreading round like wildfire, as these things do, followed by the account of the fight at Mill House where Mr Roly had tried to force Mr Elliott, who was now the legal owner of the house, to pack his things and bugger off. Those were his very words according to the men working on clearing the ruins of High Clough and it was for the most part true. It was reported to Mr Harry Sinclair by Mr Hardcastle himself that Mr Roly had gone post haste to consult him but Mr Hardcastle told him there was really nothing that could be done. Mill

House belonged legally to Mr Harry Sinclair; oh, didn't Mr Roly Sinclair know that? Yes, old Mr Sinclair, being something of a traditionalist, had stated in his will that the elder son should inherit the house, knowing, of course, that Mr Harry would not see his younger brother without a home but as soon as Mr Roly married Miss Bracken and moved into Bracken House Mr Harry had seen fit to dispose of it to . . . Yes, Mr Elliott. Oh dear, please, Mr Sinclair, I cannot allow you to fling things about in such a . . . really, Mr Sinclair, that kind of language . . .

Mr Hardcastle's clerk reported to a fellow clerk who was employed at the bank that he and Mr Hardcastle had feared for their own safety but thankfully Mr Roly had thrown himself out of the office and on to the back of his poor horse and positively whipped it down the street!

*   *   *

Now that it was no longer necessary for Lally to see to the running of the Sinclair mills she allowed herself to drift into that trance-like state which her fourth pregnancy induced in her. She was a breeding animal, waiting the birth of her young and though she had thought she would miss the busy, one might even say the exciting battle of her days with Susan and Adam at High Clough, she was content to let one day run into another as the spring moved gently towards summer.

'I wonder why we haven't heard from Roly,' Harry said lazily to Lally a week or two later, and then again several weeks after that. It was said idly as though it did not really matter. Harry Sinclair was happy with his life and he could not, in his somewhat tranced state, believe that there was anything in the world that could spoil it. The two mills, West Heath and South Royd, were going flat out twenty-three hours a day and were producing almost, if not quite, the same quantity of worsted yarn as the three mills had done in the past, but orders, come from Brice Heaton whom Harry had not even met, were flooding in and most of his operatives, glad to be employed after the disaster, accepted the shift system that he had put into place. Later he was to wonder why he had been so complacent regarding the whereabouts and activities of his brother.

'I think I'm going to try a walk in the garden,' Susan told Lally out of the blue one day as they both sat gazing dreamily from Susan's window at the long stretch of lawn that led down to the lake. Barty and Froglet were cleaning the edge of the lake of the weeds which, if not constantly checked, clogged up the clear water. The water-lilies were wide open to the sun and even from the house they could see the carp snapping at the flies on the surface of the lake. The swans and the ducks were on the far side well out of the way, though they kept a sharp lookout for the children who fed them regularly. Jamie, Alec and small Jack who was promising to be clever, though he was not yet two years old, were chanting something Philly was teaching them. Lally knew Boy was with them, just sitting quietly, since he could neither read nor write and would have a special lesson on his own with Philly when the others had raced off outside. He was beginning to ease gently out of the stunned state his ordeal had cast about him but he was inclined to cling still to Susan when he was allowed. Lally and Susan waited patiently for the day when he would play and shout and laugh with the other children but then they did not know what his life had been *before* the explosion. No one had claimed him so had he ever been loved, cared for, valued, cherished, which is the right of all children? It didn't seem so or surely someone would have been looking for him. Perhaps his mother had been killed in the explosion. Still, they were making up for it as best they could and at least he was healthy, well nourished and the maidservants made much of him, poor little chap, they said.

'*Walk in the garden?*' Lally was astounded. 'But you haven't even been downstairs yet and if John—'

'Never mind John. Adam and I have been walking round this room and down the hallway for a week now. Oh, I didn't tell you because I knew you would fuss and so would John. With Adam beside me I'm in no danger of falling.'

'*Fuss!* I should think so and I shall have a word or two to say to Adam Elliott when next I see him.' Lally was appalled and her face became very serious so that Susan laughed and without any help stood up and tottered to the window where she leaned on the sill. Lally did her best to struggle to her feet to give her a hand but she was the one who needed a hand as she tried to heave herself up from Susan's deep and comfortable armchair.

'Dear God, I don't know who is the more incapacitated, you or me. I swear I'm having twins, the size of me, but please . . . please sit down, Susan. Your legs have only just come out of splints

449

and are still very wasted. John says—'

'Ask Carly and Ben to carry me down, please, Lally. I shall go mad if I have to stay up here for much longer. And the sooner I can walk the length of the aisle the sooner Adam and I can be married. He is urging me to name the day but at the same time he knows I won't until I can walk. Please, Lally . . . please . . .'

And so Barty and Froglet were startled to see the two men, their arms linked to form a chair, carry Mrs Harper down the front steps and across the path to the seat they themselves had placed for Miss Lally and Mr Sinclair to rest on. It was becoming a firm favourite with those who were recovering from disasters and Barty was forever telling Froglet they had picked a good spot there. The sun caught it and the wonderful scent of the clusters of wallflowers hung about and really, he confided to his right-hand man, he often felt he wouldn't mind a nice sit down there himself. Smoke a pipe in the peaceful sunshine. And would you look at Miss Lally with her—he nearly said with her belly out to here but stopped himself in time—so near her time, sidling about at the back of them as though she were afraid Carly and Ben might drop Mrs Harper.

They placed her carefully on the seat and down the lawn ran Jenny and Clara with cushions and rugs though it was warm enough to fry eggs on the path, Barty remarked to Froglet in an undertone.

'Leave her in my care, Carly. She can take my arm if needs be,' sang out Miss Lally, as though she could give an arm to anyone never mind a woman who could hardly walk, but he and Froglet hurried up from the lake and promised to keep an eye on

450

them, both of them feeling enormously important.

Carly and Ben, Jenny and Clara, with many a worried backward glance, for both ladies were very vulnerable, trotted back to their duties and the minute they'd gone, bless me if Mrs Harper didn't stand up and so did Miss Lally.

'Nay,' Barty admonished, but the pair of them set off along the path until he, taking it upon himself to act as nursemaid, firmly turned them back and sat them down.

'Now you wait 'ere, Mrs Harper. I've just the thing for yer. Eeh, yer know yer shouldn't be leanin' on Miss Lally like tha'. Stop there, Froglet, an' if yer let one of 'em put a foot to't ground I'll clout yer one.'

They sat obediently while Froglet, speechless but determined, hovered about them until Barty, out of breath but wreathed in smiles, hurried round the corner of the house. He carried two walking sticks and a saw.

'See, stand up, lass,' he said to Susan. 'Steady 'er, Froglet, see she don't fall,' and before five minutes had gone by he had measured the sticks against Susan's height and, using the saw with great accuracy and with vast mutterings of 'a bit off this'un . . . another 'alf an inch . . . there, that does it . . .', Susan and Lally, Susan on her sticks, Barty to one side and Froglet on the other, were slowly walking on the flat bit beside the flowerbeds.

'I knew them sticks o' me dad's'd come in 'andy one day,' Barty told them.

John, of course, pulled his lip and frowned when he saw her the next day, another gloriously sunny afternoon, but it was clear he was only being cautious. He had come, he said, to check up on the

451

lad, meaning Boy, which he did every few days, not just on Susan, and it was noticed in the kitchen that he stayed to have a cup of tea with Miss Philly, herself a doctor's daughter so it seemed natural enough, those in the kitchen told one another, that they should find a common interest.

'Give over,' Barty told them with a snort of laughter. 'Common bloody interest indeed.' Hadn't he seen the pair of them holding hands on the other side of the lake when they thought no one could see them? Not much got past Barty, he added, tapping his nose.

So perhaps there were to be two weddings, they whispered to one another in the kitchen. Eeh, two weddings and a babby! Life was grand, it really was, and what a difference to all those weeks back when the mill had blown up. Mr Harry had still been mazed, Mrs Harper and that poor little lad had been trapped and injured and now would you look at them all. Mr Harry riding out each day to watch his grand new mill going up, Mr Elliott round here every evening to court Mrs Harper, Miss Lally blooming, that lad they called Boy beginning to respond to a bit of human kindness and them young rascals larking about, keeping everyone on their toes and it'd be Miss Caterina next since she was all over the place trying to follow them. Toddling on unsteady legs, she was now, falling over, picking herself up, laughing, shouting in her own language for them to wait for her. The house was so filled with love and laughter it fair took your breath away, they told one another, believing in their innocence that the bad corners had been turned.

Roly Sinclair looked at his wife who sprawled on the sofa opposite him, her thin body with its vast stomach ungainly and repulsive! His mother-in-law sat beside her, doing her eternal embroidery so that Roly wondered if there was a baby born in this bloody parish with as big a wardrobe as this thing was going to have. They had dined, the five of them, for the youngest son of the family, Robert, was still unmarried and living at home, but his father-in-law, lucky bastard, had escaped to his study with Robert saying they had some accounts to go over and would the ladies excuse them. He did not speak to his son-in-law whom he had never forgiven for dragging his precious daughter through that awful scene at Mill House and which had been all over Halifax by the end of the day. Thank God, said Roly to himself, Briar House would be ready for them to move into by the end of July and he would be shut of the lot of them. Not Anne, of course, since she was his wife, the source of plenty of cash for his racing and his gambling, and must, unfortunately, come with him. And their child would be born by then, he supposed, so they would be what was known as a 'happy family'. In the name of all that was holy, how was he to stand it? he wondered, but there would be plenty of diversions and he could come and go as he pleased without the Brackens' disapproval forever ringing in his ears.

With a muttered oath he sprang to his feet, noticing that his wife flinched as he did so. He had been forced to slap her a time or two when she had reproached him over something or other and he

453

hoped his bloody father-in-law would not find out but then what if he did? Anne was his wife, *his* to do with as he liked and old George could do nothing about it.

'I'm off out,' he told the ladies on the sofa.

'Roly, do you not think that with Anne as she is it would be . . .' his mother-in-law began, but Roly only shook his head in exasperation, bowed mockingly to the ladies and left the room. He bounded up the stairs, making for the bedroom in which he now slept, as it was considered his wife was too delicate to share her husband's bed, for which he was heartily thankful. Opening his wardrobe he took out a pair of field glass lenses. They were the very latest model which had a good magnification and had cost him twelve guineas. Letting himself out of a side door he walked round to the stable yard and shouted for one of the grooms to saddle Foxfire, his chestnut gelding who was reliable, even in the dark.

It took him no more then fifteen minutes to reach Penfold Meadow. He tethered Foxfire to a handy tree and slithering down a slight incline found the spot he was looking for. It was still only eight o'clock and not yet dark so he could see quite clearly the growth of the great mill that his brother was building. The scaffolding was like a cobweb against the handsome stone which had reached the first floor, and even now at this time of the evening while there was still light men could be seen working, for it seemed his brother was in a hurry to get it up.

He watched for half an hour, playing his binoculars over every part of the building, then, with a smile on his face that would have disturbed his brother had he seen it, he stood up, placed the binoculars in their case, slung them on his saddle, leaped gracefully on to Foxfire's back and set off at a gallop towards the fleshpots of Halifax.

*   *   *

With the greatest of ease and a speed that took them all by surprise, Lally gave birth to her son at the end of the July, called Martin after his grandfather. The house was in a ferment since they had all believed they were in for a long and harrowing night but though she only began her labour at four in the afternoon while taking the air on the bench Barty had set out for her by the wallflowers, they got her into her bed, sent for Mr Harry and the baby came squalling into the world at eight. By half past, Lally, much to the disapproval of the nurse who was not, in anyone's opinion, needed, was sitting up in bed eating strawberries and cream with a bright blue ribbon in her well-brushed hair.

'Lass, lass, they'll give you indigestion,' Biddy protested, casting an anxious glance at Mr Harry who was walking about the bedroom, his son in his arms, a besotted expression on his face. Susan was there, also looking anxious, for she and Adam were to be married on the Saturday and how was Lally to get to the wedding? She'd postpone it, Susan said, but Lally told her not to be so daft. Today was Monday and she'd be up and about by Saturday, she said cheerfully, spooning strawberries into her mouth, to which remark Biddy, Susan and Harry all looked at her as if she were mad and began at once to protest.

455

They had all gone and she and Harry were alone, 'and about bloody time', Harry said as he cradled her in his arms. 'What with the children all over you, though I must admit to a certain indifference to the baby on Jamie's part, I couldn't get near you. I suppose for a big boy of four who already shares his nursery with what sometimes seems dozens of children, one more isn't anything to get excited about. He was disappointed it wasn't a puppy, he told me. He dearly wants a puppy of his own and I feel inclined to get him one.' He lifted her face up to his and kissed her with a love that bathed her in its warmth and gladness.

'They'll all want one then,' she said sleepily, her eyelids drooping, and at once he was ready to bound off the bed and leave her to her rest but she clutched at him fiercely. 'Don't you dare leave me, Harry Sinclair. I want my husband in my bed from now on with his arms about me and soon . . .'

'Dear God, woman, you can't mean . . .?' He laughed delightedly.

'I do, my darling, but for tonight just you beside me in our bed with our arms about each other will be enough.'

'That nurse will have my hide if she finds me in here with you. She has already indicated that she finds my presence prejudicial to "mother".'

'To hell with her.'

Harry's arms tightened round her and he sighed in utter content. 'This has been a day like no other, d'you know that? A time like no other. My wife loves me, my son is here at last and in a few weeks we will be opening the new mill at Penfold. What a celebration that will be. They shall all come, all the children and of course . . . what d'you think of

Martin for the boy?' he asked her diffidently but when he looked down enquiringly at her she was fast asleep.

*   *   *

At Briar House another child had been born that day, a girl whose grandmother took one look at her and fainted at her daughter's bedside. A pretty child with fair fluffs of what would be curls on her tiny skull but whose left arm finished in a stump at the shoulder and whose left foot had no toes. It was as though at the beginning of her pregnancy the foetus in Anne's womb had given up forming certain parts, leaving bits missing.

On the bed the exhausted mother wept for her husband, who was not here to hold her in his comforting arms and tell her how harrowing it all was, and no, she told the nurse, she did not want to hold her baby in her arms.

When it was known at the Priory that Anne Sinclair had given birth to a deformed child they all shook their heads sadly. It was noticed that Doctor John who had called to see Lally looked somewhat pensive as though some mystery had suddenly become clear to him.

'Roly Sinclair seems to be a most objectionable man but from what I have heard of him he was not always like that. From what you tell me, Lally, he was once quite an endearing character.'

'He was, John. Chris and I were very fond of him but he changed over the years. He was always wild but never . . . well, I hate to say it, but he seems to have become almost insane.'

'Yes, I agree,' John mused but refused to say any

457

more.

When Roly finally staggered home a day or two later it seemed he cared nothing for the child!

*   *   *

Lally was proved right in her declaration that she would be up and out of her bed in time for Susan and Adam's wedding which took place at the same church in which she and Harry had been married and where Chris Fraser had been in his grave these last three years.

Susan's first marriage had been a plain and simple one, for she and Jack Harper had been hard pressed to find the money for the parson. Many of her contemporaries in the same position didn't bother with an official ceremony but simply moved in together, probably bearing their first child within six months.

This time it was not exactly a lavish affair, for that was not Susan's style, but with Lally urging her on, since Lally wanted her friend to have the very best, she had submitted to a ceremony to which all the servants from the Priory were invited along with Doctor John and one or two of his associates who had attended her when she was in hospital, accompanied by their wives. The tenants from the farms came, all dressed up in their Sunday best, even Mrs Cannon and her handmaidens from Mill House, for they were Adam's servants and would be Susan's when she moved in after the honeymoon in the northern dales of Yorkshire that Adam had insisted upon. Adam's parents came, proud as punch with their son who had done so well and the sensible lass he had chosen as his wife.

They were not so sure about Jack, who was a lively lad, merry and cheerful and noisy in the church where he insisted upon beating time to the hymns on the back of the pew with the wooden animal he had been given to keep him quiet!

The small church was full. The only ones left behind were Cat and the new baby, Martin, and so as not to disappoint Dora, who was the backbone of the nursery, Polly McGinley produced a niece, seventeen and good with children, who was looking out for a job as a nursemaid. She came a day or two before the wedding and proved so reliable Lally employed her on the spot, to work under Dora, of course, for with four young children, one of them not even a week old, it was decided Dora needed help. Jack and Boy, who was devoted to Susan, would naturally go with her to Mill House.

Susan looked lovely in the silk gown she had chosen, the colour of apple blossom with a wide crinoline which almost brushed the ends of each pew as she walked towards her groom on the arm of Harry who told Lally later he was convinced there was not really enough room for someone as unnecessary as himself. The skirt was flounced, the waist, though not exactly tiny, was neat, for Susan could not now be considered slender, the bodice, separate from the skirt, fitted her splendid bosom and was adorned round the neck and at the wrists with the tiniest of silk rosebuds. Her bonnet, worn at the back of her head, had ribbons to match her gown and under the brim was a froth of white lace and pink rosebuds, a posy of which, real this time and handpicked by Barty that morning, matched them. Her bridegroom, apart from his face which was bright and smiling, was sombre in the plain

459

grey and white that was traditional. Susan's face glowed with happiness, for this was something she had never expected to happen to her again, she confided to Lally and it was thanks to her that it was taking place at all.

They had a real 'wick' time of it after the wedding back at the Priory or, as Polly said to Sean when she could get her breath, 'Clogs'll spark toneet.' Lally, conscious that so many of their friends were what was called in higher circles 'the lower classes', had made the celebrations something they could enjoy. They poured into the ground-floor rooms where the food was abundant, all prepared by Biddy and the maids in her charge. Vast platters of steaming chicken, a haunch of mutton, meat patties stuffed with mushrooms, a boiled round of beef followed by rhubarb tartlets, jellies, blancmange and wonder of wonders, since none of them had ever tasted it, strawberry ice cream. And all washed down with ale, wine for those who liked it and champagne to toast the bride and groom who took themselves off afterwards, for they had a journey to make and wished to arrive before nightfall, the ardent bridegroom said, his eyes on his serenely smiling bride.

Lally was to wonder what the doctors' wives thought of it all but they seemed to enjoy it and when the dancing in the wide hallway started, country dancing, they joined in, their skirts whirling, their curls bobbing, their faces flushed. She herself, no more than a few days out of her childbed and watched by her husband who never left her side, was carried upstairs by him when no one was looking and made to rest for an hour but

460

no one, it seemed, missed her, except Biddy who fussed about the pair of them until Harry told her to see to the guests in the absence of the mistress of the house. Biddy sniffed, knowing she was being told that Harry Sinclair was now taking care of his wife and would do till the end of his days. She gave in.

There was a small hiccup when Susan and Adam climbed into the carriage that was to take them to the station in Halifax, for Jack wailed, believing he was to go too and why shouldn't he, he demanded to know and Boy went quite white with apprehension at the thought of Susan leaving him alone for a week but strangely it was the new nursemaid, named Becky, who calmed him down and was to be seen playing 'tig' with him and Jack at the far end of the lawn as the happy couple drove off.

Their guests had all gone, thank the Lord, said Harry with a heartfelt tone in his voice and they lay in bed, Mr and Mrs Sinclair, their arms about one another and pondered on how long it would be before they could make love. Lally was all for it now, she said, placing a hand on Harry's stomach and hearing him groan but Harry said best wait for a few days at least though it was bloody hard with her hand on his private parts.

They were almost asleep when he murmured, 'I thought we would have heard from Roly by now but he . . .' His voice was drowsy and he fell asleep in mid-sentence.

CHAPTER THIRTY-TWO

It was October now, a lovely autumn day, warm and sunny, on which it was possible to saunter along with the tribe of children, down to the lake to feed the raucous ducks and the swans which honked in annoyance when they missed a bit of bread, then on to the paddock where the two older boys were heaved up on to the backs of their ponies.

'Knees in, Master Jamie, sit in't middle o't saddle, Master Alec, an' look up, not down,' Carly would admonish sternly. The boys would obey him at once, for they held him in some awe knowing he would stand no nonsense, aware that their mother and Aunt Susan were watching and that if they did not do as they were told Carly would threaten to put young Jack up on Snowy or Teddy's back, or even Miss Cat who would do better than they could, 'an' none o' yer old buck', he would roar at one or the other should they try to answer back. They adored Carly, but at the same time respected him, knowing just where they stood with him. Father, as they called Harry, and who had once more appeared in their young lives and was accepted without question, was away all day and available only at the weekends when he would take them out into the woods and play exciting games from a book which he promised to read to them when they were older. It was called *The Last of the Mohicans* which they found tricky to say. It was about Red Indians who lived in a far-off place called America and the games involved hiding and pretend fights which they loved. Between them Father and Carly fulfilled all their childish needs, one with books and play acting, the other with their beloved ponies.

The baby, now nearly three months old, would chortle away to himself as though it wouldn't be long before he would be up there showing them how things were really done and Lally would sigh at the perfection of her life and Susan would slip her arm through hers in perfect understanding. They were in calm waters now, both of them.

The little procession left the paddock area and moved towards the woodland. The great oaks were beginning to throw their acorns, forming a dense carpet which would not stay long on the ground, for they would be seized by hordes of birds and squirrels, and by the boys when they were about. The beech trees were showing their vivid autumn colours, glowing and glorious with a mosaic of flaming orange, russet and gold which would gradually darken to a dull copper, leaves already spiralling lazily to the ground. Beside the oak and beech were sycamore and hornbeam. Dora pushed the perambulator ahead of them, trundling it over the acorns and fallen leaves, joggling the baby, keeping her eye on Cat who did her usual performance of tottering, falling, picking herself up, talking to herself, kneeling to admire some plant or perhaps a worm that wriggled out of her baby grasp.

'I wanted you to be the first to know, apart from Adam, of course . . .' Susan smiled secretly and bent her head.

'What . . . what is it that makes you look so . . . don't tell me you are pregnant?' Lally bent her

463

head to peer into Susan's rosy face then swept her into her arms and kissed her soundly. 'Well, I must say you didn't waste much time. I might have known that Adam would have you with child the minute he got you into bed.'

'*Lally!*' Susan laughed. 'You really are the limit . . .'

'Susan, so are you . . .'

Dora turned round to look at the two women who clutched each other in an ecstasy of mirth and could you wonder, Dora thought. They had both been through so much in the last few years, pain and sorrow, a burden of adversity that would have felled most women and yet they were splitting their sides in a way that made Dora fear for their sanity! Really they were a pair but they deserved to laugh, to be joyful with their husbands and children and those in the household who loved them. There were great comings and goings in preparation for the vast celebrations that were to take place at Penfold Meadow which, Dora had been told by the other servants, was to commence work next Monday. The wonderful new mill which even Dora had walked over to see was finally finished and what a grand and stately place it was, an' all. They were all to go, the servants, the children and the folk who were to work there to a grand opening, a feast the likes of which had never been seen before. A whole oxen roasted on a spit, hams the size of a cartwheel, loins of pork, meat pies, pickles and cheeses, beef steak puddings, home-made bread, and apple pies and cream enough to feed an army. Barrels of ale and cider and two old chaps who would play their fiddles to accompany the vigorous country dances that would follow. The

464

meal was timed for five o'clock on the Saturday to take place in the mill's combing shed so that the operatives who were to start work on the Monday at the crack of dawn would have a day to get over the worst of their merrymaking. They were all looking forward to it, for it was not often that this sort of thing happened in their hardworking lives.

The laughter of the two women pealed out over the autumn woodland, lifting with the fragrance of the woodsmoke, reaching even Barty and Froglet, busy with a bonfire while 'them lads' were elsewhere—for it was a right to-do-ment to keep the little imps from enthusiastically flinging everything in sight into the flames—but what the mistress and her friend were laughing about they couldn't tell you!

*   *   *

The mill was a marvel and a testament to the skill and ingenuity of the modern young architects who had designed it. Harry had, after many discussions with Adam and the operatives who were to work in it, for their ideas came from the horse's mouth, so to speak, decided against the slightly rigid plans of Albert Watson. Albert muttered about 'bloody new men and their bloody new ideas' but as he was to build the thing and would make an enormous profit he hid his animosity with smiles and much rubbing of his hands.

It was massive, four floors and along the length of each floor were fifty tall windows to let in the maximum of light and each window made to open so that the operatives might have space, light, warmth *and fresh air*. There were four majestic towers, one at each end and two spaced down its centre and across the front in huge letters was the sign, SINCLAIR. MANUFACTURER OF WORSTED GOODS.

Already, in the acres of land about the mill, the foundations for the new cottages that were to house the operatives had begun and Albert Watson rubbed his hands together with glee, confiding to his wife in the privacy of their bedroom where she was performing her marital duties in his bed that if Sinclair went on as he was doing she might have that new mansion in the country she had set her heart on!

*   *   *

There were six men, big, loutish chaps who looked as though they'd sell their own mothers for the price of a pint of ale, gathered with their leader outside the gates that led into the wide, cobbled yard that surrounded the mill at Penfold Meadow.

'Bloody 'ell, there must be two 'undred winders,' one muttered to another, but the man who led them, a tall, well-built man in a dark outfit and cap pulled down over his forehead, turned on them fiercely. 'There'll probably be a night watchman and we will have to break in, but for God's sake be as quiet as you can about it. We don't want to wake the population before we've done what we've come to do.'

'What 'e's come ter do, more like,' one whispered to another. 'As long as I gets me brass I don't care what 'e's up to.'

They all stared, impressed for a moment, at the bulky outline of the building that filled their vision

466

from horizon to horizon. There was a moon and the mill seemed to be lit by some unearthly light that reflected in the hundreds of windows across its front but there was no sign of life. It was just past midnight and there was a sense of waiting surrounding the mill, a waiting for it to spring into life, for the machines to start their new lives, which would make an enormous difference to those who were lucky enough to work there. For the moment they must remain in their hovels in St Margaret's Passage and its environs but within months, so it was promised, the workers would all be moved to the newly built houses and enjoy the open spaces in which they stood.

The glass made an almost silent sound as it broke under the stone held in Roly Sinclair's hand and tinkled to the cobbles beneath. The watchman in his little hut to the side of the gate had been dozing in front of a good fire, the frying pan with his bacon and sausages in it waiting to be placed on the flames. He thought he heard a faint noise then the cat which haunted the grounds crept round the opening to his hut and he relaxed and dozed again.

Roly wriggled through the window, feeling his way round to the enormous door set in a doorway big enough to accommodate the horses and wagons that deposited the raw fleeces in the yard and took away the worsted cloth his brother's operatives would weave. He smiled as the thought entered his head, for there would be none of that here if he had his way, and this time he would.

The men crowded in one upon the other. The moon shone on the silent machinery and on Roly Sinclair's white teeth as he grinned in the darkness. Not until they were inside did they light their torches and with shouts and yells that woke the watchman from his doze they ran loose over the first floor until a warning shout from Roly halted them.

'Take the top floor first, you fools, or you'll get burned to death. All of you now, the top floor.'

Although this was the most modern, up-to-date mill in the county with spinning frames and weaving looms made from metal there was a lot of wood about. Beams and supporting posts and even the floors which, though not yet soaked with oil and scattered with waste, were ready to feed the fires. The men with Roly Sinclair had also been armed with heavy sledge-hammers which they aimed at the machines with a savagery that sprang from their unthinking minds. They smashed them apart and then at a shout from Roly moved down to the next floor and the next, on each one smashing and burning while Roly stayed behind to make sure the wood on each floor was well alight.

The men were panting with excitement as they erupted from the building and watched the fire begin to dance alight, sweeping from one end to the other. Windows burst open and pennants of flames blew out and the watchman who had dozed in his hut was seen to be running like a hare down the lane that led from the mill. One or two of the men were all for running after him, for their blood was on fire like the building, but they were halted in their stride by a scream, high and desperate, lifting the hairs at the backs of their necks. The scream came from their backs, from *inside* the mill and they turned in horror, for thugs though they were they were capable of horror.

'Bloody Mary,' one whispered, backing away

468

from the building which by now was well alight.
' 'Oo the 'ell . . . ?'

They looked about them and for the first time noticed that the man who had employed them on this night's work, and who had promised them a considerable sum of money to do it, was not among them.

'It must be 'im. Bugger it, I'm off before the bobbies arrive,' a man with the face of a prize-fighter told the others.

' 'Ere, wha' about our brass?' another clamoured.

'If yer wanna 'ang about yer can bu' I'm off.'

The flames from the burning mill shot into the black velvet of the sky and there was a fearful roar as the machines from every floor began to crash down into the basement. The screams from within had stopped and with obscenities pouring from every mouth the men scattered into the darkness, leaving the magnificence that had always been called simply Penfold in an inferno of destroyed dreams.

*   *   *

They wept, all of them who came to look at the wreckage that lay smouldering in the yard at Penfold Meadow, even the man who had built it. He had been summoned by frantic knocking on the door of the bedroom he shared with Lally and when, still half asleep, he had failed to respond, Biddy had taken it upon herself to stumble into the room lit by the flickering flames of the fire in the grate, and shaken him violently into wakefulness. Harry had made love to his wife, leaving them both

469

languorous and satiated, sleepy in each other's arms. They were both naked, their limbs draped about each other, the sheets flung back, but Biddy was beyond caring about their modesty as she screeched in her master's ear that his magnificent new mill was ablaze from end to end.

'What . . . what . . . ?' he mumbled stupidly and it was not until she had the temerity to slap his silly face that he came fully awake.

'What the hell . . . ?' His voice was aggrieved. Behind him Lally rose up in the bed, her breasts falling forward in rosy beauty.

'The bloody mill's on fire!' Biddy shrieked in his ear so that he winced away from her, then, still stark naked, he leaped from the bed.

'Look out the winder,' Biddy shrilled and indeed when he stumbled across the room he could see the glow in the sky north towards Halifax.

'Dear sweet Jesus . . .'

'Aye, well never mind 'im. There's a chap at door . . . a bobby ses yer ter go at once. Fire engine's there and . . . Oh, dear God, what next . . . what next?' And Biddy, staunch, calm, always steady, began to weep broken-heartedly, for surely to God hadn't these two suffered enough?

It was all over by the time Harry and Lally got there, Harry on Piper, Lally on Merry, both wearing an assortment of clothing they had just flung on any old how. Lally had picked up the first garment that came to hand, the silk gown she had worn to dinner the evening before, riding astride with her nightgown, the one Harry had taken from her in a leisurely fashion only an hour or two ago, flung on beneath it and beneath the gown the kid breeches and boots she wore for riding. Adam was there, leaning bonelessly against one of the big square pillars that supported the gates, his arm round Susan. For that moment they were both mindless, blindly seeking comfort from one another, waiting to be told what to do next, where to go next, how to cope with this latest disaster. What was left of the mill was still burning fiercely but the fire brigade, with several engines, realising they could do nothing, were standing silently away from the building. A great company of police, as they had done when High Clough was destroyed, stood helplessly by, hanging their heads as though in shame that they could do nothing, failing to look directly at Mr Sinclair who had only just recovered from the last disaster and was doing his best to help so many in this township. It was not to be borne and how was he to bear it, they asked one another. His fine new mill which was to open on Monday gutted so ferociously and how the hell had it happened?

There were crying women and even men, crowds of them, who had thanked the Lord for a man like Harry Sinclair who was to make their hard lives bearable and now how was he to mend it all, if he was?

A police inspector approached Harry and cleared his throat apologetically. Neither Harry nor Adam, still dazed by the catastrophe, had thought to ask about casualties. There was no one in the mill and it would not have been until Saturday—which it now was—when the great party was to be held for the men and women who were to be employed in this huge mill, now lying wounded and dying before their eyes, that it would be filled with people. But the inspector, having caught Harry's unfocused eye, put a hand on his arm as gently as a mother will to a desolate child.

Harry, still clinging to Lally as though she were the one firm piece of ground in this quagmire in which he found himself, turned his head and stared at the inspector.

'Mr Sinclair, I'm sorry . . .'

'Thank you,' he answered politely.

'No, sir, it's not just the mill . . .'

'I beg your pardon?' he quavered.

Lally tightened her grip on him, for this beloved man was not to fall if she had anything to say about it and anybody else who upset him would have her to answer to.

'I'm sorry, sir, but there's a body.'

'A body . . . ?' Harry could feel his sluggish mind beginning to function. 'The watchman?'

'No, sir, he's safe.'

'Then . . . ?'

'He was trapped under one of the machines. Not . . . er . . . burned; the machine sheltered him but it fell into the basement and he . . . went with it.'

'He . . . ?'

'Will have to be identified by a member of his family. I'm sorry, sir.'

'But what has that to do with my husband?' Lally asked fiercely, edging herself in front of Harry like a kitten spitting into the face of a bulldog.

'He . . . we think . . . it might be your brother.'

*   *   *

For several days they all despaired, particularly Lally, that Mr Sinclair would never recover from

472

this blow that had struck him. Not only had he lost the magnificent building of which he had been so proud, but it was his own brother who had done this to him. He mourned the Roly they had known for only Harry, and perhaps Lally herself, could remember when Roly had been a slip of a boy getting into scrapes with Chris Fraser, a young lad, handsome and wild but basically good-hearted. What had twisted him? What demon had turned him into the man neither of them recognised?

Though he had ruined their hopes, perhaps for ever, the men and women who had hoped to work at the new and splendid Sinclair mill turned out for his funeral, crowding the churchyard so completely his family had to struggle through the masses to get into the church. His young widow, clothed from head to foot in black with a veil so dense her face could not be seen, moved slowly between her mother and father, followed by her brother and sister-in-law though it was noticed they did not speak. Poor soul, they said, to be widowed so young, knowing nothing of the ways in which the dead man had done his best to destroy not only his own brother but had given her the black eye that was fading beneath the veil.

Carriages stretched up the length of the lane that led to the church gate, bringing the wealthy manufacturing classes to see one of their own put tidily away, though many of them were fully aware of the scandalous ways young Roly Sinclair had adopted. None knew, of course, that it was he who had burned down his brother's mill else they would not have come to pay their respects at his funeral. The general belief was that he had died in perhaps some heroic manner trying to save the mill and

Harry had done nothing to enlighten them. Black coats, trousers and mourning bands, black swathes of veils, and afterwards there were refreshments at the Priory, reminding Lally of the day of Chris's funeral when there had been Harry to console her.

Lally stayed close to Harry lest he slip back into that strange and sombre mood that had separated him from her just after the mill fire and Roly's death but she need not have worried, for Adam Elliott was eager to embark on the rebuilding not only of Harry's mill but his own life and would not allow Harry time to consider the enormity of it. Adam was not about to brood over the demise of a man who had done his best to destroy them all but was over the day after the funeral, bringing with him the plans that had been drawn for Penfold Meadow and also what he now considered to be his family.

They were all in black still, though Lally meant to alter that as soon as she was able.

'Let's all walk over to Tangle Wood,' Adam insisted. 'It's a grand day to be out,' staring up into the mild blue sky. The air was soft and warm and at the back of the house where the farms lay men and women were bringing the harvest in, their cheery calls to one another echoing over the rooftops. 'We could pick blackberries. Mrs Stevens has promised a blackberry and apple tart with cream for tea; oh yes, we have all been invited, and then Harry, after tea you and I, and the ladies, of course, since they have had a hand in the whole thing, can go over the plans for a new mill. Now don't tell me you want more time because, with a family to provide for, like me, you need to look to the future.'

Harry began to laugh, the first time he had done so since the fire. 'Bloody hell, man, you don't mince words, do you, nor waste time. And remind me to watch my language when my children are about.' He turned to look at the lawn where Jamie was showing Jack how to do what he considered to be a cartwheel. Harry's face was relaxed and Lally exchanged a heartfelt glance with Susan and was confounded when her friend winked at her, lifted her skirts, shocking Barty and Froglet who were watching, and performed a perfect cartwheel, to the wide-eyed admiration of the children.

'Dear God, my wife never fails to amaze and delight me,' Adam spluttered, running down the slope to catch her before she did another. Harry took Lally's hand, following slowly, and as she watched him as she had done for the past week, she knew he was going to be all right. He would recover from this blow as he had done others. He would build another mill with Adam's help. He would fulfil the dream that she had shared with him and the housing community, the school, the park, the library would all come to fruition. They would better the lives of those who worked for them and perhaps others would follow.

The blackberries were thick as the stars on a clear night, the children eating as many as they gathered. They had to laugh, which they found came more easily as the afternoon wore on, for they had brought nothing in which to put their harvest. The perambulator containing the amazed baby who had been propped up by Dora and who didn't know where to look to keep all these clever people in his fascinated view, was found to be the most sensible place and without further ado

Martin was lifted out, hefted on to his father's hip and the blackberries were piled on to the waterproof mat which was placed in the bottom.

'I bet I've picked the most,' boasted Jamie, who fancied himself the leader of the gang of children, six in all, though he was not the eldest.

'Well, we'll never know,' his mother said placidly, her own mouth stained with blackberry juice. She smiled as her husband kissed her lips, licking his own to show he relished the taste.

'I think Boy's done very well,' Susan remarked, always wanting to give the lad a bit of praise to boost his confidence.

'No, he hasn't,' Jamie shouted but they were all silenced by the boy himself.

'My name's not Boy,' he said patiently, as though to reprove them all. 'It's Sam.'